"As Above,
Psycho-Spiritual Techniques of Inner Power"

Planetary Magick provides you with a thorough understanding of the essential practical heart of Western Magick. It is a complete ceremonial system and makes available a vast range of hitherto unpublished magical techniques and workings. Through the use of this book, level after level of the psyche will be opened up harmoniously and safely; its perceptions and powers will be balanced and strengthened; and your creative potential will be enhanced and directed to the achievement of powerful and positive magical benefits for yourself and others. *Planetary Magick* provides a key whereby you can understand, work with and direct the forces which fashion your destiny, and bring to fulfillment true magical effects in the material and astral worlds.

Here is a magically potent, authentic piece of ancient knowledge and wisdom which has hitherto been obscured in the splitting of Astrology and Magick as different studies. It is now restored, but set free from archaic forms and conventions. The ritual texts given in this book, although fully traditional in basis and spirit, and retaining their power in operation, are streamlined to contemporary needs, simple to grasp and to perform, and can be given as elaborate or as plain a setting as may be desired.

Planetary Magick gives an effective means of restoring and developing the power of the psyche to respond to the great cosmic archetypes: a power essential to our plenitude of life, but drastically diminished for many people by the common choice between formalistic religion and no religion at all.

Some of the major points covered in this book include:
- Millennia-old secrets of Planetary Magick now for the first time published.
- A complete system of ritual magick *ready for use* by individuals and by groups.
- Powerfully effective rituals in straightforward, easy-to-do form, in full detail.
- Guidelines for individual interpretation and development of workings.
- A considerable number of authentic magical techniques of the Western Mystery Tradition are here made public for the first time.
- Extensive tables of the Planetary Correspondences, with both familiar and previously unpublished material.
- The forces that make astrology work will work for you!
- Planet Power, traditional mirror magick, ancient knot magick, visionary ascent in the planetary Spheres, raising and sending planetary forces, invocations of the beneficent and wonderful Olympic Planetary Spirits—all within the scope of this system and of this book.

You will gain a dynamic and harmonious expansion of magical potential and ability through the use of this one self-contained system.

As the ancient script has it: "As above, so below". The powers which exist in the cosmos have their focal points also in you. The directing force of Mind which operates in and beyond the cosmos is the very source of your inner being. By directing the planetary powers as they exist within your psyche—in the Deep Mind—you can achieve inner harmony, happiness, prosperity, love. You can help others. You can win your heart's desire.

About the Author

Melita Denning and Osborne Phillips are internationally-recognized authorities on the mainstream Western Mysteries and the foremost living exponents of the Ogdoadic Tradition, that premier Hermetic school whose keywords are *Knowledge and Regeneration*. Whowe symbols are the Eight-rayed Star and the Fivefold Pattern of the Temple, and whose influence and works are historically traceable for the past one thousand years.

The authors received their major esoteric training in the magical Order Aurum Solis, a society which was founded in 1897 and which has continued in active existence to the present day. On July 8, 1987, the authors, then heads of Aurum solis, retired from the Order, butr on June 23, 1988, at the unanimous request of the members, they resumed office. Currently, Melita Denning a Grand Master of the order and Osborne Phillips is Preceptor.

Melita has traveled extensively in Europe and the Middle East. She has studied Jungian psychology under the direction of the late Buntie Wills, a disciple of Carl G. Jung's friend and collegue Toni Sussmann, Buntie, called "the Blonde Sphinx" by the French novelist Colette, of whose Paris circle she was a member, was a spiritual mentor to both Melita and Osborne, and her profound wisdom and gentle guidance inspired the witing of *The Magical Philosophy* series of books.

Over and above their extensive knowledge and experience in occult matters, Denning and Phillips owe their high reputation as writers to three special qualities: their loyalty to traditional standards of magical learning and practice, the forthright clarity with which they present true magical knowledge, and their manifest desire to guide students of High Magick honestly, safely and thoroughly in the development of insight and power.

Denning and Phillips have lived and worked in the U.S.A. for ten years, producing many successful books and tapes in close collaboration with Llewellyn Publications. In 1989 they moved to Europe to embark upon new adventures, to explore new avenues of research and endeavor, and to refresh and delight their souls in the magical ambience of the Isle of Albion.

To Write to the Author

If you wish to contact the author or would like more information about this book, please write to the author in care of Llewellyn Worldwide, and we will forward your request. Both the author and publisher appreciate hearing from you and learning of your enjoyment of this book and how it has helped you. Llewellyn Worldwide cannot guarantee that every letter written to the author can be answered, but all will be forwarded. Please write to:

Denning and Phillips
c/o Llewellyn Worldwide
P.O. Box 64383-193, St. Paul, MN 55164-0383, U.S.A.

Please enclose a self-addressed, stamped envelope for reply, or $1.00 to cover costs. If outside U.S.A., enclose international postal reply coupon.

Free Catalog from Llewellyn

For more than 90 years Llewellyn has brought its readers knowledge in the fields of metaphysics and human potential. Learn about the newest books in spiritual guidance, natural healing, astrology, occult philosophy and more. Enjoy book reviews, new age articles, a calendar of events, plus current advertised products and services. To get your free copy of the *Llewellyn's New Worlds*, send your name and address to:

Llewellyn's New Worlds
P.O. Box 64383-193, St. Paul, MN 55164-0383, U.S.A.

ABOUT LLEWELLYN'S AURUM SOLIS SERIES

To share in the action of a Living, internationally functioning Order is an exciting adventure. Besides the use of ritual techniques going far beyond general awareness there is the expertise that comes only from a deep familiarity with matters magical.

This skill can only be transmitted through the minds of present-age adepts who have been fostered in the Lore of timeless wisdom and who have "won their spurs" through years of dedicated service in the Great Work.

This magical participation can indeed be gained from books—*but only if the right books are to be had.*

Now the right books are here! In a series that not only sets forth the teachings of a Living magical order, but which analyzes one after another aspect of that vital psychic and magical know-how, and sets it forth in fascinating and practical detail, *you* are invited to realize the fullness of your magical selfhood, to realize yourself as a person of power in the scheme of things.

And what an order has given these teachings and opened the portal of genuine advancement! Rooted firmly in the basic Ogdoadic Mystery Tradition of the Western world, the Aurum Solis, established in 1897, draws from its historical roots a power and understanding unparralled in the history of magick.

Having its far origin in the teachings of Thrice-Greatest Hermes, the Ogdoadic Tradition has only sparingly—but always with great significance—blossomed into public view. The Templars, the Alchemists, the primal inspiration of the Renaissance, the intricate development of the Qabalah, the "Antiquarian Movement" of the 18th and 19th centuries_through all of these the Ogdoadic tradition can be traced.

And this underlying tradition—the historical forerunner of Freemasonry and of Rosicrucianism—is crystallized and focused in the present age in the *Order Aurum Solis.*

Denning and Phillips, authors of the Aurum Solis series, are leading adepts of their order. By their special knowledge and ability they show you the way to real magical power. Famed for the clarity and integrity of their writings, their books on occult and psychic subjects are known across the world. The heart of their published work is the Aurum Solis series, even as the Order Aurum Solis embodies the heart of their reaching.

These books are initiatory, illuminating. They show you how to learn and what to learn. Followed faithfully, they will make clear to you the Ways of Power and the highest secrets of the Western Mystery Tradition.

Llewellyn's Aurum Solis series does not provide you with a rewrite of previously published materials: it presents the authoritative teaching and practice of a society of magicians who have received, and who are impelled to share to share, the insight of a thousand years of mainstream magical endeavor.

OTHER BOOKS FROM THE AUTHORS

The Magical Philosophy—A Study of the Western Mystery Tradition
Revised in Three Volumes

    Volume 1 *Foundations of High Magick:* The Meaning & Method of the Western Mysteries *being a revision and expansion of Books I and II of the First Edition.*

    Volume 2 *The Sword and the Serpent:* The Magical Structure of Cosmos and Psyche *being a revision and expansion of Books III and IV of the First Edition.*

    Volume 3 *Mysteria Magica:* The Practice and Power of Magick *being a revision and expansion of Book V of the First Edition.*

The Llewellyn Practical Guide(s) to:
Astral Projection, 1979
Creative Visualization, 1980
Psychic Self-Defense & Well-Being, 1980
The Development of Psychic Powers, 1981
The Magick of Sex, 1982
The Magick of the Tarot, 1983

The Llewellyn New Age Series:
The Inner World of Fitness (by Melita Denning), 1987

The Llewellyn Mystery Religion Series:
Voudoun Fire: The Living Reality of Mystical Religion, 1979

The Llewellyn Deep Mind Tape(s) for:
Astral Projection and the Out-of-Body Experience, 1981
The Llewellyn Deep Mind Tape for Creative Visualization, 1987

The Llewellyn Inner Guide(s) to:
Magical States of Consciousness, 1985

The Llewellyn New Worlds Kit
Gateways to the Astral World, 1988

For current information on books & tapes and other activities of the authors, and regarding the Order Aurum Solis, see *The Llewellyn New Times* bimonthly news magazine and catalog from:

LLEWELLYN PUBLICATIONS
P.O. Box 64383-193
St. Paul, MN 55164-0383, U.S.A

Llewellyn's Inner guide Series

PLANETARY MAGICK

by

Denning & Phillips

Invoking and Directing the Powers of the Planets.
A complete system of positive magick for psycho-spiritual wholeness,
development of creative magical power, exploration of the Inner Planes,
evocation of spirits, and material prosperity.

1992
Llewellyn Publications
St. Paul, Minnesota 55164-0383, U.S.A.

FIRST EDITION
Third Printing, 1992

Cover Painting by Lissanne Lake
The Olympic Planetary Spirits by Martin Cannon
Greek and Babylonian Deities by Merle Insinga
Magical Images of the Spheres by Lissanne Lake
Book Design by Jack Adair

Library of Congress Cataloging-in-Publication Data
    Denning, Melita.
        Planetary magick / by Denning & Phillips.
          p.   cm. — (Llewellyn's High Magick series)
    Bibliography: p.
    ISBN 0-87542-193-8
    1. Magic. 2. Planets—Miscellanea. I. Phillips, Osborne.
II. Title. III. Series.
BF1621.D47   1989   82-83316
    133.4'3—dc20   CIP

Llewellyn Publications
A Division of Llewellyn Worldwide, Ltd.
P.O. Box 64383, St. Paul, MN 55164-0383

For José Feola, Ph.D.,
Scientist, Parapsychologist
and Cosmopolite,
with love and esteem

Acknowledgements

The authors would like to extend their thanks to those devoted friends whose skills and dedication to perfection helped this manuscript become a book. Special thanks to Jack Adair, Phyllis Galde, Terry Buske, Lissanne Lake, Martin Cannon, Merle Insinga, and Christopher Wells.

CONTENTS

PART TWO

YOUR PLACE OF WORKING AND EQUIPMENT

PART THREE

PLANETARY MAGICK IN ACTION AND RESULT

the operator's consciousness through their corresponding focal points in the Deep Mind. Their magical dynamism fills the consciousness.

These rites are intended for group use, and, besides fulfilling their true magical intent, they also promote that psychic bonding of the group which makes for progressively more effective working together. As the main intent of each of these rites, the group prepares a magical fluid, vibrant with the potency of the planet of the working: in drinking of this, each person is inwardly infused with the creative energies of the Sphere. A special feature of the introductory paragraphs to these rites is the list of wines suggested as magically appropriate for use as the materium *for the elixir of each Sphere.*

These rites, for individual use, are positive personal attunements with the age-old dedication of the seven days of the week to the Planetary Powers. No matter what your day's program, the governing force of the planet of the day's dedication is a constant influence. To place yourself within its tutelary power is to gain a great strength for inward and outward harmony and success.

OTHER RITES OF ATTUNEMENT
The above Rites of Attunement are intended for general Qabalistic use. However, some students with a love for the deities of a specific Pantheon may desire to make their daily attunement accordingly. We give here a series of Rites of Attunement dedicated to the Gods of Egypt; and, following this, an outline formula which can be used in conjunction with the Tables of Correspondences to construct further Rites of Attunement.

These rites are for group use. Combining ceremonial and meditative techniques, they provide a method of visionary exploration of the seven planetary modalities: a method capable of yielding an unlimited richness and variety of experience.

One of the distinctive features of these rituals is the scope they offer for the development of spontaneous gesture.

Most matters of decision-making or forecast on which people seek counsel with the Cards would fall within the scope of one of the Seven planets: a number of such subject areas, with their planetary rulership, are listed in the paragraphs introducing these rites. To make the reading within the positive magical ambience of this ruling planet will intensify the focus of the reading, and will enhance the questioner's rapport with the archetypal power of the planet. For individual use.

This rite for individual use combines several of the most potent methods of traditional and ancient Magick: cord and knot Magick, Creative Visualization, positive affirmation and reiterated speech, and the making of a talisman. It is "sevenfold" because the object of the "Heart's Desire" is ritually brought down through the creative powers of the Seven Spheres in succession, from the first Saturnian formulation through its bringing to Earth by Luna.

APPENDICES

Of considerable interest to students of Qabalah and to all who use traditional Hebrew texts for meditative or ceremonial purposes, whether in the original or in translation, these notes reveal something of the depth and richness of meaning to be found in a famous and controversial 17th-century text by the application of a simple key.

The seven Planetary Gestures given in the Table of Correspondences carry certain meanings from the Mithraic Degrees of Initiation, for which they are named. Since each of these Gestures is in its own right a mode of evocation of the planetary power to which it is dedicated, these additional notes are appended to aid in their meaningful performance.

GUIDE TO CORRESPONDENCES

EGYPTIAN DEITIES

PLANETARY BLESSINGS

☽ May the power of **Luna** place at thy girdle the silver keys of liberation from material conditions.

☿ May the power of **Mercury** set upon thy shoulders the wings of thy will, to carry thee ever to thy intent.

♀ May thy countenance be radiant with life and love in the power of **Venus,** and the lodestone of attraction be upon thy brow.

☉ In the power of **Sol,** thine be the harp of tradition and the trumpet of prophecy.

♂ May the keen sword of courage ever be ready to thy hand in the power of **Mars.**

♃ In the power of **Jupiter** may thy liberality of spirit be ever as a libation poured out before the Gods.

♄ And in the power of **Saturn,** may all blessings both temporal and spiritual be accomplished.

FOREWORD

Planetary Magick is a complete system of magick that is as new as tomorrow and as old as time. I realize that this sounds like a contradiction, but it is absolutely true. The system of magick described in this book contains everything you need to work magick. It has protection rituals, rituals for enhancing your spirituality, divinatory methods, techniques for working on the astral plane, and yes, powerful methods for making changes in your life. This book alone can help you to become a powerful magician.

The system described in *Planetary Magick* has never been published before. Aspects of this system have appeared in a variety of places, from *The Greater Key of Solomon* and *The Sefer Yetzirah* to my own *Modern Magick*, but nowhere has it been so clearly explained and fully delineated as in the pages you are about to read.

As the name implies, Planetary Magick is a system that works with the influence of the planets. The term "planets" is from the Greek and means "wanderers." It applies to the objects that "wander" fastest through the sky from our viewpoint here on Earth—the Sun, the Moon, Mercury, Venus, Mars, Jupiter and Saturn—and were easily visible to the unaided eye thousands of years ago. Today many scientists scoff at this ancient idea, saying that the planets move around the Sun, implying that the peoples of long ago, by believing otherwise, were either stupid or foolish or both. In fact, all they have done is to re-define the term "planet" to meet their specifications. They have taken it out of its original meaning, ignoring the fact that from our Earthly perspective the planets *do* appear to move. Their laughter, once you understand Einstein's theory of the relativity of motion, rings hollow.

Do the planets exert an unknown energy that affects us? Possibly. Do the movements and positions of the planets reflect something that is happening to us in the deepest levels of our being? Undoubtedly. But these are arguments in favor of astrology, and this is not an astrology book. You need not have studied astrology to become an expert in Planetary Magick. However, here is a challenge to astrologers: Astronomy is the science that looks at the stars, and astrology is the science which interprets that information. Planetary Magick shows you how to use the astrological interpretations to improve your life and the lives of others. If you have gone the one step beyond astronomy to astrology, why not take the next step.

By tapping into the powers of the planets you, astrologer or not, will be able to enhance your magickal abilities. The ancients saw that certain characteristics related to the planets. For example, they associated aggressiveness to Mars and joviality to Jupiter. Once again, many scientists are implying that the ancients were stupid for believing in these ideas and didn't know any better. But is this so? True, they didn't have high-speed computers or nuclear weapons so they didn't have as much information as we do. But they were hardly stupid. They built pyramids. They designed Stonehenge to indicate astrological data. They built step pyramids in the Americas, and the colossus of Rhodes. They knew the secret healing properties of herbs. So why would they accept what modern science considers to be unscientific in relation to the planets? Perhaps it was because the ancient ideas about the planets and their Earthly correspondences *were* checked out scientifically. They could have used one of the oldest scientific methods available: trial and error. From ancient Babylon to modern times this information has been tested millions of times. It works.

Thus, Planetary Magick can be dated as far back as Babylon at least. Before that we can only wonder. Planetary Magick is also a system of Ceremonial Magick. By that I mean that it has a complexity of thought (although performance of the rituals is easy) that does not equate with what many consider to be Natural Magick—the craft of Wicca.

But this is not totally true. If anything, Planetary Magick is a bridge between Natural Magick and Ceremonial Magick. A strong focus of Natural Magick is to take into account the elements—Air, Earth, Fire, Water and Spirit (the latter also known as Aether or Akasha)—paying scant attention to the elaborate correspondences of the Qabalist. Some Natural Magicians use aspects of planetary correspondences in their work. But some, after a superficial study of the subject, will say, "I'm not going to wait six months as described in an old book to do a particular ritual for healing!" Obviously, such a point would be well taken if it was correct—but it is not.

True Planetary Magick, such as is described in this book, will allow you to do magick today. You do not have to wait six months. What is given are the optimum times for performance of a ritual. These times endlessly repeat; as a consequence, the optimum time for a ritual can occur three or even four times in a given day. If your magick is that important, is it not worth waiting an hour or two or perhaps disturbing your day and doing the ritual a few hours earlier? Magick does take planning. Magick does take dedication. With the techniques in this book you can be successful with your magick, whether you consider yourself a Ceremonial Magician or a Wiccan. You can use Planetary Magick.

*   *   *

In the past two decades more books have been published on various forms of Magick than in the previous two millennia. This has led to a rather unfortunate consequence. In earlier times you would have needed a personal teacher in order to learn the magical arts. Today all you need to do is pick up a book. In itself, this is not bad. Problems occur, however, when a person reads a book or two and then uses his or her charisma and the glamor of a few mystical terms to take advantage of others. I am personally aware of several such situations and wish to share one of these with you.

A person of my acquaintance was a member and co-leader of a rather well-known magickal group. At the time, this person was earning a living by holding "classes." In the classes this person, ostensibly the teacher, would do nothing except assign others to give reports on the topics that were to be covered in the class. In other words, the students paid for the privilege of searching out the information that the teacher didn't have.

But this "teacher" did have charisma. As a result of the teacher's urgings, many of the students became members of the Magickal Order. When this person thought that the group was packed with enough followers, a coup was attempted. But real magickal groups work on a magickal current from higher planes, and not on popularity contests. As a result, the coup failed and this person left the Order and set up a new one.

When I knew the above person it was my perception that this individual had no magickal ability and little magickal knowledge. I feel sorry for those who have fallen prey to such a person's charisma for they are inevitably fated to have problems with their magical work and delays in their spiritual development. With computers there is a saying, "Garbage in, garbage out." The same thing goes for occult teachers.

At the beginning of Aleister Crowley's *Magick in Theory and Practice,* it is pointed out that other occult teachers have said "Believe me!" Crowley, on the other hand, says "Don't believe me." By this he means check out all the information for yourself. There are many books out there in which the most ridiculous ideas are pawned off as occult wisdom. Such is not the case with *Planetary Magick.*

Denning and Phillips are exemplary researchers, metaphysicians, occultists and magicians. But don't take my word for it—check out everything that they have written. You will find that they are accurate. For example, there is a short text known as "The 32 Paths of Wisdom." It is a commentary on the *Sefer Yetzirah* and is attributed to Joannes Stephanus Rittangelius (although according to one of the translators of the *Sefer Yetzirah,* Knut Stenring, the author is unknown). Thus, on these pages you will see that it is listed as being by Rittangelius and not part of the *Sefer Yetzirah* per se. Since the "32 Paths" (as well as another text known as the "50 Gates of Intelligence") usually appear with the book they comment upon, they are frequently referred to as "Yetziratic Texts," but they are not the *Sefer Yetzirah.* Recently I have seen several books that equate the "32 Paths" with the *Sefer Yetzirah.* Sometimes, this appears in books by people claiming to be Qabalists. But they are in error.

Admittedly, this is a small point. But if these other teachers are in error on one point, can you trust them on others? As the Romans said, *"Caveat emptor:"* Let the buyer beware.

*   *   *

In Jewish tradition it is believed that the commandment of honoring your mother and your father was not limited to your parents. Honor, it is felt, should be extended to any person who teaches you, for teaching is an essential function of parenthood. For over fifteen years Denning and Phillips have been teaching me, and thousands like me, through their books and articles. Before I met them over two years ago, I had an inward image of what they might be like. I have to admit that the reality did not fit with what I had imagined. Therefore, I think it might interest you to hear what they are really like.

Denning and Phillips are perfectionists and tireless workers. They want nothing of their work to leave their long-time publishers, Llewellyn Publications, that is not exactly as it should be. In short, they have strong feelings and beliefs and are (justly) proud of their work. They want it to be a true representation of themselves and they want the information they are presenting to be correctly conveyed to their readers.

Personally, they are fun to be with. They take joy in the simple things in life and share it with those around them. Both have amazing stories of lives filled with incredible experiences and occult work. And they are both quick to tell a joke and share a good laugh. They enjoy and cook gourmet food and love music. A large organ takes up space in their apartment. Spending time with them is always a treat as they are willing to share and willing to listen—not as the wise elder putting up with the silliness of youth, but as friends who care. And you could never have better friends than Denning and Phillips.

*   *   *

You now have in your hands the key to a marvelous journey. This journey is appropriate for you, whether you are a Wiccan or a Ceremonial Magician, young or old, well-practiced and versed in magick or just beginning, or if you just want to see what magick is all about.

You will not find an instant spell to bring you money and fame today. To learn this system will take many weeks or months. It will take longer to master it. But then, in the light of that mastery, you will wield the magickal powers of the Seven Planetary Heavens.

I have been a member of several magical groups. One of the most frequent comments I have heard from people on joining such groups was that it was like "coming home." I have no doubt that many of you reading this book will find *Planetary Magick* to be the place where you belong.

Welcome home!

—Donald Michael Kraig
Author of *Modern Magick*

INTRODUCTION

Not only through the course of our present lives, but through the whole development of our long evolution—through the whole development of life on Earth—the lights and influences of the cosmos have been impinging upon this planet, all in their measure calling forth development, reaction, sensory and psychic perceptions. And of all these influences none have been more potent, more intimate than those of our own Solar System: Sun, Moon, and those five nearest planets which have been known to humankind through the ages.

Visibly to physical sight the far gold of Saturn, the brighter radiance of Jupiter, red Mars, brilliant Venus, Mercury frequently indistinguishable from her for intensity of luster, move before the remote curtain of the starry multitude; these planets, with Sun and Moon, make up our ever-near, immemorially-known skyey family.

Astronomy tells us of the orbits and brightnesses of these seven luminaries, of their constituents and atmospheres. Astrology tells us of the effects upon us and upon our lives of the varying and blending light reflected visibly and radiating invisibly from their surfaces. And Magick tells us that additionally to all this, originating, empowering and acting through the luminaries, are great creative impulses, the archetypes of the Divine Mind.

This is by no means to deny the deep-reaching and subtle powers of the more distant and more recently recognized planets of our system; nor that of the stars beyond, whether of those which are familiar collectively in the zodiacal signs, or of those less known but sometimes formidable in their influence singly or as a star-group. But it

xxxiii

remains true now, as it was when first observed in millennia past, to say that those celestial bodies whose light and movement relative to Earth impinge most strongly on our physical senses are the ones to which our inner response is the most plainly recognized, and the ones whose powers—both objectively and subjectively manifest to us— are the most amenable, within the compass of our personal life and influence, to magical direction and control.

The special and profound responsiveness of the psyche to these luminaries is due to the existence in its depths—in the Deep Mind of each individual—of "counterparts" which are reflections, as it were, of the cosmic archetypes of the planets.

Something of the long history of human awareness of these counterparts is given in this book. Their relationship with their cosmic originals, however, is from the magical viewpoint only the beginning of the story.

The planetary powers of the cosmos are far beyond our inter-vention, both in magnitude and in their mode of being. But their counterparts in the deeps of the psyche, although they are equally "not ours," are within our reach by certain special meditative and ritual methods; and when one of the counterparts is thus stirred by our action, it produces effects of the same character as those which typify its cosmic original. This is the domain of Planetary Magick; and it is precisely the purpose of the present book to provide you with the authentic keys and the esoteric knowledge that you need in order to bring about these effects skillfully, confidently and with their full magical power.

Because of the continual reciprocity of the divine archetypes and the planetary counterparts in the Deep Mind, Planetary Magick is perennially exciting and intensely creative. Through its methods your response to the planetary powers will be strengthened, both for the enjoyment of the planetary experiences themselves and for the increased vitality and resonance of your inner being; and you will direct the force of your Deep Mind to purposes of benefit to yourself or others, promoting happiness, prosperity and all the good of life.

Planetary Magick is an art which has to create, very literally within its circle, a universe of chosen conditions and phenomena suited to the specific working. The factors necessary to make this synthesis are set forth in this book, with options which you may choose to build up a particular emotive tone or to give dimension to a special magical atmosphere.

Guidelines and suggestions to aid personal creativity are provided here, and no less than 65 never-before-published magical rites are given in full detail.

This book is in fact a complete and self-contained system of ceremonial magick, and is dependent upon no other material to complete its requirements. It comprises many levels and types of operation, and it brings to you the first comprehensive exposition of the authentic art of Planetary Magick to be made in centuries.

In writing this book we have drawn considerably upon the treasury of teachings of Aurum Solis.* That Order has since its foundation in 1897 guarded and perpetuated the venerable traditions of Planetary Magick, putting them into practice in the Sphere-workings which are a part of its Second Hall program. Ideas and presentations, language and magical approaches, have been regularly reviewed and updated by the Order, and that procedure has continued in our hands: in this book, as a consequence, simplicity and directness and a contemporary tone characterize the various psycho-spiritual techniques and the magical processes of the art.

To explore the invisible worlds, to have questions answered in dreams, to encounter wonderful spirit beings in beautiful and picturesque forms, to be able to send good influences to one's friends, to be able ritually, step by step, to bind and seal the achievement of one's heart's desire: the need for these things is ever with us—

To reach out in aspiration to the infinite cosmic glories, and to seek to raise power from the depths of the psyche: yearnings which seem intensely contrasted, but yet are mirror-images one of another in the striving for maturity of our inner being—

The fulfillment of those needs and the answer to these paradoxical yearnings are alike within the compass and gift of Planetary Magick.

---

* Other aspects of Aurum Solis teaching and practice are presented in the series *The Magical Philosophy* and in *Magical States of Consciousness,* all by the present authors and published by Llewellyn Publications, St. Paul.

PART ONE

Essentials of Planetary Magick

---

1 *PLANETARY FOCAL POINTS*

Planetary Magick is the art of evoking, intensifying, experiencing and directing the forces which derive from, or are associated with, one or another of the traditional seven planets: Saturn, Jupiter, Mars, Sol, Venus, Mercury and Luna.* Of the "new" planets, it may be recalled here that the astrologers have allocated these as "higher octaves" of certain of the traditional seven. The seven still comprehend among their number every aspect of human life, activity and aspiration.

On the Tree of Life, these forces are represented by the seven planetary Sephiroth, from the third through the ninth: Binah, Chesed, Geburah, Tiphareth, Netzach, Hod and Yesod corresponding to the planets in the order given. Planetary Magick has, indeed, been a vital factor in the long evolution of the great Qabalistic body of mystical and magical formulations; one of the first traceable stimuli in that evolution appearing at an immemorially early period, when the priests of Babylon adopted from Sumeria the attribution of the planets to the principal deities as a basis for divination and propitiation.

The greatness of the Qabalistic system however, as it has been developed and elaborated through many centuries in many lands, consists in its presenting a potent interpretation of the universe at all levels. This interpretation, applied also to the human psyche, has produced an insight which in the present age is becoming more clearly apprehended, and more evidenced, as non-occult knowledge advances into greater harmony with it.

Here the Qabalistic concept of the four "Worlds," or levels of existence, can relevantly be summarized.

---

* Throughout this book, "the planets" and "planetary" are used in the sense generally accepted astrologically, to include the Sun of our solar system, and Earth's Moon, as well as the planets properly so called.

The highest of the four is Atziluth: the World of deity transcendent, pure Spirit, pure dynamic Being which manifests, but is not limited by, attributes of divinity as humanly apprehended. In particular, this living Reality exists in those ten "modes" or "voices" of being, which are the Sephiroth in Atziluth: the ten primal, archetypal Sephiroth. Of these ten, each one—imageless, formless, all-potent—is no less divine than any other; each one is as entirely and completely divine as the Kether of Atziluth from which the rest in balanced progression emanate.

Among those ten primal Sephiroth of Atziluth—a pattern of interrelated archetypes* which remain an integral part of the Divine Mind—are the seven which we designate as "planetary," and which are the particular subject of this present study. In both the Hebrew and the Greek Qabalah, they are characterized in abstract terms as Understanding (Sphere of Saturn), Magnificence (Sphere of Jupiter), Strength (Sphere of Mars), Beauty (Sphere of the Sun), Victory (Sphere of Venus), Splendor (Sphere of Mercury), and Foundation (Sphere of the Moon): titles which give only a suggestion of their rich implications, and of the mighty and multiform power of each archetype. In these we find the power-source of every impulse of our lives, and the fount of all practical Magick.

Below Atziluth extends the World of Briah, of Mind. Its forces, emanated from those of Atziluth, are altogether a replica of the Atziluthic but are more accessible to human contact. In Briah the archetypes are more recognizable to us. Although in themselves they are focal centers of pure mental force in their individual Sephirothic modalities, their power is clothed in high and noble imagery of human formulation. Born of whatever human culture, only those concepts which correspond truly to the divine archetypes can attach to them and thus find place in the World of Briah: spontaneously, without conscious reference to Qabalistic philosophy, we apply such terms as "sublime," "exalted," "lofty," to those concepts. Whether we envisage them as gods, archangels, or "Briatic images" simply, these great "archetypal images"—more truly, "imaged archetypes"—form a necessary link in our contact with the divine power-sources.

Below the World of Briah and emanated from it is the richly colorful, diversified, soul-stirring World of Yetzirah, the "Astral Light." Here

---

* Philo (1st century) and Augustine (5th century) discern the archetypes as creative modalities in the Divine Mind. C.G. Jung discerns them as powerfully and creatively present to the depths of the human psyche, without being constituents of it; see for example *Structure & Dynamics of the Psyche*, throughout. The *Poimandres* of Hermes Trismegistus (probably 2nd century) clearly regards the archetypes as of divine origin, but places their action in the World of Mind (Briah), whence it is carried to fruition in the lower Worlds by other agencies.

human perception and imagination can run riot among innumerable Sephirothic and elemental actualities as well as among its own creations: without close mental discipline or deliberate magical action there is no guarantee of the archetypal "rightness" and viability of any astral formulation.

Below the World of Yetzirah again is the World of Assiah, the material universe. This is so directly emanated from Yetzirah, and so influenced by it, that the Astral World is often termed the Causal World in relation to the material. Here the lasting spiritual influences, and the transitory ones of lower origin, are all made manifest in the greatest confusion.

We need not and should not be victims of this confusion. The Four Worlds just enumerated are present and should be realized in every person: taking body and psyche together, we are native to every level of existence. To be aware and "alive" at every level of our being, and to bring about and enjoy the harmonious interaction of those levels— that is true holism, and that is the principal secret of magical power.

In Qabalistic thought, the Divine Flame which is the center and summit of each being is the Yechidah: a nucleus in the Divine Mind in Atziluth, at once the origin and the goal of the individual existence. (Completing with the Yechidah, the inmost spiritual life and inspiring force within the psyche are two other archetypal components, which however do not concern us directly in the scope of the present study: the *Chiah* and the *Neshamah,* corresponding to the Sephirah Chokmah and the supernal aspect of Binah.) Sent forth from the divine nucleus is the mind, the *Ruach,* native to the World of Briah. The *Nephesh,* which is the emotional instinctual level of the psyche and is emanated from the Ruach, is of the astral stuff of Yetzirah. So likewise the physical body, the instrument of the Nephesh and of the whole psyche, is native to, and an integral part of, the material universe.

To every level of the individual person therefore, just as to every level of the universe at large, the Sephirothic archetypes are present. As a similitude we can say that in every random sample of water that may be gathered—whether taken as vapor from the clouds, or run from a city faucet, or chopped solid from an iceberg, or dipped from a mountain cavern—no matter what else may be present, the underlying hydrogen-oxygen compound will be constant. Even thus, throughout the fabric of being, the Ten Sephiroth are present: even in any one Sephirah, say Qabalists, exist the ten. They are present in the divine power of the central Flame of our being, they are present in the mind-action of our Ruach, they are present in the fabric and the workings of our physical body. They are present in a very powerful and remarkable manner to our Nephesh; and here two important facts converge:

1. Vital though the non-planetary archetypes are in the development and integration of the psyche, the archetypes which relate to the planetary Sephiroth are those which govern every impulse of our lives and provide the fount of all practical magick.

2. While the action and power of every level of a person is needed in magical working, it is the Nephesh, with its immeasureable power to stir the creative Astral Light, which makes the action truly magical.

From the ancient times it has been recognized that each of the planetary powers bestows a corresponding "imprint," or evokes a corresponding "counterpart," in the psyche. For example, Franz Cumont writes in *The Mysteries of Mithra*:

> The most potent of these sidereal deities, those which were most often invoked and for which were reserved the richest offerings, were the Planets. Conformably to astrological theories, the planets were endowed with virtues and qualities for which it is frequently difficult for us to discover adequate reasons. Each of the planetary bodies presided over a day of the week, to each some one metal was consecrated, each was associated with some one degree in the initiation, and their number has caused a special religious potency to be attributed to the number seven. In descending from the empyrean to the earth, the souls, it was thought, successively received from the planets their passions and qualities.*

We know from their initiatory grades that the Persian followers of the Mithraic Mysteries, in common doubtless with others of their time and region, placed the planetary powers in just the same sequence as that which is intrinsic to the Qabalah. The purpose of these Mysteries was, in fact, to aid the initiate in mastering successively, from the lowest—Luna—to the highest—Saturn—the planetary influences to which at his incarnation he had been subjected.

Such rites have never been regarded as acting solely upon the conscious, rationally-controlled areas of the psyche of the recipient: were they so limited in effect, they would be little needed and of little worth. The importance of the Nephesh in initiatory and magical workings is that it will give access, granted the appropriate key stimuli,

---

* *The Mysteries of Mithra* by Franz Cumont (Dover 1956), p. 120.

not only to the conscious emotions and to the instincts associated with bodily well-being, but also to the Deep Mind: that unconscious region of the emotional-instinctual nature whose caverns descend through and beyond the personal life, into the mysterious deeps of the Collective Unconscious.

It is within the depths of the psyche that every person, no matter what his or her individual temperament and character, has a "focal point" corresponding to each of the planets. Undoubtedly these "focal points" or "counterparts" tend to respond to, and interact with, the influences of their corresponding luminaries; but it is as "reflections" of their great archetypes in Atziluth that they function within the Nephesh as mighty sources of magical power.

Thus Hermes Trismegistus, whose philosophy may be termed the wellspring of the Western Mystery Tradition, declares in one of the surviving "Excerpts" of his work:

> "Seven wandering stars are there which move in spheres before Olympus' gate. ... To these stars the human race is committed: we have within us Mene, Zeus, Ares, Paphie, Kronos, Helios, Hermes. By this means are we destined to draw from the living aether of the Kosmos our tears, mirth, anger, our parenthood, our converse, our sleep and every desire." (Excerpt 29, from the book *Isis to Horus.*)

The perception of these planetary archetypes as mirrored deep within the psyche is precisely the "old view" of which Carl Jung, in his book *Mysterium Coniunxionis,* makes a clearly positive acknowledgement: that the psyche comprises a "constellation" of functions corresponding to the planetary powers.

This "old view" has survived through millennia because it corresponds to reality. A contemporary author, Thomas Moore, shows that this same realization is taken as understood in the work of Marsilio Ficino, the fifteenth-century Florentine whose contribution to European thinking is so great and so basic that until recently few scholars have been able to focus their minds upon it. Thomas Moore says of Ficino's astrological texts, "The planets correspond, then, to deeply felt movements in the soul ... Mars is not simply a surface tendency to anger, nor is Venus the trappings of body awareness. These planetary centers are deep in the psyche, generating many complexes, fantasies, and behaviors."*

---

* *The Planets Within: Marsilio Ficino's Astrological Psychology,* by Thomas Moore (Bucknell University Press, 1982), p. 126. This book is thoroughly recommended to those who wish to investigate the historical development of Western Planetary Magick and its underlying psychology.

The planets in the heavens, and the high archetypal forces which they transmit, thus act upon us through the reciprocity of their intensely creative counterparts in our Deep Mind. The archetypal reflections which are thus present to the unconscious depths of the psyche are, like all archetypes and archetypal images, "seminal" in nature: that is to say, the impulses, concepts and attitudes which they engender will multiply and proliferate their kind, thus influencing the feelings, thoughts and actions of the person to a considerable extent.

However, not only those counterparts, but the whole of the Deep Mind itself is creative—most potently creative—to an extent, and with a reality, which many doctors, psychologists, clergy and other observers are only just now beginning to comprehend. Whatever suggestions the Deep Mind accepts, from whatever source, it will seek to bring to fulfillment: not only inwardly, but in the outer world. Further, it has a very mysterious and unmeasured power to achieve its purposes. This is a truth which is both terrible and wonderful.

It is terrible because, as many instances have demonstrated, the Deep Mind can accept suggestions which are likely to bring about things we neither desire nor need in our lives: suggestions which, remaining in the unconscious, are not weeded out by the rational mind, or which in some cases were accepted in childhood before personal judgment was developed.

But it is also most wonderful because, with knowledge and understanding, we can implant or make fruitful in our Deep Mind those suggestions which we do want to see achieved. This is true even for such general psychic activities as psychokinesis or creative visualization; while, for any magical project which has a planetary affinity—healing a specific disorder, advancing in a specific occupation, making a talisman for a definite purpose, etc., as well as for more general aims such as well-being, or the healing ability, prosperity and the like—Planetary Magick provides a swift, sure method of stimulating the Deep Mind into the appropriate activity. Because of the reflection within the psyche of the planetary archetypes, linked constantly with their divine and cosmic originals, and because of the Deep Mind's readiness of response to these inner counterparts, to bring any one of them into play is a most potent means to fulfill the magical purpose.

For the inner life of the practitioner, the benefits of Planetary Magick can be immense. In the contemporary culture, where for many people the choice lies between a formalistic exoteric worship and no worship at all, the psyche's powers of response to the divine archetypes are nearly starved of awareness, of activity, of nourishment. The range of life experience which falls within the domain of the traditional Seven Planets comprises, in broad terms, the whole of our existence in this world. If, within the psyche itself, the living counterparts of those planetary powers are pinched and diminished by neglect, they can respond but feebly to their celestial originals, allowing us to live with only a fraction of our natural potential to feel, to know, to will and to direct our lives.

As Crowley declares in *Magick in Theory and Practice,*

> "Each element of oneself is . . . sterile and without meaning, until it fulfills itself, by 'love under will', in its counterpart in the Macrocosm."

Ficino's doctrine of care for the soul is based upon that same conviction.

To re-establish awareness of, and in, these inner focal points; to enhance their reciprocity with their cosmic originals; to control and direct within the psyche the influences of the seven luminaries, or to project their impelling force upon the external universe in order to bring creative purpose to tangible result: these are fruits within the compass of Planetary Magick. Its methods—meditation, ritual, drama, every way of formulating earthly or astral environments in attunement to the influence to be evoked—have grown through many centuries of observation and experiment, in many lands.

Considering the tremendous access to archetypal and cosmic power which can be gained through Planetary Magick, it is not surprising that it has become the basis upon which the main structure of Western magical procedure rests. The Paths of the Tree of Life open great doors inwards, and give approaches to traverse the psyche's boundless realms; but the Spheres establish potent and vital contacts with the illimitable deeps and glorious cosmic forces beyond the psyche.

This book is designed to take the reader through both simple and elaborate usages of Planetary Magick. Thus the underlying unity of method may become apparent, and at the same time the wide spectrum of intents and purposes which are suited to Planetary Magick may be demonstrated. Planetary Magick represents both a journey of adventure, and a homecoming: as a joyous and thrilling exploration it leads its practitioners, in reality, through essential phases of spiritual and magical progress, yet, just as truly, the planetary powers themselves are, have been and remain, an integral part of our being. For we are, surely and unalterably, throughout our whole fabric of body and psyche, children of our solar system, our home in the Cosmos.

2 *PLANETARY CHARACTERS*

A Legacy of the Ancient World

Three centuries before the present era, and probably earlier, the Greeks, to whom we owe the very name of astrology, had given that art a far wider and more magical connotation than it had previously possessed. Extending the ancient principle whereby certain objects and qualities were held sacred to certain deities—a principle well established in Greco-Egyptian magick for instance—they set afoot the concept of planetary correspondences, *Symbola*, in every area of interest or inquiry known to them. Living creatures, parts of the human body, minerals, drugs and the ailments amenable to them, countries, cities—besides colors, numbers and perfumes—everything was, and is, allocated to one or other of the seven planets, in accord with the affinity of its nature or of its effect. Arab and Jewish practitioners and scholars of Art Magick quickly perceived the logic, cogency and power of the concept; and the correspondences, classified according to planetary or sephirothic affinity, became an integral part of the expanding structure of the Qabalah. Subsequently, too, the zodiacal and elemental correspondences were formulated.

Two millennia, at any event, is a reasonable average age to give for the development of the main concepts concerning the *symbola*, as well as for many of the correspondences themselves which are still employed in Planetary Magick; while through succeeding centuries further attributions have been established by the Neoplatonists, the Persian Magi, the Alchemists, the Hermetists and many others.

The Medieval Picatrix

In the eleventh century, a most influential exponent of the use of

11

correspondences in Planetary Magick was Maslama b. Ahmad al-Majriti (of Madrid), who, drawing upon Greek and Arabic sources, laid heavy emphasis on the needful attunement of the magician to the Sphere of the proposed working. Going into seclusion so as to be untroubled by other influences, the magician was recommended to fast during a preliminary period; but then, in direct preparation for the rite itself, he was bidden to choose his food according to the correspondences of the planet whose Spirit he intended to invoke, and to use for the rite appropriately colored garments, with the corresponding incense and perfumes. Somewhat later in the Middle Ages, al-Majriti's work was translated into Latin under the name of *Picatrix*, and the manifest appeal of its ideas to astrologers, alchemists and magicians spread the fame of those ideas through literary Europe.

A Contemporary Perspective

Interestingly, various branches of social psychology at the present day, in their researches upon environmental influences, are making some productive studies on the effects of previously disregarded factors upon mental and emotional states, reactions and consequent performance. Their classification of their findings is, obviously, not Qabalistic; but the potent emotive and behavioral effects of colors, odors, and specific types of music for instance—effects which stir the Deep Mind in modes which may run contrary to the subject's conscious perspective—are confirmed without question.

The Magical Process

In Planetary Magick, where the synthesizing of a harmonious environment is an essential basis of the work, the correspondences perform a vital function; for from them is built up that requisite framework of symbolism whereby the unique character of the intended Sphere of operation is delineated and its ambience established.

This ambience, while having its own objective dynamism in the external earthly and astral worlds, is operative also upon and within the psyche of the magician. For the influences of both the physical and the astral correspondences—sound, color, gesture, symbolic shapes, odors, etc., even the manner and tone of the practitioner personally— are carried via the sensory and autonomic nerves to the Deep Mind of the practitioner, presenting it with a synthesis of some essential attributes of the relevant Sphere. The Deep Mind being thus stirred to echoic activity, the planetary counterpart within is spontaneously stimulated and accessed to the mighty powers of its cosmic and archetypal originals.

Within this "planetary matrix," whose intrinsic potency is immeasurably greater than the sum of effects of the individual *symbola* composing it, the processes of the rite are blended and brought to fruition of resolve, as within an alchemical crucible, conformably to the bounds of the chosen working.

Holographing the Powers

The correspondences are not the whole of Planetary Magick, but they are an essential part of its machinery. Certainly the practitioner should develop a familiarity with them as they exist in tabulated form, reflecting upon them freely and frequently so as to develop an imaginative perception of the powers which are characterized thereby; but, pre-eminently, they will be made real and vital to the psyche by their actual employment in the workings of Art Magick. This familiarity and use will bond them for the student to their planetary modality by the juxtaposition and reiteration of patterns of words and ideas, and, too, by all the coding mechanisms by which the bonds of association can be reinforced, to impress engrams on astral as well as on brain-cell circuits. The use of the correspondences will thus become, as it should be, an act of the conscious and unconscious levels in unity.

The following tables of correspondences, then, are intended to serve both as a reference guide to the symbolism of the Spheres and as a practical tool for the actual workings of Art Magick. These lists are by no means exhaustive, and valid alternatives in each case may well suggest themselves to the student and to the experienced practitioner. Individual style and creative initiative in magical working are objectives to be prized; and when once the underlying principles of the Spheres and of their correspondences have been grasped, improvisation—particularly for a specific working and its specific purpose—can greatly enhance the quality and power of a particular rite.

3 CORRESPONDENCES OF SATURN

PLANETARY SIGN
   1.   ♄

PLANETARY NAME
   2.   **In English:** Saturn
   3.   **In Greek:** Kronos
   4.   **In Hebrew:** Shabbathai

PLANETARY PROFILE
   5.   Lofty, autocratic, cold, sometimes mournful or brooding. The forces of constriction and crystallization. Has an affinity with the land and the depths of the Earth, with advancing age and long passage of time; but also with artistic creativity, the bringing of ideas into material form.

TITLE OF SEPHIRAH
   6.   **In Hebrew:** Binah
   7.   **In Greek:** Sophia*
   8.   **In English:** Understanding

TEXT FROM THE THIRTY-TWO PATHS OF WISDOM†
   9.   The third Path is the Consecrating Intelligence: it is the underlying principle of the Wisdom of the Beginning, which is named the Pattern of Faith and is its root, Affirmation (Amen). It is the parent of faith, for from its essential nature faith proceeds.

---

* The feminine aspect of Holy Wisdom.
† A.S. translation of the work by Joannes Stephanus Rittangelius (1642). For our commentary and notes, see Appendix A.

ETEMOLOGY OF SATRN
SATRN IN HEBREW

ELEMENTAL AFFINITY OF PLANET
10.   Earth

SYMBOLS AND MAGICAL IMPLEMENTS
11.   **Specific to Sphere:** Scythe, Keys, Hourglass, Drawing
      Compasses, Astrolabe. Cauldron, Mural Crown, Starry
      Robe, Double Axe (as symbols of the Great Mother).
      Suitable, but having other magical use: The Black Cloak.
      Ears of Corn or Barley. The Grail (as symbol of the
      Great Mother).

PRESIGILLA
12.   **Planetary:**   **Supernal:**

NUMBER AND GEOMETRIC FORM
13.   **Qabalistic number:** 3
14.   **Medieval number:** 8
15.   **Plane figure:** Triangle
16.   **Star:** 3-pointed star

QUALITIES OF DESIGN
17.   Abstract designs based on natural shapes, concentric circles
      and geometric designs suggesting spatial perspective.

COLORS
18.   **In Atziluth:** Dove grey
19.   **In Briah:** Indigo
20.   **In Yetzirah:** Soft red-brown
21.   **In Assiah:** Grey with fulvous shades
22.   **Ptolemaic color:** Grey

MUSIC FOR PLANETARY MOODS
23.   **Ideal qualities:** Brooding, transformative, mystical, obscure.
24.   **Selected examples:** *Finlandia* (Sibelius). *Pavane for a Dead
      Infanta* (Ravel). Saturn (*The Planets,* Holst). *Symphony No.
      8 in D Minor* (Ralph Vaughan Williams).

SUITABLE INSTRUMENTS AND SOUND EFFECTS
25.   Tambura. Deep-toned gong. Wood blocks. Ticking clock.
      Strident, clangorous sounds. Recorded ocean sounds.

ANIMALS AND MYTHOLOGICAL BEINGS

26.   Ass. Goat. Antelope. Goose. Peacock. Cuckoo. Dove. Seamew. Bat. Spider. Fish-Goat. Chimaera.

TREES AND OTHER VEGETATION

27.   **Trees:** Yew. Elm. Cypress. Mountain Pine. Ebony. Acacia. Pomegranate.

28.   **Herbs:** Violet. Trillium. White lilies (all types). Opium poppy. Nightshade (Belladonna). Horsetail. Amaranth (Love-lies-bleeding). Mullein.

29.   **Incenses, Perfumes, etc.:** Myrrh. Spikenard. Guiac wood (Lignum Vitae). Tamarind. Cassia. Patchouli.

GEMSTONES AND OTHER MINERALS

30.   **Metals:** Lead. Antimony.

31.   **Gemstones:** Diamond. Jet. Black Onyx.

32.   **Other minerals:** Basalt. Slate. Anthracite. Geodes. Asbestos. Obsidian. Pumice. Glass (smoked or clear).

THE PLANETS AND HEALTH

33.   **Physiological functions:** Formation and maintenance of skin, bone structure, teeth and cartilage. Governance of the spleen, the skeleton generally and the knees in particular, the glands generally and the ductless glands in particular.

34.   **Pathological effects (bodily):** Skin afflictions such as leprosy, scurvy, eczema. Restrictive afflictions such as impeded circulation, rheumatism, ankylosed joints, atrophies, spinal maladies. Maladies of congelation and solidification such as arteriosclerosis, phlebitis, stone, gravel. Chronic health problems generally, including organic and nerve deafness.

35.   **Pathological effects (psychic):** Apathy, depression or over-mastering fears, possibly sapping the natural powers of recuperation, causing afflictions of the skin, or inhibiting normal glandular action. Excessive care of material resources, which may prevent the taking of early or adequate curative measures.

PLANETARY GESTURE

36.   **The Gesture Pater (Father), accomplished as follows:**

The Celestial Queen

1st point, "the Wand." Erect stance, arms at sides.

2nd point, "Orante." Arms are raised forwards, elbows flexed, until upper arm is horizontal and forearm raised to about 45° above horizontal; palms are forwards, fingers not separated.

3rd point, "Attis." In one flowing movement, the left arm swings downwards to the left side and somewhat away from the body, palm upwards, balancing the right arm which is raised aloft and maintained with the cupped palm upwards, fingers to the back. The head meanwhile is raised to look towards the right hand, and the right foot is advanced, toes resting lightly on the ground and heel raised, completing the balance of the entire figure. This changes smoothly to:

4th point, "Cybele." Right arm is brought down and forward to about horizontal. The palm is upwards, forefinger and middle finger are extended together, the third and little finger are closed but not tightly. Left palm is turned downwards, the arm raised to the horizontal but not rigid. The head turns to look along the left arm. At the same time, the right foot is brought back beside the left.

5th point, "Uplifting the World." Head forward, both hands sweep around slowly in incurving crescent movements to reach a symmetrical position, arms raised forward, elbows bent and pointing down, palms upwards and held on high, as if raising (for instance) a sheaf of wheat or similar offering which lies across the forearms.

6th point, "the Wand." Erect stance, arms at sides.

MAGICAL IMAGES OF THE SPHERE

37(a). **Celestial Queen:** A powerful and maternal female figure with a face of unutterable sweetness and high spirituality is seated upon a massive throne. Upon her head is a mural crown of gold, from beneath which her hair descends, framing her face in long dark tresses, adorned with sparkling points of silver light. The throne is of lustrous black stone, like polished jet, and has a silver step or foot rest: it is firmly and steadily established upon luminous dark blue water which gently swells. In the distance towards

The Ancient

the horizon the sky is bright, but above it is dark, with a single large multi-pointed star shining high over the head of the seated figure. She wears a long and ample robe of luminous whiteness, which is open in front to disclose a garment of deep black beneath. Her robes conceal her feet. Her right hand is raised in blessing, while in her left hand she holds up a triangular prism. From this prism arcs a rainbow, its seven bands of brilliant color spreading wide as they descend into the waters.

37(b). **The Ancient:** An aged male figure with beard and shoulder-length hair of grey is seated on a low outcrop of rock in level, fertile ground. This rock stands between two ancient yew trees, whose dark foliage and pale sinewy branches are densely interwoven so as to form an arch above the seated figure. Beyond this dark arch can be seen a sunlit orchard. The figure wears a draped garment, dusky in color with highlights of gold: this covers the lower part of his body to the ankles and passes over the right shoulder, leaving his arms and part of his chest bare. Upon his brow is a threefold burst of splendor, emitting rays of brilliant light. On the upper part of both arms are heavy barbaric bracelets of gold: his bare feet rest upon the Earth. In the palm of his upraised left hand he holds a large faceted diamond, which emits a dazzling radiance: his right arm supports a sheaf of corn.

MICROCOSMIC KEYWORDS OF THE SPHERE
38.   **Quality in Ruach:** Fulfillment
39.   **Responsive Ruach functions:** Inspiration, Renewal
40.   **Quality in Nephesh:** Stability
41.   **Responsive Nephesh functions:** Reverence, Endurance

AURUM SOLIS DIVINE AND ARCHONTIC NAMES
42(a).   **Supernal Divine Name (Atziluth):** Turana
42(b).   **Planetary Divine Name (Atziluth):** Ialdabaoth
43.   **Archon (Briah):** Menestheus
44.   **Power (Yetzirah):** Ascherias
45.   **Intelligence (Yetzirah):** Aschia
46.   **Spirit (Yetzirah):** Abethes

PLANETARY STANZA FROM THE SONG OF PRAISES

47.   **Stanza XXXII, Tau:**

Thine is the Sign of the End, Being fulfilled
                    Sum of existences:
Thine is the ultimate Door opened on Night's
                    unuttered mystery:
Thine, the first hesitant step into the dark
                    of those but latterly
          Born to the Labrinth!

OLYMPIC PLANETARY SPIRIT

48(a).   **Spirit of Saturn:** Aratron

48(b).   **His Sigil:**

48(c).   **Yetziratic manifestation of Spirit:** A tall, large-framed
        but thin male figure with dark grey hair and beard. He
        is dressed in a full-skirted robe completely encrusted
        with metallic crystals, in which continually flashes a
        cold fire. On the feet of this figure are dark sandals
        similarly ornamented. The countenance of Aratron is
        austere but benign, with a look of latent power and
        authority. The eyes are deep-set, dark, brilliant and
        steadily gazing. The thin hands, heavily ringed, are
        raised in a gesture of greeting and blessing. Without
        moving, he awaits the magician's will. (See color plate of
        Aratron after page 204.)

HEBREW DIVINE AND ANGELIC NAMES

49.   **Divine Name (Atziluth):** Yahveh Elohim *or* Yahweh
        Elohim *or* Yod Heh Vau Heh Elohim *or* Tetragrammaton
        Elohim
50.   **Archangel (Briah):** Tzaphqiel
51.   **Angelic Chora (Yetzirah):** Aralim, "the Thrones."
52.   **Planetary Angel (Yetzirah):** Kassiel
53.   **Sigil of Planetary Angel:**
54.   **Intelligence (Yetzirah):** Agiel
55.   **Spirit (Yetzirah):** Zazel

PLANETARY STANZA FROM THE SEVENFOLD AFFIRMATION*
56.   Therefore through the worlds is he acclaimed: he is
mighty.
Therefore is he praised, who has the patience of ages;
Anger passes, times go by, his truth is unchanging:
Those who come in trust to him, to new life he bringeth.
Therefore most exalted he, and through the worlds of
Life his name is glorious!

NEOPLATONIST DIVINE NAME
57(a). **Supernal Divine Name (Atziluth):** Hagios Athanatos,
"Holy Immortal One"
57(b). **Planetary Divine Name (Atziluth):** Aionos Kyrios,
"Lord of the Ages"

SACRED VOWEL OF GREEK QABALAH
58.   O (the letter *Omega*)

VOWEL TONES OF THE COSMIC HARMONY
59(a). **Contemporary Magical Mode:**

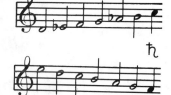

59(b). **Greek Gnostic Mode:**

GREEK DEITIES
60(a). **Hera.**
Her epithets: The Concealed One. The Revealed One.
Queen of Heaven. All-powerful Mistress. The Chaste.
The Ox-eyed. The Luminous Bride. The Virgin Mother.
The Young Mother. The Widow. The Purposeful One.
Lady of Flowers. Bringer to Birth. Bringer to the Day.
Helper of Women. Helper of Heroes.
Her Attributes: The diadem of Stars. The Torch (as patron-
ess of marriage and as the flame of divine perception
illumining the Earth). The Pomegranate. The Standing
Stone. The Monolith. The Pillar of Wood. Cuckoo. Peacock.
Cow.

---

* A hymn extolling the Divine Nature, adapted from the text of the tenth century AMRV LALHIM of
Kalonymos. Aurum Solis Translation.

Hera

60(b). **Kronos.**

His epithets: Lord of Primal Innocence. Lord of the Golden Age. Father of Gods. Devourer. The Great One. The Ancient One. Dweller in Shadows. Father of Time. Father of All Things. Maker of Seasons. The Reaper.

His Attributes: The Sickle. The Throne. The Dark Robe. Chariot drawn by Winged Serpents.

60(c). **Aphrodite Ourania.**

Her epithets: The All-Holy. The Undying Light. Celestial Beauty. Mother of Gods and Men. Mother of the World. Mother of Life. Queen of Love. The Starry One. Lady of the Deeps. Sovereign Protectress. The Victorious One.

Her attributes: The Crown. The Sphere (upon which she is represented, as indicating her ascendancy over all things mutable). The richly broidered vestment. The Girdle. Swan. Poppy.

ROMAN DEITIES

61(a). **Iuno.**

Her epithets: Queen of Heaven. Saturnia. Lady of Childbirth. Preserver. Lady of the Shades of the Dead. Bringer to Light.

Her character: Iuno is the powerful and universal ruling Goddess. She is patroness of all women; likewise the personal Holy Guardian of each individual woman is called, in Roman style, her Iuno. The Goddess' most ancient aspect, and the meaning of her name, is probably as The Maiden; but as invoked goddess of weddings and guardian of marriage she is usually represented as a youthful, dignified matron. Equally, she is anciently the female counterpart of Ianus the Gatekeeper, who is the God of January. Iuno herself is in a special sense the Guardian of the gates: she was celebrated at Rome on the day of the New Moon every month, and as Iuno Lucina she opened the gates of life for every child.

Her attributes: The Crescent Diadem. The Matron's Robe. The Scepter. Chariot, Arms and Armor (as Preserver). The Marriage Torch. The Throne. The Goose. The Cuckoo.

Attendant: Iris (Goddess of the Rainbow), her messenger.

Kronos

61(b). Saeturnus.

His epithets: The Sower. Divine Abundance. The Bareheaded One. Ruler of the Golden Age. The Old One. Lord of Peace.

His character: Saeturnus is from ancient times an agricultural deity of sowing and harvest, fertility, peace and plenty. The name of his consort Ops signifies "Abundance," but sometimes he is partnered with Lua ("Destruction," "Fire") as indicating the clearing away of the debris of past seasons. Besides being the God of Saturday, he presides over the Winter Solstice festival of the Saturnalia, December 19 through 26. This is the great midwinter celebration with feasting, drinking and gift-giving, the traditional gifts being candles and dolls. Above all, Saeturnus is ruler of the Golden Age, the time which is looked back upon nostalgically when the Earth brought forth her abundance without toil, when the climate was totally genial, and when war was unknown. The joy of that era lingers in the character and worship of Saeturnus.

His attributes: The Billhook. Ears of Corn. Fruit-laden branches.

ETRUSCAN DEITY

62.   **Uni:** Queen of Heaven. Sky-mother, or All-mother, consort of Tinia. Supreme female deity. *Crown. Pomegranate. Violet.*

BABYLONIAN DEITIES

63(a). Ea.

His ephithets: Princely Antelope. Lord of the Earth. Lord of Wisdom. Lord of the sacred Eye. God of Mighty Power.

His Character: Primarily Ea is Lord of the Water Deep, the Apsu, the mighty and unfathomable river of fresh water which is conceived of as encompassing or supporting the Earth. Giving the Water Deep its mystical meaning, Ea is enthroned upon that Abyss of darkness which keeps concealed the Supernal Mysteries. Worshiped with his consort Damkina as givers of counsel and of oracles, and as defenders of humankind against non-material

Ea

foes, Ea is particularly the patron of all who work in gold and gems, stone, clay and wood. Sometimes he is represented as the Fish-Antelope (now the Fish-Goat symbolizing zodiacal Capricorn); sometimes in human form with streams of water springing from his shoulders, or from a vessel which he carries.

63(b). **Ishtar.**

Her epithets: Lady of Starry Heaven. She whose seat is on high. Queen of the Gods. Queen of the Mountain. Mother of All.

Her Character: Ishtar's name is a translation of the older Sumerian name—Ininni, Lady of Heaven—of the supreme Mother Goddess. Along with her association with the planet Venus, Ishtar remains always in character the Saturnian "Great Mother," comprising and transcending the nature of all seven Planetary Spheres. This is the significance of a famous episode in the story of her love for the divine youth Tammuz. To rescue him, she braves the descent through the seven adverse spheres. As she goes, she pays forfeit of one of her adornments at each gate; finally, as her unveiled supernal self, withstanding triumphantly the deepest malice of the underworld. The Saturnian Ishtar appears wearing a crown, enthroned, and holding the Ring of Divinity; or standing with both hands raised in blessing, or as Mother of All offering her breasts.

HINDU DEITIES

64(a). **Parvati.**

Her epithets: The Elevated One. Dweller upon the Height. The Great Goddess. Mother Goddess of the World. Power of Shiva. The Shining One. The Abiding One. Encompassing Protection. She who Delights in Blessing. The Generous One. She who brings to Birth. Perfection of Bliss. The Enthroned One. Mistress of the Play of Reality. The Pure Spirit. Celestial Light.

Her Attributes: Beautiful and meditative countenance. The Tiara. Rich earrings, necklaces, bracelets and anklets. The Goddess is seated upon a dais. Her right leg is folded horizontally before her. Her left leg is extended downwards

Ishtar of Erech

off the dais. Her right hand is raised in blessing. Her left hand is extended, palm upwards, conveying a sense of "the touch of the divine" which lifts one out of the self into supernal ekstasis.

64(b). **Kali (the dark aspect of Parvati).**

Her epithets: The Dark One. The Dark Mother. Power of Shiva. Drinker of Blood. She in whom is seen all holiness. The Irresistible One. She who Nourishes the World. The Devourer. She to whom Life pays its due. Mother Goddess of the World. Taker and Giver of Life. Awesome Beauty. Mother of Freedom. The Ultimate Desire.

Her Attributes: Two, four or six arms. Dark skin. Red eyes and palms of the hands. Bloodstained face and breasts. Protruding fangs and tongue. Disordered hair (sometimes imaged as intense rising flames). The Necklace of Skulls. The Girdle (composed of human hands or of a serpent). The Noose. The Sword. The Goat (as her sacrificial animal).

64(c). **Shiva (as Supernal Nataraja).**

His epithets: Lord of the Dance. The Great God. Principle of Change. Principle of Dissolution. The Divine Dancer. He whose Whirling calls forth the ferment of creation. Enchanter of Demons. Transformer of Demons. Lord of Ecstasy. Lord of Entrancement. Master of Clear Vision. He whose Footfall disperses illusion. God of the Dance of Truth. He who draws all beings to Himself. God of the Trance of Perfection. He who is Manifest in the circling Worlds. He who rings the Worlds with Whirling Fire. He of the Fiery Nimbus. Swift Flame of Frenzy. Vortex of Oblivion. He who Dances within the Heart.

His attributes: The Third Eye. The Serpent Necklet. Many arms, expressing mudras or holding flames or varied emblems of his divinity. The encircling Nimbus of Cosmic Fire.

64(d). **Brahma**

His epithets: Dweller in the Waves. He of the Four Faces. The Golden Womb. The Witness. Mountain of Crystal. Sea of Nectar. The Highest Truth. The Changeless. Creator of All Things from Himself. He who Creates by Meditation. Originator of All. Possessor of Nothing.

The Beloved. The Impartial Judge. Light-giver. The Sacred Presence.

His attributes: The Goose, the Swan or the Peacock (upon which he rides). Appearing four-armed, the God holds the Vedas in one hand and in the other three a Rosary, a Lustral Vessel and a Libation Spoon.

EGYPTIAN DEITIES

65(a). **Net (Neith)**

Her epithets: She-who-is. Mystery. The Self-born. The Self-existent One. The Everlasting Goddess. The Concealed One. Mistress of the Spindle and the Loom. Mother of the Gods. First Mother. Powerful Mother. Mother-Father. Lady of the Heavens. Lady of the West. Lady of Sais. She who Opens the Paths. She who ties the magical knots of protection. Weaver of the Veil.

Her Image: The Goddess wears the Red Crown; or she is adorned with the Old Kingdom headdress surmounted by the symbol of the Shuttle. She carries the two crossed Arrows (her most ancient token) and the Bow; or she bears the Ankh, and either the Papyrus Scepter or the Ouas (the Scepter of Peaceful Authority).

65(b). **Ptah.**

His epithets: Celestial Artificer. First Father. Primal Power. Father of the beginnings. The Ancient One, the Dweller on the Horizon of Everlastingness. He whose youth is constantly renewed. God of the Shining Eyes. Fashioner of the Firmament. Fashioner of the Pattern of Sun and Moon. Master of Metals. Divine Craftsman. Architect of all that is. Establisher of Maat. He whose Feet are upon the Earth. He whose Head is in the Heavens. Lord of Stability. Opener of the Mouth.

His Image: Seated upon his throne, or standing, the God wears the ceremonial beard, and an encircling band upon his bald head. His body is tightly enswathed (signifying his character as the spirit which moves within the wrappings of form). He bears the Ankh and the Ouas. He carries also the Tet-symbol, or this may be upreared behind his throne (in either instance signifying his nature as "Lord of Stability").

4 CORRESPONDENCES OF JUPITER

PLANETARY SIGN
1.   ♃

PLANETARY NAME
2.   **In English:** Jupiter
3.   **In Greek:** Zeus
4.   **In Hebrew:** Tzedeq

PLANETARY PROFILE
5.   Majestic, expansive, organizing, optimistic. Has an affinity
with the blue sky and the sea; an overview of the unity of
life gives a sense of responsible concern. Religious and
civic leadership. All that is conducive to health, prosperity
and advancement. Justice interpreted to fulfill the needs
of those involved. Benevolent power.

TITLE OF SEPHIRAH
6.   **In Hebrew:** Gedulah, *also* Chesed
7.   **In Greek:** Doxa
8.   **In English:** Majesty, *also* Loving Kindness

TEXT FROM THE THIRTY-TWO PATHS OF WISDOM
9.   The Fourth Path is the Measuring, Collecting or Receptive
Intelligence: so named because it holds within it all the
high potencies, and from it issues forth all the successive
modalities of spirit in their highest being, each emanated
from another through the power of the first Emanation,
Kether.

ELEMENTAL AFFINITY OF PLANET
10.   Water

SYMBOLS AND MAGICAL IMPLEMENTS
11.   **Specific to Sphere:** Oak-leaf crown. The Jupiterian Cup
(as symbol of abundance). Cornucopia. Royal Scepter.
Shepherd's Staff. Trident (Oceanic Chesed). Thunderbolt.
Suitable, but having other magical use: Aspergil. Gavel.

PRESIGILLUM

12.   Z⚶

NUMBER AND GEOMETRIC FORM
13.   **Qabalistic number: 4**
14.   **Medieval number: 4**
15.   **Plane figure:** Square
16.   **Star:** 4-pointed star

QUALITIES OF DESIGN
17.   Regular rhombic and rectangular forms, squares, parallelo-
grams, intersecting lines.

COLORS
18.   **In Atziluth:** Lilac
19.   **In Briah:** Blue
20.   **In Yetzirah:** Light royal blue
21.   **In Assiah:** Nacreous green-blue merging into shell-pink
22.   **Ptolemaic color:** White

MUSIC FOR PLANETARY MOODS
23.   **Ideal qualities:** Majestic, joyful, uplifting
24.   **Selected examples:** "Air on a G String" (Bach). "Symphonic
Variations Op. 78" (Dvorak). "The Moldau" (*Vltava*,
Smetana). "Fingal's Cave" (Mendelssohn).

SUITABLE INSTRUMENTS AND SOUND EFFECTS
25.   Cello. Double bass. Saxophone. Bass drum. Conch shell.
Hand-clapping. Recorded electrical storm.

ANIMALS AND MYTHOLOGICAL BEINGS

26. Eagle. Owl (Widsom aspect). Swan. Whale. White bull. Centaur. Hippogriff. Unicorn.

TREES AND OTHER VEGETATION

27. **Trees:** All true Oaks. Cedar. Pine. Olive. Juniper. Hickory. Sassafras. Maple. Chestnut. Horse chestnut. Lime. Sycamore.

28. **Herbs:** Flax. Borage. Brooklime. Liverwort. Green Ti plant. Agrimony. Purple Betony. Sages generally.

29. **Incenses, Perfumes, etc.:** Nutmeg. Pine gum. Clove. Sarsaparilla. Hyssop.

GEMSTONES AND OTHER MINERALS

30. **Metals:** Tin. Zinc. Antimony.

31. **Gemstones:** Sapphire. Lapis Lazuli. Amethyst. Turquoise. Labradorite. Aquamarine.

32. **Other minerals:** Porphyry. Tektites. Any substance charred or fused by lightning.

THE PLANETS AND HEALTH

33. **Physiological functions:** Maintenance of cellular development. Integration and preservation of the soft tissues of the body, the intestines in particular with the liver and the digestive processes: the region of the hips and thighs: the arteries: the feet.

34. **Pathological effects (bodily):** Afflictions of the heart and liver, high blood pressure, varicose veins, apoplexy, stroke. Excess weight. Fatty degeneration. Diabetes. Pleurisy. Disorders of the teeth.

35. **Pathological effects (psychic):** Heedless self-indulgence, particularly in matters of food, drink, and indolence, so as to impair the body's powers of resistance: however, those powers where there is an overabundance of Jupiterian influence will also tend to be unusually robust.

PLANETARY GESTURE

36. **The Gesture Heliodromos, (Path of the Sun), accomplished as follows:**
1st point, "the Wand." Erect stance, arms at sides.

2nd point, "the Thunderer." Left arm is raised upwards and back to "hurling" position, the fingers curved as if grasping a thunderbolt; at the same time right arm is raised straight forward, horizontally from shoulder, left foot stepping back.

3rd point, "Chesed." Right arm is drawn back from above position, to rest palm on left shoulder. At the same time, left foot is brought forward to standing position beside right foot. The left arm is lowered to rest horizontally across the front of the body.

4th point, "Kaph." Elbows to sides, both forearms are raised forward horizontally. The left hand turned palm upwards, cupped: the right hand turned palm downwards, flat, with fingers straight.

5th point, "the Wand." Erect stance, arms at sides.

MAGICAL IMAGE OF THE SPHERE

37. **Priest King:** A mature male figure, majestic but benign of countenance, is seated upon a throne of lapis lazuli. This throne, with its dais of four steps, is securely established in the bright blue firmament. The figure has luxuriant dark hair and beard, his head crowned with a simple gold circlet which is set with square-cut sapphires. He wears a purple robe, square-necked and extending to his ankles; this robe has a single narrow vertical stripe, centrally placed, of electric blue. The sleeves are full and simple. Upon his feet are sandals. In the right hand of this figure is a scepter, the head of which is in the shape of an eagle with outstretched wings. The left hand, raised high and out to the side, holds a massive goblet. From the four quarters of this goblet there spring up and over the lip, fountain-wise, streams of clear liquid: these four streams fall vertically, without touching either the figure or the throne. Upon the lowest of the four steps of the dais rests a cornucopia, a Horn of Plenty with ripe and beautiful fruits spilling out from it.

MICROCOSMIC KEYWORDS OF THE SPHERE

38. **Quality in Ruach:** Breadth of Purpose
39. **Responsive Ruach functions:** Benignity, Moderation

Priest King

40. **Quality in Nephesh:** Elevation
41. **Responsive Nephesh Functions:** Compassion, Responsibility.

AURUM SOLIS DIVINE AND ARCHONTIC NAMES

42. **Divine Name (Atziluth):** Zaraietos
43. **Archon (Briah):** Orthoter
44. **Power (Yetzirah):** Kapaios
45. **Intelligence (Yetzirah):** Zathanat
46. **Spirit (Yetzirah):** Demoros

PLANETARY STANZA FROM THE SONG OF PRAISES

47. **Stanza XXI, Kaph:**

Cup that receives and bestows, generous palm
garnering, scattering,
Thine are the bountiful rains, thine is the fount
purpled and perilous:
Thine is dominion to cast down to the pit,
thine to give sanctuary—
Yea, to give liberty!

OLYMPIC PLANETARY SPIRIT

48(a). **Spirit of Jupiter:** Bethor

48(b). **His Sigil:** ⊢⊔⊔

48(c). **Yetziratic manifestation of Spirit:** A male figure of medium height and robust physique. The beard is full, dark and glossy, the eyes are large, bright and widely spaced, and the face has a genial but thoughtful expression. The attire is a rich and flowing robe of white brocade, patterned with deep blue arabesques, and pointed shoes of the same fabric. He wears a gold turban, on the front of which is a sapphire aigret with a peacock feather. On his left hip, through a sash of heavy white silk is thrust a short, curved sword, the scabbard of which is of varied metals patterned like a bird's plumage, and adorned with shining blue gemstones; the pommel of the sword is carved in the form of an eagle's head. The aspect of Bethor is commanding but entirely peaceable. In his left hand he grasps a long-necked metal vase, from which streamers of many-colored smoke swirl and rise. (See color plate of Bethor following page 204.)

HEBREW DIVINE AND ANGELIC NAMES
49. **Divine Name (Atziluth):** El
50. **Archangel (Briah):** Tzadqiel
51. **Angelic Chora (Yetzirah):** Chasmalim, "Brilliant Ones."
52. **Planetary Angel (Yetzirah):** Sachiel
53. **Sigil of Planetary Angel:**
54. **Intelligence (Yetzirah):** Yophiel
55. **Spirit (Yetzirah):** Hismael

PLANETARY STANZA FROM THE SEVENFOLD AFFIRMATION
56. Kingly is his throne established, founded in justice,
Righteousness, magnificence, and wisdom of judgment.
Earth and sea are in his hand, the world and the heavens;
All he doth sustain, and all in equity ruleth.
Therefore most exalted he, who nurtureth the souls that
long for justice.

NEOPLATONIST DIVINE NAME
57. **Divine Name (Atziluth):** Pantokrator, "All-Mover"

SACRED VOWEL OF GREEK QABALAH
58. U (the letter *Upsilon*)

VOWEL TONES OF THE COSMIC HARMONY
59(a). **Contemporary Magical Mode:**

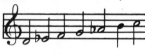

59(b). **Greek Gnostic Mode:**

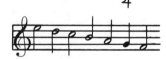

GREEK DEITIES
60(a). **Zeus.**
His epithets: Father-Mother. All-powerful. All-knowing. King of Heaven. Sovereign of the Deathless Ones. Divine Fire. Radiant Immortal Head. Wielder of the Stars. Mover

Zeus

Athene

of the Forces of Heaven. Zeus of the Starry Beard. King of Earth. Sustainer of Earth. Glory of the Deep Cavern. Lord of Bright Day. Thunderer. Gatherer of Storms. Splendid Swan of Heaven. Mighty White Bull. Giver of abundance. Giver of Shining Dew. Giver of Golden Rain. Liberator. Counselor. Zeus the Friend. The Just One. Everlasting Fountain of Justice. Lord of Boundaries. Champion of Supplicants. Protector of Companions. Patron of Strangers. He who brings to achievement.

His attributes: The Thunderbolt. Lightning. The Cup. The Throne. The Scepter. Eagle. Oak.

60(b). **Athene.**

Her epithets: Parthenos (the Maiden). The Grey-eyed. Bearer of Victory. Daughter of the Firmament. Daughter of Justice. Giver of Wisdom. Giver of the Arts of Peace. Bountiful Giver of the Olive. Mistress of the Loom. Builder of Ships. Dweller before the Shrine. Lady of Warm Brightness. Keeper of Hidden Mystery. Guardian of the Innocent. Champion. The Active One.

Her Attributes: The Aegis (Breastplate with the head of Medusa). The Helmet. The Spear and Shield. The Peplos. The Image of Nike (the Winged Victory, held in her right hand). Olive branch. Owl. Cock. Serpent (related to the Corbis, the "basket of holy things" which lies sometimes at her feet).

60(c). **Poseidon.**

His ephithets: Ruler of Ocean. Blue-haired Poseidon. Commander of Tempest. Giver of Calm Seas. Leader of the Nymphs. Guide of Seafarers. Poseidon of the Headlands. Preserver. Healer of Tenos. Bull-Poseidon. Grasper of Earth. Earth Shaker. Lord of Horses.

His Attributes: The Trident. The Chariot. The Sacred Spring. The Ship. The Horse. The Dolphin. Pine tree. Wreaths of pine.

Attendants: Nymphs. Naiads. Nereids.

ROMAN DEITIES

61(a). **Iuppiter.**

His ephithets: Best and Greatest. Bright Father. Ruler of the Celestial Assembly. Sender of Light. God of Day.

Poseidon

Sender of Lightning. King of Gods and Men. Father.

His Character: As Sky-father, Iuppiter is invoked not only in matters relating to the weather, but in matters relating to rectitude and "the light of conscience." He is the supreme divine witness of solemn oaths, lofty and moral in character, and inspirer of "the sense of duty." His temples are most often on hilltops. Nights of the Full Moon are sacred to him; so also are places (including trees) which have been struck by lightning. As "Sender of Lightning" he had at Rome an altar on the Field of Mars. The cultivation of the vine is in his care.

His attributes: Eagle. Serpent. Oak and Pine trees. The Thunderbolt (sometimes represented by ancient worked flints).

Attendants: The Dii Consentes (the Twelve Consenting Gods).

61(b). **Minerva.**

Her epithets: Wisdom Victorious. Minerva of the Spear. The Strong One. Guardian of the Skillful. The Virgin Spirit.

Her Character: This Goddess forms a trine with Iuppiter and Iuno, both of whom have, at least, strong affinities with their Etruscan counterparts Tinia and Uni. Minerva herself is entirely Etruscan in origin, her earlier name being *Menrva.* Her principal temple in Rome became a recognized meeting place for guilds of artists, craftspeople and actors, Minerva being patroness and protector of all professions and artistic occupations. Her name signifies "Mind"; she exemplifies mind dominating and expressing itself through matter. She is the warrior aspect of Wisdom. Minerva is a tall and stately woman wearing a long robe with helmet, breastplate and spear of Athene. Like Athene too she may carry the winged image of Victory, which holds aloft the laurel wreath.

Her attributes: Helmet. Breastplate. Spear. The Screech Owl.

ETRUSCAN DEITIES

62(a). **Tinia:** The Thunderer. Sky-father, lord of all climatic manifestations. In agreement with other leading deities,

Marduk

he is controller of human destinies. *Thunderbolt. Scepter. Eagle.*

62 *(b)*. **Menrva:** Faithful Wisdom. See *Minerva* (entry 61b in this table). Note however that the Etruscan Menrva is winged.

62 (c). **Nethun:** This deity, like Poseidon, represents the aquatic aspect of Chesed. Originally a divinity of fresh water, in particular the deep springs which do not fail in summer's heat: only later, as the Roman Neptune, is he associated with ocean. *Horse. Winged Horse. Hippocamp (forequarters of horse, with fish tail). Bull. Pine tree.*

BABYLONIAN DEITIES

63(a). **Marduk (Amar-Uduk, Merodak).**

His epithets: Light of his Father. Young Steer of Day. King of Heaven. Glorious Word of Power. Overseer who is good. Guardian of the Four quarters. Lord of Life. Citadel of Prayer. Shepherd of the Gods. Shepherd of the Stars. Master of Magick. Restorer of Joy to Humankind.

His character: To Marduk, son of Ea and Damkina, the planet Jupiter is assigned. He is however one of the most widely powerful of the Babylonian deities, and assumes on occasion the function of almost every other deity in the pantheon. Early seen as the bestower of green plants and ripe harvests through the beneficent influence of the sky-forces, he is later, through the movements of the luminaries, the arbiter of each person's destiny. He is "Shepherd of the Gods," keeping justice among them as well as ruling the four quarters of the world. When he speaks, fire blazes from his mouth. The gemstones owe to him their luster; with that gift he rewarded their loyalty to him, at a time when half the world of nature had risen against his laws. In a special way he is Master of Magick: particularly with regard to the banishing of demons, and to the many positive energies which can be conveyed by the magical uses of water. In one aspect Marduk, in normal human form, wields a curved sword, often in combat against a winged dragon. His attributes, however, vary widely in the various aspects of his divinity: he carries, as appropriate, spear, scepter, bow and quiver, thunderbolt, club, or the magick net which restrains doers of evil. Upon his head is the crowned helmet, and upon his hand a royal signet ring. He may appear as a winged bull-centaur,* or in colossal human form with multiple eyes and ears. Essentially, in all aspects he is a being of healing, regenerative light, shimmering in rainbow colors, in whose glory his form is scarcely visible.

63(b). **Adad.**

His epithets: Thunderer. Lord of Storms. Lord of Prevision.

His Character: Thunder, lightning, howling winds and lashing rain are at the command of Adad: but so are the gentle lifegiving showers and the flooding rivers which renew the fruitfulness of dry Earth. Into the mind, likewise, Adad can pour the light and the fruitful dew of insight which brings a perception of the future. Adad stands upright with one foot on the back, one on the head, of a running bull. In each hand he wields a thunderbolt. He wears a cylindrical crown, and his garment is adorned with golden stars.

HINDU DEITIES

64(a). **Indra**

His epithets: Great Indra. King of Heaven. The Incomparable One. The Immense One. Thunderer. Master of the Thunderbolt (Vajra). Cloud Rider. The Mighty One. Aid of Warriors. Kind Provider. He who delights in the Soma. Hero. Regent of the Movable. Regent of the Immovable. He who Succours. Opener of the Clouds. Giver of Rain. He who Revels in the Tempest. Maker of River-channels. Dweller upon Meru.

His Attributes: The Vajra (itself a magical entity, which the God can send to give humans such help as accords with its nature). The Bow. The Chariot. The Horse or the Elephant (as his mount).

64(b). **Sarasvati**

Her epithets: The Abundant Waters. Reservoir of Life. Goddess of Wisdom. The Transcendent One. Power of Brahma. Brahma Herself. The Eloquent One. The Gentle Light. Giver of the Sacred Script. Mother of the Vedas.

---

* Not to be confused with the human-headed winged bull guardians, who are tutelary spirits of a lesser order.

Adad

Breath of the Poets. Maker of Music. She who Inspires. Light of the Sages. The Living Meditation.

Her attributes: Beautiful countenance. Radiant and graceful form. The Tiara. The Necklace. Bracelets. The Garland. The Rosary. The Scriptures. The Vina (her stringed instrument). The Lotus (which she extends in offering).

EGYPTIAN DEITIES

65(a). Hapi

His epithets: The Vast One. The Unsearchable. Lord of the Celestial River. Father of the Gods. He who Makes to Live. Sustainer of Life. Giver of Abundance. Giver of the Fertile Waters. Source of Joy. Creator of Blessings. Aegis of the People. The Nourisher. Giver of Peace. Father of Increase. Lord of the Papyrus. Lord of the Lotus. Fountain of Divine Power.

His image: The God wears headdress, collar and girdle. His form is male but with pendant breasts. In his hands he bears the Lotus and the Papyrus. As Lord of the Two Niles the God may appear in double image: as Hapi of the South his adornments are white and he is crowned with Lotus, as Hapi of the North his adornments are red and he is crowned with Papyrus.

65(b). Maat

Her epithets: That which is True. Perfect Measure. Maat the Beautiful. Law. Justice. Truth. The Good Gift. Sustainer of the Sun. Tracer of the Course of the Sun. The Changeless. The Undeviating. Twofold Truth. Lady of the Hall of Judgment. Lady of the Heavens. Queen of Earth. Directress of the Underworld. The Measure of the Heart. Right Order.

Her image: This dignified and stately Goddess may appear winged. She bears the Ankh and the Papyrus Scepter. She wears a deep collar, and upon her Old Kingdom headdress is bound the single Feather of Truth.

65(c). Amun-Ra

His epithets: The Hidden One. The Only One. The First. The Peerless. The Sacred God. King of the Gods. He who Lives by Right and Truth. Creator of all that is.

Creator of all that is to be. Lord of Infinite Space. Upholder of the Universe. King of Kings. Primal Might. Glorious Flame. Light of the World. Governor of the World. Lord of Time, Master of Eternity. Provider. Mighty Bull of his Mother. The Ram. The Great Cackler. Lord of the Double Plumes. He whose Heart is rejoiced by adoration. He who appoints the Sun to be his Envoy. Inviolate Essence ever concealed amid his manifestations. The Beloved. Protector of the Beloved of his Heart. He who desires the Good. He who comes in Power. He who grants eternal life. He whose statutes endure forever.

His image: The God appears wearing kilt, corselet and collar. He has the ceremonial beard, and his flat-topped helmet is surmounted by the Double Plumes (each plume having seven sections divided vertically), or by the Solar Disk and the Plumes. In his right hand he bears the Ankh, in his left the Ouas (the Scepter of Peaceful Authority). He may be Ram-headed, bearing the Ankh and the Ouas, and wearing the Old Kingdom headdress surmounted by Disk and Plumes; or he may appear in the full form of the Ram with curling horns.

5 CORRESPONDENCES OF MARS

PLANETARY SIGN
1.   ♂

PLANETARY NAME
2.   **In English:** Mars
3.   **In Greek:** Ares
4.   **In Hebrew:** Madim

PLANETARY PROFILE
5.   Dynamic energy, enthusiasm and resolution. The flame and heat of fire are its elemental expessions. Courage, strength of body and acuity of mind all typify the character of Mars. Besides these primal connotations, this is the sphere of fraternal comradeship, as of brothers in arms who have shared many perils. This is the sphere also of engineering, and all work in iron or steel; and of the voice of the people, since the day of Mars was anciently the day of public assemblies.

TITLE OF SEPHIRAH
6.   **In Hebrew:** Geburah
7.   **In Greek:** Dynamis
8.   **In English:** Strength

TEXT FROM THE THIRTY-TWO PATHS OF WISDOM
9.   The fifth Path is the Root Intelligence, so named because it is itself the essence equaling the Unity. It is linked with Binah, the intelligence which emanates from the unfathomed deeps of Wisdom, Chokmah.

51

ELEMENTAL AFFINITY OF PLANET
    10.   Fire

SYMBOLS AND MAGICAL IMPLEMENTS
    11.   **Specific to Sphere:** Lance. Shield. Scourge. Helmet.
        Suitable, but having other magical use: The Magick
        Sword. The Krater (chafing dish). Body paints.

PRESIGILLUM
    12.

NUMBER AND GEOMETRIC FORM
    13.   **Qabalistic number:** 5
    14.   **Medieval number:** 9
    15.   **Plane figure:** Pentagon
    16.   **Star:** Pentagram

QUALITIES OF DESIGN
    17.   Zigzag and pointed forms.

COLORS
    18.   **In Atziluth:** Amber
    19.   **In Briah:** Red (spectrum red)
    20.   **In Yetzirah:** Fiery Red
    21.   **In Assiah:** Mingled pale yellow and cerise: green-blue
        tinge
    22.   **Ptolemaic color:** Red (fiery red)

MUSIC FOR PLANETARY MOODS
    23.   **Ideal qualities:** Powerful, warlike, dominating
    24.   **Selected examples:** "Ride of the Valkyrie" (Wagner). "Mars"
        (*The Planets*, Holst). "Sword Dance" (Khachaturian),
        "Sousa Marches" (as preferred). Gaelic and Celtic war-
        songs generally.

SUITABLE INSTRUMENTS AND SOUND EFFECTS
    25.   Trumpet. Side drum. Bagpipes. Stamping feet. Steel strik-
        ing upon steel or iron. Recorded sounds of raging fire, of
        volcanic eruption, or of battle.

ANIMALS AND MYTHOLOGICAL BEINGS
26.   Ram. Wolf. Woodpecker. Vulture. Scorpion. Serpent. Wasp. Hell's Angel. Basilisk. Salamander. Werewolf.

TREES AND OTHER VEGETATION
27.   **Trees:** Ash. Mountain Ash (Rowan). Holly. Pepper tree. White Fig. Mountain Mahogany. Arbutus.

28.   **Herbs:** Thistles generally. Cacti generally. Dandelion. Snapdragon (Antirrhinum). Stinging nettle. Arrowroot. High John Conqueror. Bloodroot. Wild Ginger. Bamboo.

29.   **Incenses, Perfumes, etc.:** Opoponax. Dragonsblood. Nicotiana. Peppermint. Mustard. Cumin. Asafoetida. Turmeric. Sweet Woodruff. Galangal.

GEMSTONES AND OTHER MINERALS
30.   **Metals:** Iron. All Steels. Nickel. Strontium. Magnetized iron filings.

31.   **Gemstones:** Ruby. Garnet. Red Agate. Bloodstone. Rhodochrosite.

32.   **Other minerals:** Red Jasper. Lodestone. Flint (worked flints particularly).

THE PLANETS AND HEALTH
33.   **Physiological functions:** Development and well-being of limbs and external organs (the nose, the ears as regards their health and safety, the external sexual organs); the excretory systems; the gall bladder; the red corpuscles of the blood; the motor nerves; the region of the face. Regulation of metallic trace elements in the system, and of energy levels.

34.   **Pathological effects (bodily):** Inflammation of accidental injuries. Hemorrhage. Smallpox and eruptive maladies generally. Infectious and contagious sicknesses generally; those in particular which produce acute fever. Neuralgia. Hyperactivity. Hypertension.

35.   **Pathological effects (psychic):** Anger, obstinacy, excitability, frustration, can be sufficient to cause malfunction in the nervous and glandular systems, thus opening the way to injury or to infection.

PLANETARY GESTURE

36. **The Gesture Persis (the Persian), accomplished as follows:**

1st point, "the Wand." Erect stance, arms at sides.

2nd point, "Gradivus." In one movement, step forward and left with left foot; then, in one movement, step forward and right with right foot. (Feet are thus firmly planted astride).

3rd point, "Quintus." In one movement, both hands are brought up to shoulders and flung out sideways, so that arms are horizontal and the five digits of each hand are spread wide.

4th point, "Paratus." Upper torso is twisted to left.

5th point, "Anhur." Both fists being clenched meanwhile, upper torso is twisted violently to right: as the torso is twisted to the right, the left fist is moved to the breast and the right fist is raised, right upper arm horizontally out sideways from shoulder, forearm raised vertically, as if about to hurl a spear.

6th point, "the Wand." Erect stance, arms at sides.

MAGICAL IMAGE OF THE SPHERE

37. **Warrior:** A mighty male figure stands in an iron chariot, in the midst of a dark and lurid sky of roiling clouds which smolder with inner fire. Each of the chariot wheels has five spokes, and a long, curved blade projecting from the hub. The rider is clean shaven, and wears a helmet with a high, flowing horsehair crest, and a gleaming breastplate over a scarlet undertunic. With his right hand he holds a spear poised horizontally above his shoulder as if to hurl it. With his left hand he holds, effortlessly, the reins of the two chestnut roan horses drawing the chariot: of these, the right hand one is rearing erect in mettlesome impatience, while the other, with head held low, is moodily pawing at the stormy vapor.

MICROCOSMIC KEYWORDS OF THE SPHERE

38. **Quality in Ruach:** Judgment, Decision
39. **Responsive Ruach functions:** Purification
40. **Quality in Nephesh:** Elevation

The Warrior

41.   **Responsive Nephesh Functions:** Courage, Cooperation

AURUM SOLIS DIVINE AND ARCHONTIC NAMES
42.   **Divine Name (Atziluth):** Sabao
43.   **Archon (Briah):** Doryxenos
44.   **Power (Yetzirah):** Kasartes
45.   **Intelligence (Yetzirah):** Zostheme
46.   **Spirit (Yetzirah):** Nazirias

PLANETARY STANZA FROM THE SONG OF PRAISES
47.   **Stanza XXVII, Peh:**

> Play of the Breath and the Word, Life and the Law,
>   counterchange intricate
> Weaving the ground of our days: this is our strength,
>   this is our jeopardy.
> Spirit oracular, tell: knowledge and love,
>   will they keep unity
>   Or, opposed, shatter us?

OLYMPIC PLANETARY SPIRIT
48(a).   **Spirit of Mars:** Phalegh

48(b).   **His Sigil:**

48(c).   **Yetziratic manifestation of Spirit:** A muscular, well-proportioned male figure, wearing a sleeveless tunic which covers the trunk but leaves the legs bare. This garment is of heavy cloth, bright red, projecting above the shoulders in pointed epaulets: it is girt with a wide leather belt ornamented with studs of steel and of red gold. Behind the wearer's left shoulder is slung a massive circular shield. Phalegh's head and body, including his gleaming hair and beard, are entirely of living, flexible but invulnerable bronze. His head and feet are therefore uncovered. His eyes are deep slits of flame. On both his arms, at the wrists and above the elbows are heavy bracelets of red gold. His right arm is extended sideways, to hold with point aloft a long sword, the upper part of the blade rich with fantastic designs in inlaid metals and enamels. His left arm is extended at a lower level, to hold a dagger whose wavy serpentine blade points vertically down.

The formulation of this figure of Phalegh being completed, the inward ear is at the same time to apprehend the distinct sound of a single reverberating shout, joyous and challenging. (See color plate of Phalegh following page 204.)

HEBREW DIVINE AND ANGELIC NAMES

49. **Divine Name (Atziluth):** Elohim Gebor
50. **Archangel (Briah):** Kamael
51. **Angelic Chora (Yetzirah):** Seraphim, "Burning Ones."
52. **Planetary Angel (Yetzirah):** Zamael
53. **Sigil of Planetary Angel:**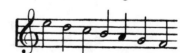
54. **Intelligence (Yetzirah):** Graphiel
55. **Spirit (Yetzirah):** Bartzabel

PLANETARY STANZA FROM THE SEVENFOLD AFFIRMATION

56.   Powerfully doth he forge and fashion all beings;
     His the strength that makes them strong; his might
                    magnifies them.
     Great and terrible is he, and true in each scruple:
     To and fro beneath the sun like sparks run his Watchers.
     Therefore most exalted he austere, who forms and governs
                    every creature.

NEOPLATONIST DIVINE NAME

57. **Divine Name (Atziluth):** Ischyros, "Mighty One"

SACRED VOWEL OF GREEK QABALAH

58.   O (the letter *Omicron*)

VOWEL TONES OF THE COSMIC HARMONY

59(a). **Contemporary Magical Mode:**

59(b). **Greek Gnostic Mode:**

GREEK DEITIES

60(a). **Ares.**

     His epithets: The Mighty One. Lord of War. The

Ares

Hephaistos

Consuming Flame. The Furious. The Strong One. Voice of Power. Lord of the Fiery Field. Giver of Courage. Inspirer of Daring Deeds. Preserver of Right. Upholder of Law. The Leveler. Father of Harmony. Lord of the Chariot.

His attributes: The Iron Sword. The Shield. The Spear. The Burning Torch (for conflagration and katharsis). The Helmet. Armor. Dog. Vulture.

Attendants: Deimos (Panic). Phobos (Fear). Enyo (Goddess of War). Eris (Strife). The Keres (Goddesses of Death, comparable to the Valkyren).

60(b). **Hephaistos.**

His epithets: The Lame One. The Outcast. Purifier of Guilt. Manifestor of Holiness. The Visible Fire. The Divine Craftsman. The Divine Armorer. Maker of Glorious Habitations. Captor of Beauty in texture of steel. Nurseling of the Sea. Divinity Manifest on Earth. Maker of the Ship of the Sun.

His Attributes: Fire. The Forge. The Hammer. Pincers. Pilos (workman's cap). Leather apron. The Volcano.

ROMAN DEITIES

61(a). **Mars (Mavors).**

His ephithets: Lord of the Measured Pace. The Warlike One. The Spear. The Watchful. The Forester. Protector of the Fields. Father.

His Character: Mars is the principal deity of warfare: not only human warfare, but also the defense of crops, herds and land against depredation and other mischance. He is the God of March, the month of new beginnings, new hope: of setting forth in every kind of activity. In Rome the chief organization in his honor was that of the Salii, the warrior priests who celebrated his great public festivals with their dancing and processions: he was patron also of the Arval Brotherhood, whose members were dedicated to safeguarding farm stock and crops against disease, flood, etc. The wolf is associated with him for its fierce spirit and for the unity of the pack: and in particular the she-wolf who rescued his sons, Romulus and Remus. The woodpecker, Picus, accompanies him: it is the awakener and sounder of the alarm.

His attributes: The Sword. The Spear. The Sacred Shields. Helm and Armor. The Fig Tree. Wolf. Wood-pecker.

61(b). **Volcanus.**

His epithets: The Subduer. Lord of the Devouring Flame. Lord of volcanoes. Guardian of Cities. Guardian of sustenance. Protector of the Hearth.

His Character: Volcanus is the God of fire, of volcanoes and of furnaces, of the smelting and casting of metals. As deity of fire he is associated with Vesta the Hearth goddess, whose dedicated maidens tend the never-extinguished flame. As protector against the destructive power of volcanic eruptions and of conflagrations he is guardian of cities and of their stocks of grain, oil and other food-stuffs; in these aspects he has as allies the Nymphs, who bring water in abundance from spring and river. Besides being the protector of Earth generally, he is also the mystic guardian of the sacred from the profane.

His attributes: Tunic leaving right shoulder bare. The volcanic peak. In later times, all the attributes of Hephaistos.

ETRUSCAN DEITIES

62(a). **Maris:** The Angry One. God of War, fomentor of unrest and discord. Inspirer of courage. *Wolf. Vulture.*

62(b). **Sethlans:** Deity of Fire. Comparable to the primitive Roman Vulcan.

BABYLONIAN DEITIES

63(a). **Ninurta.**

His ephithets: Lord of the Fields. Bringer of Fertility. Champion of the High Gods. Mighty Destroyer of Evil. Divine Strength.

His Character: Ninurta has a strong agricultural aspect. Following an ancient syncretistic confusion he is some-times ascribed to Saturn; but the error of this is manifest. He is essentially a deity of combat and pursuit. The club which is his characteristic weapon is sometimes shown as his symbol, in which case it is flanked by two undulating

Ninurta

serpents. Sometimes, however, Ninurta holds the club in his right hand, while with his left he grasps, like a falcon of the chase, an eagle with wings outspread.

63(b). **Nusku.**

His epithets: Wise Prince. Flame of Heaven. Exalter of the Sacred Torch.

His character: Nusku, deity of fire, is particularly associated with the fire of the temple. He it is who carries to the Gods the fragrance of incense, and the essence of burnt offerings and of sacred feasts. His activity is represented also by the volcanic fires which raise the mountains into high cones, and by the spiritual fire which enlightens human darkness. He it is also who, bathed in splendor, hurls down from on high the meteoric fire of heaven. He carries a lamp of archaic form, or a shining scepter. "Nusku of the Brilliant Scepter" is one of his titles.

HINDU DEITIES

64(a). **Agni.**

His epithets: Sustainer of the Cosmos. Primal Priest. Priest of the Hearth. All-powerful. He of the Two Faces. The Red One. The Sacrificer. The Sacrifice. The Essential Flame. Heart of the Sun. The Hungry One. Devourer. Purifier. Guardian. Intermediary between Heaven and Earth. Divine Oracle. Giver of Abundance. The Beneficent One. The Violent One.

His Attributes: Two faces. Three legs and seven arms (representing the asymmetrical forms of fire). Flames springing from his mouths. Wood. Torch. Fan. Axe. The Spoon for making priestly libations. The Brahmanic Cord. The Ram (upon which he rides).

64(b). **Durga.**

Her epithets: The Unapproachable. The Calmly Invincible. Radiant in Battle. Virgin Power. Patroness of Multitudes. Slayer of Demonkind. Victorious in War. Protector of the Just. She whose Beauty is Unchanging. The Dangerous One.

Her Attributes: The Tiara. Serene and beautiful countenance at all times. The Sword; the Bow; the Spear; many arms wielding Swords or other weapons of war. The Lion (upon which she rides).

EGYPTIAN DEITIES

65(a). **Heru-Behutet (Horus of Edfu).**

His epithets: Great One. Son of the Sun. The Mighty Guardian. Remover of the Head of Sutekh. He who enchains the forces of darkness. The Hawk upon his Column. Restrainer of the Serpent. The Master Iron-worker. Patron of Ironworkers. Lord of the Forge. He whose Splendor consumes. He whose Light purifies. The winged Disk whose Uraei flame forth terror. Furious in the Combat. The Victorious One. Thrice-crowned Lion.

His image: Of Hawk-headed human form, the God wears the Skhemti (the conjoined crowns of Upper and Lower Egypt) upon his Old Kingdom headdress. He is garmented in kilt, battle corselet and collar. He bears the Iron Mace, the Spear or the Bow.

65(b). **Sekhet (Sekhmet).**

Her epithets: Great Goddess. The Sacred One. The Powerful One. The Vehement One. The Red-garmented. She who Dominates. The Mighty Flame. Flame of Protection. Flame of Retribution. Eye of Ra. Uraeus of Ra. The Greatly Beloved One. Strength. Mighty in Heaven. Mighty among the Gods. The Pre-eminent. She who Purifies. Guardian of Souls.

Her image: Lioness-headed female form. Of immense dignity, the Goddess bears the Papyrus Scepter and the Ankh. Her Old Kingdom headdress is surmounted by the Solar Disk and encircling Uraeus, or by the Disk and Horns of Hathor superposed upon two tall multi-sectioned plumes, or by the Uraeus alone, upreared in power. The Goddess may appear standing or she may be enthroned.

6 CORRESPONDENCES OF SOL

PLANETARY SIGN
1.   ☉

PLANETARY NAME
2.   **In English:** Sun
3.   **In Greek:** Helios
4.   **In Hebrew:** Shemesh

PLANETARY PROFILE
5.   Authoritative, creative, equable; courage and leadership
without aggressiveness. Attuned to abundance, health-
fulness and spiritual illumination. The life-giving warmth
and light of day express its impartial action. Direction
and distribution of energies and materials, and the giving
of wise counsel, even prophetically. Equilibrium.

TITLES OF SEPHIRAH
6.   **In Hebrew:** Tiphareth
7.   **In Greek:** Kalon
8.   **In English:** Beauty

TEXT FROM THE THIRTY-TWO PATHS OF WISDOM
9.   The Sixth Path is the Intelligence of the Mediatory Influence:
it is so named because therein is gathered the influx from
all the Emanations, so that it in turn causes the mediatory
influence to flow into the founts of each of the benign
Powers, with which they are linked.

ELEMENTAL AFFINITY OF PLANET
    10. Air

SYMBOLS AND MAGICAL IMPLEMENTS
    11. **Specific to Sphere:** Solar Diadem. Breastplate. Tripod of
         Prophecy. Sunburst. Solar Sacramental Cup (symbol of
         Ruach as recipient of Supernal draught of inspiration).
         Suitable, but having other magical use: Topaz Lamen.
         Thyrsus. Holy Oil. The Alchemical Crucible.

PRESIGILLUM
    12.

NUMBER AND GEOMETRIC FORM
    13. **Qabalistic number:** 6
    14. **Medieval number:** 1
    15. **Plane figure:** Hexagon
    16. **Star:** Hexagram

QUALITIES OF DESIGN
    17. Radial forms, swirling spirals.

COLORS
    18. **In Atziluth:** Pale Greenish-yellow
    19. **In Briah:** Yellow
    20. **In Yetzirah:** Pale golden yellow
    21. **In Assiah:** Intense yellow-white, rayed scarlet
    22. **Ptolemaic color:** Gold

MUSIC FOR PLANETARY MOODS
    23. **Ideal qualities:** Noble, generous, spiritually inspiring.
    24. **Selected examples:** "Emperor Concerto" (Beethoven).
         "The Ninth" (Beethoven). "Magic Fire Music" (Wagner).
         "Concierto de Aranjuez" (Rodrigo).

SUITABLE INSTRUMENTS AND SOUND EFFECTS
    25. French horn. Brazen gong. Lyre. Autoharp. Recorded heart-
         beat or dawn-song of birds.

ANIMALS AND MYTHOLOGICAL BEINGS

26. Lion. Tiger. Panther. Leopard. Bull (sacrificial). Hawk. Birds of Paradise. Bantam. Salmon. Golden Carp. Bee. Griffin. Egyptian Sphinx. Phoenix. Winged Horse. Winged Serpent.

TREES AND OTHER VEGETATION

27. **Trees:** Pine. Walnut tree. Date palm. Oaks generally. Witch hazel. Mimosa. Acacia.

28. **Herbs:** Sunflower. Camomile. Yellow rose. Chrysanthemum. Marigold. Eyebright. Larkspur. Pineapple. Mistletoe. St. John's Wort. Laurel.

29. **Incenses, Perfumes, etc.:** Cinnamon. Frankincense. Saffron. Vanilla. Heliotropin. Cashew nuts. Copal.

GEMSTONES AND OTHER MINERALS

30. **Metals:** Gold. All yellow and lustrous alloys.

31. **Gemstones:** Tiger eye. Topaz. Goldstone. Zircon (blue or white). Citrine. Chrysoberyl.

32. **Other minerals:** Yellow Jasper. Phosphorus. Any rock or pebble showing a concentric eye-like banding.

THE PLANETS AND HEALTH

33. **Physiological functions:** Governance of the heart, the eyes as regards their health and safety (traditionally, the right eye in males and left eye in females); the upper region of the back, the circulation of the blood and the distribution of all vital fluids. Generation and maintenance of life energy; the growth of children and young people.

34. **Pathological effects (bodily):** Just as the visible and measurable radiations of the Sun can, by their intensity, harm in the living organism the very faculties and qualities which they have nurtured, so do the Sun's occult powers act similarly. Disorders of the heart's action, whether of the nature of simple palpitations or angina. Spinal afflictions, particularly those affecting the upper back. Bilious ailments and those affecting the spleen. Ills affecting the eyes, other than simple optical maladjustments. Fevers producing delirium.

35. **Pathological effects (psychic):** Superabundnace of vital

energies can disorganize the structures and rhythms of
their physical vehicle: or powerful inner vision may turn
the psyche away from earthly seeing.

PLANETARY GESTURE

36. **The Gesture Leo (Lion), accomplished as follows:**
1st point, "the Wand." Erect stance, arms at sides.
2nd point, "Calathus." The forearms are raised vertically in
front of the chest, with their undersides touching each
other from elbow to wrist. Maintaining this position, the
two hands are bent backwards until their palms are as
nearly horizontal as possible, the fingers bent to suggest
a shallow cup shape.
3rd point, "Flamma." From this formulation, the arms are
raised with an outward curving motion, until the hands
curve inwards allowing fingers and thumbs to formulate
a fire triangle $\triangle$ at maximum height overhead.
4th point, "Catinus." The arms form the *Psi* position Ψ
At the same time, the right foot steps back and the body
inclines backwards, head thrown back.
5th point, "Ignis." Right foot is restored to normal standing
position, body restored to vertical, while the hands again
formulate the fire triangle but this time on breast.
6th point, "the Holy." Left foot is advanced, body bends
forward, middle fingers touch floor in front of feet.
7th point, "the Wand." Erect stance, arms at sides.

MAGICAL IMAGES OF THE SPHERE

37(a). **Solar King:** A strong and beautiful male figure, as of an
athlete, is clad in a short white tunic which is clasped
about his waist by a broad belt: this belt is patterned with
hexagrams and hexagons, each hexagon being set with a
central topaz. Over the tunic, a cloak of bright blue bordered
with gold is flung back from the shoulders. Upon the
shining hair of this figure is a golden crown with seven
outward-pointing rays, and upon the breast of the tunic
is a golden winged disc in the center of which sparkles a
large deep ruby. The figure stands astride, holding in his
left hand the mighty orb of the Sun, resplendent in the
intense radiance of its golden light. His right hand is raised

The Solar King

The Eternal Child
Puer Aeternus

high, palm forward in blessing. The whole figure, including the bright solar orb, is seen within a sphere of brilliant light, continually flashing and pulsating, which emanates from the figure itself.

37(b). **Puer Aeternus (The Eternal Child):** A boy of about seven years of age, strong and graceful, stands with feet astride upon the summit of a rock. His arms are extended sideways, hands slightly above shoulder level: with his right hand he grasps a thyrsus, with his left he holds up a cup of wine, which he tilts so as to pour forth its contents. Amid his thick curling dark hair a serpent is enwreathed, raising its head between the budding bull-horns above his forehead. His only garment is a scarlet square cape, fastened upon his right shoulder with a heavy gold brooch set with a single large topaz: this cape leaves bare his right arm and falls diagonally to his left side. Behind him is the glorious orb of the rising Sun, surrounding him with its splendor.

MICROCOSMIC KEYWORDS OF THE SPHERE
38. **Quality in Ruach:** Integration
39. **Responsive Ruach function:** Sincerity
40. **Quality in Nephesh:** Leadership
41. **Responsive Nephesh function:** Organization

AURUM SOLIS DIVINE AND ARCHONTIC NAMES
42. **Divine Name (Atziluth):** Onophis
43. **Archon (Briah):** Pyloros
44. **Power (Yetzirah):** Agamanos
45. **Intelligence (Yetzirah):** Baltha
46. **Spirit (Yetzirah):** Sobias

PLANETARY STANZA FROM THE SONG OF PRAISES
47. **Stanza XXX, Resh:**

Rise in thy splendor, O King!—glorious brow
gaze on thy governance
Gladdening all who behold! Soaring as song,
rule and illuminate:
Crysoleth gleaming thy crown, rise and inspire,
Lion-gold, Falcon-flight,
Joyous, ambrosial!

OLYMPIC PLANETARY SPIRIT

48(a). Spirit of Sol: Och

48(b). His Sigil:

48(c). Yetziratic manifestation of Spirit: A vigorous male figure, youthful but not boyish, rides upon a magnificent red lion. The rider is resplendent in a robe of metallic gold which falls in heavy folds and which has, scattered over it, sparkling clusters of green, blue and violet gems. Upon the head of this figure is a golden crown too bright to look upon. Beneath the wide sleeves of the robe of gold are inner sleeves of a sky-blue silken gauze, gathered to the wrist; while wide Oriental trousers of the same sky-blue appear below the hem of the robe. Golden shoes with long upturned points complete the rider's attire. The aspect of Och is intensely vital, noble and generous. As he raises his hands in a superb gesture of greeting, rays of golden light stream from them towards the magician, even though the specific will of the magician may not yet have been uttered. (See color plate of Och following page 204.)

HEBREW DIVINE AND ANGELIC NAMES

49. **Divine Name (Atziluth):** Yahveh Eloah V'Daath *or* Yahweh Eloah V'Daath *or* Yod Heh Vau Heh Eloah V'Daath *or* Tetragrammaton Eloah V'Daath

50. **Archangel (Briah):** Raphael
51. **Angelic Chora (Yetzirah):** Malekim, "Kings."
52. **Planetary Angel (Yetzirah):** Mikael
53. **Sigil of Planetary Angel:**

54. **Intelligence (Yetzirah):** Nakiel
55. **Spirit (Yetzirah):** Sorath

PLANETARY STANZA FROM THE SEVENFOLD AFFIRMATION

56.   Reckoning of days and years unceasing he maketh;
    He to all existence giveth times, giveth seasons,
    Sending glory forth amid the High Lords assembled,
    Giving mind of knowledge clear to hearts that love
                      wisdom.

Therefore most exalted he, beneath whose burning gaze the
rocks are parted.

NEOPLATONIST DIVINE NAME
57. **Divine Name (Atziluth):** Theios Nous, "Divine Intelligence"

SACRED VOWEL OF GREEK QABALAH
58. I (the letter *Iota*)

VOWEL TONES OF THE COSMIC HARMONY
59(a). **Contemporary Magical Mode:**

59(b). **Greek Gnostic Mode:**

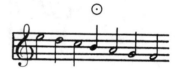

GREEK DEITIES
60(a). **Apollo.**

His epithets: Lord of Light. Far-Shooter. Slayer of
Darkness. Lord of Delos. Phoebus (the Bright One).
Healer. Prophet. Leader of the Muses. Shield against evil.
Purifier. Champion of Right. Apollo of the Song of
Triumph.

His attributes: Lyre. The Silver Bow. The Prophetic
Tripod. The Golden Throne of Truth. The Laurel Wreath.
Wolf. Roe deer. Mouse. Hawk. Griffin.

Attendants: The Nine Muses (Klio, Euterpe, Thalia,
Melpomene, Terpsichore, Erato, Polyhymnia, Ourania,
Kalliope).

60(b). **Dionysos.**

His epithets: Son of the God. Nobly-born. Twice-born.
Son of Heaven's Fire. Son of Two Mothers. Mystery. The
Many-formed. Lion of Light. Serpent-crowned. Mountain
Bull. Wild Goat of the Heights. The Youthful Victim. The
Noisy One. Priest of the Night. Lord of the Chorus of
Night. Bringer of Ecstasy. Divine Intoxication. Divine

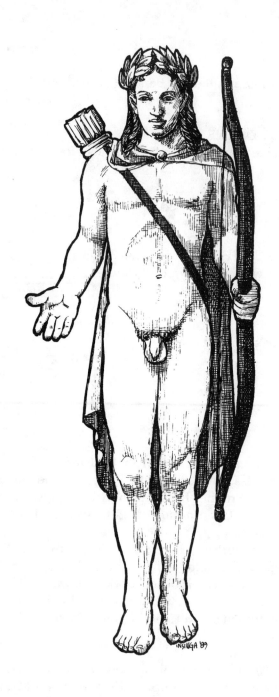

Apollo

Dionysos

Madness. Leader of Frenzy. Lord of the Dance. He whom the dancing fires of heaven obey.

His attributes: The Ivy Wreath. The Thyrsus. The Bassara (the long robe). The Kantharos (the drinking cup). The Timbrel. The Drum. The Vine. The Phallos. Lion. Snake. Goat. Panther. Bull. Tiger.

His attendants: Satyrs. Maenads. Bassarids.

60(c). **Helios.**

His epithets: The All-Seeing Sun. The Exceedingly Brilliant One. The Undying Flame. Far-riding. Giver of Light. Healer giving sight. Lord of the Hours. Witness of the Oath.

His attributes: The Quadriga (chariot drawn by four horses). The many-rayed Crown. The Sun-orb. The Golden Ship of the Night Journey.

ROMAN DEITY

61. **Sol (Nomius).**

His ephithets: The Wandering Herdsman. Inspirer of Prophecy. Seer of Hidden Truth. Bestower of Vital Force. Mighty Helper. The Invincible Sun.

His character: Crowned with effulgent rays and traversing the heavens in a chariot drawn in early times by white swans, but later by four powerful steeds, glorious Sol is imaged by the visible Sun. He surveys all that is in the tangible and the hidden worlds, and those whom he inspires can proclaim truths which were before unknown. The rays of his crown are seven in number, for his own light and that of the other wandering luminaries is, in essence, one. In his aspect as healer this is significant: maladies governed by every planetary influence are under his healing and vitalizing overlordship. Spiritually, Sol exemplifies for us an unconquerable power: daily we see him set and rise again, and from Winter he reappears in life-giving brightness every Spring. In this, as some mystics have perceived from ancient times, Sol shows forth for us not merely that round of birth and death in which spiritual evolution proceeds only slowly. Rather, what is suggested is the immortal triumph of the Higher Self, which is to flood us with an illumination enduringly

Helios

greater and more wonderful than our brightest previous noonday life: true regeneration.

Attributes: The crown of seven rays. Cornucopia. Dolphin. Swans. Horses (or Horses' heads). Ripe fruits. The Laurel.

ETRUSCAN DEITIES

62(a). **Catha:** The Radiant One. The solar deity as giver of light and life. *The Solar Chariot. Ripe fruits and ears of grain.*

62(b). **Hercle:** The solar force as strong hero, neither quite Herakles nor yet Hercules. *Garment of lion skin. Mighty Club.*

BABYLONIAN DEITY

63. **Shamash.**

His epithets: Mighty Lord of Light. Lord of All Living. Judge of Heaven and Earth. Lord of Judgment.

His character: The solar deity, named Babbar, "Shining One," is better known by his title of Shamash, "Sun." He is characterized by courage, justice and energy. Brilliant beams of golden light spring from his shoulders and sides, and he carries the key of the Gate of the East. In the chariot of the Sun he traverses the sky to the Gate of the West by day, returning by night through the underworld. All-illuminating and all-seeing, he is judge of all, and giver of knowledge through divination. Besides astrological computation and the ancient practice of examining the liver of a sacrificed animal, the soothsayers of Babylon employed another divinatory system which was sacred to Shamash. After prayers to him for revelation of the future, oil was poured on the surface of water and the shapes thus formed were interpreted. Shamash is represented in his chariot, or mounting the eastern hill with the key in his hand; or enthroned as judge, holding a scepter and the Ring of Divinity.

HINDU DEITY

64. **Vishnu.**

His epithets: The Preserver. Principle of Continuance. The Active One. The Self-existent. The All-

Shamash

pervading Light. Ocean of Bliss. Ocean of Majesty. He whose Beauty claims the Heart. He whose Sweetness intoxicates the Soul. He who Descends. He who Manifests. Savior. Helper of Evolution. Upholder of the Universe. Life of the Universe. Captor of Souls. Liberator of Souls. The Blue One. The Mighty God. Celestial Refuge. He who Loves. The Beneficent One. Lord of Fortune. Vanquisher of Demons. He who Moves upon the Waters. He who Rests upon the Waters.

His attributes: The Tiara. Large and prominent earrings. The Breast-whirl. The White Lotus (as his throne). The Golden Kite Garuda (as his mount). The Seven-headed Serpent Ananta-Sesha (upon which he sleeps during "The Night of God," the periods of cosmic inactivity). Appearing four-armed, the God holds the conch, the Lotus, the Mace and the Disk.

EGYPTIAN DEITY

65. **Ra**

His epithets: Great One. Old One. Self-generator. Creator. Breath of Life. Exalted Power. Father of the Gods. Lord of Light. Divine Love. Radiant of Face. Winged Splendor. The Disk. He who Advances. The Strong Youth. Lord of Bright Beams. The Enthroned One. King of Heaven. He whose Uraeus sends forth mighty flame. Prince of Eternity. Governor of the World. Lord of the City of the Sun. Indweller of the Lofty Shrine. Truth. The Beautiful God. He who Goes Forth in the Boat of the Morning. He whose Heart is rejoiced by the winds. Golden Glory of the Day. He to whom the planets chant in praise. He who Proceeds in the Boat of the Evening. He whose Glory the unsetting stars extol. Manifestor of the Invisible. Master of Inexorable Words. Avenger. Slayer of Darkness.

His image: The Hawk-headed One wears the Solar Disk and Uraeus upon the headdress of the Old Kingdom. In his right hand he holds the Ankh, in his left he grasps the Ouas (the Scepter of Peaceful Authority).

7
CORRESPONDENCES OF VENUS

PLANETARY SIGN
1. ♀

PLANETARY NAME
2. **In English:** Venus
3. **In Greek:** Paphié
4. **In Hebrew:** Nogah

PLANETARY PROFILE
5. Joyous, benign. Good luck with love or with money. Kindliness and affection. All that makes for concord. The beauty and vitality of the natural world, and all artistic and congenial surroundings, express the influence of this sphere. Music, dancing, happy love and all reconciliation of differences. Harmony, synthesis.

TITLES OF SEPHIRAH
6. **In Hebrew:** Netzach
7. **In Greek:** Nike
8. **In English:** Victory

TEXT FROM THE THIRTY-TWO PATHS OF WISDOM
9. The Seventh Path is the concealed Intelligence, so named because it is the dazzling resplendence of all the qualities of Mind, which are discerned by intellectual vision and by the gaze of faith.

81

ELEMENTAL AFFINITY OF PLANET
  10.   Fire.

SYMBOLS AND MAGICAL IMPLEMENTS
  11.   **Specific to Sphere:** The Mirror. The Necklace. The
         Girdle. Seashells.
         Suitable, but having other magical use: Sistrum. Flaming
         torch. Garland.

PRESIGILLUM *

  12.

NUMBER AND GEOMETRIC FORM
  13.   **Qabalistic number: 7**
  14.   **Medieval number: 6**
  15.   **Plane figure:** Heptagon
  16.   **Star:** Heptagram

QUALITIES OF DESIGN
  17.   Branching forms; flowing, harmonious lines; arabesques.

COLORS
  18.   **In Atziluth:** Greenish blue
  19.   **In Briah:** Green
  20.   **In Yetzirah:** Light turquoise
  21.   **In Assiah:** Luminescent greenish-white
  22.   **Ptolemaic color:** Saffron

MUSIC FOR PLANETARY MOODS
  23.   **Ideal qualities:** Sensuous, passionate, fiery, playful.
  24.   **Selected examples:** "Venusberg Theme" (*Venus and
         Tannhauser,* Wagner). "Barcarolle" (*Tales of Hoffmann,*
         Offenbach). "O Fortuna" (*Carmina Burana,* Orff). "Concerto
         a Due Chori" (*F.1., No. 60,* Vivaldi). "Allegro Moderato"
         (from *Violin Concerto in D Major, Op. 35,* Tchaikovsky).
         Flamenco guitar generally.

SUITABLE INSTRUMENTS AND SOUND EFFECTS
  25.   Clarsach (Celtic harp). Classical guitar. Violin. Castanets.

Zills. Sitar. Tambourine. Gently flowing or falling water, humming bees, nature's voices of the day.

ANIMALS AND MYTHOLOGICAL BEINGS
26. Lynx. Cat (Felis domesticus). Rabbit. Seal. Dolphin. Porpoise. Tortoise. Flamingo. Dove. Sparrow. Bee. Fauns. Mermaids. Sirens.

TREES AND OTHER VEGETATION
27. **Trees:** Apple and Pear trees. Lemon. Lime. Orange. Sweet Cherry. Cinchona. Beech. Elder. Common Fig.
28. **Herbs:** Red Rose. Hawthorn. Vervain. Myrtle. Columbine. Wild Anemone. Strawberry. Periwinkle. Cyclamen. Hyacinth. Foxglove. Tulip. Hibiscus.
29. **Incenses, Perfumes, etc.:** Siamese Benzoin. Red Storax. Red Sandalwood. Vetivert. Valerian. Geranium. Licorice. Tonka Beans. Cardamom. Spearmint. Lemon Verbena.

GEMSTONES AND OTHER MINERALS
30. **Metals:** Copper. All Bronzes.
31. **Gemstones:** Emerald. Malachite. Peridot. Jade (green, pink, white). Rose Quartz. Amazonite.
32. **Other minerals:** Coral. Amber. Pearl shell. Sandstone. Sea Salt.

THE PLANETS AND HEALTH
33. **Physiological functions:** Governance of the internal sexual organs generally, the kidneys, the veins generally; the mouth, throat and sinuses, the neck generally, the lower region of the back. The lymphatic system. The skin as regards its functions in breathing, absorption and exudation. The nerves and muscles generally as regards tone and relaxation. Health and well-being of scalp and hair.
34. **Pathological effects (bodily):** Tonsilitis, goiter, ailments of the throat generally. Maladies affecting the kidneys or the lymphatic system. Fibrositis of neck and shoulder. Lumbago. Cramps generally. Venereal ailments generally.
35. **Pathological effects (psychic):** The reality of health may be neglected while its appearance is cultivated. Strong

emotions may disrupt the regimen, in particular through a "compensating" indulgence.

PLANETARY GESTURE

36. **The Gesture Miles (Soldier), accomplished as follows:**

1st point, "the Wand." Erect stance, arms at sides.

2nd point, "Denial." Right palm is placed on left shoulder. Then, right arm, with palm now turned out, sweeps vigorously around in a semicircle, upwards and over to rest extended horizontally from right shoulder, palm forward.

3rd point, "I aspire!" Left hand is raised, cupped, overhead with slightly flexed elbow to allow the cupped palm to take a horizontal position. The eyes follow this action of the left hand.

4th point, "Active Repose." Hands crossed, right over left, on breast.

5th point, "Dedication." The left hand is lowered in front of the body, palm down and horizontal, while the right hand signs the Sigillum Tau on the brow.

6th point, "Passive Repose." Hands placed on breast, left over right.

7th point, "Victory." In one simultaneous movement, the arms are raised in the Psi position Ψ , the head is thrown back, and the right foot is advanced to stamp once.

8th point, "the Wand." Erect stance, arms at sides.

MAGICAL IMAGE OF THE SPHERE

37. **Flame of the Sea:** A luminous and graceful female figure stands upon a sandy shore, upon which seashells are scattered: the ocean, from which she has arisen, is behind her. She is nude but for a girdle, richly jeweled with pearls and emeralds, which encircles her waist. It is early morning. The Sun has not yet appeared, but the sky is bright with opalescent colors whose reflections change and shimmer in the dancing waves. The waves run in, sparkling, to the shore: they break into ripples about the feet of the lovely radiant figure, then flow back into the sea, only to return. Her long, luxuriant hair, in golden tresses, streams out upon a warm but vigorous sea breeze.

Flame of the Sea

In her right hand she holds out a green sprig upon which blooms a five-petaled rose, emblem of the gifts she brings to the Earth: her left hand is lowered towards her vulva, which she indicates with the extended middle finger.

MICROCOSMIC KEYWORDS OF THE SPHERE
38. **Quality in Ruach:** Creativity
39. **Responsive Ruach functions:** Artistic perception, Intuition
40. **Qualities in Nephesh:** Vitality, Reciprocity
41. **Responsive Nephesh function:** Candidness

AURUM SOLIS DIVINE AND ARCHONTIC NAMES
42. **Divine Name (Atziluth):** Albaphalana
43. **Archon (Briah):** Zothalmios
44. **Power (Yetzirah):** Amerophes
45. **Intelligence (Yetzirah):** Anaitos
46. **Spirit (Yetzirah):** Izethos

PLANETARY STANZA FROM THE SONG OF PRAISES
47. **Stanza XIV, Daleth:**

Doorway of vision fulfilled, bringer of dreams
forth to adventuring,
Sacred to thee are the red portals of dawn,
sacred the emerald
Gates of the jubilant spring, Mother of deeds
manifest, multiform—
Mother of destiny!

OLYMPIC PLANETARY SPIRIT
48(a). **Spirit of Venus:** Hagith

48(b). **Her Sigil:**

48(c). **Yetziratic manifestation of Spirit:** A beautiful, graceful female form, warmly attractive and winning but with a sense of great dignity and power. A garland of roses, red and yellow, encircles the dark and undulating hair whose profusion descends over her shoulders. Sparkling jewels adorn the ears, neck and arms. Apart from these adornments, the figure is nude to the waist. The lower part of the figure is covered by a long, saffron colored, sheathlike skirt, held closely around the hips by a wide scarf of sea green patterned with small flowers of many hues, the center of each flower being randomly a small pearl or a stud of coral, amber or turquoise. This scarf is knotted in front so that its long fringed ends swing at the wearer's ankles. Sea green slippers are upon the slender feet. In her right hand Hagith holds a slender leafy spray fashioned of copper. "She, the Holy" raises it to her lips and breathes upon it, and bright flames run from the tips of the shining leaves to shimmer in the air before rising and vanishing away. Then she breathes upon it again and thrusts the base of the stem into the Earth. The whole spray is turned to living green. Its tip swells to a large bud, which bursts open, and a white bird springs from it to soar upwards and disappear in turn. Hagith folds her arms and regards the magician. (See color plate of Hagith following page 204.)

HEBREW DIVINE AND ANGELIC NAMES

49.   **Divine Name (Atziluth):** Yahveh Tzabaoth *or* Yahweh Tzabaoth *or* Yod Heh Vau Heh Tzabaoth *or* Tetragrammaton Tzabaoth

50.   **Archangel (Briah):** Haniel

51.   **Angelic Chora (Yetzirah):** Elohim, "Gods."

52.   **Planetary Angel (Yetzirah):** Anael

53.   **Sigil of Planetary Angel:**

54.   **Intelligence (Yetzirah):** Hagiel

55.   **Spirit (Yetzirah):** Qedemel

PLANETARY STANZA FROM THE SEVENFOLD AFFIRMATION

56.   Designate is he the chief of multitudes holy,
      Glorious before them all, and all-overcoming;
      His the portal of the shrine, within which his path lies,
      He acclaimed of holiness the Triumph, the Beauty!
   Therefore most exalted he, whose pathway lies within the shrine
                                                         supernal!

NEOPLATONIST DIVINE NAME

57.   **Divine Name (Atziluth):** Charis, "Grace."

SACRED VOWEL OF GREEK QABALAH
58. E (the letter *Eta*)

VOWEL TONES OF THE COSMIC HARMONY
59(a). **Contemporary Magical Mode:**

59(b). **Greek Gnostic Mode:**

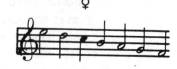

GREEK DEITY
60. **Aphrodite.**

Her epithets: The Most Holy One. The Victorious One. Adonia. She who is to be adored. Ruler of the world. Queen of Love. Chryse (the Golden One). Anadyomene (the Foam-born). The Kyprian. The Beauteous One. The Amorous One. Mother of Passion. Mother of Peace. The Preserver. She whose touch gladdens the Earth. She whose footfall is music. She of the flower-laden breath. Lady of the Myrtle Grove. She who unites. Maker of Joy. Goddess of the unexpected glance. Giver of blessing. Giver of Rapture.

Her Attributes: The Girdle. The Mirror. The Necklace of Pearls, The Diadem. Rose. Myrtle. The Dove. The Delta.

Attendants: The Charites (Aglaia, Euphrosyne, Thalia). Eros.

ROMAN DEITY
61. **Venus.**

Her epithets: The Adored One. Ruler of All. Lady of Gardens. Protectress of the Vine. Giver of Life. Giver of Delight. Queen of Love and Beauty.

Her character: The name of Venus has become without doubt the most widely renowned of all names of the Queen of Love and Beauty. Initially she is mistress and guardian of the beauty of Nature: not, as Artemis, of that

Aphrodite

beauty unadorned, but the carefully tended beauty of the classical garden with its shaded walks, its flowers and fruits, its water courses and its sacred shrine. As goddess of beauty and love in human life, her worship has customarily been celebrated in gardens and in other scenes of beauty. The arts by which all objects of charm and elegance, great or small, are produced are within her domain, with music and dancing, laughter and happy love, that the delight which is the truest devotion to her may be complete.

Her attributes: Rose. Apple and other fruits. Myrtle bush. Dove. Sparrow. Ram. Dolphin.

Attendants: Cupid. The Three Graces. The Seasons.

ETRUSCAN DEITY

62. **Turan:** Lady of Love. The Queen of Beauty and of Love, usually represented reclining and contemplating her reflected loveliness. *Mirror.*

BABYLONIAN DEITY

63. **Ishtar.**

Her epithets: Lady of Heaven. Queen of the morning and the evening. Divine Lover. Giver of Life. Lady of Battles. Goddess Most Courageous. Giver of Victory.

Her character: Even in her Venusian aspect, this most dominant Goddess appears in two distinct characters. She is the supremely powerful deity of love: not only the divine inspirer of passion, but herself a mighty lover among both Gods and men. Her other Venusian character, which has come down to us in Qabalistic and magical indications, is that of Lady of Battles. In that character she rides forth, bow in hand and carrying also the Ring of Divinity, in a chariot drawn by seven lions; or she stands armed in the midst of a battle scene, one foot resting upon a crouching lion. She gives courage, with something of her own indomitable nature: the confident attack which leads to victory, be the situation one of physical or of moral confrontation. She is planetary Venus as "Lady Luck."

HINDU DEITIES

64(a). **Ushas.**

Ishtar of Arbela

Her epithets: Lady of Dawn. Virgin of Dawn. Daughter of Heaven. The Gracious One. Bountiful Splendor. Light-bringer. Life-giver. Revealer of Night's Treasures. Bringer of Health and of Hope. Renewer of Love's Ardor. Youth Immortal. Awakener of the Breath of Life. Awakener of the Virtuous. Mother of the Sun. She who is heralded by singing birds. She who abides from aforetime. Giver of Abundance. Irresistible Loveliness. She who confers blessings.

Her Attributes: Many-colored flowing draperies. Jewels and garlands in profusion. Blossoms and budding stems. Her glittering Chariot, drawn by Red Heifers.

64(b). **Lakshmi.**

Her epithets: The Radiant One. Born from the Waters (of the Sea of Milk). Gift of the Waters. The White-robed. Daughter of the Lotus. She who is revealed within the Lotus. Power of Vishnu. Beloved of Heaven and Earth. Beloved of All. She who breathes forth all sweetness. She whose Hands are rosy buds of Lotus. The Exquisite One. The Perfumed One. The Golden One. Bestower of Love. Bestower of Good Fortune. The Blessed One. The Fickle One. The Self-luminous. She who smiles. Bountiful Goddess. She whose Hands shower coins of gold.

Her attributes: Divine beauty of form, showing every perfection of womanhood. Many necklaces and gems. Large and prominent earrings. The Lotus, upon which she stands or is seated. Sometimes the Goddess is attended by elephants, who sprinkle her with the waters of Mother Ganga.

EGYPTIAN DEITIES

65(a). **Hat-herut (Hat'hor)**

Her epithets: House of Heaven. Mother of Light. Mother of Life. Mother of All the Gods. She who is adorned with stars. The Golden Goddess. Throne of Peace. Bearer of the Sistrum. Bearer of Joy. Mistress of Gladness. Inspiration of Delight. Graceful Power. Milk of Life. Face of Beauty. Maker of Festival. Bringer of Prosperity. Lady of the Tomb. Lady of the Sycamore of the South. Benefactress of Souls. Nourisher of Souls. Divine Goodness.

Her image: Appearing in human form of superb beauty, the Goddess may be enthroned or standing. She wears the festal collar and the Menat (representing the joy of union). Her Old Kingdom headdress is surmounted by Horns and Disk, and upon her brow is the uraeus; or she may be adorned with the Vulture headdress surmounted by uraei and lotus-blossoms. Sometimes her human face has the ears of a cow and is framed by luxuriant hair. She bears the Ankh, and the Papyrus Scepter or the Ouas (the Scepter of Peaceful Authority). The Sistrum is especially sacred to her: it is her herald and her secret voice.

65(b). **Bast**

Her epithets: The Blessed One. Lady of the East. Eye of Ra. Flame of the Sun. Protector of Kings. Life of the Heart of Kings. Most Powerful Mother. Enkindler of New Life. Lady of the Springtime. The Green-robed. Beloved Lady of Bubastis. She who rejoices the people. Dweller in the High Temple. Dweller in the Grove-encircled Temple. The Concealed One.

Her image: Appearing in human form with the head of a Cat, the Goddess bears the Sistrum and the Shield of Protection (upon which is the head of a Lioness). Sometimes she bears also the Corbis (the woven basket of "hidden and holy things"). When appearing in the fullness of her tutelary power with the head of a Lioness, the Goddess wears the Old Kingdom headdress surmounted by the Uraeus, and bears the Ankh and the Papyrus Wand.* Her ancient form is entirely that of a Cat; when in this form she is adorned with rich collar and earrings and upon her breast is the Eye of Tahuti (symbolizing her vigilance and power during the night hours).

---

* The Lioness-headed manifestation of Bast resembles one of the forms of Sekhet, save that Bast is robed in green, Sekhet in red.

8 CORRESPONDENCES OF MERCURY

PLANETARY SIGN
1.　　☿

PLANETARY NAME
2. **In English:** Mercury
3. **In Greek:** Hermes
4. **In Hebrew:** Kokab

PLANETARY PROFILE
5. Intelligent, communicative, discursive and divisive; unresting, dual or even multiple in aspect, but expressive of truth. Travel, calculation, analysis, learning and teaching are among the expressions of the nature of this Sphere. The invisible and changeful force of the wind is an apt symbol. Gifts of Mercury are often freakish or "chance" happenings.

TITLES OF SEPHIRAH
6. **In Hebrew:** Hod
7. **In Greek:** Lamprotesis
8. **In English:** Splendor

TEXT FROM THE THIRTY-TWO PATHS OF WISDOM
9. The Eighth Path is called the Absolute or Perfect Intelligence, because it is the instrument of the Primordial, which has no root by which it can hold fast or abide save in the hidden regions of Gedulah, Magnificence, which emanate from its own nature.

ELEMENTAL AFFINITY OF PLANET
    10.   Water.

SYMBOLS AND MAGICAL IMPLEMENTS
    11.   **Specific to Sphere:** The Winged Staff. The Hermetic Scroll. The Stylus.
        Suitable, but having other magical use: The Hood. Sacred Tomes. Sandals. The countercharged vestment. Lustral vessel. Bell.

PRESIGILLUM
    12.

NUMBER AND GEOMETRIC FORM
    13.   **Qabalistic number:** 8
    14.   **Medieval number:** 5
    15.   **Plane figure:** Octagon
    16.   **Star:** Octagram

QUALITIES OF DESIGN
    17.   Segmented forms; countercharged patterns; mirrored images.

COLORS
    18.   **In Atziluth:** Yellow ochre
    19.   **In Briah:** Orange
    20.   **In Yetzirah:** Light apricot
    21.   **In Assiah:** Yellowish-white merging into greenish-white
    22.   **Ptolemaic color:** Shimmering opalescence (as mother of pearl)

MUSIC FOR PLANETARY MOODS
    23.   **Ideal qualities:** Well-ordered, graceful, intellectual
    24.   **Selected examples:** "Canon in D Major" (Pachelbel). "Bolero" (Ravel). "Brandenburg Concert No. 6" (Bach). "Eine Kleine Nachtmusik"(Mozart).

SUITABLE INSTRUMENTS AND SOUND EFFECTS
    25.   Xylophone. Vibraphone. Electric guitar. Tabla. Pan pipes.

Glockenspiel. Bell. Human voices. Recorded sounds of rushing wind.

ANIMALS AND MYTHOLOGICAL BEINGS

26.   Fox. Giraffe. Zebra. Cheetah. Gazelle. Baboon. Jackal. Platypus. Mule. Ostrich. Carrier pigeon. Magpie. Swift. Butterfly. Greek Sphinx. Wyvern.

TREES AND OTHER VEGETATION

27.   **Trees:** Birch. Aspen. Almond. Mulberry. Lombardy poplar. Pistachio. Magnolia.

28.   **Herbs:** Marjoram. Lavender. Ferns generally. Medicinal herbs generally (as an alternative to their individual attributions). Castor palm. Angelica. Mandrake. Parsley. Stillengia.

29.   **Incenses, Perfumes, etc.:** Mace. Star Anise. Mastic. Gum Arabic. Yellow Sandalwood. Spikenard (for Hermes psychopompos). Orange. Bergamot. Styrax (Liquid Storax). Lemongrass. Walnut. Fennel oil. Lavender oil. Clove oil.

GEMSTONES AND OTHER MINERALS

30.   **Metals:** Quicksilver. Aluminum. Aircraft alloys. Lanthanum.

31.   **Gemstones:** Fire Opal. Carnelian. Cairngorm. Sard. Banded Agate.

32.   **Other minerals:** Chance-found small coins or other artifacts. Curious pebbles, particularly variegated ones.

THE PLANETS AND HEALTH

33.   **Physiological functions:** Governance of cerebrospinal nervous system and to some extent the sympathetic systems; the organs of respiration and speech, the ears as regards hearing: nervous and muscular coordination. Hands and arms generally; the tactile sense; gesture as communication. The thyroid gland with its various functions. The region of the waist. The functioning of the brain-mind faculties, as memory, association, deduction, etc.

34.   **Pathological effects (bodily):** Maladies associated with

the nerves, as neurasthenia, amnesia, asthma, speech disorders. Bronchitis. Laryngitis. Abnormal conditions of the thyroid. Shingles. Any accident or condition affecting hands, arms or waist. Nervous tic.

35. **Pathological effects (psychic):** Somnambulism, talking in the sleep. Periods of intense study may cause or increase problems relating to digestion or respiration.

PLANETARY GESTURE

36. **The Gesture Kryphios (the Concealed), accomplished as follows:***

   1st point, "the Wand." Erect stance, arms at sides.

   2nd point, "Priest of Babylon." Forearms are held horizontally so that hands are palm to palm in front of the solar plexus, right hand palm down over left hand palm up. The fingers of both hands are closed, each hand enfolding the fingers of the other. The thumbs lie closely alongside the forefingers.

   3rd point, "Herald." Right foot is advanced with knee flexed. At the same time, right arm is raised forward to horizontal, left arm raised backwards to horizontal. Left heel is raised, body inclines forward in straight line with left leg.

   4th point, "the Hidden One." Both hands are raised simultaneously to draw the hood swiftly over the face. Then, head is bowed, forearms are crossed in front of head, left arm on outside, palms forward.

   6th point, "the Wand." Erect stance, arms at sides (hood still covering face).

   7th point, "the Revealed." Both hands simultaneously throw back hood.

MAGICAL IMAGES OF THE SPHERE

37(a). **The Hermit:** The figure of a mature man, grey of hair and beard, wise of countenance, but robust, powerful and very luminous, stands in the darkness of night. He wears a full cape, which shimmers with all the vivid and changeful hues of a pearly shell: as he moves, this cape parts to show a long dark robe, girt with a belt which is patterned

---

* A hood is worn for this gesture, initially thrown back upon the shoulders.

The Hermit

Divine Messenger

with alternated octagons and eight-petaled flowers. Upon his feet are sandals. In his right hand this figure holds aloft a flaming torch which he swings slowly above him, half turning his body to left and to right, so as to illumine the dark landscape. Now rocks, now trees, now gleaming water, now a pathway, flash momentarily into sight as he moves the torch. The vivid flames are reflected also in the pearly sheen of his enfolding cape, adding a quality of swiftly scintillating fire to its shimmering colors.

37(b). **Divine Messenger:** A youthful male figure, so delicate as to appear somewhat effeminate, is gliding through the air. His hair is short and dark. He is nude but for the sandals on his feet and a belt about his waist, patterned with alternate octagons and eight-petaled flowers. Springing from his shoulders are great sweeping wings, outspread for flight, with countercharged black and white plumage. His body is inclined forward not more than about 30° from the vertical, in a graceful posture with his right foot lifted slightly more than his left. In his left hand he carries a rolled scroll, with his right hand he extends before him the short staff which is the ancient token of the herald: from its head flutter two white ribbons. This figure seems to be approaching through a tunnel of many-colored light, which because of his swift movement is seen as streaming away in the opposite direction, in long changeful darts and flashes of prismatic radiance. The face of the figure is alert, and communicates something of the high importance of the message which is contained in the scroll.

MICROCOSMIC KEYWORDS OF THE SPHERE

38. **Quality in Ruach:** Intellection
39. **Responsive Ruach functions:** Magical acumen, Analysis
40. **Qualities in Nephesh:** Cognition, Mobility
41. **Responsive Nephesh function:** Communication

AURUM SOLIS DIVINE AND ARCHONTIC NAMES

42. **Divine Name (Atziluth):** Azoth
43. **Archon (Briah):** Anaxephydrias
44. **Power (Yetzirah):** Haberophes

45. **Intelligence (Yetzirah):** Astaphia
46. **Spirit (Yetzirah):** Psarchias

PLANETARY STANZA FROM THE SONG OF PRAISES
47. **Stanza XII, Beth:**

> Bearing thy truth in thy heart, opal-fired sealed
> > deep and inviolate,
> Over the seven-hued bridge pass to the worlds,
> > share in their variance.
> Hail to the voice of thy power, speaking all tongues,
> > many in purposes,
> > One in divinity!

OLYMPIC PLANETARY SPIRIT
48(a). **Spirit of Mercury:** Ophiel

48(b). **His Sigil:**

48(c). **Yetziratic manifestation of Spirit:** A youthful male figure, attired in a flowing robe which falls beltless from throat to ankles. The shining whiteness of this robe is varied with vertical bands of changeful hue, delicate and gleaming as the colors in mother-of-pearl. Upon the head of this figure is a tall cone-shaped helmet, deep blue in color, from the sides of which rise wings covered with tawny plumes. These wings stir and quiver continually, making a sound like delicate wind bells and an Aeolian harp, representing the essential thoughts of Ophiel in a mystical language of ethereal harmonies. His feet are bare. He stands upon a small rug which is of the proportions of an Oriental prayer rug and patterned with geometrical designs in black and orange. In his right hand Ophiel holds a slender rod of bright silver which tapers to a point. By holding out this rod he directs the rug to travel as he wills. (See color plate of Ophiel following page 204.)

HEBREW DIVINE AND ANGELIC NAMES
49. **Divine Name (Atziluth):** Elohim Tzabaoth
50. **Archangel (Briah):** Mikael
51. **Angelic Chora (Yetzirah):** Tarshishim, "the Seas."
52. **Planetary Angel (Yetzirah):** Raphael

53.   **Sigil of Planetary Angel:**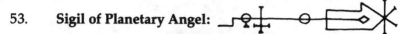

54.   **Intelligence (Yetzirah):** Tiriel

55.   **Spirit (Yetzirah):** Tapthartharath

PLANETARY STANZA FROM THE SEVENFOLD AFFIRMATION

56.   Builded in the heavens are his high habitations,
Steeps of Splendor whence he sendeth rain on the
mountains!
Even they within the deeps, the Fallen, he knoweth:
Knower of all deeds is he and Lord of the Record.
Therefore most exalted he, who foundeth in the deeps his
habitation.

NEOPLATONIST DIVINE NAME

57.   **Divine Name (Atziluth):** Alethes Logos, "True Word"

SACRED VOWEL OF GREEK QABALAH

58.   E (the letter *Epsilon*)

VOWEL TONES OF THE COSMIC HARMONY

59(a).   **Contemporary Magical Mode:**

59(b).   **Greek Gnostic Mode:**

GREEK DEITY

60.   **Hermes.**

His epithets: The Gracious One. The Great One. Exalted
Herald. Divine Messenger. The Protector. Guide of Man.
Hermes of the Cloak of Night. Psychopompos (Guide of
Souls). Bringer of Dreams. Bestower of Good Gifts. Help
in War. Lord of the Games. Lord of Oracles. He who gives
light to the mind. The Swift One. Divine Shepherd. Lord
of the Radiant Staff.

His attributes: The Caduceus. The Winged Sandals.

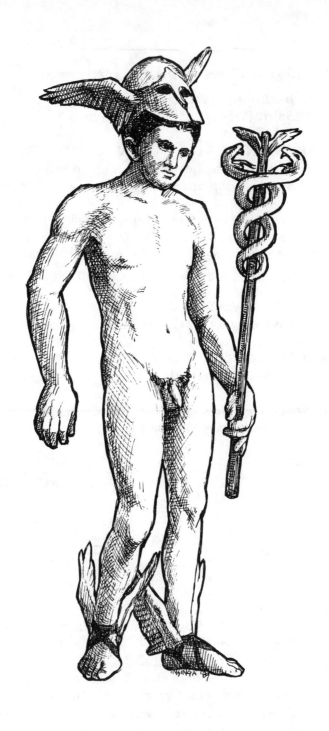

Hermes

Helmet of Invisibility. Petasos (the traveler's hat). The Cithara. The Hermes Pillar. The Ram.

ROMAN DEITY

61. Mercurius

His epithets: Divine Messenger. Guide of Heroes. Guide of Souls. Keeper of the Roads. The Sapient One. The Multiplier. Giver of Gifts. Giver of Signs. Guide of Dreams. The Encourager.

His character: Guardian of flocks, herds and the produce of the Earth; patron of trading and of all activities requiring calculation; patron of astronomy, medicine, music, of astrology, magick and the prophetic chant. Thus Mercurius assumes the character and attributes of Hermes. Unlike Hermes, however, who in his more ancient representations appears as a mature, bearded man, Mercurius is always the young, swiftly moving and sometimes tricky divinity. He is typified by brilliance of mind and quick wit, the unexpected response, the challenging enigma, the paradox. All forms of divination are in his care. Traditionally, he may be invoked to judge of a projected enterprise, the questioner throwing dice and rating the outcome according to the score. He is patron of those who pursue the arts and sciences, especially in the magical or occult aspects; patron of travelers and messengers of whatever kind; patron of those in business if they are willing that their dealings should be spiced with an element of luck.

His attributes: The Palm Branch. The "Herald's Staff." The Winged Cap. Cock. Goat.

ETRUSCAN DEITIES

62(a). **Turms:** Lord of Magick. Guardian of measure in its magical aspects. Boundary stone and threshold are sacred to him. *The Staff. Traveler's hat.*

62(b). **Cilans:** Guide of the Souls of the Dead. Comparable to Hermes Psychopompos.

BABYLONIAN DEITY

63. Nabu.

His epithets: Supreme Messenger. Herald of the Gods. Divine Scribe. Director of the World. Wielder of the

Nabu

Wand of Divination. Opener of the Wells. Far Traveler.

His character: Nabu, son of Marduk and grandson of
Ea, is by origin a water divinity. His power over human
existence is immense. He engraves the destiny of each
person, as the Gods together have decided it, on the
tablets of the sacred record; and he himself can increase
or diminish, at will, the length of any person's life span.
Nevertheless, this divine messenger is a deity worthy of
grateful devotion. He and his consort Tashmetum together
invented writing and bestowed it upon the world; also,
as his titles imply, he is lord of the arts of divination, and
particularly of the discovery of water by means of dowsing.
He is patron of all learning, both overt and occult. His
emblems are the stone tablet and writing chisel, and the
winged dragon which is initially his father's. He wears a
cap adorned with curving horns of power, and stands
with hands clasped before him in the ancient gesture
of priesthood.

HINDU DEITY
64.   Ganesha.

His epithets: Lord of Wisdom. Sixfold in Honor. He
who is crowned with Wisdom. Elephant Face. The One-
Tusked. Giver of Good Counsel. Teacher of Prudence.
Serpent-girdled Lord of Discernment. Friend of Scholars.
Friend of All. God of Writings. Divine Scribe. God of
Riches. Bringer of Abundance. Helper of Commerce.
Tamer of Demons. Inaugurator of Prayer. He who prospers
new ventures. He who confuses the way. He who makes
clear the way. Mighty Mover of Barriers.

His attributes: The Directing Wand. The Rosary. The
Bowl of Plenty. The Detached Tusk. The Tiara or rich
Head trappings. The Snake (which adorns his upper
body). The Rat (as his mount).

EGYPTIAN DEITIES
65(a).   Tahuti (Thoth)

His epithets: The One. Maker of Himself. Twice Greatest.
Thrice Greatest. Divine Scribe. He who Measures. Lord
of the Sacred Texts. He who numbers the Stars. He who

knows the boundaries of the world. Master of Knowledge. Mighty in Magick. He whose Words live. Witness of Equilibrium. Arbiter of Night and Day. Glowing Heart of Ra. Ibis of Power. Divine Peacemaker. The Persuasive One. Leader of Souls. Bestower of Eternity.

His image: The Ibis-headed One wears the kilt and headdress of the Old Kingdom, the collar and the transverse sash. Characteristically, he bears the Tablet and the Stylus. In other of his aspects, his headdress is adorned with the Lunar Disk and Crescent.

65(b). **Sefekh (Seshat)**

Her epithets: Lady of Sevenfold Power. Daughter of Heaven. Consort of Tahuti. The Great Archivist. Keeper of the Book of Life. Maker of Everlasting Words. She who inscribes the term of life. She who inscribes the duration of eternity. Maker of the Celestial habitation of the Soul. Establisher of the Celestial Alignment of the Houses of the Gods. Mistress of the Sacred Characters. She who studies the patterns of Time. She who remembers in Eternity.

Her image: The Goddess is robed in a panther skin. Her Old Kingdom headdress is surmounted by a brilliant Seven-rayed Star framed by an inverted Lunar Crescent. In her hands she holds the Tablet and the Stylus.

9 *CORRESPONDENCES OF LUNA*

PLANETARY SIGN
    1. $\mathcal{D}$

PLANETARY NAME
    2.   **In English:** Moon
    3.   **In Greek:** Mene
    4.   **In Hebrew:** Levanah

PLANETARY PROFILE
    5.   Intense, passionate yet intrinsically cold, changeful. Glamor and dreaming, sudden adventure, childlike wonder and delight. This Sphere has an affinity with the fluctuating tides of ocean, which the Moon governs, and to the ever-varying waves. The impulse of the moment, the work of caprice, the transient pleasure are typical manifestations of the Moon force; but there is also a strong cleansing and purificatory aspect. Further, the dreams of the Moon sphere are the potential realities of Earth.

TITLES OF SEPHIRAH
    6.   **In Hebrew:** Yesod
    7.   **In Greek:** Asphaleia
    8.   **In English:** Foundation

TEXT FROM THE THIRTY-TWO PATHS OF WISDOM
    9.   The Ninth Path is called the Pure Intelligence, because it purifies the manifestations of the Sephiroth: it proves

and governs the formation of their similitude, and disposes in exact measure the unity which is intrinsic to them, not lessened nor divided.

ELEMENTAL AFFINITY OF PLANET
10.   Air

SYMBOLS AND MAGICAL IMPLEMENTS
11.   **Specific to Sphere:** Silver sickle. The Bridle. The Bow. Silver Veil.
Appropriate, but having other magical use: Mask. Transparent robe. Crystal ball.

PRESIGILLUM

12.

NUMBER AND GEOMETRIC FORM
13.   **Qabalistic number:** 9
14.   **Medieval number:** 2
15.   **Plane figure:** Nonagon
16.   **Star:** Enneagram

QUALITIES OF DESIGN
17.   Circular, elliptical and mazelike forms.

COLORS
18.   **In Atziluth:** Red-Purple
19.   **In Briah:** Violet
20.   **In Yetzirah:** Lavender
21.   **In Assiah:** Pale lemon yellow, flecked white
22.   **Ptolemaic color:** Silver

MUSIC FOR PLANETARY MOODS
23.   **Ideal qualities:** Dreamlike, elfin, mysterious, disturbing
24.   **Selected examples:** "Clair de Lune" (Debussy). "La Valse" (Ravel). "Symphonie Pathétique" (Tchaikovsky). "Adagio in E Major" (from *Piano Concerto No. 1, Op. 11*, Chopin).

SUITABLE INSTRUMENTS AND SOUND EFFECTS
25.   Cymbals. Delicate bells. Mandolin. Gourd rattles. Flute. Triangle. Harp. Oboe. Vina. Celesta. Wind chimes. Recorded night-voices of nature.

ANIMALS AND MYTHOLOGICAL BEINGS
26.   Bear. Horse. Elephant. Cat (*Felis cattus*). Hare. Deer. Camel. Dog. Bull. Cow. Hyena. Pig (all kinds). Owl. Nightjar. Raven. Vulture. Minotaur. Winged bull. Ram-headed Serpent. Harpy. Hydra.

TREES AND OTHER VEGETATION
27.   **Trees:** All Willows. Coconut palm. Bay. Hazel. Papaya. Carob. Laburnum.
28.   **Herbs:** All white or purple lily-flowered plants, including hyacinths and irises. Narcissus. All gourds (squashes, cucumbers, melons, etc.). Peas. Beans. Lentils. Vetches. Turnip. Yam.
29.   **Incenses, Perfumes, etc.:** Camphor. Orris root. Galbanum. Artemisia. Wintergreen. Eucalyptus oil. Jasmine oil. Aromatic seeds generally. Ylang-ylang.

GEMSTONES AND OTHER MINERALS
30.   **Metals:** Silver. Platinum. Yttrium.
31.   **Gemstones:** Beryl. Moonstone. Alexandrite.
32.   **Other minerals:** Rock Crystal. Fluorspar. Alabaster or other white translucent rock. Mirror glass.

THE PLANETS AND HEALTH
33.   **Physiological functions:** Secretion and utilizations of fluids: tears, saliva, digestive fluids, sexual secretions and impregnation, the processes of birth. Governance of all life rhythms. The substance of the brain. The sympathetic nervous systems. The uterus. The stomach and the alimentary canal. The lungs. All mucous surfaces.
34.   **Pathological effects (bodily):** Maladies relating to accumulation of body fluids: abscesses, tumors, etc. Women's disorders. Afflictions of the stomach. Chest colds and coughs. Pneumonia. Allergies. Epilepsy. Recurring ailments generally.

35. **Pathological effects (psychic):** Irrational fears, obsessions (in the psychological meaning of the word), prejudices of any kind, if dwelt upon, may prevent a full exercise of life's healthful and healing potentials. Conditions such as anorexia nervosa can give the imagination dominance, not only over the rational mind but also over the body-related instincts. Depression and pessimism, if allowed to prevail, can lower the body's resistance to infection.

PLANETARY GESTURE

36. **The Gesture Korax (Raven), accomplished as follows:**
1st point, "the Wand." Erect stance, arms at sides.
2nd point, "Medean step." Left foot steps back, trunk turns to left confortably. At the same time, arms are raised slightly at sides, palms turned up.
3rd point, "Calling Luna." Arms are raised in a graceful flowing movement until fingers meet overhead, elbows and wrist slightly bent to curve the arms. Then, arms are lowered, still curved, to about shoulder height, then raised, without haste, overhead as before.
4th point, "Taurus." The elbows are bent decisively to bring the hands down to form the Bull Sign at brow, as follows: the two fists are clenched, palms towards brow, the outer edges of the hands touching. The two thumbs, slightly crooked, are extended to point outwards and upwards at the sides.
5th point, "the Wand." Erect stance, arms at sides.
6th point, "Active Repose." With fingers extended, arms are crossed on beast, right arm outside.
7th point, "Lunar Pronatio." Upper arms remaining close to the body, the forearms are extended downwards and slightly forward. The hands are horizontal, palms downward, closed fingertips pointing forwards and thumbs extended as in "Taurus."
8th point, "the Wand." Erect stance, arms at sides.

MAGICAL IMAGE OF THE SPHERE

37. **Lady of Night:** A tall, slender female figure of austere beauty stands erect, her bare feet upon the rock of a mountain summit. It is night time, and the large disc of

Lady of Night

the Full Moon, rising behind her, frames her head and shoulders. Upon her head is a diadem of glittering stones, which flash continually with every hue. From beneath this diadem her dark hair flows down over her bare shoulders, for, save for a lunula—a crescent-shaped necklet—she is unclothed to the waist. Around her waist is a girdle, clasped in front with a shining buckle whose shape suggests the moon-disc between left-facing and right-facing crescents: and from this girdle a skirt of filmy whiteness descends in deep folds to her ankles. In its wide embroidered border, spiral grows out of spiral in such a way that each spiral is like a circular maze, but their progression is like the waves of the sea. The arms of the figure are extended forwards, both palms facing forwards in a gesture of giving. Around each arm from shoulder to wrist is entwined a serpent, dark in color, its head extended before her palm. These serpents are full of life and power, for they represent the mighty astral forces which she controls and directs.

MICROCOSMIC KEYWORDS OF THE SPHERE
38. **Quality in Ruach:** Individuation
39. **Responsive Ruach functions:** Aspiration, Self-respect
40. **Qualities in Nephesh:** Fecundation, Nourishment
41. **Responsive Nephesh functions:** Imagination, Delight

AURUM SOLIS DIVINE AND ARCHONTIC NAMES
42. **Divine Name (Atziluth):** Iao
43. **Archon (Briah):** Theonoemenos
44. **Power (Yetzirah):** Armateon
45. **Intelligence (Yetzirah):** Kamaira
46. **Spirit (Yetzirah):** Ierochos

PLANETARY STANZA FROM THE SONG OF PRAISES
47. **Stanza XIII, Gimel:**
    Grace of the glimmering night, beautiful pale
    camel thou journeyest
    Comely with bridle of pearl, cloth of most fair
    silver caparisoned:
    Tracing the trackless abodes, knowing all times,
    knowing the numberless
    Seeds of the firmament!

OLYMPIC PLANETARY SPIRIT

48(a). **Spirit of Luna:** Phul

48(b). **Her Sigil:**

48(c). **Yetziratic manifestation of Spirit:** The figure is of a warrior maiden, youthful, strong, calmly fearless and with a pale face of radiant beauty. She wears a tunic of silver chain-mail over an inner tunic and wide trousers of violet. Upon her head is a silver helmet, beneath which a neck-guard of silver chain-mail covers her dark blue flowing hair. In her right hand she carries a bow, a quiver of silver arrows hangs upon her shoulder, and from a wide belt studded with pearls about her waist swings a short, crescent-shaped sword in a sheath of ivory. A long cape of brocade, silver and rose, floats from her shoulders, and silver shoes are upon her feet. Phul appears riding a winged white bull. The wings, like gigantic swan's wings in shape, are turquoise blue, and fan forth the sweetness of jasmine at every movement. Upon the bull's back is a black saddle-cloth, upon which is a mystical inscription in letters of silver signifying "Power over the Earth." Upon the ivory sheath of the crescent sword is an inscription in letters of fire which signifies "Power over the Waters"; and upon the bow which Phul bears in her hand are inscribed golden characters signifying "Power in the World of Dream." (See color plate of Phul following page 204.)

HEBREW DIVINE AND ANGELIC NAMES

49. **Divine Name (Atziluth):** Shaddai, El Chai

50. **Archangel (Briah):** Gebriel

51. **Angelic Chora (Yetzirah):** Kerubim, "Strong Ones."

52. **Planetary Angel (Yetzirah):** Gebriel

53. **Sigil of Planetary Angel:**

54. **Intelligence (Yetzirah):** Malkah b'Tarshishim

55. **Spirit (Yetzirah):** Chasmodai

Artemis

PLANETARY STANZA FROM THE SEVENFOLD AFFIRMATION

    56.   Great is he and mighty in the infinite heavens,
                 Manifest in Light is he, in Light covered wholly.
                 His Geburah, his Gedulah, strength his and greatness:
                 Might is his, and his dominion. All-Potent, Living!
    Therefore most exalted he, whose kingdom over all things
                                                is extended.

NEOPLATONIST DIVINE NAME

    57.   **Divine Name (Atziluth):** Aigle Trisagia, "Thrice-Holy Splendor"

SACRED VOWEL OF GREEK QABALAH

    58.   A (the letter *Alpha*)

VOWEL TONES OF THE COSMIC HARMONY

    59(a). **Contemporary Magical Mode:**

    59(b). **Greek Gnostic Mode:**

GREEK DEITIES

    60(a). **Artemis.**

            Her epithets: Light Giver. Lady of Lakes. Roamer of the Wilds. Sustenance of the Life of the Wilds. The Most Bountiful. The Chaste One. The Virgin Huntress. She of the Silver Bow. Sender forth of Arrows of Light. She Who Binds. The Chastizer. Savior. Afflicter. Healer. Strength of the Young Male. The Sower.

            Her attributes: The Silver Bow. The Quiver. The short robe. The Chariot drawn by hinds. Hounds of the chase. Stag. Boar. Bear.

    57(b). **Selene.**

            Her epithets: Queen of Night. Brightness of Night. The Very Manifest One. She who shines for all. The Moon. Opener of the Gate. She who calls forth. The Reward of

Hecate

Dreams. She who commands the rhythmic tides.

Her attributes: The Crescent (upon her brow), or Silver Horns. The Silver Veil. The Silver Chariot. The Cradle. The Hare.

57(c). **Hecate.**

Her epithets: Ruler of Night. Favored of Zeus. Granter of Heart's Desire. Mighty in Heaven, Earth and Ocean. Mother of Enchantment. The Far-reaching Power. She who can turn back the currents. She of the Triple countenance. Guardian of the Three Ways. She of Aforetime. The Dark One. The Many-jeweled One.

Her attributes: The spinning Wheel and the Distaff. Flaming Torches. Voluminous, trailing draperies. Brass sandals. The column at the crossroads. The Alder tree.

Attendants: Eumenides. Empusae (Succubae). Baying hounds. The Dead.

ROMAN DEITY

61. **Diana.**

Her epithets: Queen of all that lives. Diana of the Grove. Diana of the Mountains. Lady of Enchantments. Lady of the Dance. Guardian of Travelers. Guardian of Maidens. Guardian of the Wilds.

Her character: Diana is Goddess of the world of nature, of fertility and birth for all earthly beings. As Goddess of the Moon, she is the resplendent and mighty deity whose powers encompass every aspect of life. Her magical aid is invoked in all contingencies: nonetheless, as one of the great measurers of life and time, she has her own strict requirements of right dealing. She is champion of all helpless or innocent beings: she protects the traveler by night from beasts of prey, but severely avenges the wanton shooting of a stag. Young maidens are in her special care. Yet time and season are all. Diana it is—particularly in her older worship—who calls forth those of riper growth to rapturous song and dance which the moonlight inspires, in forest or on mountain, to rites of sacred orgy. But the month moves on, and behold! the Virgin of the Silver Bow is with us once more.

Her attributes: Silver Bow. Arrows. The robe girt up

Sin

for running. Hair knotted up above the brow. Garlands of flowers. Offerings of first-fruits. Stag. Hound. Ox.

ETRUSCAN DEITY

62. **Tivs:** The Shining One. Natural power of the moon in relation to animal and vegetable life. Later, the character is that of Diana.

BABYLONIAN DEITY

63. **Sin (Zu-En or En-Zu, Nannar).**

His epithets: Lord of Wisdom. Brother of the Earth. Father of the Sun. Father of the Gods. Lord of the Diadem. Calf of the Skies. The Secret-Hearted, Mysterious One.

His character: Sometimes called by his name Nannar, but more often by his title Sin or Zu-En, "Lord of Wisdom," the deity of the Moon is an old man with a beard blue as lapis lazuli, who usually wears an elaborate turban. Early in the lunar month he rides forth, wearing his turban, in the silver boat of the crescent. Alternatively, the silver crescent is at that time his crown, and he bears the title "Calf of the Skies" on account of its small horns. In either case, he later exchanges his headgear—turban or crescent horns—for the white-fire diadem of the Full Moon. He is called "Secret-hearted" and "mysterious" chiefly on account of the enigma of the Moon's phases. He is called the father of Shamash because the lunar calendar is an older institution than is the solar. We can concur, too, in his being titled Father of the Gods; for it is in the astral domain, which the Moon governs, that the Gods are clothed in the forms by which we know them. Besides being a measurer of time, Sin is one of the divine dealers of justice: by night it is his bright radiance which deters, or detects, evil doers, and the shadowy blue web of his beard can entrap them. He is counselor to Gods and humankind, bestowing chiefly an inner perception of the interpretations of astrology.

HINDU DEITIES

64(a). **Varuna.**

His epithets: The Thousand-eyed. Sovereign King. The

Almighty. The Wise One. Stablisher of the Foundations. The White Man. Guardian of the Pledged Word. Guardian of Right Order. Lawgiver of Heaven and the Deeps. Seer of Thoughts. The Omnipresent One. All-seeing by Night. Ruler of the Night Sky. Ruler of the Air. Ruler of the World of Waters. Pursuer of the Lawless. King of the Dead.

His attributes: The Lasso. The Makara (the dragon of the deeps upon which he rides). The Moon.

64(b). Shiva (as the Great Ascetic).

His epithets: The Beneficent One. The Great God. Principle of Dissolution. Blue Throat. The Three-eyed God. The White One. Supreme Ruler. The Divine Will. Leader of Ascetics. Lord of the Lawless. He in whose Hair flows the Ganges. Moon-crowned Madman. Divine Ecstasy. The Space-clad. Destroyer of Illusion. He who Fascinates. He who Draws Forth. The Great Transformer. The Profusely Generous. The Wild One. Passionate Coldness. Inexorable Lord of the Dark Forces.

His attributes: The Ascetic's Hair-knot. The Crescent Moon (upon his hair). The Third Eye. The Blue-stained Throat. The Serpent Necklet. The Double Drum. The Trident. The Deer (springing from his hand). The White Bull Nandi (as his attendant or as his mount). The Fire Tongs of the mendicant.

64(c). Uma.

Her epithets: The Generous One. Daughter of Himavat. The Devoted Ascetic. Mother of Silence. The Brilliant One. Singlehearted. Votary of God. Mirror of Contemplation. Power of Shiva.

Her character: Uma-Parvati, the maiden daughter of the mighty Himalayas, loses her heart to the divine ascetic Shiva who, entirely unheeding her existence, with fanatical austerities broods like the moonlight itself among the eternal snows. In no sense can she be his counterpart, save in taking on an existence as harsh as his own. At last, having become completely transformed to the nature of her deity, she ceases to pursue him and sits alone in contemplation on the heights. Then Shiva comes to find her; and their union crowns their inner unity.

EGYPTIAN DEITIES
65(a). Khonsu (Khonsu Nefer-hotep)

His epithets: The Swift Mover. Beautiful in his Fullness. He who stirs the womb. Fountain of Fertility. The Dweller in Peace. Establisher of Times. Lord of Vital Fruition. Dispeller of Evil. The Great Exorcist. The Great Healer. The Wonder-Worker. Countenance of Light. Royal Child. Virile Bull. The Ancient. Prince of Gladness. The Very Mighty. Restorer of Truth.

His image: The God is enthroned, and like Ptah he is enswathed. Characteristically, he wears a skull-cap adorned with the Uraeus and the single hair-tress of a prince of Egypt. He holds the Ouas (the Scepter of Peaceful Authority) centrally before him; upon the rod of the Ouas are displayed the Ankh and the Tet. In addition to the Ouas he bears the Crook and Flail. As a standing figure he appears wearing the kilt and headdress of the Old Kingdom, the headdress being surmounted by the Lunar Disk and Crescent. In other of his aspects he appears Hawk-headed; or double Hawk-headed, winged, and standing upon two crocodiles.

65(b). Ta-Urt (Taueret)

Her epithets: The Great One. Mother of the Sun. Mistress of the Gods. Consort of Sutekh. She who moves Destiny. Guardian of Women. Powerful Helper in childbirth. The Propitious One. She who abhors the Powers of Darkness. Bringer of Magical Protection. Generous Bringer of Good Fortune. Powerful Guardian of the Land. Banisher of Robbers. Slayer of Crocodiles. Kindly Guardian of Souls.

Her image: The Goddess manifests in the form of a Hippopotamus, standing upright and having hanging breasts. Characteristically, her left hand is placed upon the Sa-symbol (a folded and bound roll of papyrus denoting Magical Protection) and in that hand she may also bear the Ankh, which thus rests upon the Sa. Her right hand may also rest upon a Sa-symbol, or may be extended holding an unopened bud of papyrus. Her Old Kingdom headdress, the back of which has an ornamental continuation reaching to the ground behind her, is surmounted by Horns and Disk, or by Plumes, Horns and Disk.

10 TIMES OF POWER

For many types of magick a system of multiple forces has to be considered, to find times when our acts will produce the greatest and best results or to note other times which should be avoided. The reasons for this complexity lie in the continual fluctuations and changes which take place in and around us, physically and, more important, astrally: that is, in our Nephesh and in the Astral Light at large.

Planetary Magick is less dependent upon conditions in the external Worlds than are many other branches of magical art, while at the same time having its own immense resources of power. There is, for one thing, the Deep Mind's mysterious and immeasurable faculty, when once it has been called into action, of creating its own good from existing circumstances and of molding to its purposes even the most unlikely conditions. But the distinctive strength of Planetary Magick is its sure means of engaging the Deep Mind and sparking into potent life the meaning and purpose of the workings: the immense power-source which Planetary Magick has in the inner counterparts of the planetary archetypes. And these counterparts have their place in the strongholds of the Deep Mind itself, where fluctuations of the outer levels of being cannot disturb them.

It is on account of its unique nature and power, drawing directly upon inner rather than outer sources, that Planetary Magick has, by long tradition, its own particular methods of establishing times for its workings: methods which, for this type of magick, entirely supersede and replace a variety of considerations which are important elsewhere.

Of the many impulses which affect earthly existence in general at its material and astral levels, two have a partial significance in Planetary

Magick: *the Seasonal Tides,* which are based upon Earth's position in respect of the Sun, and *the Phases of the Moon.* In considering these two types of fluctuation, only the principal changes which they cause in the *character* of the astral energies are important here.*

> *The Seasonal Tides divide the year into four parts:*
> Spring Equinox through Summer Solstice—Tide of Sowing.
> Summer Solstice through Autumn Equinox—Tide of Harvest.
> Autumn Equinox through Winter Solstice—Tide of Reflection.
> Winter Solstice through Spring Equinox—Tide of Overturning.
>
> *The Phases of the Moon thus divide the lunar month:*
> 1st Quarter—New Moon waxing through Half Moon.
> 2nd Quarter—Half Moon through Full Moon.
> 3rd Quarter—Full Moon through Half Waned.
> 4th Quarter—Half Waned through Dark.

The effective application of these Seasonal and Lunar Tides is governed by the type of operation to be performed. For this reason the practices given in this book are designated according to their required combination of these tides, in the following categories:

Temporal Mode 1. *Practices in this category may be performed during the 1st and 2nd Quarters of the Moon, and during any Seasonal Tide except the Tide of Overturning.*

Temporal Mode 2. *Practices in this category may be performed during the 2nd Quarter of the Moon, and during any Seasonal Tide except the Tide of Overturning.*

Temporal Mode 3. *Practices in this category may be performed during any Phase of the Moon except the 4th Quarter, and during all four Seasonal Tides.*

Within the general and beneficent confluence of astral currents ensured by selection of the appropriate *Temporal Mode,* Planetary Magick requires also a specific and potent focusing of Time in accordance with its own intrinsic attributions. This will now be considered.

PLANETARY DAYS AND HOURS
Works of Planetary Magick invariably have been, and are, begun during a *planetary hour* dedicated to the luminary which is the subject of the working, and, for maximum efficacy, on the *day of the week* which

---

* For other aspects of the Tides, in relation to the magical art generally, see *The Sword and the Serpent* (Llewellyn's "The Magical Philosophy" series).

is ruled by that same luminary.

The planetary attributions of the days of the week are: Sunday, *the Sun.* Monday, *the Moon.* Tuesday, *Mars.* Wednesday, *Mercury.* Thursday, *Jupiter.* Friday, *Venus.* Saturday, *Saturn.* The planetary "Seven" is built into our very concept of the week.

If you wish to trace the origins of the names of the days, the English language gives a remarkably unimpaired planetary sequence; but in any European language you will find the same overall pattern and sequence of attribution with, usually, one or two historically interesting avoidances where ancient popular loyalties were considered too strong to be safe. This basically unanimous sequence of the seven planetary powers as associated with the days of the week is, for the whole of Western culture, imprinted as a powerful egregor in the Astral Light and in the deep levels of the human psyche.

The order in which these planetary powers are so unanimously given seems at first sight arbitrary, and certainly it has no mythological basis. In fact it is not arbitrary at all, but follows with simple mathematical inevitability from the descending order of the Seven Planetary Sephiroth of the Tree of Life. As a starting point, all that needs to be accepted is that it is the first hour of each day—that is, the hour following sunrise—which gives the day its attribution. Taking the planets in their sephirothic order—Saturn, Jupiter, Mars, Sun, Venus, Mercury, Moon—in rotation, on Sunday we must begin therefore with the Sun. The twenty-four hours for that day, then, work out in this way:

1. ☉	7. ♂	13. ♃	19. ♄
2. ♀	8. ☉	14. ♂	20. ♃
3. ☿	9. ♀	15. ☉	21. ♂
4. ☽	10. ☿	16. ♀	22. ☉
5. ♄	11. ☽	17. ☿	23. ♀
6. ♃	12. ♄	18. ☽	24. ☿

The next planetary power on our rotating list is ☽, which arrives just as it should to be Hour 1 on Monday.

These attributions of the days and hours are integral to Planetary Magick. A planetary working, harmoniously planned as regards its other correspondences and taking place upon the day, and beginning in the hour, of the planet of its dedication, is an operation of vital and glorious power, a living link in an ages-old, mighty tradition.

Because of the deep responsiveness of the psyche to the planetary archetypes, such a working is dynamic not only in its cosmic effectiveness, but also in the inward joy and inspiration of those who participate, knowing and profoundly feeling that all is rightly and fittingly done.

The next requirement, then, in deciding when an intended planetary working shall take place, is to determine when feasible hours of the planet's attribution will occur. To avoid the labor and complexity of setting out the twenty-four hourly attributions singly for each day of the week, the planetary hours are summarized for ease of reference in the following chart:

Key to Planetary Hours

Mon	Tues	Wed	Thu	Fri	Sat	Sun	Hours ruled by indicated planet
☽	♂	☿	♃	♀	♄	☉	1, 8, 15, 22
♄	☉	☽	♂	☿	♃	♀	2, 9, 16, 23
♃	♀	♄	☉	☽	♂	☿	3, 10, 17, 24
♂	☿	♃	♀	♄	☉	☽	4, 11, 18
☉	☽	♂	☿	♃	♀	♄	5, 12, 19
♀	♄	☉	☽	♂	☿	♃	6, 13, 20
☿	♃	♀	♄	☉	☽	♂	7, 14, 21

Examples of the use of the "Key to Planetary Hours"
The chart shows that on each day of the week, the hours of the ruling planet of that day are the 1st, 8th, 15th and 22nd. For each planet, the greatest power for a working is to be gained by performing a working on its own day and in one of those hours. To do this, however, is not always feasible. The following examples relate to the use of the planetary hour alone, which is still very potent where it occurs on other days.

(1) If you wish to know what hours are ruled by the Moon throughout the week, find the Moon symbol in the vertical column for each day successively. The information in the final column shows that the Moon rules the 1st, 8th, 15th and 22nd hours on Monday, the 5th, 12th and 19th hours on Tuesday, the 2nd, 9th, 16th and 23rd hours on Wednesday, and so on.

(2) Supposing you wish to perform a ritual of Venus, but you are only free to do so in the 19th or 20th hours; on what days of the week can you perform your ritual? Finding the number 19 in the final column, trace back horizontally to the Venus sign in the same line; this is in the vertical column for Saturday. Now, finding the number 20 in the final column, trace back horizontally to the Venus sign in that line. This is in the vertical column for Monday. You can, therefore, perform your ritual of Venus in the hour of Venus, in the 19th hour on Saturday or in the 20th hour on Monday.

(3) Supposing you have unexpectedly to take an important journey on a Saturday morning; you wish therefore to perform a ritual of Mercury, for safety and a good outcome, on the previous day, Friday. In the vertical column for Friday you find the Mercury sign, then from this trace horizontally to the final column. This tells you that the hours of Mercury on a Friday are the 2nd, 9th, 16th and 23rd; four to choose from.

In all cases it should be noted that if a working is to take more than one hour, or if you cannot begin your working until the hour of its attribution is partly spent, there is no problem. The important thing is that the working begins during the hour of its attribution, no matter what may be the attribution of the hour it proceeds into: just as the day itself has the attribution of its first hour. Here, however, another question must be answered: *How long is a magical hour?*

Magical Hours and Planetary Hours

Hours in Planetary Magick are not hours of the mechanical clock. There are twelve hours from sunrise to sunset, and twelve from sunset to sunrise, so the hours of day and night will only be equal to each other (and to 60 minutes) twice in the year, on the days which for that reason are called the Equinoxes. At the Solstices of summer and winter, the difference of duration of day and night is most extreme, the extent of that difference depending upon your distance from the Equator. All you need to know in order to make your necessary calculation, however, is the time of sunrise and of sunset on the intended day of your working. If you wish to do this on a regular basis, to make your calculation once a week should be sufficient.

Generally you will not need to work out the magical hours for both day and night in planning for your working. However, to show the simplicity of the whole thing, the calculations for a specimen day and night follow here.

Finding the Planetary Hours—An Example

Let us suppose that on the day in question the sun rises at 6:11 a.m., and sets at 7:35 p.m. If this day is before the Summer Solstice the *next* sunrise will in fact be fractionally earlier, but for practical purposes we can assume this night will extend from 7:35 p.m. to the next 6:11 a.m.

Our period of daylight, from 6:11 to 7:35 consists of 13 hours and 24 minutes; that is, 804 minutes. Dividing this number by 12, we find each magical hour of daylight is 67 minutes long; that is, 67 minutes are given to each planetary attribution in turn.

We can at once conclude from this that each of the magical hours of night is 53 minutes long; but this can easily be confirmed, if desired, since the period from 7:35 p.m. to 6:11 a.m. is 10 hours and 36 minutes, or 636 minutes, which if divided by 12 gives 53 minutes.

Following from this simple calculation, a complete table of the clocktimes for the beginning of each magical hour of day and night can now be made out, beginning at 6:11 a.m. (sunrise), adding 67 minutes for each of the twelve magical hours until sunset, and thereafter adding only 53 minutes for each of the twelve magical hours until sunrise. But, to complete the example, let us suppose our specimen day to be a Monday, and give to each magical hour the attribution which will make it a true Planetary Hour:

SPECIMEN CHART OF MAGICAL HOURS
(Sun rising at 6:11 a.m. and setting at 7:35 p.m. on a Monday)

Day Hours

Number of Magical Hour	Clock time of Hour's beginning	Planetary Attribution
1	6:11 a.m.	Moon
2	7:18	Saturn
3	8:25	Jupiter
4	9:32	Mars
5	10:39	Sun
6	11:46	Venus
7	12:53 p.m.	Mercury
8	2:00	Moon
9	3:07	Saturn
10	4:14	Jupiter
11	5:21	Mars
12	6:28	Sun

Night Hours

Number of Magical Hour	Clock time of Hour's beginning	Planetary Attribution
13	7:35 p.m.	Venus
14	8:28	Mercury
15	9:21	Moon
16	10:14	Saturn
17	11:07	Jupiter
18	12:00	Mars
19	12:53 a.m.	Sun
20	1:46	Venus
21	2:39	Mercury
22	3:32	Moon
23	4:25	Saturn
24	5:18	Jupiter

Fifty-three minutes later, at 6:11 a.m., the day of Mars (Tuesday) will begin at sunrise with the hour of Mars.

The preceding example is not, of course, meant to be used as it stands. The degree of latitude at which you are, as well as the exact time of year, will affect the relative times of sunrise and sunset and thus the proportions of day and night. In the period from Autumn Equinox up to Spring Equinox, the magical hours will be shorter during the day than during the night, and the day hours will be shortest of all around the Winter Solstice.

To make the appropriate chart for your working, therefore, proceed as follows:

1. Find the true times of sunrise and sunset for the day of your intended working. (If you are practicing Planetary Magick regularly, do this once a week.)

2. Calculate the number of hours and minutes in the day and in the night.

3. Divide each of these numbers by twelve to find the length of a magical day hour, and of a magical night hour.

4. Beginning at the time of sunrise, add on the length of a day hour to find the beginning time of magical day hours 2 through 12. Number the hours as you list them. If your calculations are right, when you add the length of a day hour to the beginning time of Hour 12, you will find it gives the time of sunset.

5. That time of sunset is the beginning of Hour 13, your first magical hour of the night. So add to it the length of a night hour, to find the beginning of Hour 14. Proceed with the night

hours through Hour 24. If your calculations are right, adding the length of a night hour to the beginning of Hour 24 should bring you to the same time of sunrise that you used for this day.

6. Starting with the planet of the day's attribution, put in the names or signs of the planets in rotation (that is, in recurring sephirothic sequence). Or, simply by looking at the Key to Planetary Hours, you can see which hours are attributed to the planet of your working for the day of the week you have chosen.

7. If you wish to work out the night hours only, the bottom line but one of the Key to Planetary Hours gives you the planetary attribution for Hour 13—that is, the magical hour which begins at sunset—for every day of the week.

In summary, it is to be observed that due to the direct link which Planetary Magick has with the great inner resources of the psyche, there are very few outer-world conditions to be complied with when choosing a time for a planetary working. Those which are taken into account—the Seasonal and Lunar Tides—are for the purposes of this book systemized in the three *Temporal Modes.* Specific reference to these is made for every practice of Planetary Magick given in this book.

Within the compass of the appropriate Temporal Mode the student needs only to establish the distinctive focusing of time by calculating a *Planetary Hour* suitable to the working.

All requirements for *Times of Power* in Planetary Magick are thereby fulfilled.

PART TWO

Your Place of Working and Equipment

1   *THE PLACE OF WORKING*

On many occasions the practitioner of Planetary Magick will wish to follow the example of his spiritual forebears in the Art, by conducting particular workings in specific locales: a rite of Jupiter upon a hilltop or within the secret domain of an oak wood; a rite of Venus upon the seashore or in the delicate surroundings of an enclosed formal garden. A place of secluded and awesome natural beauty may be his choice; or he may seek out an ancient sacred site wherein to make adoration and invocation of the power to which he aspires. Again, he may be moved to celebrate his planetary ritual during the night hours, in open country, bathed in the light of the Full Moon or with the planet of the working exalted in living splendor among the stars. Such occasions are unforgettably precious; they hold a sense of sublime mystery, a character of special and profound magick which is born of their unique confluence of time, place and purpose.

For the generality of planetary workings, however, beauty, rightness and effectiveness are to be sought within an established *temenos:* that is to say, within a place made sacred by the regular and accustomed practice of the Magical Art. It matters little whether this chosen place be a lofty hall, a basement, a gazebo, the garage or the spare bedroom; whether it be without mundane furniture, or whether the furniture be, for a ritual occasion, removed or put aside. On every occasion of magical use, with the interaction of the various levels of being which is engendered thereby, the place of working is imbued with the particular dignity and resplendence of the sphere of operation and is suffused with a vibrancy which sustains the whole unqualified potential of that sphere. It thus becomes truly a *Place of Light,* and its nature utterly transcends the mundane environment. When, moreover, this *temenos* is the place of regular magical working it will, in course of time, become an astro-physical locale of power, a nexus between the worlds, and herein the forces of abundant life will progressively, and ever more readily, respond to invocation.*

For each working of Planetary Magick, the equipment and arrangement of the place of working can be as simple or as elaborate as may be desired. The magician may choose to build up, by means of symbols, implements, colors, sounds and so on from the appropriate Table of Correspondences, as exact a representation of the Sphere as possible. Alternatively, by a few vital indicators drawn from the same source, an instant "portrait" of the sphere may be called up irresistibly in the imagination. The choice must depend upon the nature and purpose of the rite, the character of the planet and the will of the magician; for neither of these methods, nor one of the moderate choices which lie between them is in itself to be preferred above the rest.

The directions given regarding ritual equipment in the rest of this book, even where recommendation for specific appurtenances is made, should not be taken as deciding the question of elaboration or simplicity, for in no case are they intended to show more than a basic setting for the specified rite. The Correspondences offer the possibility of introducing many accessories beyond these indications; which, if any, of such additional accessories shall be used must remain a matter of individual taste and initiative.

Two items of equipment are, however, constant factors in the furnishing of the place of working: the *Bomos* and the *Symbol of the Spiritual Ideal.* These will now be considered.

The Bomos

This is the typical altar of the Western Mystery Tradition, and its form recalls the upright altar of the ancient world.

Some ancient Middle Eastern altars, carved from marble or other rock, have "horns of power" shaped at the four upper corners, while the vertical faces of Greek examples show beautiful emblematic designs in low relief. The modern magical tradition favors natural wood,

---

* If the place of working has on occasion to be used for mundane purposes—a lounge or living room, for instance, or that spare bedroom—a sensitive visitor is likely to be aware of a latent magical dynamism. The latent ambience, however, is neutral and unconditioned, and the erstwhile place of working will simply be felt to have *atmosphere*. In such circumstances the magical forces are entirely in abeyance between workings and will only become operative again upon invocation. If magical working is discontinued in such a place for a considerable period of time, the nexus will dissolve.

By contrast, it may be observed that the nexus formed by the due and potent consecration of a magical temple is stronger and more lasting, and although here too the ambience is latent between workings, the guards of protection and the specific consecratory links remain operative at all times.

however, with the emphasis on design and proportion rather than on adornment.

Traditionally, the Bomos is proportioned as one cube resting upon another. The lower cube represents the visible light of the world of mundane life, the upper represents the concealed splendor of the spiritual world; the whole being a statement of Hermetic dictum "As above, so below." To emphasize this significance, the lower cube of the altar is sometimes colored white, the upper cube black. This recalls the deeply venerated banner of the Knights Templar, which similarly showed a black square above a white square. However, the knowledge of this mystery does not need to be manifested in painting, and the beauty of natural materials has a rightness which is suited to all occasions.

For the significance of the altar can validly be re-interpreted according to the varying circumstances of time, place and purpose:

It is the Column of Power, symbol of the Father.

It is the Hearthstone of the World, sacred to the Mother.

It is the Boundary Stone, standing between the realms of Gods and Men.

It is the Fruitful Rock from which springs Mithras, Light of Inspiration.

It is a representative part of all Earth, as if it were a mound, chosen by the magician in a wilderness yet not losing its oneness with all the surrounding environment.

It is a symbol of the Material World, which in itself is the receptacle of all the forces of the universe, yet which is subject to the magician and resonant to the gavel of his will.

It is the World Ash; it is the prophetic Oak of Zeus; and it is the Tree of Crystal wherein Tammuz shines as flame.

It is a symbol of the magician himself, and thus it betokens the great secret of Alchemy: that whatever we do in, or to, the outer world is done also within ourselves. For truly, it is upon the altar of our inner being that all our works of power are performed.

This altar, then, is to be established in the place of working: this *Bomos*, among whose mystical titles are "Ark of the Perfect Light," "Lodestone of Infinite Power," and "The Anvil." The magician may choose that in his *temenos* its form should be the "Altar of the Double Cube," whether of natural wood or colored in symbolic black and white; or another form may be preferred.

The simple norm for a magical altar, as established by antiquity, esthetics and functional utility, is that it should be upright—that is, of a width less than its height—of convenient dimensions for practical working, and, preferably, symmetrical in form. Any kind of pedestal may be chosen: the upper surface may be square, polygonal or circular. One magician might for instance have a tiered pyramid, like the curio stand chosen as an "Altar of Nature" by Goethe in his boyhood: another might delight in a modern pedestal in the form of an inverted cone upon a basal disk. The essential is that the individual mage should see that altar as "right" in the *temenos,* and should be physically and emotionally able to work harmoniously with it.

The Symbol of the Spiritual Ideal.

In a way which may not be obvious until the matter is considered at some depth, one's magical work needs a sufficient overall purpose and tension to give it validity. We might indeed say, "to give it reality"; for without a deep sense of tension, an unfailing awareness of a need which must be fulfilled, it is to be doubted whether a true magical act is possible. To cover the whole span of one's magical work, therefore— that which one may resolve upon in the future as well as that of past and present—no less a purpose will suffice than the "highest common denominator" of all the motives of one's life, the one ultimate aspiration towards which, whether implicitly or explicitly, all one's minor aspirations tend: that divine reality—no matter how obscurely one's life may adumbrate it—which lies at the heart of all being. And this objective of one's aspirations is necessarily—again, whether implicitly or explicity—the ultimate objective of all one's magical work.

Fittingly, therefore, to put us in mind of it and to give precision and force to our magical will, at every working there should be present upon the Bomos a symbol to represent to us this central divine reality, either in its own nature simply or as fusing with the earthly life which aspires to it.

This symbol, once chosen, should not lightly be changed: as time passes it will become, with use and familiarity, progressively more meaningful and more precious. It can be a three-dimensional object or a two-dimensional representation. It need not be complex.

The Aurum Solis uniformly employs a "Tessera,"* a square tablet of natural wood with two interlaced squares inscribed upon it, one in red outline and the other in white, the diagonals of the one sharing a

---

* For further information on the Tessera and its significance in Aurum Solis practice, see *Mysteria Magica* (Volume 3 of the 2nd edition of The Magical Philosophy, Llewellyn Publications), pages 253 through 262.

common center with the diagonals of the other but being turned from them at an angle of forty-five degrees. This simple symbol denotes the closely interwoven unity of the material and spiritual levels of existence, whose balance and reciprocity show forth the perfection of each.

The Triangle, the Eye within the Triangle, the simple eight-rayed Star which was the emblem of godhead in Babylonia, the Moebius or Infinity Curve of modern physics and medieval Islamic mathematic: all are venerable tokens of the divine nature as conceived of in itself. Symbols expressing the interrelation or the fusion of temporal and eternal, on the other hand, include the Serpent upon the Tau Cross (representing the divine nature entwining with and vivifying material being); the Pyramid upon the Cube (matter crowned by the fire of Spirit); the Hexagram (the holy symbol of "the Everlasting Arms," the upward and downward pointing triangles of the glyph indicating respectively in this context the divine power *per se*, the "right hand of God," and that power as it acts through the causes and effects of the contingent world, the "left hand of God" traditionally so called).

Again, the symbol may be a photograph of a spiral nebula, symbolizing the Sephirah Kether, power-source of creation. It may be a statue or other representation of the Greek Sphynx, winged, with woman's head and breasts, lion's body, and tail formed of a serpent; this being an ancient emblem of the Great Mother in her universal aspect, combining within herself all levels of being from the divine to the material.*

Spiritual reality is unchanging, but the symbols by which we express it in this age may take forms altogether contemporary. A computer abstract, for instance, may represent the presence of infinity in the finite by suggesting boundless perspectives within its small plan.

These are, however, only a few of the innumerable possible ways of symbolizing the Spiritual Ideal. The vital symbol may present itself from the realms of nature, of art, of science, of philosophy. Everywhere there is imagery suggesting the action of unseen forces, and there is beauty and order where chaos might have been expected. It is for the magician to choose, as he wills.

---

* Get lost, Oedipus!

2 THE LAMEN

The Lamen is a form of pentacle or medallion which is worn only on the occasion of a magical working. In assuming the Lamen, the magician affirms the basis of his magical authority and the context in which that authority is to be exercised: a signal directed not only to his subliminal faculties, to engage their attention and to ensure their cooperation, but also to the forces of the external universe, to announce his "power in presence" and to invoke their witness.

Ideally, the Lamen for Planetary Magick should symbolize a harmonious unity and interaction of the Seven Planetary Powers, together with a central device representing the higher directing faculties of the psyche. The following diagram illustrates a Lamen fulfilling these requirements, and traditional for rites of Planetary Magick in the Order Aurum Solis.

The design of this Lamen itself shows forth the reason why only the one Lamen need be, or should be, employed for whatever rites of Planetary Magick are performed within the system given in this book. Certainly in a rite of Planetary Magick a single planetary power is invoked, but always within the context of the balance and harmony of the whole, both cosmic and microcosmic. An unbalanced force tends to be an uncontrolled force, and only from the strength of one's inner harmony is any force controllable. No matter, therefore, whether in a program of inner development we perform rites of each planetary power in rotation, or whether we perform a significant number of rites of one planet consecutively for a special purpose, the use of this composite Lamen expresses—and keeps us in mind of—our underlying aim to maintain our life and our personal universe in wholeness, equilibrium and the invincible power of the Light.

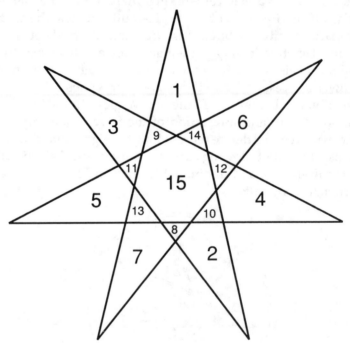

A) The major design of the Lamen is formed by the seven-pointed star, signifying the planetary powers in their spiritual and cosmic aspects. This figure is defined by one continuous interlace, a reflection of the fact that the planetary powers are, in essence, modifications of one original power, whether we consider this at the spiritual or at the cosmic level. The interlace is colored white, representing that radiance of the Divine Mind which infuses and sustains all the planetary emanations. This interlace may be outlined delicately with black to ensure clear definition of the design.

B) Within the rays of the heptagram the Presigilla of the planetary powers (*Entry 12*, Tables of Correspondences) are shown in Briatic colors (*Entry 19*, Tables of Correspondences), each against a background of its complementary color:

1. Presigillum of Saturn, indigo (or black) on white.
2. Presigillum of Jupiter, blue on orange.
3. Presigillum of Mars, red on green.
4. Presigillum of Sol, yellow on violet.
5. Presigillum of Venus, green on red.
6. Presigillum of Mercury, orange on blue.
7. Presigillum of Luna, violet on yellow.

These Presigilla are characteristic "signatures" of the planetary forces at astral level, pragmatically established as potent whether to represent or to awaken the forces in question. Their use is integral to the system here set forth; and in addition to their depiction upon the Lamen they are employed as signs to be "cut" or traced in the air in some instances of the actual invocation of planetary forces.

C) The sections numbered 8 through 14 on the *key diagram* form a smaller and inverted seven-pointed star within the major heptagram. In context, this lesser star signifies the microcosmic aspect of the planetary powers, their reflection in the Deep Mind, contingent to the spiritual and cosmic aspects and nurtured by them. Each of these sections is filled with the Briatic color of its planetary attribution, as follows:

8 – Indigo or black (for Saturn).
9. – Blue (for Jupiter).
10. – Red (for Mars).
11. – Yellow (for Sol).
12. – Green (for Venus).
13. – Orange (for Mercury).
14. – Violet (for Luna).

D) Within the heptagon, numbered 15 on the *key diagram*, at the center of the whole figure, is depicted the *Sign of the Quintessence*. The Quintessence is a concept of medieval philosophy which signifies at once the light of the heavenly bodies as their perfected distillate, and the singular resplendence of the "personal Star of Destiny," that special "nucleus" in the Divine Mind which is both one's origin and goal. In our Lamen, the Sign of the Quintessence is colored gold, the heptagon which forms its background being colored silver; this signifying the manifestation of the positive Divine Fire of the Higher Self in and through the pure receptive matrix of the Soul, to the consequent ordering and right governance of the faculties of the aware and integrated individual.*

E) The surrounding circle of the Lamen is colored black, carrying a suggestion of the unmanifest from which all manifestation comes forth, of that cosmic womb wherein all powers are quickened to birth, of mystical night which is the domain of the Wandering Stars.

For making the Lamen a thin disc is needed, about 11 cm. in diameter. A basswood plaque, such as may be found in craft stores, is ideal for this purpose. Basswood can easily be sanded, drawn and painted upon, and varnished if desired, and a small screw-eye can easily be inserted into the rim for suspension.

When the Lamen is to be worn, it should be suspended about the neck by a goldtone or silvertone chain, of length sufficient to let the Lamen hang comfortably upon the sternum.

The practical making of the Lamen should be performed during the relevant planetary hours, and within the ambit of Temporal Mode 1. As may prove convenient, the practitioner is free to choose different hours of the appropriate planet for different parts of the work: for instance a background color may be applied during one of the hours of the planet of attribution, then the symbol may be added during another hour of that same planet. A procedure which takes a longer time than one planetary hour, however, in accord with accepted practice need only be begun during the hour of its planetary attribution, and can be continued into a succeeding hour.

For the different parts of the Lamen, the planetary hours to be employed are as follows:

Sanding and general preparation of the material, drafting/tracing the design—*Hour of Saturn.*

Depicting the interlaced Star (white and black lines)—*Hour of Saturn.*

Section 15 of the design (Sign of the Quintessence on silver ground)—*Hour of Saturn.*

---

* It may be noted that the use of gold on silver is a particular medieval device, in which the heraldic rules of tincture were deliberately set aside, to symbolize the unique marvel of Divine Energy infusing Creation.

Sections 1 and 8 of the design—*Hour of Saturn.*
Sections 2 and 9—*Hour of Jupiter.*
Sections 3 and 10—*Hour of Mars.*
Sections 4 and 11—*Hour of Sun.*
Sections 5 and 12—*Hour of Venus.*
Sections 6 and 13—*Hour of Mercury.*
Sections 7 and 14—*Hour of Moon.*
The enclosing black circle—*Hour of Saturn.*
The finishing operations, varnishing, affixing the screw-eye, etc.—
Hour of Saturn.

The above guidelines for the design and making of the Aurum Solis Lamen having been given, it remains to be said that for the purposes of Planetary Magick the individual practitioner who so wishes is at liberty to change or to adapt the design, or the method of making, according to his or her personal ingenium. If you have the necessary facilities you might desire for example to make the Lamen of glazed and fired ceramic. Or you might desire to make the Lamen exactly as we have detailed, but using the familiar planetary signs in place of the Presigilla. Again, you might wish to place a different symbol in the center to represent the spiritual controlling force. Or you might feel inspired to create an altogether different design for the Lamen. This would be altogether in order for your personal workings, providing only that the design should of its nature perform the same function as ours in respect of Planetary Magick. If it is to serve you for this purpose, it must by whatever imagery represent a harmonious synthesis of the planetary powers, and should indicate the inner spiritual being of yourself, the magician, as controlling and directing those powers.

3 MAGICAL APPAREL & COLOR-CHARGE

Within the place of working various objects are brought together to characterize the magical ambience, the planetary power of the working, or the identity of the magician. Such are the robes, the altar covers and the planetary lights. These principal adjuncts of a magical working, with their options, are now to be considered.

The Robes of Art.

Clothing in magical usage should differ from ordinary attire so as to fulfill two main purposes: first, it is a proclamation to the external universe and, more particularly, to the subliminal faculties of the operator, that a special work is to be accomplished; and, secondly, it is to convey to the wearer that his or her everyday personality has given place to *the Magician,* the Person of Power who is now to perform this special work.

There are two essential modes of denoting the planetary dedication of a working in one's attire. The first is to keep on all occasions to one neutral basis, and for each specific working to add for the occasion an appropriate color charge. The second is to have a set of seven robes, one for each planetary power.

For the "neutral basis" there are various possibilities:

1. In the magical context, to be prepared for the work as regards clothing can mean predominantly to remove the everyday attire. The neutral basis could thus be validly interpreted as going Skyclad.

2. It may be a white or cream-colored robe, perhaps of the popular "traditional" style, full length and with wide sleeves. Or it may have cuffed sleeves, or be sleeveless, or it may be a

short tunic. Whatever its style, however, two qualities are essential: it should be generously cut so as to allow for those dramatic gestures of power which are needful in certain operations of Planetary Magick; and it should be so designed as not to distract the wearer's attention during the working.

3. Planetary Magick is essentially *practical,* and is ever young in spirit. The magician is entitled to complete freedom of movement not only to make sweeping ritual gestures but even to dance according to the mode of the planet of the working. The truly modern magician may therefore wish to conduct his or her Planetary Magick in the superb and eminently suitable neutral basis of a white outfit designed for the Martial Arts, a form of physical and spiritual magick which has been much neglected in the Western world since the end of the Age of Chivalry, which was also an age of most potent magick. One of the great re-discoveries of this present age is the profound effectiveness in all life's activities of the way of thinking, feeling and directing the body associated with the Martial Arts traditions, and something of this may fittingly be absorbed into the spirit of Planetary Magick.

A color charge for a specific working can be given to the neutral basis by the addition of a secondary article of attire. Some possibilities are:

A cord or belt.

A stole or long scarf.

A tabard.

A hood, worn thrown back upon the shoulders.

In each of the above articles, simple Briatic color (*Entry 19,* Tables of Correspondences) may be used throughout.

To vitalize and highlight the effect of the main color charge, the complementary may be employed in edging or ornamentation. The amount of the complementary color used should not exceed 30% of the whole area of the article, lest it tend to negate the impact of the main color charge instead of fulfilling its rightful purpose of enhancing and vivifying it.

It may here be remarked that in regard to working Skyclad, the effect of belt or cincture in the planetary color is wholly dynamic. There is however a special option for the Skyclad: that of using body paints for adornment with appropriate designs in the colors of the working.

Planet	Color Charge	Highlight (optional)
Saturn	Indigo, Black	White
Jupiter	Blue	Orange
Mars	Red	Green
Sun	Yellow	Violet
Venus	Green	Red
Mercury	Orange	Blue
Moon	Violet	Yellow

For the set of seven planetary garments, the simplest is one in which the robes are made in an uncomplicated and uniform style, one in each of the planetary (Briatic) colors. To enrich these, as suggested above for the color charges, ornamentation or edging in the complementary color will be very effective so long as it is not excessive.

The set of seven planetary garments need not, however, be uniform, for an outfit could be devised in keeping with the character of each planet. Each of these costumes can be entirely different from the others, if so desired, in style, historic suggestion, and fabric: the magician might desire to perform a rite of Jupiter in a classically draped linen garment, a rite of Mercury in a Space Age outfit of metallic fabrics.

In magical attire of this kind, adherence to the planetary colors would not be essential, since the nature of the costume would itself constitute the correspondence to the Sphere. An eurhythmic dancer of Venus need not, therefore, be in green, nor need a warrior of Mars be clothed in red.

To some students these ideas may provide an added dimension and incentive in magical working. The designing and making of a collection of costumes of this kind can add to one's personal feeling of kinship with the planetary powers which they interpret; but, above all, to wear them and thus to perform the appropriate workings in garments expressive of some aspect of the nature of the Sphere is a wonderful way to lift one's whole nature into a swift rapport with that Sphere. The set of seven planetary garments thus offers a rich field for personal creativity, and for that experience of planetary qualities which embodies both the play and the deep significance of Art Magick.

When a magical working involves more than one person—and in Planetary Magick there may well be a whole group of people—the question arises as to what should be worn by those taking part, other than the leader of the working.

The magician, the leader of the working, the principal, alone wears the Lamen: strictly, there is no need of any distinction other than that. However, when several people are participating it may be a good idea to have a greater difference in attire, not only so the leading figure can be at once distinguished amid the movement of the rite, but also to save the group collectively from unnecessary expense and time-consuming preparations. Thus the whole group might be robed in the planetary color, or alternatively the principal only might wear a robe of the planetary color, while the other members might wear a simple cord or belt of that color over neutral attire. There is no rule in the matter, nor need a particular group of people always follow the same procedure. The practical details of this are a matter for taste, judgment and the specific needs of the occasion.

Altar Covers.

A set of seven drapes in the planetary colors may be provided for the Bomos: whether to cover its top, or to hang at the sides, or to cover the Bomos completely. Each drape may be of its planetary color simply, or may be edged with the complementary.

This can give a strong focal point for the color of the working; but since that color will be worn by the magician and any other participants, and may appear also elsewhere in the place of working, it may be felt that the covering upon the Bomos is not needed to fortify it. In such a case a plain white drape can be used, or, if the Bomos has a beautiful and worthy appearance, no covering may be needed.

A balanced and harmonious effect in the place of working is a main consideration, but the requirements and the spirit of each working should govern the way this is to be achieved.

Planetary Lights.

For some of the workings given in this book, a single lamp or candle of the appropriate planetary color is required; for others, the full planetary number. Where no such specification is given, the operator has the option whether to use the one light or the planetary number.

Saturn—three indigo or smoked glass lamps or black candles.
Jupiter—four blue lamps or candles.
Mars—five red lamps or candles.
Sun—six yellow lamps or candles.
Venus—seven green lamps or candles.
Mercury—eight orange lamps or candles.
Moon—nine violet lamps or candles.

Should it prove impossible to complete the number of lights in a given color, then plain white lamps or candles can be used instead. One could not for instance make up the planetary number with some colored and some white lights, since the magical unity of the number would be broken. When only white lights are employed, however, a colored cover upon the Bomos becomes necessary in order to reinforce the color charge of the working.

In all workings where a single light is employed this must be of the planetary color without exception, since its correspondence to the power of the working is not reinforced by the use of number.

The placing of the planetary lights is important too. When a single light is used it is displayed prominently, upon the Bomos or in a suitable place of honor; but when the planetary number of lights is used, these should be disposed regularly around the place of working as if forming the points of the corresponding linear figure (*Entry 15*, Tables of Correspondences) and orientated to the East.

Working within "the Star of Lights" is a venerable tradition of Planetary Magick, and is a practice having an intrinsic power whose catalytic action upon the ambience and within the psyche is profound and well-attested. Besides, it feels good!

It remains only to say a word as to the kinds of lights that can be used. The small colored "votive lights" often used for domestic table decoration are very good but cannot always be had in true, bright colors. Candles are acceptable for use instead of lamps: although giving only white light they themselves are often available in every color of the spectrum, and when illuminated by their glowing flame they do have reasonable color-presence. An excellent choice for the modern magician however is to have small electric battery lamps provided with colored shields or filters. If these shields are interchangeable, only a total of nine lamps is needed. Bright, vivid light is thus available with maximum safety and convenience, and the planetary rites can be liberated into a vibrant world of true prismatic beauty.

The kinds of electrical lighting devices and the purposes, both decorative and scientific, for which they are designed, increases continually. Thus the magician can with advantage explore what is new, what is coming from research and technology, to discover what can best be employed in the service of Art Magick.

4 INCENSE

Incense is traditionally used in Planetary Magick as a means of infusing the delicate web of the atmosphere with a distinctive quality, and, through the subtle interaction of bodily sense and psychic apperception, thus to attune the mind and consciousness of the magician to the corresponding planetary modality.

The use of incense is not, however, an essential requirement of magical practice: such effects as it is capable of inducing within the astral ambience of the place of working and within the psyche of the operator can equally well be promoted by the vibrations of light and sound, or by dramatic action and gesture. For the rites given in this book, therefore, the use of incense is entirely optional, and the magician may forego its use for any (or for all) ceremonies contained herein.

To those who feel a need or a desire for the use of incense, besides its intrinsic value as one of the great sensory correspondences, there is the wonder of the aromatic gums and resins, woods, oils and herbs which are its ingredients, the music of their names, the antiquity of their traditions, and the almost alchemical fascination of their blending. These things, with the fact that the finished incense is the magician's own work, carry a glamor which is near-kindred to the true magick in which it will participate.

Recommended incense materials will be found under *Entry 29* of the Tables of Correspondences. On occasion the magician may prefer to use a single favorite substance rather than a blend as a planetary incense. He might choose for instance the pure gentle bitterness of Myrrh for Saturn, the generous masculinity of Cedar for Jupiter, the sultry smoldering fire of Opoponax for Mars; for Sol he might choose

153

the hot, sweet flame of Cinnamon, for Venus the mysterious vibrancy of Red Storax, for Mercury, Mastic's shy and swift-winged elusiveness, and for Luna the living, penetrating dark green odor of Galbanum.

When a blend is to be used, it may appropriately be prepared during the corresponding planetary hour. The following Aurum Solis recipes for blended incenses have been selected to offer a potent but uncomplicated suffumigation for each Sphere:

Incense of Saturn

Myrrh	1 oz.
Cassia buds, crushed	½ oz.
Oil of violet	8 drops

Incense of Jupiter

Juniper berries, crushed	½ oz.
Cedar wood, fine shavings	¼ oz.
Pine gum, small grains	¼ oz.
Oil of Cedar	5 drops
Oil of Clove	4 drops

Incense of Mars

Opoponax, small grains	1 oz.
Dragonsblood, powdered	⅛ oz.
Galangal, crushed	⅛ oz.
Oil of Nicotiana	6 drops
Oil of Peppermint	3 drops

Incense of Sun

Cinnamon bark, small fragments	1 oz.
Frankincense, powdered	¼ oz.
Heliotropin crystals	⅛ oz.
Oil of Cinnamon	5 drops
Oil of Frankincense	2 drops

Incense of Venus

Siamese benzoin, small grains	1 oz.
Dried red rosebuds, pounded	¼ oz.
Lemon Verbena leaves	⅛ oz.
Oil of Rose	4 drops
Oil of Sandalwood	4 drops
Oil of Lemon	4 drops

Incense of Mercury

Mastic grains ....1 oz.
Gum Arabic, grains...¼ oz.
Lavender flowers ....⅛ oz.
Oil of Lavender..5 drops
Oil of Anise..3 drops

Incense of Moon

Galbanum, small grains..¾ oz.
Orris root, powdered...¾ oz.
Bay leaves, crushed..2
Oil of Jasmine..6 drops
Oil of Narcissus ....4 drops
Oil of Camphor ....3 drops

In every rite contained in this book, the point at which incense may be introduced is noted.

When it is decided to employ incense, the requirements for this should be placed in readiness in the place of working. The thymiaterion (a standing vessel of metal or ceramic in which to burn incense) should be placed upon a trivet or tile upon a small table or pedestal positioned conveniently, or upon the Bomos if this be desired and feasible. In either case, with the thymiaterion should be a tablet of charcoal, to be ignited at the beginning of the working, and the incense which is at the indicated moment to be cast upon the glowing charcoal.*

---

* For those who wish to have incenses without needing to prepare them or to use charcoal, commercially manufactured incense sticks and cones offer an alternative. These should likewise be burned in the thymiaterion, which can be filled with sand to accommodate them.

5 THE BATTERY

The battery is an audible signal. Its use may mark simply the beginning and ending of a rite; frequently it also marks division into sections of the magical action.

By tradition, the battery consists (as its name also implies) of a series of distinct percussive or other well-defined sounds. Their total number should be significant, and by the introduction of pauses this can be divided into lesser groups. These may have symbolic value themselves, or may serve simply to endow the whole battery with balance and symmetry, with solemnity, force, or other desirable quality. A battery of distinctive pattern, if employed consistently on every occasion of a particular type, has also the advantage of being recognized at multiple levels of the psyche, so that its message is easily accepted: as for instance with the special battery sounded at the close of a working, to recall the consciousness of participants to outward phenomena.

As to the number and pattern of sounds composing a battery, in each rite in this book these details will be given wherever a battery should occur. There is another aspect of the matter, however, on which the decision rests with the magician and upon which only guidelines and suggestions can be given here. This concerns the *quality of sound* with which, in any specific working, the battery shall be given.

There is an important magical opportunity here. It is of the very nature of a battery to claim instantly the attention of the hearer, as well as impinging upon the carefully formulated ambience within the place of working. It follows that a sound which is intimately associated with the sphere of the working will help focus the attention of the hearer thereon, and will additionally strengthen the planetary ambience.

157

In the Tables of Correspondences, Entry 25, though it also has other and larger purposes, can provide valuable indications for sounding the battery. For the Sphere of Saturn, for instance, a "deep-toned gong" might be sounded in the slow, even measure associated with a large chiming clock, although for some workings the heavy and hollow sound of wood-blocks struck together might stir the air more eloquently.

For the Sphere of Jupiter, the magician might choose for the battery the sound of a bass drum, a gavel, or, where the character of the rite warrants it, the sonorous call of a conch trumpet. For many rites, however, the authoritative clapping of the magician's hands might be most effectively Jupiterian. For the Sphere of Mars, the clash of steel on steel, or the resounding stamp of the foot, would be appropriate choices.

The instruments for the Sphere of the Sun offer glorious and resonant possibilities. The thrilling, shimmering sound of lyre and autoharp are suited to more mystical batteries than could be sounded upon French horn or brazen gong, and again the nature of the rite—for healing or for prophecy perhaps, or for celebration of solstice or equinox—would help determine suitability. The lovely and joyful music of the Sphere of Venus, too, has its sounds of deeply-felt authority: classical guitar and tambour, notably, can utter majestic and inescapable rhythms, while on occasion the gentler tones too will have their place. For the Sphere of Mercury, the swift sounds of the musical instruments named in the Correspondences, or the ringing of an etherially-toned bell, could fittingly be adapted as a "battery" in a rite of that planet; while for the Sphere of the Moon above all it must be said that the diversity of types of musical sound must match the diversity of moods possible to the rites.

So the Correspondences yield their secrets of magical power as they are scrutinized. The magician who is attached to the use of one particular instrument for sounding the battery—a favorite gavel or bell, perhaps—may feel that in that accustomed sound his magical authority flourishes and is fortified, no matter what the rite. But in such an argument something of the essential nature of Planetary Magick could be missed. It is not in the familiar practices and sensations of our Earth-Sphere that we find our strength in this magick, but in a literal ekstasis, a lifting out of ourselves, even though we may not recognize it as such: a state in which the consciousness, detached from its familiar data, and conditioned by the modality of the working, reaches out, not to its daily *persona* but to the archetypal counterpart in the Deep Mind which corresponds most nearly to that modality: that of the planet of the working. In that power, by whatever means we make contact with it, true Planetary Magic is wrought.

PART THREE

Planetary Magick in Action and Result

PRELIMINARY NOTES

I

Standard Requirements

The robes of the magician and of any other participants, as well as the coverings for the Bomos, will not be referred to further in this book. It is assumed they will be chosen within the range of options indicated in **Part Two;** also, that on every occasion the Symbol of the Spiritual Ideal will be present upon the Bomos, and the magician will wear the Lamen. Similarly, no further reference will be made to materials or vessels which may be needed for burning incense, nor to any instruments for sounding the battery. It is the responsibility and privilege of the magician to decide upon these things and, if they are required, to ensure they are ready in the place of working before the rite begins.

II

The Words of Power

Throughout the planetary rites in this book, whenever divine names are to be employed, they are given in sets of three, thus:
(1) HEBREW NAME | **(2) AURUM SOLIS NAME** | **(3) NEOPLATON-
IST NAME**

The names are invariably given in this order. It is not however intended that more than one of the three should be employed in a working, for each represents the planetary archetype, the pure essential reality of the planetary force existing in, and as part of, the World of Atziluth, the Divine Mind.

Each series of divine names is commended by a particular aptness

163

of tradition or meaning. The first series comprises the familiar names of Hebrew Qabalah; the second series comprises the Atziluthic magical formulae of the Order Aurum Solis upon whose teachings this presentation of Planetary Magick is based; while the third series comprises the beautiful divine epithets of Neoplatonist tradition.

Initially, a definite choice of the first, second or third series of names should be made; and that series should be faithfully employed by the student in exploring the various rites of Planetary Magick here following. When she has worked with these names to a degree of proficiency at which they are an intimate and potent part of her magical life, then she may, if she wishes, adopt another of the three series of names and work with it similarly. Thereafter she is free, at her discretion, to employ whichever of the two—or even three—series of names she has inaugurated.

In each of the rites of Ascent and Vision, a set of three Briatic names is also introduced. These are set out in the same sequence as the divine names. Since the divine names are Atziluthic, the Briatic names are subordinate to them, and the student will select the first, second or third Briatic name according to her choice of the divine name.

III

The Ritual Program

Apart from certain requirements of practice which are indicated where necessary, the choice and order of the rituals of Planetary Magick is open for the individual or the group to decide.

A working program suited to the proficiency and aspiration of the individual or group may be arranged according to the following guidelines:

• As a first step, the Rite of Preparation, which is intended to precede every working in this book, should initially be practiced by itself and brought to a stage of proficiency.

• As the second step, the series of seven Rites of Approach should be undertaken in ascending order.

• As the third step, the series of seven Rites of Contact should be undertaken in ascending order. *This completes the essential groundwork of Planetary Magick and establishes the student in rapport with the cosmic and microcosmic power-sources.*

• After the completion of the Rites of Approach and of Contact, the student, while proceeding with the ongoing program of Planetary Magick, should return to perform those groundwork rites often; whether in ascending sequence, or selected individually as desired. Thus the necessary channels of power, once established, will be kept open.

• When all members of a group have completed the groundwork as individuals, they may together undertake the group rituals.

Initially, to create a group aura and to bond themselves as a "magical family," the group should undertake Creating the Elixir of Virtue. For this purpose, the complete series of seven rites may be employed in ascending sequence or, validly, the Solar rite for Creating the Elixir, which has a natural quality of harmonious balance, may be employed.

Following this intial bonding, there is no limitation whatever upon the use of the Elixir rites, and they may be employed in sequence or individually as desired. At this stage too, the rites of Ascent and Vision in the Spheres may be introduced into the program, as may the rites for Beneficent Sendings.

Even when it is desired to work one or another of these series in its entirety, this need not preclude the working of other rites before the chosen series has been completed: just as individual repetition of the groundwork rituals is permissible whatever the program. Thus a group might undertake the working of all the Elixir rites in ascending order, and after completing Moon and Mercury they might be called upon to perform the Beneficent Sendings rite in Jupiter on behalf of a friend. Or a group might undertake the Elixir rites as a weekly project, and at the same time begin the rites of Ascent and Vision as a monthly project.

• When a new member is to be brought into the group, that person should complete the groundwork—the Rites of Approach and of Contact—and should thereafter be bonded with the group by Creating the Elixir of Virtue.

• The individual student, whether participating in group activity or not, should continue to develop her personal program after completion of the groundwork. Thus the Rites of Attunement should next be undertaken and, when occasion arises, Planetary Tarot Divination. But she should prefer to develop considerable confidence and familiarity with the planetary forces before proceeding to The Sevenfold Rite of the Heart's Desire and Olympic Evocation of Dreams.

• To maintain a balance of magical energies in working with planetary forces, two principles are worthy of note. First, ascending sequences of workings are intrinsically self-balancing, for they establish "the Music of the Spheres," their cosmic harmony of vibrations. Secondly, a generous mixture of the seven planetary forces employed in the workings, a vital and frequent stirring of those forces, is the surest and most natural safeguard of balanced energies both cosmic and microcosmic in origin.

1 *PREPARING THE PLACE OF LIGHT*
(How to Open your Planetary Working)

This simple but potent rite is intended to precede every operation of Planetary Magick given in this book.

If you have a favorite and customary ritual opening—such as a Golden Dawn Banishing Ceremony, the Aurum Solis Setting of the Wards or a Wiccan Circle-casting—then feel free to use that in place of the procedure here given.

Our present rite is designed to be used by one person only, whether for an individual working or for a group working. The first part of this formula—*Purification*—has a threefold virtue: it provides an initial empowerment for the operator, it delineates and protects the intended area of magical activity, and it effectively banishes adverse forces from the place of working. The second part—*Affirmation of the Septenary*—establishes a beneficent astral ambience, and a harmonious chord of planetary vibrations within which a specific planetary power will be identified and called forth in the course of the subsequent working.

RITE OF PREPARATION

Purification
1. Standing at the center facing East,* imagine above your head a globe of brilliant white light.
   Know this to be a symbol of that Supernal Light which is the inmost life of your psyche, and which is a true part of the Divine Mind.

---

* If the Bomos is stationed at the center, stand just West of center facing East across the Bomos.

2. Now imagine a continuous spiral of white light descending from the globe, whirling counterclockwise around you and disappearing into the ground at your feet.
   Feel the warmth of this downward whirling light: draw from it health, blessing and inspiration.

3. Allow the whirling spiral to fade from your consciousness, but keep awareness of the globe above your head.

4. Raise both arms to a loosely vertical position, palms facing forwards. With arms thus, and with awareness of the globe above your head, turn counterclockwise through 360° on the same spot. As you turn, visualize a wall of light, white with golden sparkles, spreading as your hands move so that it encircles the place of working. Conclude facing East again; then fold your arms upon your breast, right over left.
   Be aware of the globe above your head, and of the wall of light encompassing your place of working.

5. Lower your arms, and turn about counterclockwise to face West. Raise your arms again overhead, palms forwards, and keeping them thus, stamp once with your right foot (to assert your dominance over the forces of chaos), then proclaim the banishing charge:

   PROCUL ESTE, PROFANI!*

   As you utter the charge, know that in the power of your Higher Self (symbolized by the globe above your head) you are banishing all unbalanced forces from within your circle of light.

6. Fold your arms upon your breast, right over left.
   In imagination hear the echo of a clear space within your circle, all impure or inept forces being gone from it.

---

* "Begone afar, unholy ones": the massively powerful banishing charge of the Ausonian Mysteries of ancient Latium. Its sanctity made the phrase famous through classical and post-classical times.

Affirmation of the Septenary

7. Lower your arms to your sides and turn about counter-clockwise to face East. Again raise your arms overhead, palms forwards, and with awareness of the globe above your head turn clockwise through 360° on the same spot. As you turn, visualize a wall of light, mist-blue with silver sparkles, spreading as your hands move so that it encircles the place of working. Conclude facing East again, and fold your arms upon your breast, right over left.
   Keep awareness of the wall of blue light encompassing your place of working,* but now let the globe above your head fade from your consciousness.

8. Lower your arms to your sides, having your hands slightly away from your body with palms upcurved. Standing thus, proclaim:

   Thee we invoke, the Secret Flame that abideth in holy and luminous silence.
   Thee, the Light of the Great Gods and the Life of the Worlds.
   Thee, the Mighty and Shining One, whose Spirit filleth all things and whose holy Fire is invoked in every sanctuary of the heavens!

9. Having completed this invocation, with your right hand now trace clockwise before you the sign of the heptagram; and with the tracing of each line, utter the appropriate vowel of Greek Qabalah, as follows:

   1 to 2: Ω (Omega, pronounced as "o" in *only*)
   2 to 3: Υ (Upsilon, as German ü)
   3 to 4: O (Omicron, as "o" in *hot*)
   4 to 5: I (Iota, as "ee" in *meet*)
   5 to 6: H (Eta, as "a" in *care*)
   6 to 7: E (Epsilon, as "e" in *set*)
   7 to 1: A (Alpha, as "a" in *father*)

---

* As you prefer, the blue-silver wall may replace awareness of the white-gold wall, or both may be held in consciousness.

10. Fold your arms upon your breast, left over right. Remaining thus, re-affirm your awareness of the blue-silver wall, and feel the magical vibrancy of the place of light wherein you stand. When you are ready, allow the blue-silver wall to fade gently from your consciousness.

The place of working has been prepared, and you are strong to achieve in acts of mystery and wonder.

Chanting the Vowels

In Section 9 of the Rite of Preparation above, direction is given for the utterance of the Greek Vowels. If desired these may be chanted, as the heptagram is traced, according to the Vowel Tones of the Cosmic Harmony (*Entry 59*, Tables of Correspondences). Either series of tones may validly be employed, as follows:

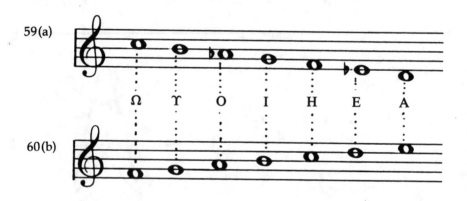

A superb effect is achieved here if the chosen sequence of tones is sounded, in unison with the chanted vowels, by a companion playing a musical instrument.

2 APPROACHING THE ARCHETYPES

The Rites of Approach given here are for individual working. They afford a means of affirming and strengthening the bond which exists between the psyche of the magician and the archetypal forces of the external cosmos. They are an essential foundation for the works of Planetary Magick, and will assist towards a permanent invigorating of the psyche's natural rapport with the planetary powers.

Initially, you should work the series of Rites of Approach in ascending planetary order—mounting the steps of "The Ziggurat of Light" from Luna through Saturn—putting all you can into each rite and drawing all you can from it.

Thereafter you may return to them as you will: whether to repeat the ascending sequence, or to select specific rites to supplement or enhance your ongoing program. It is only recommended that you should perform them often: for here is a reservoir of magical vitality and a fountainhead of joyful refreshment.

With the completion of the first ascending series you will have opened the primary "Gateways of Power," and you will have begun to develop the ability to enter effectively into the magical ambience of the planetary spheres. For this reason, all seven Rites of Approach should be accomplished before you undertake the further works of Planetary Magick given in this book.

RITE OF APPROACH IN LUNA

Temporal Mode: 3
Planetary Time Day and Hour of the Moon
Position of Bomos: Center of Place of Working
Lights: 1 Violet Light upon the Bomos

171

1. Perform the Rite of Preparation.
2. Standing just West of center facing East across the Bomos, sound the battery: 9.
3. *If you desire, now activate incense.*
4. Visualize yourself encompassed by an ovoid (an auric shape) of *violet* light and, maintaining this in awareness, proclaim:

   > I will pass through the veil of the Shining Light to accomplish the works of Yesod.
   >
   > With my highest mind and with all my being I will raise my inward gaze to the divine resplendence in the Sphere of Luna, ever more clearly to know and to apprehend that living glory.

5. Vibrate the chosen divine name of the sphere—

   SHADDAI EL CHAI | IAO | AIGLE TRISAGIA

   and as you do so visualize the ovoid changing to *red-purple* light.
6. Keeping awareness of the red-purple light surrounding you, proclaim the adoration of the divine force of the Sphere of Luna:

   > O shining and sure guide through the illimitable realm of dreams, most gracious opener of the way to those who venture into worlds unseen! Thou maker and destroyer of Illusion, thou who knowest the tides of ocean, the furthest distances of the mind and the dark places of unreason: hail to thee!

7. Still keeping the red-purple ovoid surrounding you, *mentally* intone the divine name (as in 5 above) over and over, and with each mental utterance visualize the red-purple becoming brighter and more luminous while maintaining the shape of the ovoid. *Continue in this essential practice for as long as you will, filling your consciousness with the divine name and with the red-purple light, avoiding discursive thought.*
8. Ceasing mental utterance of the divine name, keep for a while longer your awareness of the red-purple light; then visualize the ovoid changing to *violet* light.
9. Maintain the violet ovoid for several minutes, then allow it to fade gently from your awareness.
10. Sound the battery: 1.
11. Now utter the following orison of aspiration:

    > May I be sure of my course and perceptive of vision in the uncharted realm of dreams, and may the way ever be open when I seek the regions of the unseen. May that ecstatic light which gives inspiration

to Lover and poet be ever mine, not as ruling my life but as responding to my command so that at will I may step into its holy enchantment. May the might of that force which governs all growing things, the living power of the ruler of the tides and the knower of the hidden deeps, be mine to aid me in ascending the stair of the planetary powers, both outer and inner: to the fulfillment of my magical destiny and the realization of my true will. So may it be, in the name

SHADDAI EL CHAI | **IAO** | **AIGLE TRISAGIA**

12. Sound the battery: 3–5–3.

RITE OF APPROACH IN MERCURY

Temporal Mode: 3
Planetary Time: Day and Hour of Mercury
Position of Bomos: Center of Place of Working
Lights: 1 Orange Light upon the Bomos

1. Perform the Rite of Preparation.
2. Standing just West of center facing East across the Bomos, sound the battery: 8.
3. *If you desire, now activate incense.*
4. Visualize yourself encompassed by an ovoid of *orange* light and, maintaining this in awareness, proclaim:
    I will pass through the veil of the Shining Light to accomplish the works of Hod.
    With my highest mind and with all my being I will raise my inward gaze to the divine vibrancy in the Sphere of Mercury, ever more clearly to know and to apprehend that wondrous glory.
5. Vibrate the chosen divine name of the Sphere—
    ELOHIM TZABAOTH | **AZOTH** | **ALETHES LOGOS**
   and as you do so visualize the ovoid changing to *yellow ochre* light.
6. Keeping awareness of the yellow ochre light surrounding you, proclaim the adoration of the divine force of the Sphere of Mercury:
    O thou swift and unconstrained traveler in the ways between the Worlds, divine imparter of secret tidings to gods and to humankind, bountiful bestower of aid in Art Magick!—knowledge and skill, rite and high result are thine to impart! Thine are the Tongues and the

Numbers, thine the Signs and the Sigils and the words of Power. Thine it is to heal, and to teach, and to watch upon the way. Hail to thee!

7. Still keeping the yellow ochre ovoid surrounding you, *mentally intone the divine name (as in 5 above) over and over, and with each mental utterance visualize the yellow ochre becoming brighter and more luminous while maintaining the shape of the ovoid. Continue in this essential practice for as long as you will, filling your consciousness with the divine name and with the yellow ochre light, avoiding discursive thought.*

8. Ceasing mental utterance of the divine name, keep for a while longer your awarenesss of the yellow ochre light; then visualize the ovoid changing to *orange* light.

9. Maintain the orange ovoid for several minutes, then allow it to fade gently from your awareness.

10. Sound the battery: 1.

11. Now utter the following orison of aspiration:

Swift be my onward passage in the ways of knowledge!—swiftly and joyfully may I receive the bright illuminations which are given hiddenly upon that journey. May my mind be borne upon wings of inspiration to overpass all divisions between truth and truth, and may I rejoice in the twofold magick which abides in every comprehension: the magick of the realization, and the magick of its sowing for a new harvest. May the potent force which awakens all understanding, the great wind that sweeps the snows from the uplands and the dead leaves from the forest hollows, be with me to clear the inner skies of my perceptions, so that every luminary may pour its radiance into my whole being. And when with art I invoke the celestial Powers, swift, O swift be the event! So may it be, in the name

ELOHIM TZABAOTH ⎪ **AZOTH** ⎪ **ALETHES LOGOS**

12. Sound the battery: 3–5–3.

RITE OF APPROACH IN VENUS

Temporal Mode: 3
Planetary Time: Day and Hour of Venus
Position of Bomos: Center of Place of Working
Lights: 1 Green Light upon the Bomos

1. Perform the Rite of Preparation.

2. Standing just West of center facing East across the Bomos, sound the battery: 7.
3. *If you desire, now activate incense.*
4. Visualize yourself encompassed by an ovoid of *green* light and, maintaining this in awareness, proclaim:

    I will pass through the veil of the Shining Light to accomplish the works of Netzach.

    With my highest mind and with all my being I will raise my inward gaze to the divine ardor in the Sphere of Venus, ever more clearly to know and to apprehend that mystical glory.
5. Vibrate the chosen divine name of the Sphere—

    YHVH* TZABAOTH | ALBAPHALANA | CHARIS

    and as you do so visualize the ovoid changing to *greenish blue* light.
6. Keeping awareness of the greenish blue light surrounding you, proclaim the adoration of the divine force of the Sphere of Venus:

    O thou radiant giver of love, ruler of the forces of life, divinely robed in light and girded with invincible beauty! Perfect harmony and concord are as the perfumes of thy presence, and thou it is who dost create the rhythms whose pulsings call into life the sacred dance. O thou who ever sendest forth all delight, hail to thee!
7. Still keeping the greenish blue ovoid surrounding you, *mentally* intone the divine name (as in 5 above) over and over, and with each mental utterance visualize the greenish blue becoming brighter and more luminous while maintaining the shape of the ovoid. *Continue in this essential practice for as long as you will, filling your consciousness with the divine name and with the greenish blue light, avoiding discursive thought.*
8. Ceasing mental utterance of the divine name, keep for a while longer your awareness of the greenish blue light; then visualize the ovoid changing to *green* light.
9. Maintain the green ovoid for several minutes, then allow it to fade gently from your awareness.
10. Sound the Battery: 1.
11. Now utter the following orison of aspiration:

    May I ever be filled with a joyous awe as I contemplate the unity of life and love: a unity wherein all we love can be a source of spiritual life for

---

* The word YHVH may be vocalized as *Yahveh*, as *Yahweh*, as *Yod Heh Vau Heh*, or as *Tetragrammaton*, as the student prefers.

us. Lovingly may I delight in the Worlds of Life, divine and earthly and all that lies between; mine be it to love and to rejoice in the sublime and thrilling loveliness of the forces of life themselves. Thus may I be assisted by the divine force which directs them: may I be guarded by the panoply of that invincible beauty, may I walk secure within the aura of that perfect harmony and concord. So may I go forward in that mantle of radiance, that every level of my being may be empowered by the cosmic cadence of the sacred dance. So may it be, in the name

YHVH TZABAOTH | ALBAPHALANA | CHARIS

12. Sound the battery: 3–5–3.

RITE OF APPROACH IN SOL

Temporal Mode: 3
Planetary Time: Day and Hour of the Sun
Position of Bomos: Center of Place of Working
Lights: 1 Yellow Light upon the Bomos

1. Perform the Rite of Preparation.
2. Standing just West of center facing East across the Bomos, sound the battery: 6.
3. *If you desire, now activate incense.*
4. Visualize yourself encompassed by an ovoid of yellow light and, maintaining this in awareness, proclaim:
   I will pass through the veil of the Shining Light to accomplish the works of Tiphareth.
   With my highest mind and with all my being I will raise my inward gaze to the divine vitality in the Sphere of the Sun, ever more clearly to know and to apprehend that effulgent glory.
5. Vibrate the chosen divine name of the Sphere—
   YHVH ELOAH V'DAATH | ONOPHIS | THEIOS NOUS
   and as you do so visualize the ovoid changing to *pale greenish-yellow* light.
6. Keeping awareness of the pale greenish-yellow light surrounding you, proclaim the adoration of the divine force of the sphere of Sol:
   Far-riding ruler of days, all-seeing arbiter of the planetary powers! Thine is the wisdom of prophecy, the rapture of music and poesy, the

upward surging force of mystical endeavor. Thine is the vision which sees beyond all change and chance, and the clear perception of truth which dispels all shadow. In the rising and in the incomparable luster of the Day-Star thou givest a sacred image to magical ascendence, even as thy power enkindles a glory within us and elevates us to accomplish that which we seek. Hail to thee!

7. Still keeping the pale greenish-yellow ovoid surrounding you, *mentally* intone the divine name (as in 5 above) over and over, and with each mental utterance visualize the pale greenish-yellow becoming brighter and more luminous while maintaining the shape of the ovoid. *Continue in this essential practice for as long as you will, filling your consciousness with the divine name and with the pale greenish-yellow light, avoiding discursive thought.*

8. Ceasing mental utterance of the divine name, keep for a while longer your awareness of the pale greenish-yellow light; then visualize the ovoid changing to *yellow* light.

9. Maintain the yellow ovoid for several minutes, then allow it to fade gently from your awareness.

10. Sound the battery: 1.

11. Now utter the following orison of aspiration:
   May the unconquerable flame of mystical inspiration be enkindled within me, that my course may be glorious in the gaze of the sublime arbiter of the planetary powers! May my inner perception of truth be opened to the delight within all that is manifest, the rapture which is voiced in music and poesy, the spirit of prophecy which knows the currents of change and chance. So may my inner nature find its perfect equilibrium and its true fulfillment, and my magical selfhood and power arise as a star in an unclouded heaven, imparting its luster to all it beholds; and may I walk robed in the radiance which shines forth from my heart's resplendence! So may it be, in the name
   YHVH ELOAH V'DAATH | **ONOPHIS** | **THEIOS NOUS**

12. Sound the battery: 3–5–3.

RITE OF APPROACH IN MARS

Temporal Mode: 3
Planetary Time: Day and Hour of Mars
Position of Bomos: Center of Place of Working
Lights: 1 Red Light upon the Bomos

1. Perform the Rite of Preparation.
2. Standing just West of center facing East across the Bomos, sound the battery: 5.
3. *If you desire, now activate incense.*
4. Visualize yourself encompassed by an ovoid of *red* light and, maintaining this in awareness, proclaim:

   I will pass through the veil of the Shining Light to accomplish the works of Geburah.

   With my highest mind and with all my being I will raise my inward gaze to the divine potency in the Sphere of Mars, ever more clearly to know and to apprehend that indomitable glory.
5. Vibrate the chosen divine name of the Sphere—
   ELOHIM GEBOR | SABAO | ISCHYROS
   and as you do so visualize the ovoid changing to *amber* light.
6. Keeping awareness of the amber light surrounding you, proclaim the adoration of the divine force of the Sphere of Mars:

   All powerful defender of justice and truth, thou noble inspirer of courage and endurance and of bold resolve! Inculcator of loyalty, giver of the joy which springs from shared endeavor: thou divine patron of fruitful debate and of good order, thou who dost confirm the steadfast heart and the unfaltering hand! Thou mighty adversary of the powers adverse, hail to thee!
7. Still keeping the amber ovoid surrounding you, *mentally* intone the divine name (as in 5 above) over and over, and with each mental utterance visualize the amber becoming brighter and more luminous while maintaining the shape of the ovoid. *Continue in this essential practice for as long as you will, filling your consciousness with the divine name and with the amber light, avoiding discursive thought.*
8. Ceasing mental utterance of the divine name, keep for a while longer your awareness of the amber light; then visualize the ovoid changing to *red* light.
9. Maintain the red ovoid for several minutes, then allow it to fade gently from your awareness.
10. Sound the battery: 1.
11. Now utter the following orison of aspiration:

    May strength in will and deed be mine, that what I have resolved I shall to the utmost do. May I seek and find within my heart good counsel before the event: then, my plan of action decided, may I falter not. May the guardian powers of confidence and steadfastness be at all times with me, and in the ever-varying adventures of Art Magick may they bring my efforts to high success. Fortitude and faithful endurance be mine, to wrest opposing events and conditions to good avail for advancement of the Great Work; or, as I may deem it the better course, mine be the courage and power to banish that which is adverse. Mine be ever the keen sure blade of clear intent, and ever the glorious banner of aspiration which is the star of my destiny! So may it be, in the name

ELOHIM GEBOR ⎮ SABAO ⎮ ISCHYROS

12. Sound the battery: 3–5–3.

RITE OF APPROACH IN JUPITER

Temporal Mode: 3
Planetary Time: Day and Hour of Jupiter
Position of Bomos: Center of Place of Working
Lights: 1 Blue Light upon the Bomos

1. Perform the Rite of Preparation.
2. Standing just West of center facing East across the Bomos, sound the battery: 4.
3. *If you desire, now activate incense.*
4. Visualize yourself encompassed by an ovoid of *blue* light and, maintaining this awareness, proclaim:
    I will pass through the veil of the Shining Light to accomplish the works of Chesed.
    With my highest mind and with all my being I will raise my inward gaze to the divine abundance in the Sphere of Jupiter, ever more clearly to know and to apprehend that beneficent glory.
5. Vibrate the chosen divine name of the Sphere—
    EL ⎮ ZARAIETOS ⎮ PANTOKRATOR
    and as you do so visualize the ovoid changing to *lilac* light.
6. Keeping awareness of the lilac light surrounding you, proclaim the adoration of the divine force of the Sphere of Jupiter:
    Royal and magnanimous giver of abundance from a cup unfailing, Shepherd of the golden Stars, Lord of the tides of fortune! Glorious dispenser of mercy, divine patron of paternal and filial love! Thou dost bless peace and amity between all beings: thou great Father of benevolent rule and of priesthood, and of that loving wisdom which sublimates authority! Hail to thee!

7. Still keeping the lilac ovoid surrounding you, *mentally* intone the divine name (as in 5 above) over and over, and with each mental utterance visualize the lilac becoming brighter and more luminous while maintaining the shape of the ovoid. *Continue in this essential practice for as long as you will, filling your consciousness with the divine name and with the lilac light, avoiding discursive thought.*

8. Ceasing mental utterance of the divine name, keep for a while longer your awareness of the lilac light; then visualize the ovoid changing to *blue* light.

9. Maintain the blue ovoid for several minutes, then allow it to fade gently from your awareness.

10. Sound the battery: 1.

11. Now utter the following orison of aspiration:

> May I be blessed with the generous spirit which both gives and attracts the bounties of all levels of existence: mine be that cup unfailing, overflowing and ever replenished by the powers of celestial abundance! Mine be the far vision which transcends the images and emotions of the moment, mine the regardful love which seeks the highest good in all and for all; mine be it to dispose with true wisdom all matters which fall within my judgment. May my heart be filled with the royal freedom, the divine gladness of the blue illimitable skies; and may that bright amplitude exalt my mind to share in its magnificence, so that my whole being may be imbued, and may give forth again its high peace and sublime felicity. So may it be, in the name
>
> **EL | ZARAIETOS | PANTOKRATOR**

12. Sound the battery: 3–5–3.

RITE OF APPROACH IN SATURN

Temporal Mode: 3
Planetary Time: Day and Hour of Saturn
Position of Bomos: Center of Place of Working
Lights: 1 Indigo (or Black) Light upon the Bomos

1. Perform the Rite of Preparation.

2. Standing just West of center facing East across the Bomos, sound the battery: 3.

3. *If you desire, now activate incense.*

4. Visualize yourself encompassed by an ovoid of *indigo* light and,

maintaining this in awareness, proclaim:

> I will pass through the veil of the Shining Light to accomplish the works of Binah.
> With my highest mind and with all my being I will raise my inward gaze to the divine creativity in the Sphere of Saturn, ever more clearly to know and to apprehend that undying glory.

5. Vibrate the chosen divine name of the Sphere—

   YHVH ELOHIM | IALDABAOTH | AIONOS KYRIOS

   and as you do so visualize the ovoid changing to *dove grey* light.

6. Keeping awareness of the dove grey light surrounding you, proclaim the adoration of the divine force of the Sphere of Saturn:

> Sublime and shadowed one, austere awakener of high aspiration and mystic hope! Thou art giver of the silent will to endure, thou art patron of the spirit's creativity and of the forces of preservation and of renewal. In thy keeping are alike the scythe of the reaper and the instruments of the builder in stone; thine too is the open scroll of the past, and thine the sealed scroll which holds the mysteries of the future. Hail to thee!

7. Still keeping the dove grey ovoid surrounding you, *mentally intone the divine name (as in 5 above) over and over*, and with each mental utterance visualize the dove grey becoming brighter and more luminous while maintaining the shape of the ovoid. *Continue in this essential practice for as long as you will, filling your consciousness with the divine name and with the dove grey light, avoiding discursive thought.*

8. Ceasing mental utterance of the divine name, keep for a while longer your awareness of the dove grey light; then visualize the ovoid changing to *indigo* light.

9. Maintain the indigo ovoid for several minutes, then allow it to fade gently from your awareness.

10. Sound the battery: 1.

11. Now utter the following orison of aspiration:

> Constant and unswerving be my progress in the holy Mysteries! Though the further distance be veiled from my present vision, as in the pregnant darkness of an ancient shrine, still may I the more fervently aspire to that onward way. May my confidence endure and come to stronger growth beneath the holy face of that all-creative Night. May I reap in understanding the harvest of past action, and make a fresh sowing of the seeds of my experience. May my magical will shine

forth as a pure flame from that austere cradle; and, in the immense silence of transcended Time, may I learn awareness of my own heart's true and inward voice! So may it be, in the name

YHVH ELOHIM | **IALDABAOTH** | **AIONOS KYRIOS**

12. Sound the battery: 3–5–3.

3 CONTACTING THE POWER-DEEPS

These Rites of Contact, like the Rites of Approach, are for individual working.

Whereas the Rites of Approach look "outwards," establishing the magician in the power of the cosmic life-forces, these look "inwards," stimulating the inner planetary focal points to vital activity.

In each instance, the power of the cosmic archetype which has, in the Rite of Approach, already illumined the higher levels of the psyche, is now brought through its counterpart in the Deep Mind, and is thence called upwards into consciousness. In this way it is made one's own: supplying for working the vital link between cosmos and microcosmos, and carrying too an additional charge of magical potential from the profound treasury of the Collective Unconscious.

She who in the Rite of Approach was enrobed in the light of the sphere of operation, and imbued with its benison, is here suffused with its magical dynamism; and suffused with it in a personal realization of that power arising within her.

Just as with the Rites of Approach, the Rites of Contact should initially be worked in ascending planetary order (Moon through Saturn). Devote yourself to an entire attunement with each step in its turn of "The Ziggurat of Light," and complete all seven Rites of Contact before you proceed with the further works of Planetary Magick given in this book.

After completing the series in this way, take care, again as with the Rites of Approach, to keep open within your psyche the channel for each of the planetary powers to cultivate for yourself the effectiveness of these rites by frequent repetition, whether you employ the ascending sequence or select specific rites for your ongoing program.

Considered together the Rites of Approach and of Contact form the essential groundwork for the practice of Planetary Magick. They are root processes whose vitality, sustaining power and magical avail increase proportionately with use as the magician wins proficiency and might in her art.

RITE OF CONTACT IN LUNA

Temporal Mode: 3
Planetary Time: Day and Hour of the Moon
Position of Bomos: Just East of Center
Lights: 1 Violet Light or Star of Nine Lights

1. Perform the Rite of Preparation.
2. Standing at center facing East across the Bomos, sound the battery: 9.
3. *If you desire, now activate incense.*
4. Visualize yourself encompassed by an ovoid of *violet* light, and maintaining this in awareness proclaim:

   I will enter into the Light of Yesod, and approaching the inmost shrine of the Foundation I will invoke the Living Flame of the First Heaven.

   Encompassed by that resplendence and established upon the first step of the Ziggurat of Light, I will call forth within my soul the holy powers of Luna.

   So shall the glories of the worlds invisible be vividly present to my inner realization and the eye of my mind, and so shall I be indued with every virtue of the realm of Levanah that I may need in the workings of Art Magick.

5. Visualize the ovoid changing to *red-purple* light, and maintaining this vibrate the chosen divine name of the Sphere nine times:
   SHADDAI EL CHAI | IAO | AIGLE TRISAGIA
6. Now visualize the ovoid changing to *violet* light, and maintaining this make invocation as follows:

   Stainless, most luminous, mighty one! Leader of Night's holy enchantments! The brightness of thy triple countenance maddens the howlers of the wastelands: thy dominance speeds forth upon arrows, it rides the shining arrows of thy light. O thou who bringest to birth, thou who callest the dreamer forth to freedom!—thy presence and thy power I here invoke.

O thou who art ruler of the orb of Levanah, thou regent of night whose palace of Garen ha-Saphir is paved with azure; thou whose heaven is the veil of the skies, the region of silver and pearl, Tebel Vilun Shamaim;

O thou divine guardian of the sacred treaure-house: now open within me the crystalline gates of thy Sphere, that thy power may arise in my soul!

7. Having completed the invocation, allow the ovoid to fade from your awareness; then immediately proceed as follows:

8. Imagine a continuous spiral of *silver* light* ascending from the ground at your feet, whirling clockwise around you and disappearing above your head. As you hold this upward whirling spiral in visualization, vibrate the chosen divine name of the Sphere nine times—

SHADDAI EL CHAI | IAO | AIGLE TRISAGIA

9. Having completed the vibration of the divine name, allow the whirling spiral to fade from your consciousness.

10. Now, after the close of the deliberate visualizations, give at least 5 or 10 minutes to experiencing the contact you have established with this Sphere. Remain passive in the *feeling* of the Sphere of Luna as it has come to you through the visualizations and through vibrating the divine name; allowing ideas and images to flow unbidden and unchecked through your consciousness, as if you were dreaming.†

11. When you reach a point which you consider should end this period of reflection, sound the battery: 1.

12. Visualize yourself encompassed by an ovoid of *violet* light, and maintaining this utter the closing orison:

Ever may the Living Flame of the First Heaven light my path; and may its reverberation in Tebel Vilun Shamaim, arising within my soul, increasingly bestow upon me the bounteous gifts of imagination and the true perception of the Foundation.

13. Allow the violet ovoid to fade from your consciousness, then sound the battery: 3–5–3.

---

* This section of the rite employs the Ptolemaic color correspondences of the Spheres (*Entry 22*, Tables of Correspondences). These attributions are imbued with the influence of age-long magical tradition and potent usage, and are markedly appropriate where, as here, in a planetary context the need is to engage the deeps of the psyche and the mighty aid of the Collective Unconscious.

† At a later time you may if you wish review the content of your reflection, comparing the correspondences occurring therein with the list of Correspondences for the Planet. For each of these Rites of Contact, this subsequent review is recommended. It gives a good opportunity to verify the validity of the correspondences occurring in the reflection; further, it may provide new insights into their significance, new interpretations of material already known. It is also likely, on occasion, to enable you to add new material to your lists of correspondences, when this impresses you as being convincingly appropriate.

RITE OF CONTACT IN MERCURY

Temporal Mode: 3
Planetary Time: Day and Hour of Mercury
Position of Bomos: Just East of Center
Lights: 1 Orange Light or Star of Eight Lights

1. Perform the Rite of Preparation.
2. Standing at center facing East across the Bomos, sound the battery: 8.
3. *If you desire, now activate incense.*
4. Visualize yourself encompassed by an ovoid of *orange* light, and maintaining this in awareness proclaim:

    I will enter into the Light of Hod, and approaching the inmost shrine of Splendor I will invoke the Wondrous Flame of the Second Heaven. Encompassed by that vibrancy and established upon the second step of the Ziggurat of Light, I will call forth within my soul the holy powers of Mercury.

    So shall the glories of the worlds invisible be vividly present to my inner realization and the eye of my mind, and so shall I be indued with every virtue of the realm of Kokab that I may need in the workings of Art Magick.
5. Visualize the ovoid changing to *yellow ochre* light, and maintaining this vibrate the chosen divine name of the Sphere eight times:

    ### ELOHIM TZABAOTH | AZOTH | ALETHES LOGOS
6. Now visualize the ovoid changing to *orange* light, and maintaining this make invocation as follows:

    Multiple, dual, yet ever indivisible in thy unity: thou goest powerfully in light and in darkness! Subtle art thou as water, tenacious as fire. Thy power is a sure staff to the wayfarer and a crown of knowledge to the mage. Swift must be the words that call thee, swift but most trenchant!— a rushing wind is the language of this my invocation.

    O thou who art ruler of the orb of Kokab, thou protector and guide who dwellest in the graceful palace of Thushiah; thou whose chosen heaven is Reqia'a, the profound and splendid firmament itself: now let thine auspicious gaze rest upon my earnest explorations, and open within me the hidden gates of thy Sphere, that thy power may arise in my soul!
7. Having completed the invocation, allow the ovoid to fade from

your awareness; then immediately proceed as follows:

8. Imagine a continuous spiral of *shimmering opalescence* ascending from the ground at your feet, whirling clockwise around you and disappearing above your head. As you hold this upward whirling spiral in visualization, vibrate the chosen divine name of the Sphere eight times—

    ELOHIM TZABAOTH | AZOTH | ALETHES LOGOS

9. Having completed the vibration of the divine name, allow the whirling spiral to fade from your consciousness.

10. Now, after the close of the deliberate visualizations, give at least 5 or 10 minutes to experiencing the contact you have established with this Sphere. Remain passive in the *feeling* of the Sphere of Mercury as it has come to you through the visualizations and through vibrating the divine name; allowing ideas and images to flow unbidden and unchecked through your consciousness, as if you were dreaming.

11. When you reach a point which you consider should end this period of reflection, sound the battery: 1.

12. Visualize yourself encompassed by an ovoid of *orange* light, and maintaining this utter the closing orison:

    > Ever may the Wondrous Flame of the Second Heaven give wings to my mind; and may its reverberation in Reqia'a, arising within my soul, increasingly bestow upon me the precious gifts of magical understanding and the illuminations of Splendor.

13. Allow the orange ovoid to fade from your consciousness, then sound the battery: 3–5–3.

RITE OF CONTACT IN VENUS

Temporal Mode: 3
Planetary Time: Day and Hour of Venus
Position of Bomos: Just East of Center
Lights: 1 Green Light or Star of Seven Lights

1. Perform the Rite of Preparation.
2. Standing at center facing East across the Bomos, sound the battery: 7.
3. *If you desire, now activate incense.*
4. Visualize yourself encompassed by an ovoid of *green* light, and

maintaining this in awareness proclaim:

> I will enter into the Light of Netzach, and approaching the inmost shrine of Victory I will invoke the Mystical Flame of the Third Heaven. Encompassed by that ardor and established upon the third step of the Ziggurat of Light, I will call forth within my soul the holy powers of Venus.
>
> So shall the glories of the worlds invisible be vividly present to my inner realization and the eye of my mind, and so shall I be indued with every virtue of the realm of Nogah that I may need in the workings of Art Magick.

5. Visualize the ovoid changing to *greenish blue* light, and maintaining this vibrate the chosen divine name of the Sphere seven times:

   YHVH TZABAOTH | **ALBAPHALANA** | **CHARIS**

5. Visualize the ovoid changing to *green* light, and maintaining this make invocation as follows:

   > Radiant and strong ally, victorious friend, swift healer and helper!— giver of gladness, bathing all beings in the light of thy golden eyes! Song and sweet laughter evoke thee, and thy glory calls forth song and sweet laughter again. Bestower of life, bestower of love, my heart and soul find ecstasy in thee.
   >
   > O thou who are ruler of the orb of Nogah, bestower of blessing and of rapture, who dwellest in thy palace of the celestial forest, the festive palace of Otz Shamaim; thou who in the languid heaven of misty Shecheqim shinest in brilliance: now, in love and in peace, open within me the kindly gates of thy Sphere, that thy power may arise in my soul!

7. Having completed the invocation, allow the ovoid to fade from your awareness; then immediately proceed as follows:

8. Imagine a continuous spiral of *saffron* light ascending from the ground at your feet, whirling clockwise around you and disappearing above your head. As you hold this upward whirling spiral in visualization, vibrate the chosen divine name of the Sphere seven times—

   YHVH TZABAOTH | **ALBAPHALANA** | **CHARIS**

9. Having completed the vibration of the divine name, allow the whirling spiral to fade from your consciousness.

10. Now, after the close of the deliberate visualizations, give at least 5 or 10 minutes to experiencing the contact you have established with this Sphere. Remain passive in the *feeling* of the Sphere of Venus as it has come to you through the visualizations and

through vibrating the divine name; allowing ideas and images to flow unbidden and unchecked through your consciousness, as if you were dreaming.

11. When you reach a point which you consider should end this period of reflection, sound the battery: 1.

12. Visualize yourself encompassed by an ovoid of *green* light, and maintaining this utter the closing orison:

> Ever may the mystical Flame of the Third Heaven inspire joy in my life: and may its reverberation in Shecheqim, arising within my soul, increasingly bestow upon me the abundant gifts of spiritual vitality and the celestial fire of Victory.

13. Allow the green ovoid to fade from your consciousness, then sound the battery: 3–5–3.

RITE OF CONTACT IN SOL

Temporal Mode: 3
Planetary Time: Day and Hour of the Sun
Position of Bomos: Just East of Center
Lights: 1 Yellow Light or Star of Six Lights

1. Perform the Rite of Preparation.

2. Standing at center facing East across the Bomos, sound the battery: 6.

3. *If you desire, now activate incense.*

4. Visualize yourself encompassed by an ovoid of *yellow* light, and maintaining this in awareness proclaim:

> I will enter into the light of Tiphareth, and approaching the inmost shrine of Beauty I will invoke the Effulgent Flame of the Fourth Heaven.
>
> Encompassed by that vitality and established upon the fourth step of the Ziggurat of Light, I will call forth within my soul the holy powers of the Sun.
>
> So shall the glories of the worlds invisible be vividly present to my inner realization and the eye of my mind, and so shall I be indued with every virtue of the realm of Shemesh that I may need in the workings of Art Magick.

5. Visualize the ovoid changing to *pale greenish-yellow* light, and maintaining this vibrate the chosen divine name of the Sphere

six times:

YHVH ELOAH V'DAATH | ONOPHIS | THEIOS NOUS

6. Now visualize the ovoid changing to *yellow* light, and maintaining this make invocation as follows:

Effulgent prince of day!—through thine all-giving and most potent gaze we are wrought of star-fire, and kin to the glories beyond the spheres. Thine is the measure of Time and thine to bestow are the gifts that outpass Time: delight of life, rapture of life renewed! Thou art the Love which illumines our love and the Beauty which shines forth in the beauty of every being. Thou are present in all: yet now above all and apart from all I invoke thy glorious power.

O thou who are ruler of the orb of Shemesh, thou triumphant hero who dwellest in the delightsome palace of Ratzon; thou whose own heaven is many-hued Zabul, the wide region which is the resplendent dwelling of thy glory: now in thy great excellence, that I may partake in the wonder-working beneficence of thy rays, open within me the luminous gates of thy Sphere, that thy power may arise in my soul!

7. Having completed the invocation, allow the ovoid to fade from your awareness; then immediately proceed as follows:

8. Imagine a continuous spiral of *gold* light ascending from the ground at your feet, whirling clockwise around you and disappearing above your head. As you hold this upward whirling spiral in visualization, vibrate the chosen divine name of the Sphere six times—

YHVH ELOAH V'DAATH | ONOPHIS | THEIOS NOUS

9. Having completed the vibration of the divine name, allow the whirling spiral to fade from your consciousness.

10. Now, after the close of the deliberate visualizations, give at least 5 or 10 minutes to experiencing the contact you have established with this Sphere. Remain passive in the *feeling* of the Sphere of Sol as it has come to you through the visualizations and through vibrating the divine name; allowing ideas and images to flow unbidden and unchecked through your consciousness, as if you were dreaming.

11. When you reach a point which you consider should end this period of reflection, sound the battery: 1.

12. Visualize yourself encompassed by an ovoid of *yellow* light, and maintaining this utter the closing orison:

Ever may the Effulgent Flame of the Fourth Heaven illumine the sanctuary of my heart; and may its reverberation in Zabul, arising within my soul, increasingly bestow upon me the most sacred gifts of magical dedication and the high ecstasies of Beauty.

13. Allow the yellow ovoid to fade from your consciousness, then sound the battery: 3–5–3.

RITE OF CONTACT IN MARS

Temporal Mode: 3
Planetary Time: Day and Hour of Mars
Position of Bomos: Just East of Center
Lights: 1 Red Light or Star of Five Lights

1. Perform the Rite of Preparation.
2. Standing at center facing East across the Bomos, sound the battery: 5.
3. *If you desire, now activate incense.*
4. Visualize yourself encompassed by an ovoid of *red* light, and maintaining this in awareness proclaim:

   I will enter into the Light of Geburah, and approaching the inmost shrine of Strength I will invoke the Indomitable Flame of the Fifth Heaven.

   Encompassed by that potency and established upon the fifth step of the Ziggurat of Light, I will call forth within my soul the holy powers of Mars.

   So shall the glories of the worlds invisible be vividly present to my inner realization and the eye of my mind, and so shall I be indued with every virtue of the realm of Madim that I may need in the workings of Art Magick.

5. Visualize the ovoid changing to *amber* light, and maintaining this vibrate the chosen divine name of the Sphere five times:

   ELOHIM GEBOR | SABAO | ISCHYROS

6. Now visualize the ovoid changing to *red* light, and maintaining this make invocation as follows:

   Pure flame of valor! With ringing voice and upraised countenance be thine invocation made! Glory of fortitude, glory of achievement are in thy hand, and that inward joy of attainment which lifts the heart more than the acclaim of trumpets. Infuser of strong resolve into the blood of those who aspire: in courage and confidence I call upon thy might.

O thou who art ruler of the orb of Madim, thou intrepid champion who dwellest in the exalted palace of Zakoth; thou whose domain among the heavens is flame-bright Ma-on, habitation of the valorous and stronghold of protection to the just: now in thy sustaining care, that I may advance in justice and truth, open within me the massive gates of thy Sphere, that thy power may arise in my soul!

7. Having completed the invocation, allow the ovoid to fade from your awareness; then immediately proceed as follows:

8. Imagine a continuous spiral of *fiery red* light ascending from the ground at your feet, whirling clockwise around you and disappearing above your head. As you hold this upward whirling spiral in visualization, vibrate the chosen divine name of the Sphere five times—

ELOHIM GEBOR | SABAO | ISCHYROS

9. Having completed the vibration of the divine name, allow the whirling spiral to fade from your consciousness.

10. Now, after the close of the deliberate visualizations, give at least 5 or 10 minutes to experiencing the contact you have established with this Sphere. Remain passive in the *feeling* of the Sphere of Mars as it has come to you through the visualizations and through vibrating the divine name; allowing ideas and images to flow unbidden and unchecked through your consciousness, as if you were dreaming.

11. When you reach a point which you consider should end this period of reflection, sound the battery: 1.

12. Visualize yourself encompassed by an ovoid of *red* light, and maintaining this utter the closing orison:

Ever may the indomitable Flame of the Fifth Heaven guard my life and my works; and may its reverberation in Ma-on, arising within my soul, increasingly bestow upon me the high gifts of magical adventure and the unfailing confidence of Strength.

13. Allow the red ovoid to fade from your consciousness, then sound the battery: 3–5–3.

RITE OF CONTACT IN JUPITER

Temporal Mode: 3
Planetary Time: Day and Hour of Jupiter
Position of Bomos: Just East of Center
Lights: 1 Blue Light or Star of Four Lights

1. Perform the Rite of Preparation.
2. Standing at center facing East across the Bomos, sound the battery: 4.
3. *If you desire, now activate incense.*
4. Visualize yourself encompassed by an ovoid of *blue* light, and maintaining this in awareness proclaim:

   > I will enter into the Light of Chesed, and approaching the inmost shrine of Loving-kindness I will invoke the Beneficent Flame of the Sixth Heaven.
   >
   > Encompassed by that abundance and established upon the sixth step of the Ziggurat of Light, I will call forth within my soul the holy powers of Jupiter.
   >
   > So shall the glories of the worlds invisible be vividly present to my inner realization and the eye of my mind, and so shall I be indued with every virtue of the realm of Tzedeq that I may need in the workings of Art Magick.

5. Visualize the ovoid changing to *lilac* light, and maintaining this vibrate the chosen divine name of the Sphere four times:

   EL ⏐ ZARAIETOS ⏐ PANTOKRATOR

6. Now visualize the ovoid changing to *blue* light, and maintaining this make invocation as follows;

   > O most exalted wielder of the stars, supreme in all magnificence! The immense blue and purple of sky and ocean declare the breadth of thy domain, the fruitful rains affirm thy benignity. Majestic in power, compassionate in regard, beneath thy protecting hand I here invoke thee.
   >
   > O thou who art ruler of the orb of Tzedeq, most royal Father who dwellest in the beloved palace of white-pillared Ahabah; thou whose chosen region is the peaceful, the established place, the joyous realm of Makon: now in thy divine liberality, that I may arise to greater plenitude of life, open within me the spacious gates of thy Sphere, that thy power may arise in my soul!

7. Having completed the invocation, allow the ovoid to fade from your awareness; then immediately proceed as follows:
8. Imagine a continuous spiral of *white* light ascending from the ground at your feet, whirling clockwise around you and disappearing above your head. As you hold this upward whirling spiral in visualization, vibrate the chosen divine name of the Sphere four times—

   EL ⏐ ZARAIETOS ⏐ PANTOKRATOR

9. Having completed the vibration of the divine name, allow the whirling spiral to fade from your consciousness.

10. Now, after the close of the deliberate visualizations, give at least 5 or 10 minutes to experiencing the contact you have established with this Sphere. Remain passive in the *feeling* of the Sphere of Jupiter as it has come to you through the visualizations and through vibrating the divine name; allowing ideas and images to flow unbidden and unchecked through your consciousness, as if you were dreaming.

11. When you reach a point which you consider should end this period of reflection, sound the battery: 1.

12. Visualize yourself encompassed by an ovoid of *blue* light, and maintaining this utter the closing orison:

> Ever may the Beneficent Flame of the Sixth Heaven prosper my spiritual development; and may its reverberation in Makon, arising within my soul, increasingly bestow upon me the most excellent gifts of magnificence of spirit and the inner touchstone of Mercy.

13. Allow the blue ovoid to fade from your consciousness, then sound the battery: 3–5–3.

RITE OF CONTACT IN SATURN

Temporal Mode: 3
Planetary Time: Day and Hour of Saturn
Position of Bomos: Just East of Center
Lights: 1 Yellow Light or Star of Six Lights

1. Perform the Rite of Preparation.
2. Standing at center facing East across the Bomos, sound the battery: 3.
3. *If you desire, now activate incense.*
4. Visualize yourself encompassed by an ovoid of *indigo* light, and maintaining this in awareness proclaim:

> I will enter into the Light of Binah, and approaching the inmost shrine of Understanding I will invoke the Undying Flame of the Seventh Heaven.
>
> Encompassed by that creativity and established upon the seventh step of the Ziggurat of Light, I wil call forth within my soul the holy powers of Saturn. So shall the glories of the worlds invisible be vividly

present to my inner realization and the eye of my mind, and so shall I be indued with every virtue of the realm of Shabbathai that I may need in the working of Art Magick.

5. Visualize the ovoid changing to *dove grey* light, and maintaining this vibrate the chosen divine name of the Sphere three times:

    YHVH ELOHIM | IALDABAOTH | AIONOS KYRIOS

6. Now visualize the ovoid changing to *indigo* light, and maintaining this make invocation as follows:

    August and terrible! Thou silent, thou sublime! Through Time and Necessity thou dost rule us, through Mystery and the secret seeds of Creative Inspiration thou dost move us. Thou who bearest the scepter of elder Night, who dost govern the seasons of the spirit: thou Sower, thou Reaper, thou Regenerator!—thee now I invoke.

    O thou who art ruler of the orb of Shabbathai, thou venerable one who dwellest in the most sacred palace of Qadosh Qadoshim; thou whose domain is the vasty heaven of the glimmering plains, remote in Araboth: now in thine ever-heedful fidelity, that I may bring my labors on Earth to their full harvest, open within me the adamantine gates of thy Sphere, that thy power may arise in my soul!

7. Having completed the invocation, allow the ovoid to fade from your awareness; then immediately proceed as follows:

8. Imagine a continuous spiral of *grey* light ascending from the ground at your feet, whirling clockwise around you and disappearing above your head. As you hold this upward whirling spiral in visualization, vibrate the chosen divine name of the Sphere three times—

    YHVH ELOHIM | IALDABAOTH | AIONOS KYRIOS

9. Having completed the vibration of the divine name, allow the whirling spiral to fade from your consciousness.

10. Now, after the close of the deliberate visualizations, give at least 5 or 10 minutes to experiencing the contact you have established with this Sphere. Remain passive in the *feeling* of the Sphere of Saturn as it has come to you through the visualizations and through vibrating the divine name; allowing ideas and images to flow unbidden and unchecked through your consciousness, as if you were dreaming.

11. When you reach a point which you consider should end this period of reflection, sound the battery: 1.

12. Visualize yourself encompassed by an ovoid of *indigo* light, and maintaining this utter the closing orison:

Ever may the Undying Flame of the Seventh Heaven consecrate my upward progress with shining benediction; and may its reverberation in Araboth, arising within my soul, increasingly bestow upon me the wondrous gifts of renewal in Time and beyond Time and the sure counsels of Understanding.

13. Allow the indigo ovoid to fade from your consciousness, then sound the battery: 3–5–3.

4 CREATING THE ELIXIR OF VIRTUE

These rites are intended for group use. They may be undertaken in ascending planetary order, or from the outset they may be selected at need or will.

In each instance the group conjointly prepares a magical fluid, vibrant with the potency of the planet of the working; and in drinking of the same, each is inwardly infused with the creative energies of the sphere of operation. The ongoing benefits of these rites include not only the heightened ability of the recipients to work in harmony with the powers of the Spheres, but also their continuing and subtly-increasing apperception of the plantetary modalities as they operate in cosmos and microcosmos.

As an additional good, these rites effectively promote that transpersonal interactive process termed "magical group bonding"; unifying the participants at psychic and emotional levels, fostering the development of a group aura, and establishing a psycho-spiritual ambience wherein energy may be freely shared and rightly equilibriated.

For each planetary working in this series, the wine which is to be employed as the materium may be appropriately chosen from the following:

Saturn—Retzina. Elderberry. Entre Deux Mers. Campari.
Jupiter—Burgundy. Dubonnet. Byrrh. Ruby Port.
Mars—Ginger Wine. Asti Spumante. Bull's Blood. Chablis.
Sun—Muscatel. Claret. Commanderie St. John. Commanderia. Chianti. Barsac.
Venus—Moselle. Rosé. Sparkling Rosé. Mead. Champagne.
Mercury—Vermouth. Old Tokay. Blanc de Blancs. Reisling.
Moon—Liebfraumilch. Sauternes. Sylvaner. Palm Wine.

If desired, the dramatic effect of these rites, and consequently their appeal to the Nephesh, can be enhanced by the introduction of additional correspondences. For example:

A.   Each participant may wear a circlet of flowers or foliage upon the head (see *Entries 27, 28*, Tables of Correspondences). To do so is an ancient tradition of the Mysteries, and emphasizes both the sacerdotal and the joyful nature of the celebration.

B.   An appropriate magical implement may be employed in Section 11 of each rite, for the tracing of circle and presigillum (see *Entry 11*, Tables of Correspondences). For Saturn, perhaps an hourglass or a large key might be selected; for Venus, a lighted taper or a shell of elongated form.

C.   In Section 16 of each rite, during the pause for meditative reflection, evocative music suitable to the Sphere may be played (see *Entries 23, 24*, Tables of Correspondences).

CREATING THE ELIXIR IN LUNA

Temporal Mode: 2
Planetary Time: Hour of the Moon
Position of Bomos: Center of the Place of Working
Lights: 1 Violet Light or Star of Nine Lights
Other Requirements: A Cup with Wine upon the Bomos

(At the opening of the rite all participants stand in a circle around the place of working: the director stationed at the West.)

1.   The director advances to the West of the Bomos and performs the Rite of Preparation.
2.   The battery is sounded: 9.
3.   *If desired, incense is now activated.*
4.   The director begins the invocation:
     Let us open the mystic portals of the Shrine of Silver by invocation of the sacred name, that the resplendent glory of the divine presence may illumine us and raise our work into the Sphere of Yesod.
     She vibrates the chosen divine name of the Sphere once—
     SHADDAI EL CHAI ⎮ **IAO** ⎮ **AIGLE TRISAGIA**
     All now say:
     Thou giver of dreams, maker of all enchantments, ruler of the sacred light whereof is wrought the frame of things to be!—thou most faithful

in thy governance who art called the changeful one! As thou bringest all things to birth and growth and to their earthly fulfillment, now be thy mighty power with us in the working of Art Magick.

The director resumes her place in the circle. All link hands and utter the chosen divine name of the Sphere—

SHADDAI EL CHAI | IAO | AIGLE TRISAGIA

Hands are unlinked.

5. The director advances to West of Bomos. Raising the cup in both hands she makes the dedication:

O life-giving and potent

SHADDAI EL CHAI | IAO | AIGLE TRISAGIA

to thee we raise, in the cup of our aspiration, the wine which is to be the talisman of our united magical will!—asking thee, O Shining One, to receive this materium of our rite into the light of thy presence. So as we proceed in preparation of the Elixir of the Moon, charging the astral substance of this wine with the creative energies of Levanah, shall we achieve a true alchemical ferment, mighty in Yetzirah and vitalized by thy blessing.

And in partaking of this mystery, let there be unto us vitality of soul upon the first step of the Ziggurat of Light, increase of perception and heightened experience of the wonders of thy Sphere.

The cup is replaced on the Bomos, and the director resumes her place in the circle.

6. All link hands and make one complete clockwise circumambulation of the place of working; visualizing, as they do so, a wall of *violet* light whirling rapidly clockwise about their circle. This done, hands are unlinked and the wall of light is allowed to fade from awareness.

7. Beginning with the director and proceeding clockwise around the circle of participants, each in turn advances to the West side of the Bomos, holds the cup at heart level with both hands, and says:

Creature of Wine who art established upon the first step of the Ziggurat of Light: by the vital force of my breath, in this Hour of the Moon, I create a magical link between thee and me for the perfecting of this operation of Holy Magick in the realm of Levanah.

The participant then breathes once upon the wine, replaces the cup, and returns to his place in the circle.

8. All link hands and circumambulate the place of working nine times clockwise. This being done, hands are unlinked.

9. The director now raises power by the Ptolemaic formula, as follows:

   She imagines a continuous spiral of *silver* light ascending from the ground at her feet, whirling clockwise around her and disappearing above her head. As she holds this whirling spiral in visualization, she vibrates the chosen divine name of the Sphere once—

   SHADDAI EL CHAI | **IAO** | **AIGLE TRISAGIA**

   Having completed the vibration of the divine name, she allows the whirling spiral to fade from her consciousness.

   Each participant in turn, clockwise around the circle, now raises power by the Ptolemaic formula, visualizing the upward whirling light and vibrating the divine name.

   This being done, all link hands and vibrate once the chosen divine name of the Sphere—

   SHADDAI EL CHAI | **IAO** | **AIGLE TRISAGIA**

   Hands are unlinked.

10. The director leading, all now extend their hands towards the cup upon the Bomos, palms raised forwards; visualizing beams of *silver* light emanating from each palm and entering into the cup.

    After a few moments, the director ceases to visualize the beams of light and folds her arms upon her breast, left over right. All do likewise.

    Following the director, all lower arms to sides.

11. The director advances to West of Bomos. With her right hand she traces in horizontal plane a clockwise circle about the cup. Then with her right hand she traces in vertical plane above the cup the Presigillum of the planet (beginning from the point marked *), meanwhile vibrating the chosen divine name of the Sphere—

    SHADDAI EL CHAI | **IAO** | **AIGLE TRISAGIA**

12. The director resumes her place in the circle. All link hands and make one complete circumambulation of the place of working. Hands are unlinked.

13. The battery is sounded: 1.

14. The director advances to West of Bomos. She raises the cup and proclaims:

    Behold the Elixir of the Moon, mighty in Tebel Vilun Shamaim!
    For all and for each it is prepared!
    Let each and all receive its magick virtue!

She drinks of the wine, replaces the cup upon the Bomos and resumes her place in the circle.

15. One by one the other participants, clockwise around the circle, approach to West side of Bomos. Each raises the cup, makes the following declaration, then drinks (the last participant draining the cup):

Be the ferment of our spiritual alchemy mighty in the crucible of my soul!

Having drunk, each returns to his place in the circle.

16. After a pause for meditative reflection, the battery is sounded: 1.
17. All link hands and circumambulate once. Hands are unlinked.
18. The director utters the valediction:

O life-giving and potent

SHADDAI EL CHAI | IAO | AIGLE TRISAGIA

we who have entered into the Treasury of thy Light in Yesod, and have drunk of the mighty Elixir of the Moon, salute thee!

And as now we close again from outer awareness the mystic portals of the Shrine of Silver, grant us, O shining One, to keep the joy of this mystery of Luna in our hearts and to feel its wonder increasing within our souls.

All respond:

Thus shall it be!

19. The battery is sounded: 3–5–3.

CREATING THE ELIXIR IN MERCURY

Temporal Mode: 2
Planetary Time: Hour of Mercury
Position of Bomos: Center of the Place of Working
Lights: 1 Orange Light or Star of Eight Lights
Other Requirements: A Cup with Wine upon the Bomos

(At the opening of the rite all participants stand in a circle around the place of working: the director stationed at the West.)

1. The director advances to the West of the Bomos and performs the Rite of Preparation.
2. The battery is sounded: 8.
3. *If desired, incense is now activated.*
4. The director begins the invocation:

Let us open the mystic portals of the Shrine of Pearl by invocation of the sacred name, that the shimmering glory of the divine presence may illumine us and raise our work into the Sphere of Hod.

She vibrates the chosen divine name of the Sphere once—

ELOHIM TZABAOTH | **AZOTH** | **ALETHES LOGOS**

All now say:

Thou whose domain is all swiftness!—swifter than the wind, swifter than the course of light is the flashing of thought wherein thou dost move. Thou who goest ever between high heavens and fruitful earth, now as we call upon thee thou art with us.

The director resumes her place in the circle. All link hands and utter the chosen divine name of the Sphere—

ELOHIM TZABAOTH | **AZOTH** | **ALETHES LOGOS**

Hands are unlinked.

5. The director advances to West of Bomos. Raising the cup in both hands she makes the dedication:

O self-luminous and vibrant

ELOHIM TZABAOTH | **AZOTH** | **ALETHES LOGOS**

to thee we raise, in the cup of our aspiration, the wine which is to be the talisman of our united magical will!—asking thee, O Swift-winged One, to receive this materium of our rite into the light of thy presence.

So, as we proceed in preparation of the Elixir of Mercury, charging the astral substance of this wine with the creative energies of Kokab, shall we achieve a true alchemical ferment, mighty in Yetzirah and vitalized by thy blessing.

And in partaking of this mystery, let there be unto us vitality of soul upon the second step of the Ziggurat of Light, increase of perception and heightened experience of the wonders of thy Sphere.

The cup is replaced on the Bomos, and the director resumes her place in the circle.

6. All link hands and make one complete clockwise circumambulation of the place of working; visualizing, as they do so, a wall of *orange* light whirling rapidly clockwise about their circle. This done, hands are unlinked and the wall of light is allowed to fade from awareness.

7. Beginning with the director and proceeding clockwise around the circle of participants, each in turn advances to the West side of the Bomos, holds the cup at heart level with both hands, and says:

Creature of Wine who art established upon the second step of the

Ziggurat of Light: by the vital force of my breath, in this Hour of Mercury, I create a magical link between thee and me for the perfecting of this operation of Holy Magick in the realm of Kokab.

The participant then breathes once upon the wine, replaces the cup, and returns to his place in the circle.

8. All link hands and circumambulate the place of working eight times clockwise. This being done, hands are unlinked.

9. The director now raises power by the Ptolemaic formula, as follows:

She imagines a continuous spiral of *shimmering opalescence* ascending from the ground at her feet, whirling clockwise around her and disappearing above her head. As she holds this whirling spiral in visualization, she vibrates the chosen divine name of the Sphere once—

ELOHIM TZABAOTH | AZOTH | ALETHES LOGOS

Having completed the vibration of the divine name, she allows the whirling spiral to fade from her consciousness.

Each participant in turn, clockwise around the circle, now raises power by the Ptolemaic formula, visualizing the upward whirling light and vibrating the divine name.

This being done, all link hands and vibrate once the chosen divine name of the Sphere—

ELOHIM TZABAOTH | AZOTH | ALETHES LOGOS

Hands are unlinked.

10. The director leading, all now extend their hands towards the cup upon the Bomos, palms raised forwards; visualizing beams of *shimmering opalescence* emanating from each palm and entering into the cup.

After a few moments, the director ceases to visualize the beams of light and folds her arms upon her breast, left over right. All do likewise.

Following the director, all lower arms to sides.

11. The director advances to West of Bomos. With her right hand she traces in horizontal plane a clockwise circle about the cup. Then with her right hand she traces in vertical plane above the cup the Presigillum of the planet (beginning from the point marked *), meanwhile vibrating the chosen divine name of the Sphere—

ELOHIM TZABAOTH | AZOTH | ALETHES LOGOS

12. The director resumes her place in the circle. All link hands and

make one complete circumambulation of the place of working. Hands are unlinked.

13. The battery is sounded: 1

14. The director advances to West of Bomos. She raises the cup and proclaims:

> Behold the Elixir of Mercury, mighty in Reqia'a!
> For all and for each it is prepared!
> Let each and all receive its magick virtue!

She drinks of the wine, replaces the cup upon the Bomos and resumes her place in the circle.

15. One by one the other participants, clockwise around the circle, approach to West side of Bomos. Each raises the cup, makes the following declaration, then drinks (the last participant draining the cup):

> Be the ferment of our spiritual alchemy mighty in the crucible of my soul!

Having drunk, each returns to his place in the circle.

16. After a pause for meditative reflection, the battery is sounded: 1.

17. All link hands and circumambulate once. Hands are unlinked.

18. The director utters the valediction:

> O self-luminous and vibrant
>
> ### ELOHIM TZABAOTH | AZOTH | ALETHES LOGOS
>
> we who have entered into the Treasury of thy Light in Hod, and have drunk of the mighty Elixir of Mercury, salute thee!
> And as now we close again from outer awareness the mystic portals of the Shrine of Pearl, grant us, O Swift-winged One, to keep the joy of this mystery of Mercury in our hearts and to feel its wonder increasing within our souls.

All respond:

> Thus shall it be!

19. The battery is sounded: 3–5–3.

CREATING THE ELIXIR IN VENUS

Temporal Mode: 2
Planetary Time: Hour of Venus
Position of Bomos: Center of the Place of Working
Lights: 1 Green Light or Star of Seven Lights
Other Requirements: A Cup with Wine upon the Bomos

ARATRON ♄

BETHOR 4

PHALEGH ♂

OCH ☉

HAGITH ♀

OPHIEL ☿

PHUL 🌙

(At the opening of the rite all participants stand in a circle around the place of working: the director stationed at the West.)

1. The director advances to the West of the Bomos and performs the Rite of Preparation.
2. The battery is sounded: 7.
3. *If desired, incense is now activated.*
4. The director begins the invocation:

> Let us open the mystic portals of the Shrine of Amber by invocation of the sacred name, that the radiant glory of the divine presence may illumine us and raise our work into the Sphere of Netzach.

She vibrates the chosen divine name of the Sphere once—

YHVH TZABAOTH | ALBAPHALANA | CHARIS

All now say:

> Thou who callest forth gladness and peace and beauty in our lives, upon thee do we call! Thou who dost move ever to music heard and to music beyond all hearing, thou whose smile fills the air with sparkling light and with fragrance of a myriad blossoms!—now upon thee we call, that thy power may be with us in this rite.

The director resumes her place in the circle. All link hands and utter the chosen divine name of the Sphere—

YHVH TZABAOTH | ALBAPHALANA | CHARIS

Hands are unlinked.

5. The director advances to West of Bomos. Raising the cup in both hands she makes the dedication:

> O radiant and gentle
>
> **YHVH TZABAOTH | ALBAPHALANA | CHARIS**
>
> to thee we raise in the cup of our aspiration, the wine which is to be the talisman of our united magical will!—asking thee, O Loving One, to receive this materium of our rite into the light of thy presence. So, as we proceed in preparation of the Elixir of Venus, charging the astral substance of this wine with the creative energies of Nogah, shall we achieve a true alchemical ferment, mighty in Yetzirah and vitalized by thy blessing.
>
> And in partaking of this mystery, let there be unto us vitality of soul upon the third step of the Ziggurat of Light, increase of perception and heightened experience of the wonders of thy Sphere.

The cup is replaced on the Bomos, and the director resumes her place in the circle.

6. All link hands and make one complete clockwise circumambulation of the place of working; visualizing, as they do so, a wall of

green light whirling rapidly clockwise about their circle. This done, hands are unlinked and the wall of light is allowed to fade from awareness.

7. Beginning with the director and proceeding clockwise around the circle of participants, each in turn advances to the West side of the Bomos, holds the cup at heart level with both hands, and says:

> Creature of Wine who art established upon the third step of the Ziggurat of Light: by the vital force of my breath, in this Hour of Venus, I create a magical link between thee and me for the perfecting of this operation of Holy Magick in the realm of Nogah.

The participant then breathes once upon the wine, replaces the cup, and returns to his place in the circle.

8. All link hands and circumambulate the place of working seven times clockwise. This being done, hands are unlinked.

9. The director now raises power by the Ptolemaic formula, as follows:

She imagines a continuous spiral of *saffron* light ascending from the ground at her feet, whirling clockwise around her and disappearing above her head. As she holds this whirling spiral in visualization, she vibrates the chosen divine name of the Sphere once—

YHVH TZABAOTH | **ALBAPHALANA** | **CHARIS**

Having completed the vibration of the divine name, she allows the whirling spiral to fade from her consciousness.

Each participant in turn, clockwise around the circle, now raises power by the Ptolemaic formula, visualizing the upward whirling light and vibrating the divine name.

This being done, all link hands and vibrate once the chosen divine name of the Sphere—

YHVH TZABAOTH | **ALBAPHALANA** | **CHARIS**

Hands are unlinked.

10. The director leading, all now extend their hands towards the cup upon the Bomos, palms raised forwards; visualizing beams of *saffron* light emanating from each palm and entering into the cup.

After a few moments, the director ceases to visualize the beams of light and folds her arms upon her breast, left over right. All do likewise.

Following the director, all lower arms to sides.

11. The director advances to West of Bomos. With her right hand she traces in horizontal plane a clockwise circle about the cup. Then with her right hand she traces in vertical plane above the cup the Presigillum of the planet (beginning from the point marked *), meanwhile vibrating the chosen divine name of the Sphere—
     YHVH TZABAOTH | ALBAPHALANA | CHARIS

12. The director resumes her place in the circle. All link hands and make one complete circumambulation of the place of working. Hands are unlinked.

13. The battery is sounded: 1.

14. The director advances to West of Bomos. She raises the cup and proclaims:
     Behold the Elixir of Venus, mighty in Shecheqim!
     For all and for each it is prepared!
     Let each and all receive its magick virtue!
     She drinks of the wine, replaces the cup upon the Bomos and resumes her place in the circle.

15. One by one the other participants, clockwise around the circle, approach to West side of Bomos. Each raises the cup, makes the following declaration, then drinks (the last participant draining the cup):
     Be the ferment of our spiritual alchemy mighty in the crucible of my soul!
     Having drunk, each returns to his place in the circle.

16. After a pause for meditative reflection, the battery is sounded: 1.

17. All link hands and circumambulate once. Hands are unlinked.

18. The director utters the valediction:
     O radiant and gentle
     YHVH TZABAOTH | ALBAPHALANA | CHARIS
     we who have entered into the Treasury of thy Light in Netzach, and have drunk of the mighty Elixir of Venus, salute thee!
     And as now we close again from outer awareness the mystic portals of the Shrine of Amber, grant us, O Loving One, to keep the joy of this mystery of Venus in our hearts and to feel its wonder increasing within our souls.
     All respond:
     Thus shall it be!

19. The battery is sounded: 3–5–3.

CREATING THE ELIXIR IN SOL

Temporal Mode: 2
Planetary Time: Hour of the Sun
Position of Bomos: Center of the Place of Working
Lights: 1 Yellow Light or Star of Six Lights
Other Requirements: A Cup with Wine upon the Bomos

(At the opening of the rite all participants stand in a circle around the place of working: the director stationed at the West.)

1. The director advances to the West of the Bomos and performs the Rite of Preparation.
2. The battery is sounded: 6.
3. *If desired, incense is now activated.*
4. The director begins the invocation:

    Let us open the mystic portals of the Shrine of Gold by invocation of the sacred name, that the dazzling glory of the divine presence may illumine us and raise our work into the Sphere of Tiphareth.

    She vibrates the chosen divine name of the Sphere once—
    YHVH ELOAH V'DAATH | ONOPHIS | THEIOS NOUS

    All now say:

    Thou glorious giver of light and life, master of inward vision and the flashing flame of prophecy!—thou whose ensign fills the heavens with darts of golden fire!
    Divine bearer of healing and of hope, bestower of unconquerable joy, all-seeing Lord of Day, now be thy power with us.

    The director resumes her place in the circle. All link hands and utter the chosen divine name of the Sphere—
    YHVH ELOAH V'DAATH | ONOPHIS | THEIOS NOUS

    Hands are unlinked.

5. The director advances to West of Bomos. Raising the cup in both hands she makes the dedication:

    O peerless and jubilant
    YHVH ELOAH V'DAATH | ONOPHIS | THEIOS NOUS
    to thee we raise in the cup of our aspiration, the wine which is to be the talisman of our united magical will!—asking thee, O Brilliant One, to receive this materium of our rite into the light of thy presence. So, as we proceed in preparation of the Elixir of the Sun, charging the astral substance of this wine with the creative energies of Shemesh, shall we achieve a true alchemical ferment, mighty in Yetzirah and vitalized

by thy blessing.
And in partaking of this mystery, let there be unto us vitality of soul upon the fourth step of the Ziggurat of Light, increase of perception and heightened experience of the wonders of thy Sphere.

The cup is replaced on the Bomos, and the director resumes her place in the circle.

6. All link hands and make one complete clockwise circumambulation of the place of working; visualizing, as they do so, a wall of *yellow* light whirling rapidly clockwise about their circle. This done, hands are unlinked and the wall of light is allowed to fade from awareness.

7. Beginning with the director and proceeding clockwise around the circle of participants, each in turn advances to the West side of the Bomos, holds the cup at heart level with both hands, and says:

Creature of Wine who art established upon the fourth step of the Ziggurat of Light: by the vital force of my breath, in this Hour of the Sun, I create a magical link between thee and me for the perfecting of this operation of Holy Magick in the realm of Shemesh.

The participant then breathes once upon the wine, replaces the cup, and returns to his place in the circle.

8. All link hands and circumambulate the place of working six times clockwise. This being done, hands are unlinked.

9. The director now raises power by the Ptolemaic formula, as follows:

She imagines a continuous spiral of *gold* light ascending from the ground at her feet, whirling clockwise around her and disappearing above her head. As she holds this whirling spiral in visualization, she vibrates the chosen divine name of the Sphere once—

YHVH ELOAH V'DAATH | ONOPHIS | THEIOS NOUS

Having completed the vibration of the divine name, she allows the whirling spiral to fade from her consciousness.

Each participant in turn, clockwise around the circle, now raises power by the Ptolemaic formula, visualizing the upward whirling light and vibrating the divine name.

This being done, all link hands and vibrate once the chosen divine name of the Sphere—

YHVH ELOAH V'DAATH | ONOPHIS | THEIOS NOUS

Hands are unlinked.

10. The director leading, all now extend their hands towards the cup upon the Bomos, palms raised forwards; visualizing beams of *gold* light emanating from each palm and entering into the cup. After a few moments, the director ceases to visualize the beams of light and folds her arms upon her breast, left over right. All do likewise.

11. The director advances to West of Bomos. With her right hand she traces in horizontal plane a clockwise circle about the cup. Then with her right hand she traces in vertical plane above the cup the Presigillum of the planet (beginning from the point marked *), meanwhile vibrating the chosen divine name of the Sphere—
    YHVH ELOAH V'DAATH | **ONOPHIS** | **THEIOS NOUS**

12. The director resumes her place in the circle. All link hands and make one complete circumambulation of the place of working. Hands are unlinked.

13. The battery is sounded: 1.

14. The director advances to West of Bomos. She raises the cup and proclaims:
    Behold the Elixir of the Sun, mighty in Zabul!
    For all and for each it is prepared!
    Let each and all receive its magick virtue!
    She drinks of the wine, replaces the cup upon the Bomos and resumes her place in the circle.

15. One by one the other participants, clockwise around the circle, approach to West side of Bomos. Each raises the cup, makes the following declaration, then drinks (the last participant draining the cup):
    Be the ferment of our spiritual alchemy mighty in the crucible of my soul!
    Having drunk, each returns to his place in the circle.

16. After a pause for meditative reflection, the battery is sounded: 1.

17. All link hands and circumambulate once. Hands are unlinked.

18. The director utters the valediction:
    O peerless and jubilant
    YHVH ELOAH V'DAATH | **ONOPHIS** | **THEIOS NOUS**
    we who have entered into the Treasury of thy Light in Tiphareth, and have drunk of the mighty Elixir of the Sun, salute thee!
    And as now we close again from outer awareness the mystic portals of the Shrine of Gold, grant us, O Brilliant One, to keep the joy of this

mystery of the Sun in our hearts and to feel its wonder increasing within our souls.

All respond:

Thus shall it be!

19. The battery is sounded: 3–5–3.

CREATING THE ELIXIR IN MARS

Temporal Mode: 2
Planetary Time: Hour of Mars
Position of Bomos: Center of the Place of Working
Lights: 1 Red Light or Star of Five Lights
Other Requirements: A Cup with Wine upon the Bomos

(At the opening of the rite all participants stand in a circle around the place of working: the director stationed at the West.)

1. The director advances to the West of the Bomos and performs the Rite of Preparation.
2. The battery is sounded: 5.
3. *If desired, incense is now activated.*
4. The director begins the invocation:
   Let us open the mystic portals of the Shrine of Garnet by invocation of the sacred name, that the fiery glory of the divine presence may illumine us and raise our work into the Sphere of Geburah.

   She vibrates the chosen divine name of the Sphere once—
   ELOHIM GEBOR | **SABAO** | **ISCHYROS**

   All now say:
   Steadfast gaze of indomitable eyes, unfailing champion of just cause! A sharp spear thou dost forge from the needs of the hour. In that which here we do, Most Strong One, in power and presence be with us: thine arm above us, thy shield before us, in confidence we go forward.

   The director resumes her place in the circle. All link hands and utter the chosen divine name of the Sphere—
   ELOHIM GEBOR | **SABAO** | **ISCHYROS**

   Hands are unlinked.
5. The director advances to West of Bomos. Raising the cup in both hands she makes the dedication:
   O inexorable and inspiriting
   ELOHIM GEBOR | **SABAO** | **ISCHYROS**

> to thee we raise in the cup of our aspiration, the wine which is to be the talisman of our united magical will!—asking thee, O Most Valorous, to receive this materium of our rite into the light of thy presence. So, as we proceed in preparation of the Elixir of Mars, charging the astral substance of this wine with the creative energies of Madim, shall we achieve a true alchemical ferment, mighty in Yetzirah and vitalized by thy blessing.
>
> And in partaking of this mystery, let there be unto us vitality of soul upon the fifth step of the Ziggurat of Light, increase of perception and heightened experience of the wonders of thy Sphere.

The cup is replaced on the Bomos, and the director resumes her place in the circle.

6. All link hands and make one complete clockwise circumambulation of the place of working; visualizing, as they do so, a wall of *red* light whirling rapidly clockwise about their circle. This done, hands are unlinked and the wall of light is allowed to fade from awareness.

7. Beginning with the director and proceeding clockwise around the circle of participants, each in turn advances to the West side of the Bomos, holds the cup at heart level with both hands, and says:

> Creature of Wine who art established upon the fifth step of the Ziggurat of Light: by the vital force of my breath, in this Hour of Mars, I create a magical link between thee and me for the perfecting of this operation of Holy Magick in the realm of Madim.

The participant then breathes once upon the wine, replaces the cup, and returns to his place in the circle.

8. All link hands and circumambulate the place of working five times clockwise. This being done, hands are unlinked.

9. The director now raises power by the Ptolemaic formula, as follows:

She imagines a continuous spiral of *fiery red* light ascending from the ground at her feet, whirling clockwise around her and disappearing above her head. As she holds this whirling spiral in visualization, she vibrates the chosen divine name of the Sphere once—

ELOHIM GEBOR | SABAO | ISCHYROS

Having completed the vibration of the divine name, she allows the whirling spiral to fade from her consciousness.

Each participant in turn, clockwise around the circle, now raises power by the Ptolemaic formula, visualizing the upward whirling light and vibrating the divine name.

This being done, all link hands and vibrate once the chosen divine name of the Sphere—

ELOHIM GEBOR ⎮ SABAO ⎮ ISCHYROS

Hands are unlinked.

10. The director leading, all now extend their hands towards the cup upon the Bomos, palms raised forwards; visualizing beams of *fiery red* light emanating from each palm and entering into the cup.

   After a few moments, the director ceases to visualize the beams of light and folds her arms upon her breast, left over right. All do likewise.

   Following the director, all lower arms to sides.

11. The director advances to West of Bomos. With her right hand she traces in horizontal plane a clockwise circle about the cup. Then with her right hand she traces in vertical plane above the cup the Presigillum of the planet (beginning from the point marked *), meanwhile vibrating the chosen divine name of the Sphere—

   ELOHIM GEBOR ⎮ SABAO ⎮ ISCHYROS

12. The director resumes her place in the circle. All link hands and make one complete circumambulation of the place of working. Hands are unlinked.

13. The battery is sounded: 1.

14. The director advances to West of Bomos. She raises the cup and proclaims:

   Behold the Elixir of Mars, mighty in Ma-on!
   For all and for each it is prepared!
   Let each and all receive its magick virtue!

   She drinks of the wine, replaces the cup upon the Bomos and resumes her place in the circle.

15. One by one the other participants, clockwise around the circle, approach to West side of Bomos. Each raises the cup, makes the following declaration, then drinks (the last participant draining the cup):

   Be the ferment of our spiritual alchemy mighty in the crucible of my soul!

   Having drunk, each returns to his place in the circle.

16. After a pause for meditative reflection, the battery is sounded: 1.

17. All link hands and circumambulate once. Hands are unlinked.

18. The director utters the valediction:
    O inexorable and inspiriting
    ELOHIM GEBOR | **SABAO** | **ISCHYROS**
    we who have entered into the Treasury of thy Light in Geburah, and
    have drunk of the mighty Elixir of Mars, salute thee!
    And as now we close again from outer awareness the mystic portals
    of the Shrine of Garnet, grant us, O most Valorous, to keep the joy of
    this mystery of Mars in our hearts and to feel its wonder increasing
    within our souls.
    All respond:
    Thus shall it be!
19. The battery is sounded: 3-5-3.

CREATING THE ELIXIR IN JUPITER

Temporal Mode: 2
Planetary Time: Hour of Jupiter
Position of Bomos: Center of the Place of Working
Lights: 1 Blue Light or Star of Four Lights
Other Requirements: A Cup with Wine upon the Bomos

(At the opening of the rite all participants stand in a circle around the
place of working: the director stationed at the West.)
1. The director advances to the West of the Bomos and performs
   the Rite of Preparation.
2. The battery is sounded: 4.
3. *If desired, incense is now activated.*
4. The director begins the invocation:
    Let us open the mystic portals of the Shrine of Alabaster by invocation
    of the sacred name, that the bounteous glory of the divine presence
    may illumine us and raise our work into the Sphere of Chesed.
    She vibrates the chosen divine name of the Sphere once—
    EL | **ZARAIETOS** | **PANTOKRATOR**
    All now say:
    Divine Father of immortals, compassionate Father of earthly life! Thou
    who art ever with us to sustain us in being, be with us now in the work-
    ing of our art!—thou abundance more liberal than light of summer
    skies, thou majestic power more potent than the surge of ocean's
    deep!

The director resumes her place in the circle. All link hands and utter the chosen divine name of the Sphere—

EL ⏐ ZARAIETOS ⏐ PANTOKRATOR

Hands are unlinked.

5. The director advances to West of Bomos. Raising the cup in both hands she makes the dedication:

O great and beneficent

EL ⏐ ZARAIETOS ⏐ PANTOKRATOR

to thee we raise, in the cup of our aspiration, the wine which is to be the talisman of our united magical will!—asking thee, O Most Splendid, to receive this materium of our rite into the light of thy presence. So, as we proceed in preparation of the Elixir of Jupiter, charging the astral substance of this wine with the creative energies of Tzedeq, shall we achieve a true alchemical ferment, mighty in Yetzirah and vitalized by thy blessing.

And in partaking of this mystery, let there be unto us vitality of soul upon the sixth step of the Ziggurat of Light, increase of perception and heightened experience of the wonders of thy Sphere.

The cup is replaced on the Bomos, and the director resumes her place in the circle.

6. All link hands and make one complete clockwise circumambulation of the place of working; visualizing, as they do so, a wall of *blue* light whirling rapidly clockwise about their circle. This done, hands are unlinked and the wall of light is allowed to fade from awareness.

7. Beginning with the director and proceeding clockwise around the circle of participants, each in turn advances to the West side of the Bomos, holds the cup at heart level with both hands, and says:

Creature of Wine who art established upon the sixth step of the Ziggurat of Light: by the vital force of my breath, in this Hour of Jupiter, I create a magical link between thee and me for the perfecting of this operation of Holy Magick in the realm of Tzedeq.

The participant then breathes once upon the wine, replaces the cup, and returns to his place in the circle.

8. All link hands and circumambulate the place of working four times clockwise. This being done, hands are unlinked.

9. The director now raises power by the Ptolemaic formula, as follows:

She imagines a continuous spiral of *white* light ascending from the ground at her feet, whirling clockwise around her and disappearing above her head. As she holds this whirling spiral in visualization, she vibrates the chosen divine name of the Sphere once—

EL | **ZARAIETOS** | **PANTOKRATOR**

Having completed the vibration of the divine name, she allows the whirling spiral to fade from her consciousness.

Each participant in turn, clockwise around the circle, now raises power by the Ptolemaic formula, visualizing the upward whirling light and vibrating the divine name.

This being done, all link hands and vibrate once the chosen divine name of the Sphere—

EL | **ZARAIETOS** | **PANTOKRATOR**

Hands are unlinked.

10. The director leading, all now extend their hands towards the cup upon the Bomos, palms raised forwards; visualizing beams of *white* light emanating from each palm and entering into the cup. After a few moments, the director ceases to visualize the beams of light and folds her arms upon her breast, left over right. All do likewise.

Following the director, all lower arms to sides.

11. The director advances to West of Bomos. With her right hand she traces in horizontal plane a clockwise circle about the cup. Then with her right hand she traces in vertical plane above the cup the Presigillum of the planet (beginning from the point marked *), meanwhile vibrating the chosen divine name of the Sphere—

EL | **ZARAIETOS** | **PANTOKRATOR**

12. The director resumes her place in the circle. All link hands and make one complete circumambulation of the place of working. Hands are unlinked.

13. The battery is sounded: 1.

14. The director advances to West of Bomos. She raises the cup and proclaims:

Behold the Elixir of Jupiter, mighty in Makon!

For all and for each it is prepared!

Let each and all receive its magick virtue!

She drinks of the wine, replaces the cup upon the Bomos and resumes her place in the circle.

15. One by one the other participants, clockwise around the circle,

approach to West side of Bomos. Each raises the cup, makes the following declaration, then drinks (the last participant draining the cup):

Be the ferment of our spiritual alchemy mighty in the crucible of my soul!

Having drunk, each returns to his place in the circle.

16. After a pause for meditative reflection, the battery is sounded: 1.
17. All link hands and circumambulate once. Hands are unlinked.
18. The director utters the valediction:

O great and beneficent

EL ǀ ZARAIETOS ǀ PANTOKRATOR

we who have entered into the Treasury of thy Light in Chesed, and have drunk of the mighty Elixir of Jupiter, salute thee!

And as now we close again from outer awareness the mystic portals of the Shrine of Alabaster, grant us, O Most Splendid, to keep the joy of this mystery of Jupiter in our hearts and to feel its wonder increasing within our souls.

All respond:

Thus shall it be!

19. The battery is sounded: 3–5–3.

CREATING THE ELIXIR IN SATURN

Temporal Mode: 2
Planetary Time: Hour of Saturn
Position of Bomos: Center of the Place of Working
Lights: 1 Indigo (or Black) Light or Star of Three Lights
Other Requirements: A Cup with Wine upon the Bomos

(At the opening of the rite all participants stand in a circle around the place of working: the director stationed at the West.)

1. The director advances to the West of the Bomos and performs the Rite of Preparation.
2. The battery is sounded: 3.
3. *If desired, incense is now activated.*
4. The director begins the invocation:

Let us open the mystic portals of the Shrine of Onyx by invocation of the sacred name, that the sublime glory of the divine presence may illumine us and raise our work into the Sphere of Binah.

She vibrates the chosen divine name of the Sphere once—
>**YHVH ELOHIM | IALDABAOTH | AIONOS KYRIOS**

All now say:
>Thou mighty one of elder time!—thou whose far glory reveals by slow degrees the wondrous mystery of our being! As like ever responds to like, enkindle thou by inspiration the deep creative fire within our souls. Be with us now in thy power, as thou art ever with us in the truth of spirit.

The director resumes her place in the circle. All link hands and utter the chosen divine name of the sphere—
>**YHVH ELOHIM | IALDABAOTH | AIONOS KYRIOS**

Hands are unlinked.

5. The director advances to West of Bomos. Raising the cup in both hands she makes the dedication:
>O vast and sublime
>**YHVH ELOHIM | IALDABAOTH | AIONOS KYRIOS**
>to thee we raise, in the cup of our aspiration, the wine which is to be the talisman of our united magical will!—asking thee, O Exalted One, to receive this materium of our rite into the light of thy presence. So, as we proceed in preparation of the Elixir of Saturn, charging the astral substance of this wine with the creative energies of Shabbathai, shall we achieve a true alchemical ferment, mighty in Yetzirah and vitalized by thy blessing.
>And in partaking of this mystery, let there be unto us vitality of soul upon the seventh step of the Ziggurat of Light, increase of perception and heightened experience of the wonders of thy Sphere.

The cup is replaced on the Bomos, and the director resumes her place in the circle.

6. All link hands and make one complete clockwise circumambulation of the place of working; visualizing, as they do so, a wall of *indigo* light whirling rapidly clockwise about their circle. This done, hands are unlinked and the wall of light is allowed to fade from awareness.

7. Beginning with the director and proceeding clockwise around the circle of participants, each in turn advances to the West side of the Bomos, holds the cup at heart level with both hands, and says:
>Creature of Wine who art established upon the seventh step of the Ziggurat of Light: by the vital force of my breath, in this Hour of Saturn, I create a magical link between thee and me for the perfecting of this

operation of holy Magick in the realm of Shabbathai.

The participant then breathes once upon the wine, replaces the cup, and returns to his place in the circle.

8. All link hands and circumambulate the place of working three times clockwise. This being done, hands are unlinked.

9. The director now raises power by the Ptolemaic formula, as follows:

    She imagines a continuous spiral of *grey* light ascending from the ground at her feet, whirling clockwise around her and disappearing above her head. As she holds this whirling spiral in visualization, she vibrates the chosen divine name of the Sphere once—

    YHVH ELOHIM | **IALDABAOTH** | **AIONOS KYRIOS**

    Having completed the vibration of the divine name, she allows the whirling spiral to fade from her consciousness.

    Each participant in turn, clockwise around the circle, now raises power by the Ptolemaic formula, visualizing the upward whirling light and vibrating the divine name.

    This being done, all link hands and vibrate once the chosen divine name of the Sphere—

    YHVH ELOHIM | **IALDABAOTH** | **AIONOS KYRIOS**

    Hands are unlinked.

10. The director leading, all now extend their hands towards the cup upon the Bomos, palms raised forwards; visualizing beams of *grey* light emanating from each palm and entering into the cup.

    After a few moments, the director ceases to visualize the beams of light and folds her arms upon her breast, left over right. All do likewise.

    Following the director, all lower arms to sides.

11. The director advances to West of Bomos. With her right hand she traces in horizontal plane a clockwise circle about the cup. Then with her right hand she traces in vertical plane above the cup the Presigillum of the planet (beginning from the point marked *), meanwhile vibrating the chosen divine name of the Sphere—

    YHVH ELOHIM | **IALDABAOTH** | **AIONOS KYRIOS**

12. The director resumes her place in the circle. All link hands and make one complete circumambulation of the place of working. Hands are unlinked.

13. The battery is sounded: 1.

14. The director advances to West of Bomos. She raises the cup and proclaims:
    Behold the Elixir of Saturn, mighty in Araboth!
    For all and for each it is prepared!
    Let each and all receive its magick virtue!
    She drinks of the wine, replaces the cup upon the Bomos and resumes her place in the circle.

15. One by one the other participants, clockwise around the circle, approach to West side of Bomos. Each raises the cup, makes the following declaration, then drinks (the last participant draining the cup):
    Be the ferment of our spiritual alchemy mighty in the crucible of my soul!
    Having drunk, each returns to his place in the circle.

16. After a pause for meditative reflection, the battery is sounded: 1.

17. All link hands and circumambulate once. Hands are unlinked.

18. The director utters the valediction;
    O vast and sublime
    YHVH ELOHIM ⏐ IALDABAOTH ⏐ AIONOS KYRIOS
    we who have entered into the Treasury of thy Light in Binah, and have drunk of the mighty Elixir of Saturn, salute thee!
    And as now we close again from outer awareness the mystic portals of the Shrine of Onyx, grant us, O Exalted One, to keep the joy of this mystery of Saturn in our hearts and to feel its wonder increasing within our souls.
    All respond:
    Thus shall it be!

19. The battery is sounded: 3–5–3.

5 DAILY PLANETARY ATTUNEMENT

These rites are for individual use. They constitute positive personal attunements with the ages-old dedication of the seven days of the week to the planetary powers.

Ideally, and as presented here, each of the rites should be performed in the morning of the appropriate day of the week, during the 1st magical hour which begins at sunrise; but the 8th, 15th or 22nd magical hours of the day may validly be selected for the work as opportunity or preference suggests.

The benefits of these rites derive from a deep, simple and therefore most powerful level. No matter what your day's program, or how many varied forces may have a bearing upon it, the governing force of the planet of the day's dedication is a constant, knowable, modifying influence. To place yourself consciously in a daily rapport with that influence, and within its tutelary power is to gain at once a great strength for inward and outward harmony, order, and ongoing success in your life.

The essential magical act of each attunement is the formulation of a channel for the deific force of the working. Thus the aspirant builds up in imagination a Magical Image appropriate to the Sphere (automatically formulating it thereby in the thought-responsive substance of the Astral World), then vitalizes this image by vibration of a relevant divine name. Upon the inner planes the image flashes to life, resonating to the reality it represents and becoming a localized vehicle for the operation and transmission of the divine energies. In this sense, the aspirant truly stands "before the Presence"; her adoration is directed to a specific nexus of spiritual vitality within the space-time continuum, and she is bathed in the light and blessing radiating therefrom.

In the early stages of practice the aspirant can and should enjoy the happiness and peace of mind of *knowing* that the daily attunement is being made, that the day's activities are placed with the strong guardianship of the planetary power. When however the deeper awareness begins to develop of what is taking place spiritually, then that awareness will develop rapidly. The experience of attunement will become ever richer; the joy and confidence with which the aspirant knows herself to stand daily before the day's tutelary power will progressively increase; and the day thus begun in beauty, peace and inspiration will be thrillingly transformed.

RITE OF ATTUNEMENT FOR SUNDAY

Temporal Mode: 3
Planetary Time: Day and Hour of the Sun
Position of Bomos: Center of Place of Working
Lights: 1 Yellow Light upon the Bomos (initially unlighted)
Other Requirements: A lighting taper upon the Bomos

1. Standing just West of center, facing East across the Bomos, perform the Rite of Preparation.
2. Sound the battery: 6.
3. Now proclaim:

    On this Day of the Sun I, true Priest of the Temple of Shemesh and Servitor of the Sacred Flame of the Fourth Heaven, seek attunement with the spiritual power of Beauty.

    Wherefore I pass from darkness into the light of this mystery by intonation of the Sacred Vowel of the Cosmic Harmony.

    Immediately following the proclamation, vibrate, or chant according to its specified tone, the vowel of the Sphere—

    I (pronounced as "ee" in *meet*)

4. Kindle the taper, then proceed to the East side of the Bomos and face East. With the lighted taper, trace in the air before you the Presigillum of the planet. Then turn to face West and light the yellow lamp upon the Bomos. Resume your place at the West side of the Bomos, facing East, and extinguish the taper.
5. *If you desire, now activate incense.*
6. Now make invocation, as follows:

O most mighty
YHVH ELOAH V'DAATH | **ONOPHIS** | **THEIOS NOUS**
triumphant chieftain of the shining and many-colored days, O divine
exemplar of heroes and princes, thou most benign in jubilation, most
peaceable in sovereignty! Numberless as the rays of thy peerless
crown are the noble and glorious beings who surround thee. These
thou sendest forth to bestow thy royal bounties, scattered at large or
as particular gifts: all precious beyond reckoning. In thy power thy
radiant emissaries endow with joy of spirit, and with that perception of
beauty which is life's purest gold. To thee, life-giving, all seeing, all
beneficent, to thee I make this invocation.

7. Having completed the invocation, close your eyes. Visualize
before you the Magical Image of "The Solar King" or of the "Puer
Aeternus," as you prefer (*Entries 37a and 37b*, Correspondences of
Sun); then, holding the image in your awareness, powerfully vibrate
the chosen divine name of the Sphere to charge and vitalize it—
YHVH ELOAH V'DAATH | **ONOPHIS** | **THEIOS NOUS**

8. Standing before this "Presence," breathing evenly and deeply,
allow yourself to feel the awakened current of divine energy and
to be inwardly uplifted in joyful and reverent response thereto.

9. When you are so moved, make salutation with your right hand; then
open your eyes, ceasing to hold the image in your awareness, and
re-center your consciousness in your material environment.

10. Sound the battery: 1.

11. Finally, proclaim:
Salutation and thanks be unto thee, O thou Sovereign Genius of
Kalon, who dost now uphold me in the light of thy blessing, and who dost
receive all my works of this day into the harmony of thy power.

12. Sound the battery: 3–5–3.

RITE OF ATTUNEMENT FOR MONDAY

Temporal Mode: 3
Planetary Time: Day and Hour of the Moon
Position of Bomos: Center of Place of Working
Lights: 1 Violet Light upon the Bomos (initially unlighted)
Other Requirements: A lighting taper upon the Bomos

1. Standing just West of Center, facing East across the Bomos, perform
the Rite of Preparation.

2. Sound the battery: 9.
3. Now proclaim:
> On this Day of the Moon I, true Priest of the Temple of Levanah and Servitor of the Sacred Flame of the First Heaven, seek attunement with the spiritual power of the Foundation.
>
> Wherefore I pass from darkness into the light of this mystery by intonation of the Sacred Vowel of the Cosmic Harmony.

Immediately following the proclamation, vibrate, or chant according to its specified tone, the vowel of the Sphere—

A (pronounced as "a" in *father*)

4. Kindle the taper, then proceed to the east side of the Bomos and face East. With the lighted taper, trace in the air before you the Presigillum of the planet. Then turn to face West and light the violet lamp upon the Bomos. Resume your place at the West side of the Bomos, facing East, and extinguish the taper.
5. *If you desire, now activate incense.*
6. Now make invocation as follows:
> O most mighty
> **SHADDAI EL CHAI | IAO | AIGLE TRISAGIA**
> thou radiant ecstasy, manifest glory of the night!—far-riding maker of enchantment, stooping low above Earth to fulfill thy purposes! Thou whisperest to hidden seeds in dark of earth, that they burst forth to life. Thou criest aloud to the hearts of humankind, that they cry response to thee: the soul cries in yearning for its own greater life, in response to thee. Ever swift thou art to guard all young beings, and to keep safe the ardent following whose hands are raised to thee. Over all these watch thy gentle and mighty ones with unsleeping eyes of light, the tall-winged and vigorous flashings-forth of thy pure brilliance. To thee O nurturing, to thee most widely potent, O sovereign of threefold empire, I make my invocation.

7. Having completed the invocation, close your eyes. Visualize before you the Magical Image of "The Lady of Night" (*Entry 37*, Correspondences of the Moon); then, holding the image in your awareness, powerfuly vibrate the chosen divine name of the Sphere to charge and vitalize it—

SHADDAI EL CHAI | IAO | AIGLE TRISAGIA

8. Standing before this "Presence," breathing evenly and deeply, allow yourself to feel the awakened current of divine energy and to be inwardly uplifted in joyful and reverent response thereto.

9. When you are so moved, make salutation with your right hand; then open your eyes, ceasing to hold the image in your awareness, and re-center your consciousness in your material environment.
10. Sound the battery: 1.
11. Finally, proclaim:
    Salutation and thanks be unto thee, O thou Sovereign Genius of Asphaleia, who dost now uphold me in the light of thy blessing, and who dost receive all my works of this day into the harmony of thy power.
12. Sound the Battery: 3–5–3.

RITE OF ATTUNEMENT FOR TUESDAY

Temporal Mode: 3
Planetary Time: Day and Hour of Mars
Position of Bomos: Center of Place of Working
Lights: 1 Red Light upon the Bomos (initially unlighted)
Other Requirements: A lighting taper upon the Bomos

1. Standing just West of center, facing East across the Bomos, perform the Rite of Preparation.
2. Sound the battery: 5.
3. Now proclaim:
   On this Day of Mars I, true Priest of the Temple of Madim and Servitor of the Sacred Flame of the Fifth Heaven, seek attunement with the spiritual power of Strength.
   Wherefore I pass from darkness into the light of this mystery by intonation of the Sacred Vowel of the Cosmic Harmony.
   Immediately following the proclamation, vibrate, or chant according to its specified tone, the vowel of the Sphere—
   O (pronounced as "o" in *hot*)
4. Kindle the taper, then proceed to the East side of the Bomos and face East. With the lighted taper, trace in the air before you the Presigillum of the planet. Then turn to face West and light the red lamp upon the Bomos. Resume your place at the West side of the Bomos, facing East, and extingtuish the taper.
5. *If you desire, now activate incense.*
6. Now make invocation as follows:
   O most mighty
   ELOHIM GEBOR | **SABAO** | **ISCHYROS**

thou glory of valor, who dost enkindle within the soul the fires of energy and of daring! The heart leaps in eager emulation of thy hardihood, the pulse of thy measured tread sings in the blood. Not the warrior only, not alone the seeker-out of bold exploit, win thine all-powerful assistance. For thou sendest forth thy flashing cohorts, lithe and sinuous flames of thine own living effulgence: theirs it is to give enthusiasm and inspiration, and to quicken the fierce innocency of the will to go forward, to prosper and to attain. With the ardent fire of the heart and the steel of the mind, and the high soaring shafts of quenchless resolve, thus do I invoke thee.

7. Having completed the invocation, close your eyes. Visualize before you the Magical Image of "The Warrior" (*Entry 37*, Correspondences of Mars); then, holding the image in your awareness, powerfully vibrate the chosen divine name of the Sphere to charge and vitalize it—

ELOHIM GEBOR | SABAO | ISCHYROS

8. Standing before this "Presence," breathing evenly and deeply, allow yourself to feel the awakened current of divine energy and to be inwardly uplifted in joyful and reverent response thereto.

9. When you are so moved, make salutation with your right hand; then open your eyes, ceasing to hold the image in your awareness, and re-center your consciousness in your material environment.

10. Finally, proclaim:

Salutation and thanks be unto thee, O thou Sovereign Genius of Dynamis, who dost now uphold me in the light of thy blessing, and who dost receive all my works of this day into the harmony of thy power.

12. Sound the battery: 3–5–3.

RITE OF ATTUNEMENT FOR WEDNESDAY

Temporal Mode: 3
Planetary Time: Day and Hour of Mercury
Position of Bomos: Center of Place of Working
Lights: 1 Orange Light upon the Bomos (initially unlighted)
Other Requirements: A lighting taper upon the Bomos

1. Standing just West of center, facing East across the Bomos, perform the Rite of Preparation.

2. Sound the battery: 8.

3. Now proclaim:

   On this Day of Mercury I, true Priest of the Temple of Kokab and Servitor of the Sacred Flame of the Second Heaven, seek attunement with the spiritual power of Splendor.

   Wherefore I pass from darkness into the light of this mystery by intonation of the Sacred Vowel of the Cosmic Harmony.

   Immediately following the proclamation, vibrate, or chant according to its specified tone, the vowel of the Sphere—

   E (pronounced as "e" in *set*)

4. Kindle the taper, then proceed to the East side of the Bomos and face East. With the lighted taper, trace in the air before you the Presigillum of the planet. Then turn to face West and light the orange lamp upon the Bomos. Resume your place at the West side of the Bomos, facing East, and extinguish the taper.

5. *If you desire, now activate incense.*

6. Now make invocation as follows:

   O most mighty

   ELOHIM TZABAOTH | **AZOTH** | **ALETHES LOGOS**

   thou swift and self-luminous, whose aspect is refreshing as welcome news: far-seeing friend, sure guide, true counselor! The lore of herb and gem is in thy gift, words and the charm of words, and the magical might of number. Thine are the bright ethereal messengers, gladsome as flashing waves of the sea, ever eager and youthful! Leader and chief art thou also, potent and subtle, among the children of High Magick: for the hidden ways of life and death, and of every mystery, are alike thy free approaches, and thou movest scintillant but unseen between earth and the heavens. Here I invoke thee, I who love and venerate thee: O giver of knowledge, giver of power, thou immortal Energy bathed in dew of light divine!

7. Having completed the invocation, close your eyes. Visualize before you the Magical Image of "The Hermit" or of "The Divine Messenger" (*Entries 37a, 37b,* Correspondences of Mercury); then, holding the image in your awareness, powerfully vibrate the chosen divine name of the Sphere to charge and vitalize it—

   ELOHIM TZABAOTH | **AZOTH** | **ALETHES LOGOS**

8. Standing before this "Presence," breathing evenly and deeply, allow yourself to feel the awakened current of divine energy and to be inwardly uplifted in joyful and reverent response thereto.

9. When you are so moved, make salutation with your right hand;

then open your eyes, ceasing to hold the image in your awareness, and re-center your consciousness in your material environment.

10. Sound the battery: 1
11. Finally, proclaim:

> Salutation and thanks be unto thee, O thou Sovereign Genius of Lamprotesis, who dost now uphold me in the light of thy blessing, and who dost receive all my works of this day into the harmony of thy power.

12. Sound the Battery: 3–5–3.

RITE OF ATTUNEMENT FOR THURSDAY

Temporal Mode: 3
Planetary Time: Day and Hour of Jupiter
Position of Bomos: Center of Place of Working
Lights: 1 Blue Light upon the Bomos (initially unlighted)
Other Requirements: A lighting taper upon the Bomos

1. Standing just West of center, facing East across the Bomos, perform the Rite of Preparation.
2. Sound the battery: 4.
3. Now proclaim:

> On this Day of Jupiter I, true Priest of the Temple of Tzedeq and Servitor of the Sacred Flame of the Sixth Heaven, seek attunement with the spiritual power of Loving-kindness.
> Wherefore I pass from darkness into the light of this mystery by intonation of the Sacred Vowel of the Cosmic harmony.

Immediately following the proclamation, vibrate, or chant according to its specified tone, the vowel of the Sphere—
ϒ (pronounced as German ü)

4. Kindle the taper, then proceed to the East side of the Bomos and face East. With the lighted taper, trace in the air before you the Presigillum of the planet. Then turn to face West and light the blue lamp upon the Bomos. Resume your place at the West side of the Bomos, facing East, and extinguish the taper.
5. *If you desire, now activate incense.*
6. Now make invocation as follows:

> O most mighty

EL | **ZARAIETOS** | **PANTOKRATOR**

thou who dost direct the illimitable powers of the heavens, thou who out of the frenzy of the elements bringest sustenance for the earth! O thou most magnificent: the lightnings are thine to impel, and to do thy bidding thou dost summon a multitude more swift, more refulgent, more vital than thy lightnings. The minds of humankind, contemplating thy majestic splendor, are illuminated and empowered with the freedom of new visions: at thy hands thy children receive wondrous gifts. Royal arbiter of justice, paternal lavisher of mercy, by thine ancient titles—Father of the Heavens, best and greatest—do I invoke thee.

7. Having completed the invocation, close your eyes. Visualize before you the Magical Image of "The Priest King" (*Entry 37*, Correspondences of Jupiter); then, holding the image in your awareness, powerfully vibrate the chosen divine name of the Sphere to charge and vitalize it—

   EL | ZARAIETOS | PANTOKRATOR

8. Standing before this "Presence," breathing evenly and deeply, allow yourself to feel the awakened current of divine energy and to be inwardly uplifted in joyful and reverent response thereto.

9. When you are so moved, make salutation with your right hand; then open your eyes, ceasing to hold the image in your awareness, and re-center your consciousness in your material environment.

10. Sound the battery: 1.

11. Finally, proclaim:

    Salutation and thanks be unto thee, O thou Sovereign Genius of Doxa, who dost now uphold me in the light of thy blessing, and who dost receive all my works of this day into the harmony of thy power.

12. Sound the battery: 3–5–3.

RITE OF ATTUNEMENT FOR FRIDAY

Temporal Mode: 3
Planetary Time: Day and Hour of Venus
Position of Bomos: Center of Place of Working
Lights: 1 Green Light upon the Bomos (initially unlighted)
Other Requirements: A lighting taper upon the Bomos

1. Standing just West of center, facing East across the Bomos, perform the Rite of Preparation.

2. Sound the battery: 7.

3. Now proclaim:

On this day of Venus I, true Priest of the Temple of Nogah and Servitor of the Sacred Flame of the Third Heaven, seek attunement with the spiritual power of Victory.

Wherefore I pass from darkness into the light of this mystery by intonation of the Sacred Vowel of the Cosmic harmony.

Immediately following the proclamation, vibrate, or chant according to its specified time, the vowel of the Sphere—

H (pronounced as "a" in *care*)

4. Kindle the taper, then proceed to the East side of the Bomos and face East. With the lighted taper, trace in the air before you the Presigillum of the planet. Then turn to face West and light the green lamp upon the Bomos. Resume your place at the West side of the Bomos, facing East, and extinguish the taper.

5. *If you desire, now activate incense.*

6. Now make invocation as follows:

O most mighty

YHVH TZABAOTH | ALBAPHALANA | CHARIS

thou beauteous, thou golden, who dost awaken the heart with inward song. Of thy giving is the love which draws us to all loveliness, whether of spirit, soul or earthly frame. Thine is the deep unity which binds all that is, the bond that lovers need no wisdom but love to discern, uniting them in the universal joyousness of thy presence. Most wonderful thou art, and wonderful are those celestial ones who, excelling in strength and beauty, show forth through the worlds thy victorious power alike with thy compassion. Thou art ruler and bestower of the gifts of Fortune. To thee who movest all the forces of life, who dost decree all concord and fruitful interplay of force and force, I make invocation.

7. Having completed the invocation, close your eyes. Visualize before you the Magical Image of "The Flame of the Sea" (*Entry 37*, Correspondences of Venus); then, holding the image in your awareness, powerfully vibrate the chosen divine name of the Sphere to charge and vitalize it—

YHVH TZABAOTH | ALBAPHALANA | CHARIS

8. Standing before this "Presence," breathing evenly and deeply, allow yourself to feel the awakened current of divine energy and to be inwardly uplifted in joyful and reverent response thereto.

9. When you are so moved, make salutation with your right hand; then open your eyes, ceasing to hold the image in your awareness,

and re-center your consciousness in your material environment.

10. Sound the Battery: 1.

11. Finally, proclaim:

> Salutation and thanks be unto thee, O thou Sovereign Genius of Niké, who dost now uphold me in the light of thy blessing, and who dost receive all my works of this day into the harmony of thy power.

12. Sound the battery: 3–5–3.

RITE OF ATTUNEMENT FOR SATURDAY

Temporal Mode: 3
Planetary Time: Day and Hour of Saturn
Position of Bomos: Center of Place of Working
Lights: 1 Indigo (or Black) Light upon the Bomos (initially unlighted)
Other Requirements: A lighting taper upon the Bomos

1. Standing just West of Center, facing East across the Bomos, perform the Rite of Preparation.

2. Sound the battery: 3.

3. Now proclaim:

> On this Day of Saturn I, true Priest of the Temple of Shabbathai and Servitor of the Sacred Flame of the Seventh Heaven, seek attunement with the spiritual power of Understanding.
>
> Wherefore I pass from darkness into the light of this mystery by intonation of the Sacred Vowel of the Cosmic Harmony.

Immediately following the proclamation, vibrate, or chant according to its specified tone, the vowel of the Sphere—

Ω (pronounced as "o" in *only*)

4. Kindle the taper, then proceed to the East side of the Bomos and face East. With the lighted taper, trace in the air before you the presigillum of the planet. Then turn to face West and light the indigo lamp upon the Bomos. Resume your place at the West side of the Bomos, facing East, and extinguish the taper.

5. *If you desire, now activate incense.*

6. Make invocation as follows:

> O most mighty
>
> **YHVH ELOHIM | IALDABAOTH | AIONOS KYRIOS**
>
> thou most revered, thou awesome in exaltation!—thou who yet art known, praised and loved in the worlds of life! Those who make and

create, they know thee when they hearken inwardly to the voice of inspiration. Children and sages are drawn to thee, and in candor of spirit they praise thee: to them time is not an enemy nor eternity a stranger. But they of the Mysteries love thee, and spiritual beings immense in power give thee all their allegiance; for to these it belongs to raise their gaze above the many-jeweled border of thy vesture and to behold the inaccessible glory of thy countenance. O dark one, O silent one, with this love and devotion do I invoke thee!

7. Having completed the invocation, close your eyes. Visualize before you the Magical Image of "The Ancient" (*Entry 37b*, Correspondences of Saturn). Then, holding the image in your awareness, powerfully vibrate the chosen divine name of the Sphere to charge and vitalize it—

   YHVH ELOHIM | **IALDABAOTH** | **AIONOS KYRIOS**

8. Standing before this "Presence," breathing evenly and deeply, allow yourself to feel the awakened current of divine energy and to be inwardly uplifted in joyful and reverent response thereto.

9. When you are so moved, make salutation with your right hand; then open your eyes, ceasing to hold the image in your awareness, and re-center your consciousness in your material environment.

10. Sound the battery: 1.

11. Finally, proclaim:

    Salutation and thanks be unto thee, O thou Sovereign Genius of Sophia, who dost now uphold me in the light of thy blessing, and who dost receive all my works of this day into the harmony of thy power.

12. Sound the battery: 3–5–3.

The above Rites of Attunement are intended for general Qabalistic use. However, some students may have a love for the deities of a specific pantheon, and may therefore desire to make their daily attunement with the appropriate deity of that pantheon.

To illustrate how this can be done, we give below a series of Rites of Attunement dedicated to the Gods of Ancient Egypt.* Following this, you will find an outline formula for the Rites of Attunement which you can use, in conjunction with the Tables of Correspondences, for constructing futher works of this type.

---

* See *Entry 65*, Tables of Correspondences.

SUNDAY: ATTUNEMENT WITH RA

Temporal Mode: 3
Planetary Time: Day and Hour of the Sun
Position of Bomos: Center of Place of Working
Lights: 1 Yellow Light upon the Bomos (initially unlighted)
Other Requirements: A lighting taper upon the Bomos

1. Standing just West of center, facing East across the Bomos, perform the Rite of Preparation.
2. Sound the battery: 6.
3. Now proclaim:

> Let your faces be towards me, O Shining Ones of the Company of Gods in celestial Heq-At: for I, even I, am the First Servant of the Great One of Annu.
>> Isis is behind me
>>> her wings protect me:
>> Horus her son is before me
>>> in the mystery of silence:
>> Nephthys
>>> is my diadem of light
>> And the serpent of power is upraised
>>> upon my brow.
> Wherefore let your faces be towards me, O Shining Ones, as now established in right and truth I seek attunement with the Divine Flame of Beauty.

Immediately following the proclamation, vibrate, or chant according to its specified tone, the vowel of the Sphere—

> I (pronounced as "ee" in *meet*)

4. Kindle the taper, then proceed to the East side of the Bomos and face East. With the lighted taper, trace in the air before you the Presigillum of the planet. Then turn to face West and light the yellow lamp upon the Bomos. Resume your place at the West side of the Bomos, facing East, and extinguish the taper.
5. *If you desire, now activate incense.*
6. Make invocation, as follows:

> O mighty Ra, Lord of Light: hail to thee! O Winged Splendor, radiant in thy appearing: hail to thee! O Ancient One who breathest forth life: hail to thee! O Creator whose power is divine love: Hail to thee! O Beautiful God, O Father of the Gods, O King of Heaven who art all truth: hail to

thee! O Lord of Bright Beams who art enthroned upon the heavens, thou to whom the unbounded winds bring gladness, thou whose glory the unsetting stars extol: hail to thee! Thou Disk, thou torch of mighty flame which manifests the invisible: hail to thee! Thou hawk-headed Governor of the World, thou Lord of the City of the Sun, dwelling place of the Phoenix, thou Prince of Eternity going forth triumphant in thy sacred boat: I adore thee and thee I invoke!

7. Having completed the invocation, close your eyes. Visualize before you the form of the God; then, holding the divine form in your awareness, powerfully vibrate the God's name—

RA

8. Standing before this "Presence," breathing evenly and deeply, allow yourself to feel the awakened current of divine energy and to be inwardly uplifted in joyful and reverent response thereto.

9. When you are so moved, make salutation with your right hand; then open your eyes, ceasing to hold the godform in your awareness, and re-center your consciousness in your material environment.

10. Sound the battery: 1.

11. Finally, proclaim:

Salutation and thanks be unto thee, O thou Great One of Annu, who dost now uphold me in the light of thy blessing, and who dost receive all my works of this day into the harmony of thy power.

12. Sound the battery: 3–5–3.

MONDAY: ATTUNEMENT WITH KHONSU NEFER-HOTEP

Temporal Mode: 3
Planetary Time: Day and Hour of the Moon
Position of Bomos: Center of Place of Working
Lights: 1 Violet Light upon the Bomos (initially unlighted)
Other Requirements: A lighting taper upon the Bomos

1. Standing just West of center, facing East across the Bomos, perform the Rite of Preparation.

2. Sound the battery: 9.

3. Now proclaim:

Let your faces be towards me, O Shining Ones of the Company of Gods in celestial Ouast: for I, even I, am the First Servant of the Great One of No-Amon.

> Isis is behind me
>> her wings protect me:
> Horus her son is before me
>> in the mystery of silence:
> Nephthys
>> is my diadem of light
> And the serpent of power is upraised
>> upon my brow.
> Wherefore let your faces be towards me, O Shining Ones, as now established in right and truth I seek attunement with the Divine Flame of the Foundation.

Immediately following the proclamation, vibrate, or chant according to its specified tone, the vowel of the Sphere—

A (pronounced as "a" *father*)

4. Kindle the taper, then proceed to the East side of the Bomos and face East. With the lighted taper, trace in the air before you the Presigillum of the planet. Then turn to face West and light the violet lamp upon the Bomos. Resume your place at the West side of the Bomos, facing East, and extinguish the taper.

5. *If you desire, now activate incense.*

6. Make invocation, as follows:

> O mighty Khonsu, thou exceeding in might: hail to thee! O thou swiftly moving one who art the Establisher of Times; hail to thee! O thou Royal Child, thou Prince of Gladness who dost stir the womb: hail to thee! O thou beautiful in thy fullness, thou Lord of Vital Fruition: hail to thee! O Virile Bull, Fountain of Fertility: hail to thee! O thou who art the Restorer of Truth, thou Healer and Exorcist of ancient power: hail to thee! O thou Wonderworker, thou Dispeller of Evil, thou enthroned Countenance of Light: I adore thee and thee I invoke!

7. Having completed the invocation, close your eyes. Visualize before you the form of the God; then, holding the divine form in your awareness, powerfully vibrate the God's name—

KHONSU NEFER-HOTEP

8. Standing before this "Presence," breathing evenly and deeply, allow yourself to feel the awakened current of divine energy and to be inwardly uplifted in joyful and reverent response thereto.

9. When you are so moved, make salutation with your right hand; then open your eyes, ceasing to hold the godform in your awareness, and re-center your consciousness in your material environment.

10. Sound the battery: 1.
11. Finally, proclaim:
> Salutation and thanks be unto thee, O thou Great One of No-Amon, who dost now uphold me in the light of thy blessing, and who dost receive all my works of this day into the harmony of thy power.
12. Sound the battery: 3–5–3.

TUESDAY: ATTUNEMENT WITH HORUS

Temporal Mode: 3
Planetary Time: Day and Hour of Mars
Position of Bomos: Center of Place of Working
Lights: 1 Red Light upon the Bomos (initially unlighted)
Other Requirements: A lighting taper upon the Bomos
1. Standing just West of center, facing East across the Bomos, perform the Rite of Preparation.
2. Sound the battery: 5.
3. Now proclaim:
> Let your faces be towards me, O Shining Ones of the company of Gods in celestial Tes-Hertu: for I, even I, am the First Servant of the Great One of Teb.
>> Isis is behind me
>>> her wings protect me:
>> Horus her son* is before me
>>> in the mystery of silence:
>> Nephthys
>>> is my diadem of light
>> And the serpent of power is upraised
>>> upon my brow.
> Wherefore let your faces be towards me, O Shining Ones, as now established in right and truth I seek attunement with the Divine Flame of Strength.

Immediately following the proclamation, vibrate or chant according to its specified tone, the vowel of the Sphere—
O   (pronounced as "o" in hot).

---

* The Egyptian Pantheon included a great number of Horus gods, of major and minor stature. Although throughout the long growth and development of Egyptian religion the functions and characters of these deities were at various periods reassessed, the great Horus gods retained their individual identities and attributes. Thus Horus son of Isis, who is essentially solar and who became in popular imagination the type of all the Horus gods, is to be distinguished from the mighty and martial Horus of Edfu who is the subject of this present invocation.

4. Kindle the taper, then proceed to the East side of the Bomos and face East. With the lighted taper, trace in the air before you the Presigillum of the planet. Then turn to face West and light the red lamp upon the Bomos. Resume your place at the West side of the Bomos, facing East, and extinguish the taper.

5. *If you desire, now activate incense.*

6. Make invocation, as follows:

   O mighty Horus, O Purifying Light: hail to thee! O Son of the Sun, inexorable guardian: hail to thee! O Hawk upon thy Column who dost restrain the Serpent: hail to thee! O Great One furious in the combat, O Victorious One of devouring splendor, O Winged Disk whose uraei flame forth terror: hail to thee! thrice crowned Lion of threefold dominion, thou Flame of Retribution ever advancing, thou who smitest fire from the anvil of the world: hail to thee! O thou Glorious in Battle who dost enchain the forces of darkness: I adore thee and thee I invoke.

7. Having completed the invocation, close your eyes. Visualize before you the form of the God; then, holding the divine form in your awareness, powerfully vibrate the God's name—

   HERU-BEHUTET

8. Standing before this "Presence," breathing evenly and deeply, allow yourself to feel the awakened current of divine energy and to be inwardly uplifted in joyful and reverent response thereto.

9. When you are so moved, make salutation with your right hand; then open your eyes, ceasing to hold the godform in your awareness, and re-center your consciousness in your material environment.

10. Sound the battery: 1.

11. Finally, proclaim:

    Salutation and thanks be unto thee, O thou Great One of Teb, who dost now uphold me in the light of thy blessing, and who dost receive all my works of this day into the harmony of thy power.

12. Sound the battery: 3–5–3.

WEDNESDAY: ATTUNEMENT WITH THOTH

Temporal Mode: 3
Planetary Time: Day and Hour of Mercury
Position of Bomos: Center of Place of Working

Lights: 1 Orange Light upon the Bomos (initially unlighted)
Other Requirements: A lighting taper upon the Bomos

1. Standing just West of center, facing East across the Bomos, perform the Rite of Preparation.
2. Sound the battery: 8.
3. Now proclaim:

> Let your faces be towards me, O Shining Ones of the Company of Gods in celestial Un: for I, even I, am the First Servant of the Great One of Khemennu.
>
> Isis is behind me
> > her wings protect me:
> Horus her son is before me
> > in the mystery of silence:
> Nephthys
> > is my diadem of light
> And the serpent of power is upraised
> > upon my brow.
>
> Wherefore let your faces be towards me, O Shining Ones, as now established in right and truth I seek attunement with the Divine Flame of Splendor.

Immediately following the proclamation, vibrate, or chant according to its specified tone, the vowel of the Sphere—

> E (pronounced as "e" in *set*)

4. Kindle the taper, then proceed to the East side of the Bomos and face East. With the lighted taper, trace in the air before you the Presigillum of the planet. Then turn to face West and light the orange lamp upon the Bomos. Resume your place at the West side of the Bomos, facing East, and extinguish the taper.
5. *If you desire, now activate incense.*
6. Make invocation, as follows:

> O mighty Tahuti, Thou Alone and Maker of Thyself: hail to thee! O Thrice Greatest God, thou Master of Knowledge, thou Divine Scribe whose words ever live: hail to thee! O Glowing Heart of Ra: hail to thee! O thou Arbiter of Night and Day, thou who dost divide and balance time and time: hail to thee! O thou Ibis of Power who art mighty in magick: hail to thee! O thou persuasive one who art the Divine Peacemaker and the Witness of Equilibrium: hail to thee! O thou who dost number the stars, thou who knowest the boundaries of the world: I adore thee and thee I invoke!

7. Having completed the invocation, close your eyes. Visualize before you the form of the God; then, holding the divine form in your awareness, powerfully vibrate the God's name—

    TAHUTI

8. Standing before this "Presence," breathing evenly and deeply, allow yourself to feel the awakened current of divine energy and to be inwardly uplifted in joyful and reverent response thereto.

9. When you are so moved, make salutation with your right hand; then open your eyes, ceasing to hold the godform in your awareness, and re-center your consciousness in your material environment.

10. Sound the battery: 1.

11. Finally, proclaim:

    Salutation and thanks be unto thee, O thou Great One of Khemennu, who dost now uphold me in the light of thy blessing, and who dost receive all my works of this day into the harmony of thy power.

12. Sound the battery: 3–5–3.

THURSDAY: ATTUNEMENT WITH AMUN-RA

Temporal Mode: 3
Planetary Time: Day and Hour of Jupiter
Position of Bomos: Center of Place of Working
Lights: 1 Blue Light upon the Bomos (initially unlighted)
Other Requirements: A lighting taper upon the Bomos

1. Standing just West of center, facing East across the Bomos, perform the Rite of Preparation.

2. Sound the battery: 4.

3. Now proclaim:

    Let your faces be towards me, O Shining Ones of the Company of Gods in celestial Ouast: for I, even I, am the First Servant of the Great One of Ouast.

    Isis is behind me
    	her wings protect me:
    Horus her son is before me
    	in the mystery of silence:
    Nephthys
    	is my diadem of light
    And the serpent of power is upraised
    		upon my brow.

> Wherefore let your faces be towards me, O Shining Ones, as now established in right and truth I seek attunement with the Divine Flame of Loving-kindness.

Immediately following the proclamation, vibrate, or chant according to its specified tone, the vowel of the Sphere—

ϒ (pronounced as German ü)

4. Kindle the taper, then proceed to the East side of the Bomos and face East. With the lighted taper, trace in the air before you the Presigillum of the planet. Then turn to face West and light the blue lamp upon the Bomos. Resume your place at the West side of the Bomos, facing East, and extinguish the taper.

5. *If you desire, now activate incense.*

6. Make invocation as follows:

> O mighty Amun, thou holy God and king of all the Gods, who dost live by right and by truth: hail to thee! O Lord of Infinite Space, thou who upholdest the marvelous universe by thy primal might: hail to thee! O Hidden One: hail to thee! O Creator of all that is and of all that yet shall be: hail to thee! O Glorious Flame, O Incomparable Light of the World: hail to thee! O thou Lord of the double Plumes, whose heart is rejoiced by adoration: hail to thee! O Inviolate Essence, ever concealed amid thy manifestations: hail to thee! O Beloved who dost come in the plenitude of thy power: I adore thee and thee I invoke!

6. Having completed the invocation, close your eyes. Visualize before you the form of the God; then, holding the divine form in your awareness, powerfully vibrate the God's name—

AMUN-RA

8. Standing before this "Presence," breathing evenly and deeply, allow yourself to feel the awakened current of divine energy and to be inwardly uplifted in joyful and reverent response thereto.

9. When you are so moved, make salutation with your right hand; then open your eyes, ceasing to hold the godform in your awareness, and re-center your consciousness in your material environment.

10. Sound the battery: 1.

11. Finally, proclaim:

> Salutation and thanks be unto thee, O thou Great One of Ouast, who dost now uphold me in the light of thy blessing, and who dost receive all my works of this day into the harmony of thy power.

12. Sound the battery: 3–5–3.

FRIDAY: ATTUNEMENT WITH HAT'HOR

Temporal Mode: 3
Planetary Time: Day and Hour of Venus
Position of Bomos: Center of Place of Working
Lights: 1 Green Light upon the Bomos (initially unlighted)
Other Requirements: A lighting taper upon the Bomos

1. Standing just West of center, facing East across the Bomos, perform the Rite of Preparation.
2. Sound the battery: 7.
3. Now proclaim:

> Let your faces be towards me, O Shining Ones of the Company of Gods in Celestial Aah-Ta: for I, even I, am the First Servant of the Great One of Ta-En-Tarerut.
>
> Isis is behind me
> > her wings protect me:
>
> Horus her son is before me
> > in the mystery of silence:
>
> Nephthys
> > is my diadem of light
>
> And the serpent of power is upraised
> > upon my brow.
>
> Wherefore let your faces be towards me, O Shining Ones, as now established in right and truth I seek attunement with the Divine Flame of Victory.

Immediately following the proclamation, vibrate, or chant according to its specified tone, the vowel of the Sphere—

> H   (pronounced as "a" in *care*)

4. Kindle the taper, then proceed to the East side of the Bomos and face East. With the lighted taper, trace in the air before you the Presigillum of the planet. Then turn to face West and light the green lamp upon the Bomos. Resume your place at the West side of the Bomos, facing East, and extinguish the taper.
5. *If you desire, now activate incense.*
6. Make invocation, as follows:

> O mighty Hat'hor, Mother of Light, Mother of Life: hail to thee! O House of Heaven, thou who are adorned with the Stars: hail to thee! O Graceful Power, Beauteous Bringer of Joy: hail to thee! Thou Golden One, thou who art bearer of the Sistrum, lotus-crowned Mistress of

Gladness: hail to thee! O Maker of Festival, Inspiration of Delight: hail to thee! O Throne of peace: hail to thee! O Lady of the Sycamore of the South, O Divine goodness, O Milk of Life: I adore thee and thee I invoke!

7. Having completed the invocation, close your eyes. Visualize before you the form of the Goddess; then, holding the divine form in awareness, powerfully vibrate the Goddess' name—

    HAT-HERUT

8. Standing before this "Presence," breathing evenly and deeply, allow yourself to feel the awakened current of divine energy and to be inwardly uplifted in joyful and reverent response thereto.

9. When you are so moved, make salutation with your right hand; then open your eyes, ceasing to hold the godform in your awareness, and re-center your consciousness in your material environment.

10. Sound the battery: 1.

11. Finally, proclaim:

    Salutation and thanks be unto thee, O thou Great One of Ta-En-Tarerut, who dost now uphold me in the light of thy blessing, and who dost receive all my works of this day into the harmony of thy power.

12. Sound the battery: 3–5–3.

SATURDAY: ATTUNEMENT WITH NEITH

Temporal Mode: 3
Planetary Time: Day and Hour of Saturn
Position of Bomos: Center of Place of Working
Lights: 1 Indigo (or Black) Light upon the Bomos (initially unlighted)
Other Requirements: A lighting taper upon the Bomos

1. Standing just West of center, facing East across the Bomos, perform the Rite of Preparation.

2. Sound the battery: 2

3. Now proclaim:

    Let your faces be towards me, O Shining ones of the Company of Gods in celestial Sap-Meh: for I, even I, am the First Servant of the Great One of Saut.

    Isis is behind me
        her wings protect me:
    Horus her son is before me

in the mystery of silence:
Nephthys
is my diadem of light
And the serpent of power is upraised
upon my brow.
Wherefore let your faces be towards me, O Shining Ones, as now
established in right and truth I seek attunement with the Divine
Flame of Understanding.

Immediately following the proclamation, vibrate, or chant according
to its specified tone, the vowel of the sphere—

Ω (pronounced as "o" in *only*)

4. Kindle the taper, then proceed to the East side of the Bomos and
   face East. With the lighted taper, trace in the air before
   you the Presigillum of the planet. Then turn to face
   West and light the indigo lamp upon the Bomos. Resume
   your place at the West side of the Bomos, facing East,
   and extinguish the taper.
5. *If you desire, now activate incense.*
6. Make invocation, as follows:

   O mighty Neith, O Mystery!—who art all that has been, that is and that
   shall be: hail to thee! Everlasting Goddess, self-existent and ever concealed: hail to thee! O self born, O Lady of the Heavens and Mother of
   the Gods: hail to thee! O Powerful Mother, O Mother-Father, thou
   Opener of the Paths who dost weave the veil of life: hail to thee! O thou
   who art mistress of the spindle and the loom, thou Lady of Sais who
   dost tie the magical knots of protection: I adore thee and thee I
   invoke!
7. Having completed the invocation, close your eyes. Visualize
   before you the form of the Goddess; then, holding the divine
   form in awareness, powerfully vibrate the Goddess' name—

   NET
8. Standing before this "Presence," breathing evenly and deeply,
   allow yourself to feel the awakened current of divine energy and
   to be inwardly uplifted in joyful and reverent response thereto.
9. When you are so moved, make salutation with your right hand;
   then open your eyes, ceasing to hold the godform in your
   awareness, and re-center your consciousness in your material
   environment.
10. Sound the battery: 1
11. Finally, proclaim:

Salutation and thanks be unto thee, O thou Great One of Saut, who dost now uphold me in the light of thy blessing, and who dost receive all my works of his day into the harmony of thy power.

12. Sound the battery: 3–5–3.

OUTLINE FORMULA FOR RITES OF ATTUNEMENT

1. Perform the Rite of Preparation.
2. Sound the battery of the Sphere.
3. (a) In terms appropriate to the chosen pantheon, proclaim yourself as magician, priest or prophet of the Sphere of operation, and/or as minister or devotee of the deity of the working; stating also that you seek attunement with the spiritual principle of the Sphere.
   (b) Utter the sacred vowel of the Sphere to stir the astral ambience and to condition it with the planetary vibration.
4. Trace the presigillum with flame, to further charge the ambience, then light the planetary lamp.
5. If you desire, now activate incense.
6. Make salutation and invocation of the deity—employing epithets, extolling the nature of the god, recounting the god's deeds—as you prefer.
7. Now prepare the channel for the power of the god:
   (a) Visualize before you the form of the god.
   (b) Holding the form in awareness, vibrate the name of the god.
8. Symbol and reality have, at this stage, fused into dynamic unity. Therefore, standing before this "Presence," breathing evenly and deeply, allow yourself to feel the awakened current of divine energy and to be inwardly uplifted in joyful and reverent response thereto.
9. Salute the god, then re-center your consciousness in your material environment.
10. Sound the battery once, to assist the process of objective re-centering.
11. Now give thanks to the deity, and proclaim the attained objective of the rite.
12. Conclude with the battery: 3–5–3.

6 *ASCENT AND VISION IN THE SPHERES*

These rites are for group use, and from the outset may be selected at need or will.

Combining within their compass both ceremonial and meditative techniques, they provide a method of visionary exploration of the seven planetary modalities: a method which is, by its very nature, capable of yielding an unlimited richness and variety of experience. In Section 9 of each rite, the direction is given for each participant to perform, in turn, the Planetary Gesture (*Entry 36*, Tables of Correspondences). This procedure, when accomplished smoothly, has the quality of magical dance; an effect which may be heightened by the playing of suitable music throughout Section 9.

However, the main consideration in Section 9 is the vital expression of the spirit and feeling of the planetary force; reproduction of the Gestures in their formal exactness as given in the Tables of Correspondences is not essential to the working. The Gestures can be very much simplified or even altered, provided only that suitability to the planetary force is maintained; while in a group which has mastered the significance and spirit of the Gestures of each Sphere, participants may in this section express the planetary characteristics by entirely spontaneous movements.

The essential planetary characteristics to be preserved in modified or in spontaneous Gestures are as follows:

Saturn—slow, deliberate, stately, with limited movement.

Jupiter—dignified, with movements carefully judged but grand and sweeping in effect.

Mars—forceful, simple, swinging, perhaps noisy (as of a stamping foot).

Sun—steady in rhythm and exact in course, going smoothly forwards.

Venus—graceful, unhurried, perhaps languorous, or employing calisthenic movements.

Mercury—rapid, light movements, with an abundance of quick, expressive gesture.

Moon—gentle swaying movement, with fanciful postures suggesting the movement of the Moon, or the play of inner fantasies.

For these rites an appropriate gemstone of the planet can be worn by all participants upon the brow, at the location of the Third Eye, the point of inner vision. This can be done by placing the stone within a folded headband, which should itself be of the planetary color or white.

ASCENT AND VISION IN LUNA

Temporal Mode: 2
Planetary Time: Hour of the Moon
Position of Bomos: Center of Place of Working
Lights: 1 Violet Light upon the Bomos
Other Requirements: Chairs for participants, around place of working

(At the opening of the rite all participants stand in a circle around the place of working, in front of their chairs; the director stationed at the East.)

1. The director moves to the West side of the Bomos and faces East. She performs the Rite of Preparation.
2. The battery is sounded: 9.
3. The director makes invocation, as follows:
   O lifegiving and potent
   SHADDAI EL CHAI | IAO | AIGLE TRISAGIA
   thou dweller in the secret place of Yesod:
   Let shine upon us in this hour the light of thy countenance, and grant us thy blessing and thine aid in this our undertaking. So shall we, ascending in the chariot of our aspiration, penetrate the coruscating gulfs of flame, the living veils of the astral and celestial firmaments of thy Sphere: to achieve true vision in the Yetziratic Heaven of Tebel Vilun Shamaim, and to experience thy mystery in the Briatic Sanctuary of Garen ha-Saphir.

4. The director resumes her place in the circle. The battery is sounded: 1.
5. The director says:
   Companions in Light, let us awaken the vibration of Levanah in this place and within ourselves.
6. *If desired, incense is now activated.*
7. All now say:
   Grace of the glimmering night, beautiful pale
   camel thou journeyest
   comely with bridle of pearl, cloth of most fair
   silver caparisoned:
   Tracing the trackless abodes, knowing all times,
   knowing the numberless
   Seeds of the firmament!
8. All link hands and vibrate, or chant according to its specified tone, the vowel of the Sphere—
   A   (pronounced as "a" in *father*)
   Hands are unlinked.
9. Beginning with the director and proceeding clockwise around the circle of participants, each in turn steps forward and, facing the Bomos, performs the Planetary Gesture; then resumes his place in the circle.
10. The last participant having resumed his place, all link hands and circumambulate the place of working nine times clockwise; visualizing as they do so, a wall of *violet* light whirling rapidly clockwise about their circle. This done, hands are unlinked and the wall of light is allowed to fade from awareness.
11. The battery is sounded: 1.
12. All now seat themselves, and the director proclaims:
    Let us now seek the deeper mysteries of the Sephirah Yesod, the Ninth Path of the Holy Tree of Life.
13. The battery is sounded: 9.
14. The director utters the following text from the Thirty-two Paths of Wisdom:
    The Ninth Path is called the Pure Intelligence, because it purifies the manifestations of the Sephiroth: it proves and governs the formation of their similitude, and disposes in exact measure the unity which is intrinsic to them, not lessened nor divided.
15. The battery is sounded: 1.
16. The Ascent and Vision in Luna now proceeds, led by the director

who guides the working at a leisurely pace by means of the following text:

*   *   *

Companions in Light, close your eyes and your mind to outer awareness. Breathe evenly and deeply. Let each one of you in this working be aware only of your self, listening to my voice guiding you in your personal experience of Ascent and Vision in this Sphere. As now this rite proceeds, YOU are the individual focal point of this adventure.

*   *   *

You are standing at the center of a vast circular temple, upon a floor of translucent moonstone. Completely encompassing the temple is a slowly swirling wall of bright silver light. The ceiling high above you is a billowing lavender radiance, and represents the veiled portal of Yesod in Yetzirah.

*   *   *

As I invoke the Olympic Guardian of the Sphere to open the portal, give your inner affirmation to my words and accept the invocation as your own.

*   *   *

O LUMINOUS PHUL, SPIRIT OF THE MOON WHO ART MIGHTY IN THE FIRST HEAVEN OF YETZIRAH, AND WHO DOST GUARD THE APPROACHES OF THE NINTH PATH OF THE HOLY TREE OF LIFE: HEAR THE VOICE OF MY POWER AND OPEN UNTO ME THE PORTAL OF THY REALM IN THE DIVINE NAME
SHADDAI EL CHAI | IAO | AIGLE TRISAGIA
THAT I MAY ASCEND WITHOUT HINDRANCE TO THE HEIGHT OF TEBEL VILUN SHAMAIM.

*   *   *

The lavender radiance above you now begins to swirl slowly in a clockwise motion about its center. Gathering momentum, it runs faster and more smoothly, its center opening and lifting away from you so that you are gazing upwards into a receding vortex of lavender radiance.

*   *   *

And now you are aware of a strong attraction drawing you towards the vortex. You are lifted from the floor of the temple, the attracting force acting more and more strongly. Suddenly, you are drawn completely into the vortex. Immediately it flashes into a new vitality, enwrapping you a whirling frenzy of lavender flame, and carrying you swiftly upwards and upwards.

*   *   *

As you continue to ascend, you become aware of the rushing and pulsating sound of the vortex; it is as though the flame itself were uttering the sacred vowel of the Sphere. You catch fragments of other sounds too: the vibrant shimmering clash of high-toned cymbals, with broken fragments of mystic chant uttered by unearthly voices in an unknown tongue.

*   *   *

Now the lavender flame whirling about you seems gradually to decrease in velocity; gradually too you feel the intense speed of your upward movement diminishing. Now you are gliding upwards, in a gently turning lavender fire which is filled with gradations of scintillant brilliance. More slowly yet you ascend, more slowly swirls the light about you. Now, with a feeling of wondering expectancy, you float in a peaceful region of gleaming lavender radiance.

*   *   *

In this light and in this vibrant stillness remain without change until I have made the invocation which is to initiate your vision in Tebel Vilun Shamaim. When the invocation has been made, the light all about you will resolve itself into a scene. Let it unfold and develop in the manner of a waking dream. You may travel therein; or you may remain to witness what befalls. Should you desire greater clarity of vision, make mental utterance of the sacred vowel of the Sphere. Should you be approached by a Being of the Sphere, mentally give it greeting in the divine name of the Sphere; then, if you will, you can accept it as your guide. Seek and explore as you desire, remembering that you have the ability to use astrally all your five senses.

*   *   *

I will now make the invocation. As I speak the words, give your inner affirmation to them and accept the invocation as your own. Then let the light about you dissolve to reveal the wonders of this astral realm.

*   *   *

BEHOLD ME, O BRIGHT ONES OF THE FIRST HEAVEN, YE MINISTERING SPIRITS OF THE NINTH PATH IN YETZIRAH: FOR I AM THE TRUE CHILD OF LEVANAH AND WITHIN ME SHINES AND MOVES THE VITAL FLAME OF THE SAME YOUR GOD, THE LIFEGIVING AND POTENT
SHADDAI EL CHAI | **IAO** | **AIGLE TRISAGIA**
WHEREFORE, DISSOLVE THE ASTRAL ETHERS OF THIS HEIGHT AND REVEAL TO MY INNER PERCEPTION THE WONDERS OF TEBEL VILUN SHAMAIM.

*   *   *

Here the director should allow a space of silence, sufficient for the development of individual inward vision by the participants. She should judge the time according to her feeling as to the progress of the rite, but generally five or ten minutes will be ample. As with sleep, some inner experiences may be curtailed by the closing of the allotted period, but no harm is done: a particiant will continue subsequently in dream any vision which is significant to the deeper self.

*   *   *

Now your vision fades, giving place at first to a nebulous indistinctness which in turn is transformed once more to lavender light. Even the ground on which you stand is assimilated into this light, so that again you are floating in a region of peaceful lavender radiance.

*   *   *

Remain thus as I now make invocation to access the Briatic level of this Sphere. As I utter the words, give you inner affirmation to them and accept the invocation as your own.

*   *   *

O GLORIOUS AND MIGHTY
GABRIEL | THEONOEMENOS | ANAKTOR
THOU CELESTIAL INTELLIGENCE WHO DOST RULE IN THE FIRST MANSION OF BRIAH AND WHO ART PRINCE AND COMMANDER OF THE SPIRITS OF THE MOON: BEHOLD ME, AND IN THE NAME OF THE SAME YOUR GOD, WHOM I ALSO WORSHIP, EVEN THE LIFEGIVING AND POTENT
SHADDAI EL CHAI | IAO | AIGLE TRISAGIA
GRANT ME TO ENTER INTO THY REALM AND TO BE ESTABLISHED IN GAREN HA-SAPHIR.

*   *   *

Now at once, for as far as you can see, the radiance in which you float is suffused with bright violet light, which swirls and sparkles, fluctuating and diversified all about you. The swirling and fluctuation slowly diminish; the new and all-pervasive light in which you are floating becomes steadied to an unvarying radiance of pure and intensely clear violet.

*   *   *

In the profound stillness and peace of this region of violet light The Lady of Night, the magical image of Yesod, manifests shiningly before you:
A tall, slender female figure of austere beauty stands erect, her bare feet upon the rock of a mountain summit. It is night time, and the large

disc of the Full Moon, rising behind her, frames her head and shoulders. Upon her head is a diadem of glittering stones, which flash continually with every hue. From beneath this diadem her dark hair flows down over her bare shoulders, for, save for a lunula—a crescent-shaped necklet—she is unclothed to the waist. Around her waist is a girdle, clasped in front with a shining buckle whose shape suggests the moon-disc between left-facing and right-facing crescents: and from this girdle a skirt of filmy whiteness descends in deep folds to her ankles. In its wide embroidered border, spiral grows out of spiral in such a way that each spiral is like a circular maze, but their progression is like the waves of the sea. The arms of the figure are extended forwards, both palms facing forwards in a gesture of giving. Around each arm from shoulder to wrist is entwined a serpent, dark in color, its head extended before her palm. These serpents are full of life and power, for they represent the mighty astral forces which she controls and directs.

*   *   *

Keeping awareness of the shining form of the Lady of Night, listen to the invocation which I shall now make, and accept its words as your own.

*   *   *

O LADY OF NIGHT WHO ABIDEST IN BRIAH, THOU MANTLE OF THE DIVINE SPIRIT OF YESOD, WHO DOST IMPART THE SACRED ENERGIES OF THE FOUNDATION TO THE LOWER WORLDS: THROUGH THEE I SEEK PLENITUDE OF BLESSING AND TRUE EXPERIENCE OF THE MYSTERY OF GAREN HA-SAPHIR. WHERE-FORE I SALUTE THEE BY THE TREMENDOUS MOST EXCELLENT NAME WHICH IS THE LIGHT OF THY LIFE:

SHADDAI EL CHAI | **IAO** | **AIGLE TRISAGIA**

*   *   *

Now the figure of the Lady of Night which stands before you is aureoled with a red-purple radiance. Rapidly this radiance extends: the figure glows with it, and bright beams of the same red-purple light dart piercingly towards you, becoming continually more brilliant. You are aware of a swift access of gladness in the influence of the powerful beams. In glorious effulgent waves, more and more of the red-purple radiance is given forth from the luminous figure. The radiance spreads, then explodes flashingly to fill the whole region. You see nothing in any direction but the red-purple light itself. You feel transformed, ecstatic, while there reverberates in your ears, clear and ringing, the sacred vowel of the Sphere. In a world of red-purple radiance you float alone and motionless, exultant and blissful.

*   *   *

For a time the encompassing radiance in which you float is altogether red-purple: then swirlings of violet appear in it. By degrees the violet light prevails more and more, until you are floating altogether in a region of luminous violet. Now in this violet light appear gleams of lavender. The lavender light spreads all about you, swirling and flashing, until at last you are floating in a region entirely of lavender radiance. Suddenly you are floating no longer in a formless world of light. You are standing at the center of a vast circular temple, upon a floor of translucent moonstone. Completely encompassing the temple is a slowly swirling wall of bright silver light, and the ceiling high above you is a billowing lavender radiance.

*   *   *

As I now speak the valediction, give your inner affirmation to my words and accept them as your own.

*   *   *

O GLORIOUS AND MIGHTY
GABRIEL | **THEONOEMENOS** | **ANAKTOR**
PRAISE AND HONOR BE UNTO THEE FOR THE SPLENDOR OF THINE OFFICE AND THE MAJESTY OF THY BEING. AND WITH YOU, O MINISTERING SPIRITS OF THE NINTH PATH IN YETZIRAH, AS LIKEWISE WITH THEE, O LUMINOUS PHUL, BE THE BLESSING OF THY GOD AND MINE, EVEN THE LIFEGIVING AND POTENT
SHADDAI EL CHAI | **IAO** | **AIGLE TRISAGIA**
AND IN THIS SAME MOST SACRED NAME WHICH IS THE LIGHT OF THY LIFE, I SALUTE THEE, O LADY OF NIGHT: WHO ART VEHICLE AND INSTRUMENT OF THE GOOD, THE BEAUTIFUL, AND THE TRUE.

*   *   *

Now the temple in which you are standing fades from your awareness, and you are surrounded by pale yellow light, flecked with white. This too fades, and you become aware once more of yourself, sitting with closed eyes amid your physical surroundings and the other Companions.

*   *   *

Now open your eyes.

*   *   *

17. The battery is sounded: 1.

18. At this point, if desired, there may be a discussion, led by the director, of the experience of Ascent and Vision. This is optional; and even when it takes place, individual members may desist from it if they wish to reserve their experiences for further meditation. Following discussion, the battery should again be sounded once.

19. All participants stand, and the director proclaims:
     Companions in Light: in unity this rite began, in unity let us bring it to a close.

20. All link hands and perform one clockwise circumambulation of the place of working. Hands are unlinked.

21. The director now utters the thanksgiving:
     Salutation and thanks be unto thee, O lifegiving and potent
     SHADDAI EL CHAI I **IAO** I **AIGLE TRISAGIA**
     for the virtue and inspiration wherewith thou hast endowed us in this operation of Holy Magick in thy Sphere of Yesod.
     All respond:
     Salutation and thanks.
     The director continues:
     And do thou grant to us, Most Mighty, the continuance of thy regard as now we go forth from this place.
     All respond:
     Thus shall it be.

22. The battery is sounded: 3–5–3.

ASCENT AND VISION IN MERCURY

Temporal Mode: 2
Planetary Time: Hour of Mercury
Position of Bomos: Center of Place of Working
Lights: 1 Orange Light upon the Bomos
Other Requirements: Chairs for participants, around place of working

(At the opening of the rite all participants stand in a circle around the place of working, in front of their chairs; the director stationed at the East.)

1. The director moves to the West side of the Bomos and faces East. She performs the Rite of Preparation.
2. The battery is sounded: 8.
3. The director makes invocation, as follows:

O scintillant and light-bedewed
>> **ELOHIM TZABAOTH** | **AZOTH** | **ALETHES LOGOS**
thou dweller in the secret place of Hod:
Let shine upon us in this hour the light of thy countenance, and grant us thy blessing and thine aid in this our undertaking. So shall we, ascending in the chariot of our aspiration, penetrate the coruscating gulfs of flame, the living veils of the astral and celestial firmaments of thy Sphere: to achieve true vision in the Yetziratic Heaven of Reqia'a, and to experience thy mystery in the Briatic Sanctuary of Thushiah.

4. The director resumes her place in the circle. The battery is sounded: 1.

5. The director says:
   Companions in Light, let us awaken the vibration of Kokab in this place and within ourselves.

6. *If desired, incense is now activated.*

7. All now say:
   Bearing thy truth in thy heart, opal-fire sealed
   >> deep and inviolate,
   Over the seven-hued bridge pass to the worlds,
   >> share in their variance.
   Hail to the voice of thy power, speaking all tongues,
   >> many in purposes,
   > One in divinity!

8. All link hands and vibrate, or chant according to its specified tone, the vowel of the Sphere—
   >> E   (pronounced as "e" in *set*)
   Hands are unlinked.

9. Beginning with the director and proceeding clockwise around the circle of participants, each in turn steps forward and, facing the Bomos, performs the Planetary Gesture; then resumes his place in the circle.

10. The last participant having resumed his place, all link hands and circumambulate the place of working eight times clockwise; visualizing as they do so, a wall of *orange* light whirling rapidly clockwise about their circle. This done, hands are unlinked and the wall of light is allowed to fade from awareness.

11. The battery is sounded: 1.

12. All now seat themselves, and the director proclaims:
    Let us now seek the deeper mysteries of the Sephirah Hod, the Eighth Path of the Holy Tree of Life.

13. The battery is sounded: 8.
14. The director utters the following text from the Thirty-two Paths of Wisdom:

> The Eighth Path is called the Absolute or perfect Intelligence, because it is the instrument of the Primordial, which has no root by which it can hold fast or abide save in the hidden regions of Gedulah, Magnificence, which emanate from its own nature.

15. The battery is sounded: 1.
16. The Ascent and Vision in Mercury now proceeds, led by the director who guides the working at a leisurely pace by means of the following text:

*   *   *

> Companions in Light, close your eyes and your mind to outer awareness. Breathe evenly and deeply. Let each one of you in this working be aware only of your self, listening to my voice guiding you in your personal experience of Ascent and Vision in this Sphere. As now this rite proceeds, YOU are the individual focal point of this adventure.

*   *   *

> You are standing at the center of a vast circular temple, upon a floor of carnelian. Completely encompassing the temple is a slowly swirling wall of shimmering opalescence. The ceiling high above you is a billowing pale tawny radiance, and represents the veiled portal of Hod in Yetzirah.

*   *   *

> As I invoke the Olympic Guardian of the Sphere to open the portal, give your inner affirmation to my words and accept the invocation as your own.

*   *   *

> O LUMINOUS OPHIEL, SPIRIT OF MERCURY WHO ART MIGHTY IN THE SECOND HEAVEN OF YETZIRAH, AND WHO DOST GUARD THE APPROACHES OF THE EIGHTH PATH OF THE HOLY TREE OF LIFE: HEAR THE VOICE OF MY POWER AND OPEN UNTO ME THE PORTAL OF THY REALM IN THE DIVINE NAME
>
> **ELOHIM TZABAOTH** | **AZOTH** | **ALETHES LOGOS**
>
> THAT I MAY ASCEND WITHOUT HINDRANCE TO THE HEIGHT OF REQIA'A.

*   *   *

> The pale tawny radiance above you now begins to swirl slowly in a clockwise motion about its center. Gathering momentum, it runs faster

and more smoothly, its center opening and lifting away from you so that you are gazing upwards into a receding vortex of pale, tawny radiance.

*   *   *

And now you are aware of a strong attraction drawing you towards the vortex. You are lifted from the floor of the temple, the attracting force acting more and more strongly. Suddenly, you are drawn completely into the vortex. Immediately it flashes into a new vitality, enwrapping you in a whirling frenzy of tawny flame, and carrying you swiftly upwards and upwards.

*   *   *

As you continue to ascend, you become aware of the rushing and pulsating sound of the vortex; it is as though the flame itself were uttering the sacred vowel of the Sphere. You catch fragments of other sounds too: the thrilling sound of flutes singing and soaring, intermittently plucked away and mingled with the cry of tremendous winds.

*   *   *

Now the tawny flame whirling about you seems gradually to decrease in velocity; gradually too you feel the intense speed of your upward movement diminishing. Now you are gliding upwards, in a gently turning tawny fire which is filled with gradations of scintillant brilliance. More slowly yet you ascend, more slowly swirls the light about you. Now, with a feeling of wondering expectancy, you float in a peaceful region of gleaming tawny radiance.

*   *   *

In this light and in this vibrant stillness remain without change until I have made the invocation which is to initiate your vision in Reqia'a. When the invocation has been made, the light all about you will resolve itself into a scene. Let it unfold and develop in the manner of a waking dream. You may travel therein; or you may remain to witness what befalls. Should you desire greater clarity of vision, make mental utterance of the sacred vowel of the Sphere. Should you be approached by a Being of the Sphere, mentally give it greeting in the divine name of the Sphere; then, if you will, you can accept it as your guide. Seek and explore as you desire, remembering that you have the ability to use astrally all your five senses.

*   *   *

I will now make the invocation. As I speak the words, give your inner affirmation to them and accept the invocation as your own. Then let the light about you dissolve to reveal the wonders of this astral realm.

*   *   *

BEHOLD ME, O BRIGHT ONES OF THE SECOND HEAVEN, YE
MINISTERING SPIRITS OF THE EIGHTH PATH IN YETZIRAH: FOR I
AM THE TRUE CHILD OF KOKAB AND WITHIN ME SHINES AND
MOVES THE VITAL FLAME OF THE SAME YOUR GOD, THE SCIN-
TILLANT AND LIGHT-BEDEWED
     ELOHIM TZABAOTH | **AZOTH** | **ALETHES LOGOS**
WHEREFORE, DISSOLVE THE ASTRAL ETHERS OF THIS HEIGHT
AND REVEAL TO MY INNER PERCEPTION THE WONDERS OF
REQIA'A.

*　　　　　*　　　　　*

*Here the director should allow a space of silence for the development of
inward vision by the participants: it will depend upon her feeling as to the
progress of the rite, five or ten minutes generally being ample.*

*　　　　　*　　　　　*

Now your vision fades, giving place at first to a nebulous indistinctness which in turn is transformed once more to pale tawny light. Even
the ground on which you stand is assimilated into this light, so that
again you are floating in a region of peaceful tawny radiance.

*　　　　　*　　　　　*

Remain thus as I now make invocation to access the Briatic level of
this Sphere. As I utter the words, give your inner affirmation to them
and accept the invocation as your own.

*　　　　　*　　　　　*

O GLORIOUS AND MIGHTY
     MIKAEL | **ANAXEPHYDRIAS** | **STHENOS**
THOU CELESTIAL INTELLIGENCE WHO DOST RULE IN THE
SECOND MANSION OF BRIAH AND WHO ART PRINCE AND
COMMANDER OF THE SPIRITS OF MERCURY: BEHOLD ME, AND
IN THE NAME OF THE SAME YOUR GOD, WHOM I ALSO WORSHIP,
EVEN THE SCINTILLANT AND LIGHT-BEDEWED
     ELOHIM TZABAOTH | **AZOTH** | **ALETHES LOGOS**
GRANT ME TO ENTER INTO THY REALM AND TO BE ESTABLISHED
IN THUSHIAH.

*　　　　　*　　　　　*

Now at once, for as far as you can see, the radiance in which you float is
suffused with bright orange light, which swirls and sparkles, fluctuating and diversified all about you. The swirling and fluctuation slowly
diminish; the new and all-pervasive light in which you are floating
becomes steadied to an unvarying radiance of pure and intensely
clear orange.

*　　　　　*　　　　　*

In the profound stillness and peace of this region of orange light The Divine Messenger, the magical image of Hod, manifests shiningly before you:

A youthful male figure, so delicate as to appear somewhat effeminate, is gliding through the air. His hair is short and dark. He is nude but for the sandals on his feet and a belt about his waist, patterned with alternate octagons and eight-petaled flowers. Springing from his shoulders are great sweeping wings, outspread for flight, with countercharged black and white plumage. His body is inclined forward not more than about 30° from the vertical, in a graceful posture with his right foot lifted slightly more than his left. In his left hand he carries a rolled scroll, with his right hand he extends before him the short staff which is the ancient token of the herald; from its head flutter two white ribbons. This figure seems to be approaching through a tunnel of many-colored light, which because of his swift movement is seen as streaming away in the opposite direction, in long changeful darts and flashes of prismatic radiance. The face of the figure is alert, and communicates something of the high importance of the message which is contained in the scroll.

*   *   *

Keeping awareness of the shining form of the Divine Messenger, listen to the invocation which I shall now make, and accept its words as your own.

*   *   *

O DIVINE MESSENGER WHO ABIDEST IN BRIAH, THOU MANTLE OF THE DIVINE SPIRIT OF HOD, WHO DOST IMPART THE SACRED ENERGIES OF SPLENDOR TO THE LOWER WORLDS: THROUGH THEE I SEEK PLENITUDE OF BLESSING AND TRUE EXPERIENCE OF THE MYSTERY OF THUSHIAH. WHEREFORE I SALUTE THEE BY THE TREMENDOUS MOST EXCELLENT NAME WHICH IS THE LIGHT OF THY LIFE:

ELOHIM TZABAOTH | AZOTH | ALETHES LOGOS

*   *   *

Now the figure of the Divine Messenger before you is aureoled with ochre-yellow radiance. Rapidly this radiance extends: the figure glows with it, and bright beams of the same ochre-yellow light dart piercingly towards you, becoming continually more brilliant. You are aware of a swift access of gladness in the influence of the powerful beams. In glorious effulgent waves, more and more of the ochre-yellow radiance is given forth from the luminous figure. The radiance spreads, then explodes flashingly to fill the whole region. You see nothing in any direction but the ochre-yellow light itself. You feel transformed, ecstatic, while there reverberates in your ears, clear and ringing, the sacred vowel of the Sphere. In a world of ochre-yellow radiance you float alone and motionless, exultant and blissful.

*   *   *

For a time the encompassing radiance in which you float is altogether ochre-yellow: then swirlings of orange appear in it. By degrees the orange light prevails more and more, until you are floating altogether in a region of luminous orange. Now in this orange light appear gleams of pale tawny radiance. The pale tawny light spreads all about you, swirling and flashing, until at last you are floating in a region entirely of tawny radiance. Suddenly you are floating no longer in a formless world of light. You are standing at the center of a vast circular temple, upon a floor of carnelian. Completely encompassing the temple is a slowly swirling wall of shimmering opalescence, and the ceiling high above you is a billowing pale tawny radiance.

*   *   *

As I now speak the valediction, give your inner affirmation to my words and accept them as your own.

*   *   *

O GLORIOUS AND MIGHTY
MIKAEL | ANAXEPHYDRIAS | STHENOS
PRAISE AND HONOR BE UNTO THEE FOR THE SPLENDOR OF THINE OFFICE AND THE MAJESTY OF THY BEING. AND WITH YOU, O MINISTERING SPIRITS OF THE EIGHTH PATH IN YET-ZIRAH, AS LIKEWISE WITH THEE, O LUMINOUS OPHIEL, BE THE BLESSING OF THY GOD AND MINE, EVEN THE SCINTILLANT AND LIGHT-BEDEWED
ELOHIM TZABAOTH | AZOTH | ALETHES LOGOS
AND IN THIS SAME MOST SACRED NAME WHICH IS THE LIGHT OF THY LIFE, I SALUTE THEE, O DIVINE MESSENGER: WHO ART VEHICLE AND INSTRUMENT OF THE GOOD, THE BEAUTIFUL, AND THE TRUE.

*   *   *

Now the temple in which you are standing fades from your awareness, and you are surrounded by yellowish white light, tinged with greenish white. This too fades, and you become aware once more of yourself, sitting with closed eyes amid your physical surroundings and the other Companions.

*   *   *

Now open your eyes.

*　　　　　*　　　　　*

17. The battery is sounded: 1.
18. At this point, if desired, there may be a discussion, led by the director, of the experience of Ascent and Vision. This is optional; and even when it takes place, individual members may desist from it if they wish to reserve their experiences for further meditation. Following discussion, the battery should again be sounded once.
19. All participants stand, and the director proclaims:
   Companions in Light: in unity this rite began, in unity let us bring it to a close.
20. All link hands and perform one clockwise circumambulation of the place of working. Hands are unlinked.
21. The director now utters the thanksgiving:
   Salutation and thanks be unto thee, O scintillant and light-bedewed
   ELOHIM TZABAOTH | **AZOTH** | **ALETHES LOGOS**
   for the virtue and inspiration wherewith thou hast endowed us in this operation of Holy Magick in thy Sphere of Hod.
   All respond:
   Salutation and thanks.
   The director continues:
   And do thou grant to us, Most Mighty, the continuance of thy regard as now we go forth from this place.
   All respond:
   Thus shall it be.
22. The battery is sounded: 3–5–3.

ASCENT AND VISION IN VENUS

Temporal Mode: 2
Planetary Time: Hour of Venus
Position of Bomos: Center of Place of Working
Lights: 1 Green Light upon the Bomos
Other Requirements: Chairs for participants, around place of working

(At the opening of the rite all participants stand in a circle around the place of working, in front of their chairs; the director stationed at the East.)

1. The director moves to the West side of the Bomos and faces East. She performs the Rite of Preparation.
2. The battery is sounded: 7.
3. The director makes invocation, as follows:
   O loving and strong
   YHVH TZABAOTH | **ALBAPHALANA** | **CHARIS**
   thou dweller in the secret place of Netzach:
   Let shine upon us in this hour the light of thy countenance, and grant us thy blessing and thine aid in this our undertaking. So shall we, ascending in the chariot of our aspiration, penetrate the coruscating gulfs of flame, the living veils of the astral and celestial firmaments of thy Sphere: to achieve true vision in the Yetziratic Heaven of Shecheqim, and to experience thy mystery in the Briatic Sanctuary of Otz Shamaim.
4. The director resumes her place in the circle. The battery is sounded: 1.
5. The director says:
   Companions in Light, let us awaken the vibration of Nogah in this place and within ourselves.
6. *If desired, incense is now activated.*
7. All now say:
   Doorway of vision fulfilled, bringer of dreams
                                  forth to adventuring,
   Sacred to thee are the red portals of dawn,
                                  sacred the emerald
   Gates of the jubilant spring, Mother of deeds
                                  manifest, multiform—
                      Mother of destiny!
8. All link hands and vibrate, or chant according to its specified tone, the vowel of the Sphere—
           H   (pronounced as "a" in *care*)
   Hands are unlinked.
9. Beginning with the director and proceeding clockwise around the circle of participants, each in turn steps forward and, facing the Bomos, performs the Planetary Gesture; then resumes his place in the circle.
10. The last participant having resumed his place, all link hands and circumambulate the place of working seven times clockwise; visualizing as they do so, a wall of *green* light whirling rapidly clockwise about their circle. This done, hands are unlinked and

the wall of light is allowed to fade from awareness.

11. The battery is sounded: 1.

12. All now seat themselves, and the director proclaims:

> Let us now seek the deeper mysteries of the Sephirah Netzach, the Seventh Path of the Holy Tree of Life.

13. The battery is sounded: 7.

14. The director utters the following text from the Thirty-two Paths of Wisdom:

> The Seventh Path is the concealed Intelligence, so named because it is the dazzling resplendence of all the qualities of Mind, which are discerned by intellectual vision and by the gaze of faith.

15. The battery is sounded: 1.

16. The Ascent and Vision in Venus now proceeds, led by the director who guides the working at a leisurely pace by means of the following text:

*   *   *

> Companions in Light, close your eyes and your mind to outer awareness. Breathe evenly and deeply. Let each one of you in this working be aware only of your self, listening to my voice guiding you in your personal experience of Ascent and Vision in this Sphere. As now this rite proceeds, YOU are the individual focal point of this adventure.

*   *   *

> You are standing at the center of a vast, circular temple, upon a floor of malachite. Completely encompassing the temple is a slowly swirling wall of saffron light. The ceiling high above you is a billowing, pale turquoise radiance, and represents the veiled portal of Netzach in Yetzirah.

*   *   *

> As I invoke the Olympic Guardian of the Sphere to open the portal, give your inner affirmation to my words and accept the invocation as your own.

*   *   *

> O LUMINOUS HAGITH, SPIRIT OF VENUS WHO ART MIGHTY IN THE THIRD HEAVEN OF YETZIRAH, AND WHO DOST GUARD THE APPROACHES OF THE SEVENTH PATH OF THE HOLY TREE OF LIFE: HEAR THE VOICE OF MY POWER AND OPEN UNTO ME THE PORTAL OF THY REALM IN THE DIVINE NAME
> **YVH TZABAOTH I ALBAPHALANA I CHARIS**
> THAT I MAY ASCEND WITHOUT HINDRANCE TO THE HEIGHT OF SHECHEQIM.

*   *   *

The pale turquoise radiance above you now begins to swirl slowly in a clockwise motion about its center. Gathering momentum, it runs faster and more smoothly, its center opening and lifting away from you so that you are gazing upwards into a receding vortex of pale turquoise radiance.

*   *   *

And now you are aware of a strong attraction drawing you towards the vortex. You are lifted from the floor of the temple, the attracting force acting more and more strongly. Suddenly, you are drawn completely into the vortex. Immediately it flashes into a new vitality, enwrapping you in a whirling frenzy of pale turquoise flame, and carrying you swiftly upwards and upwards.

*   *   *

As you continue to ascend, you become aware of the rushing and pulsating sound of the vortex; it is as though the flame itself were uttering the sacred vowel of the Sphere. You catch fragments of other sounds too: a sweet insistent rippling as of a gently flowing stream, interspersed with voices of birds giving their wild calls and sudden bursts of song.

*   *   *

Now the pale turquoise flame whirling about you seems gradually to decrease in velocity; gradually too you feel the intense speed of your upward movement diminishing. Now you are gliding upwards, in a gently turning pale turquoise fire which is filled with gradations of scintillant brilliance. More slowly yet you ascend, more slowly swirls the light about you. Now, with a feeling of wondering expectancy, you float in a peaceful region of gleaming pale turquoise radiance.

*   *   *

In this light and in this vibrant stillness remain without change until I have made the invocation which is to initiate your vision in Shecheqim. When the invocation has been made, the light all about you will resolve itself into a scene. Let it unfold and develop in the manner of a waking dream. You may travel therein; or you may remain to witness what befalls. Should you desire greater clarity of vision, make mental utterance of the sacred vowel of the Sphere. Should you be approached by a Being of the Sphere, mentally give it greeting in the divine name of the Sphere; then, if you will, you can accept it as your guide. Seek and explore as you desire, remembering that you have the ability to use astrally all your five senses.

*   *   *

I will now make the invocation. As I speak the words, give your inner affirmation to them and accept the invocation as your own. Then let the light about you dissolve to reveal the wonders of this astral realm.

* * *

BEHOLD ME, O BRIGHT ONES OF THE THIRD HEAVEN, YE MINISTERING SPIRITS OF THE SEVENTH PATH IN YETZIRAH: FOR I AM THE TRUE CHILD OF NOGAH AND WITHIN ME SHINES AND MOVES THE VITAL FLAME OF THE SAME YOUR GOD, THE LOVING AND STRONG
YHVH TZABAOTH | **ALBAPHALANA** | **CHARIS**
WHEREFORE, DISSOLVE THE ASTRAL ETHERS OF THIS HEIGHT AND REVEAL TO MY INNER PERCEPTION THE WONDERS OF SHECHEQIM.

* * *

Here the director should allow a space of silence for the development of inward vision by the participants: it will depend upon her feeling as to the progress of the rite, five or ten minutes generally being ample.

* * *

Now your vision fades, giving place at first to a nebulous indistinctness which in turn is transformed once more to pale turquoise light. Even the ground on which you stand is assimilated into this light, so that again you are floating in a region of peaceful pale turquoise radiance.

* * *

Remain thus as I now make invocation to access the Briatic level of this Sphere. As I utter the words, give your inner affirmation to them and accept the invocation as your own.

* * *

O GLORIOUS AND MIGHTY
HANIEL | **ZOTHALMIOS** | **ALALE**
THOU CELESTIAL INTELLIGENCE WHO DOST RULE IN THE THIRD MANSION OF BRIAH AND WHO ART PRINCE AND COMMANDER OF THE SPIRITS OF VENUS: BEHOLD ME, AND IN THE NAME OF THE SAME YOUR GOD, WHOM I ALSO WORSHIP, EVEN THE LOVING AND STRONG
YHVH TZABAOTH | **ALBAPHALANA** | **CHARIS**
GRANT ME TO ENTER INTO THY REALM AND TO BE ESTABLISHED IN OTZ SHAMAIM.

* * *

Now at once, for as far as you can see, the radiance in which you float is suffused with bright green light, which swirls and sparkles, fluctuating and diversified all about you. The swirling and fluctuation slowly diminish; the new and all-pervasive light in which you are floating becomes steadied to an unvarying radiance of pure and intensely clear green.

*   *   *

In the profound stillness and peace of this region of green light The Flame of the Sea, the magical image of Netzach, manifests shiningly before you:

A luminous and graceful female figure stands upon a sandy shore, upon which seashells are scattered: the ocean, from which she has arisen, is behind her. She is nude but for a girdle, richly jeweled with pearls and emeralds, which encircles her waist. It is early morning. The sun has not yet appeared, but the sky is bright with opalescent colors whose reflections change and shimmer in the dancing waves. The waves run in, sparkling, to the shore: they break into ripples about the feet of the lovely radiant figure, then flow back into the sea, only to return. Her long, luxuriant hair, in golden tresses, streams out upon a warm but vigorous sea breeze. In her right hand she holds out a green sprig upon which blooms a five-petaled rose, emblem of the gifts she brings to the Earth: her left hand is lowered towards her vulva, which she indicates with the extended middle finger.

*   *   *

Keeping awareness of the shining form of the Flame of the Sea, listen to the invocation which I shall now make, and accept its words as your own.

*   *   *

O FLAME OF THE SEA WHO ABIDEST IN BRIAH, THOU MANTLE OF THE DIVINE SPIRIT OF NETZACH, WHO DOST IMPART THE SACRED ENERGIES OF VICTORY TO THE LOWER WORLDS: THROUGH THEE I SEEK PLENITUDE OF BLESSING AND TRUE EXPERIENCE OF THE MYSTERY OF OTZ SHAMAIM. WHEREFORE I SALUTE THEE BY THE TREMENDOUS MOST EXCELLENT NAME WHICH IS THE LIGHT OF THY LIFE:

YHVH TZABAOTH | **ALBAPHALANA** | **CHARIS**

*   *   *

Now the figure of the Flame of the Sea which stands before you is aureoled with a greenish-blue radiance. Rapidly this radiance extends: the figure glows with it, and bright beams of the same greenish-blue light dart piercingly towards you, becoming continually more brilliant. You are aware of a swift access of gladness in the influence of the powerful beams. In glorious effulgent waves, more and more of the greenish-blue radiance is given forth from the luminous figure. The radiance spreads, then explodes flashingly to fill the whole region. You see nothing in any direction but the greenish-blue light itself. You feel transformed, ecstatic, while there reverberates in your ears, clear and ringing, the sacred vowel of the Sphere. In a world of greenish-blue radiance you float alone and motionless, exultant and blissful.

*   *   *

For a time the encompassing radiance in which you float is altogether greenish-blue: then swirlings of green appear in it. By degrees the green light prevails more and more, until you are floating altogether in a region of luminous green. Now in this green light appear gleams of pale turquoise. The pale turquoise light spreads all about you, swirling and flashing, until at last you are floating in a region entirely of pale turquoise radiance. Suddenly you are floating no longer in a formless world of light. You are standing at the center of a vast circular temple, upon a floor of malachite. Completely encompassing the temple is a slowly swirling wall of saffron light, and the ceiling high above you is a billowing pale turquoise radiance.

*   *   *

As I now speak the valediction, give your inner affirmation to my words and accept them as your own.

*   *   *

O GLORIOUS AND MIGHTY

HANIEL | ZOTHALMIOS | ALALE

PRAISE AND HONOR BE UNTO THEE FOR THE SPLENDOR OF THINE OFFICE AND THE MAJESTY OF THY BEING. AND WITH YOU, O MINISTERING SPIRITS OF THE SEVENTH PATH IN YETZIRAH, AS LIKEWISE WITH THEE, O LUMINOUS HAGITH, BE THE BLESSING OF THY GOD AND MINE, EVEN THE LOVING AND STRONG

YHVH TZABAOTH | ALBAPHALANA | CHARIS

AND IN THIS SAME MOST SACRED NAME WHICH IS THE LIGHT OF THY LIFE, I SALUTE THEE, O FLAME OF THE SEA: WHO ART VEHICLE AND INSTRUMENT OF THE GOOD, THE BEAUTIFUL, AND THE TRUE.

*   *   *

Now the temple in which you are standing fades from your awareness, and you are surrounded by greenish white light, gleaming and full of brightness. This too fades, and you become aware once more of yourself, sitting with closed eyes amid your physical surroundings and the other Companions.

*   *   *

Now open your eyes.

*   *   *

17. The battery is sounded: 1.
18. At this point, if desired, there may be a discussion, led by the director, of the experience of Ascent and Vision. This is optional; and even when it takes place, individual members may desist from it if they wish to reserve their experiences for further meditation. Following discussion, the battery should again be sounded once.
19. All participants stand, and the director proclaims:
    Companions in Light: in unity this rite began, in unity let us bring it to a close.
20. All link hands and perform one clockwise circumambulation of the place of working. Hands are unlinked.
21. The director now utters the thanksgiving:
    Salutation and thanks be unto thee, O loving and strong
    YHVH TZABAOTH | ALBAPHALANA | CHARIS
    for the virtue and inspiration wherewith thou hast endowed us in this operation of Holy Magick in thy Sphere of Netzach.
    All respond:
    Salutation and thanks.
    The director continues:
    And do thou grant to us, Most Mighty, the continuance of thy regard as now we go forth from this place.
    All respond:
    Thus shall it be.
22. The battery is sounded: 3–5–3.

ASCENT AND VISION IN SOL

Temporal Mode: 2
Planetary Time: Hour of the Sun
Position of Bomos: Center of Place of Working
Lights: 1 Yellow Light upon the Bomos
Other Requirements: Chairs for participants, around place of working

(At the opening of the rite all participants stand in a circle around the place of working, in front of their chairs; the director stationed at the East.)

1. The director moves to the West side of the Bomos and faces East. She performs the Rite of Preparation.
2. The battery is sounded: 6.
3. The director makes invocation, as follows:

> O jubilant and far-shining
> ### YHVH ELOAH V'DAATH ‖ ONOPHIS ‖ THEIOS NOUS
> thou dweller in the secret place of Tiphareth:
> Let shine upon us in this hour the light of thy countenance, and grant us thy blessing and thine aid in this our undertaking. So shall we, ascending in the chariot of our aspiration, penetrate the coruscating gulfs of flame, the living veils of the astral and celestial firmaments of thy Sphere: to achieve true vision in the Yetziratic Heaven of Zabul, and to experience thy mystery in the Briatic Sanctuary of Ratzon.

4. The director resumes her place in the circle. The battery is sounded: 1.
5. The director says:

> Companions in Light, let us awaken the vibration of Shemesh in this place and within ourselves.

6. *If desired, incense is now activated.*
7. All now say:

> Rise in thy splendor, O King!—glorious brow,
> gaze on thy governance
> Gladdening all who behold! Soaring as song,
> rule and illuminate:
> Crysoleth gleaming thy crown, rise and inspire,
> Lion-gold, Falcon-flight,
> Joyous, ambrosial!

8. All link hands and vibrate, or chant according to its specified tone, the vowel of the Sphere—

> I   (pronounced as "ee" in *meet*)

Hands are unlinked.
9. Beginning with the director and proceeding clockwise around the circle of participants, each in turn steps forward and, facing the Bomos, performs the Planetary Gesture; then resumes his place in the circle.
10. The last participant having resumed his place, all link hands and circumambulate the place of working six times clockwise;

visualizing as they do so, a wall of *yellow* light whirling rapidly clockwise about their circle. This done, hands are unlinked and the wall of light is allowed to fade from awareness.

11. The battery is sounded: 1.
12. All now seat themselves, and the director proclaims:

> Let us now seek the deeper mysteries of the Sephirah Tiphareth, the Sixth Path of the Holy Tree of Life.

13. The battery is sounded: 6.
14. The director utters the following text from the Thirty-two Paths of Wisdom:

> The Sixth Path is the Intelligence of the Mediatory Influence: it is so named because therein is gathered the influx from all the Emanations, so that it in turn causes the mediatory influences to flow into the founts of each of the benign Powers, with which they are linked.

15. The battery is sounded: 1.
16. The Ascent and Vision in Sol now proceeds, led by the director who guides the working at a leisurely pace by means of the following text:

> *   *   *
>
> Companions in Light, close your eyes and your mind to outer awareness. Breathe evenly and deeply. Let each one of you in this working be aware only of your self, listening to my voice guiding you in your personal experience of Ascent and Vision in this Sphere. As now this rite proceeds, YOU are the individual focal point of this adventure.
>
> *   *   *
>
> You are standing at the center of a vast circular temple, upon a floor of topaz. Completely encompassing the temple is a slowly swirling wall of bright metallic golden light. The ceiling high above you is a billowing golden yellow radiance, and represents the veiled portal of Tiphareth in Yetzirah.
>
> *   *   *
>
> As I invoke the Olympic Guardian of the Sphere to open the portal, give your inner affirmation to my words and accept the invocation as your own.
>
> *   *   *
>
> O LUMINOUS OCH, SPIRIT OF THE SUN WHO ART MIGHTY IN THE FOURTH HEAVEN OF YETZIRAH, AND WHO DOST GUARD THE APPROACHES OF THE SIXTH PATH OF THE HOLY TREE OF LIFE: HEAR THE VOICE OF MY POWER AND OPEN UNTO ME THE PORTAL OF THY REALM IN THE DIVINE NAME

YHVH ELOAH V'DAATH | **ONOPHIS** | **THEIOS NOUS**
THAT I MAY ASCEND WITHOUT HINDRANCE TO THE HEIGHT
OF ZABUL.

*   *   *

The pale golden-yellow radiance above you now begins to swirl slowly in a clockwise motion about its center. Gathering momentum, it runs faster and more smoothly, its center opening and lifting away from you so that you are gazing upwards into a receding vortex of pale golden-yellow radiance.

*   *   *

And now you are aware of a strong attraction drawing you towards the vortex. You are lifted from the floor of the temple, the attracting force acting more and more strongly. Suddenly, you are drawn completely into the vortex. Immediately it flashes into a new vitality, enwrapping you in a whirling frenzy of pale golden-yellow flame, and carrying you swiftly upwards and upwards.

*   *   *

As you continue to ascend, you become aware of the rushing and pulsating sound of the vortex; it is as though the flame itself were uttering the sacred vowel of the Sphere. You catch fragments of other sounds too: recurrently at measured intervals, sent forth in ringing waves of sound, the deep and musical reverberations of a mighty gong; and at times, rising across those reverberations, a splendid fanfare of majestic trumpets.

*   *   *

Now the pale golden-yellow flame whirling about you seems gradually to decrease in velocity; gradually too you feel the intense speed of your upward movement diminishing. Now you are gliding upwards, in a gently turning pale golden-yellow fire which is filled with gradations of scintillant brilliance. More slowly yet you ascend, more slowly swirls the light about you. Now, with a feeling of wondering expectancy, you float in a peaceful region of gleaming pale golden-yellow radiance.

*   *   *

In this light and in this vibrant stillness remain without change until I have made the invocation which is to initiate your vision in Zabul. When the invocation has been made, the light all about you will resolve itself into a scene. Let it unfold and develop in the manner of a waking dream. You may travel therein; or you may remain to witness what befalls. Should you desire greater clarity of vision, make mental utterance of the sacred vowel of the Sphere. Should you be approached by a Being of the Sphere, mentally give it greeting in the divine name of the Sphere; then, if you will, you can accept it as your guide. Seek and explore as you desire, remembering that you have the ability to use astrally all your five senses.

*   *   *

I will now make the invocation. As I speak the words, give your inner affirmation to them and accept the invocation as your own. Then let the light about you dissolve to reveal the wonders of this astral realm.

*   *   *

BEHOLD ME, O BRIGHT ONES OF THE FOURTH HEAVEN, YE MINISTERING SPIRITS OF THE SIXTH PATH IN YETZIRAH: FOR I AM THE TRUE CHILD OF SHEMESH AND WITHIN ME SHINES AND MOVES THE VITAL FLAME OF THE SAME YOUR GOD, THE JUBILANT AND FAR-SHINING
   YHVH ELOAH V'DAATH | ONOPHIS | THEIOS NOUS
WHEREFORE, DISSOLVE THE ASTRAL ETHERS OF THIS HEIGHT AND REVEAL TO MY INNER PERCEPTION THE WONDERS OF ZABUL.

*   *   *

Here the director should allow a space of silence for the development of inward vision by the participants: it will depend upon her feeling as to the progress of the rite, five or ten minutes generally being ample.

*   *   *

Now your vision fades, giving place at first to a nebulous indistinctness which in turn is transformed once more to pale golden-yellow light. Even the ground on which you stand is assimilated into this light, so that again you are floating in a region of peaceful, pale golden-yellow radiance.

*   *   *

Remain thus as I now make invocation to access the Briatic level of this Sphere. As I utter the words, give your inner affirmation to them and accept the invocation as your own.

*   *   *

O GLORIOUS AND MIGHTY
   RAPHAEL | PYLOROS | ASPIS
THOU CELESTIAL INTELLIGENCE WHO DOST RULE IN THE FOURTH MANSION OF BRIAH AND WHO ART PRINCE AND COMMANDER OF THE SPIRITS OF THE SUN: BEHOLD ME, AND IN THE NAME OF THE SAME YOUR GOD, WHOM I ALSO WORSHIP,

EVEN THE JUBILANT AND FAR-SHINING
YHVH ELOAH V'DAATH | **ONOPHIS** | **THEIOS NOUS**
GRANT ME TO ENTER INTO THY REALM AND TO BE ESTABLISHED
IN RATZON.

*   *   *

Now at once, for as far as you can see, the radiance in which you float is suffused with bright yellow light, which swirls and sparkles, fluctuating and diversified all about you. The swirling and fluctuation slowly diminish; the new and all-pervasive light in which you are floating becomes steadied to an unvarying radiance of pure and intensely clear yellow.

*   *   *

In the profound stillness and peace of this region of yellow light The Puer Aeternus, the magical image of Tiphareth, manifests shiningly before you:
A boy of about seven years of age, strong and graceful, stands with feet astride upon the summit of a rock. His arms are extended sideways, hands slightly above shoulder level: with his right hand he grasps a thyrsus, with his left he holds up a cup of wine, which he tilts so as to pour forth its contents. Amid his thick, curling dark hair a serpent is enwreathed, raising its head between the budding bull-horns above his forehead. His only garment is a scarlet, square cape, fastened upon his right shoulder with a heavy gold brooch set with a single large topaz: this cape leaves bare his right arm and falls diagonally to his left side. Behind him is the glorious orb of the rising sun, surrounding him with its splendor.

*   *   *

Keeping awareness of the shining form of the Puer Aeternus, listen to the invocation which I shall now make, and accept its words as your own.

*   *   *

O ETERNAL CHILD WHO ABIDEST IN BRIAH, THOU MANTLE OF THE DIVINE SPIRIT OF TIPHARETH, WHO DOST IMPART THE SACRED ENERGIES OF BEAUTY TO THE LOWER WORLDS: THROUGH THEE I SEEK PLENITUDE OF BLESSING AND TRUE EXPERIENCE OF THE MYSTERY OF RATZON. WHEREFORE I SALUTE THEE BY THE TREMENDOUS MOST EXCELLENT NAME WHICH IS THE LIGHT OF THY LIFE:
YHVH ELOAH V'DAATH | **ONOPHIS** | **THEIOS NOUS**

*   *   *

Now the figure of the Eternal Child which stands before you is aureoled with a primrose radiance. Rapidly this radiance extends: the figure glows with it, and bright beams of the same primrose light dart piercingly towards you, becoming continually more brilliant. You are aware of a swift access of gladness in the influence of the powerful beams. In glorious effulgent waves, more and more of the primrose radiance is given forth from the luminous figure. The radiance spreads, then explodes flashingly to fill the whole region. You see nothing in any direction but the primrose light itself. You feel transformed, ecstatic, while there reverberates in your ears, clear and ringing, the sacred vowel of the Sphere. In a world of primrose radiance you float alone and motionless, exultant and blissful.

*   *   *

For a time the encompassing radiance in which you float is altogether primrose: then swirlings of spectrum yellow appear in it. By degrees the spectrum yellow light prevails more and more, until you are float-ing altogether in a region of luminous spectrum yellow. Now in this spectrum yellow light appear gleams of pale golden-yellow. The pale golden-yellow light spreads all about you, swirling and flashing, until at last you are floating in a region entirely of pale golden-yellow radiance. Suddenly you are floating no longer in a formless world of light. You are standing at the center of a vast circular temple, upon a floor of topaz. Completely encompassing the temple is a slowly swirling wall of bright, metallic golden light, and the ceiling high above you is a billowing pale golden-yellow radiance.

*   *   *

As I now speak the valediction, give your inner affirmation to my words and accept them as your own.

*   *   *

O GLORIOUS AND MIGHTY
RAPHAEL | PYLOROS | ASPIS
PRAISE AND HONOR BE UNTO THEE FOR THE SPLENDOR OF THINE OFFICE AND THE MAJESTY OF THY BEING. AND WITH YOU, O MINISTERING SPIRITS OF THE SIXTH PATH IN YETZIRAH, AS LIKEWISE WITH THEE, O LUMINOUS OCH, BE THE BLESSING OF THY GOD AND MINE, EVEN THE LOVING AND STRONG
YHVH ELOAH V'DAATH | ONOPHIS | THEIOS NOUS
AND IN THIS SAME MOST SACRED NAME WHICH IS THE LIGHT OF THY LIFE, I SALUTE THEE, O ETERNAL CHILD: WHO ART VEHICLE AND INSTRUMENT OF THE GOOD, THE BEAUTIFUL, AND THE TRUE.

*   *   *

Now the temple in which you are standing fades from your awareness, and you are surrounded by brilliant, pale yellow light, with sudden sparkles of bright red. This too fades, and you become aware once more of yourself, sitting with closed eyes amid your physical surroundings and the other Companions.

*   *   *

Now open your eyes.

*   *   *

17. The battery is sounded: 1.
18. At this point, if desired, there may be a discussion, led by the director, of the experience of Ascent and Vision. This is optional; and even when it takes place, individual members may desist from it if they wish to reserve their experiences for further meditation. Following discussion, the battery should again be sounded once.
19. All participants stand, and the director proclaims:
    Companions in Light: in unity this rite began, in unity let us bring it to a close.
20. All link hands and perform one clockwise circumambulation of the place of working. Hands are unlinked.
21. The director now utters the thanksgiving:
    Salutation and thanks be unto thee, O jubilant and far-shining
    YHVH ELOAH V'DAATH ⎮ **ONOPHIS** ⎮ **THEIOS NOUS**
    for the virtue and inspiration wherewith thou hast endowed us in this operation of Holy Magick in thy Sphere of Tiphareth.
    All respond:
    Salutation and thanks.
    The director continues:
    And do thou grant to us, Most Mighty, the continuance of thy regard as now we go forth from this place.
    All respond:
    Thus shall it be.
22. The battery is sounded: 3–5–3.

ASCENT AND VISION IN MARS

Temporal Mode: 2
Planetary Time: Hour of Mars
Position of Bomos: Center of Place of Working
Lights: 1 Red Light upon the Bomos

Other Requirements: Chairs for participants, around place of working

(At the opening of the rite all participants stand in a circle around the place of working, in front of their chairs; the director stationed at the East.)

1. The director moves to the West side of the Bomos and faces East. She performs the Rite of Preparation.
2. The battery is sounded: 5.
3. The director makes invocation, as follows:
   > O flame-bearing and inexorable
   > **ELOHIM GEBOR ⏐ SABAO ⏐ ISCHYROS**
   > thou dweller in the secret place of Geburah:
   > Let shine upon us in this hour the light of thy countenance, and grant us thy blessing and thine aid in this our undertaking. So shall we, ascending in the chariot of our aspiration, penetrate the coruscating gulfs of flame, the living veils of the astral and celestial firmaments of thy Sphere: to achieve true vision in the Yetziratic Heaven of Ma-on, and to experience thy mystery in the Briatic Sanctuary of Zakoth.
4. The director resumes her place in the circle. The battery is sounded: 1.
5. The director says:
   > Companions in Light, let us awaken the vibration of Madim in this place and within ourselves.
6. *If desired, incense is now activated.*
7. All now say:
   > Play of the Breath and the Word, Life and the Law,
   > counterchange intricate
   > Weaving the ground of our days: this is our strength,
   > this is our jeopardy.
   > Spirit oracular, tell: knowledge and love,
   > will they keep unity
   > Or, opposed, shatter us?
8. All link hands and vibrate, or chant according to its specified tone, the vowel of the Sphere—
   > O   (pronounced as "o" in *hot*)
   Hands are unlinked.
9. Beginning with the director and proceeding clockwise around the circle of participants, each in turn steps forward and, facing the Bomos, performs the Planetary Gesture; then resumes his place in the circle.

10. The last participant having resumed his place, all link hands and circumambulate the place of working five times clockwise; visualizing as they do so, a wall of *red* light whirling rapidly clockwise about their circle. This done, hands are unlinked and the wall of light is allowed to fade from awareness.

11. The battery is sounded: 1.

12. All now seat themselves, and the director proclaims:

    Let us now seek the deeper mysteries of the Sephirah Geburah, the Fifth Path of the Holy Tree of Life.

13. The battery is sounded: 5.

14. The director utters the following text from the Thirty-two Paths of Wisdom:

    The Fifth Path is the Root Intelligence, so named because it is itself the essence equaling the Unity. It is linked with Binah, the Intelligence which emanates from the unfathomed deeps of Wisdom, Chokmah.

15. The battery is sounded: 1.

16. The Ascent and Vision in Mars now proceeds, led by the director who guides the working at a leisurely pace by means of the following text:

    *   *   *

    Companions in Light, close your eyes and your mind to outer awareness. Breathe evenly and deeply. Let each one of you in this working be aware only of your self, listening to my voice guiding you in your personal experience of Ascent and Vision in this Sphere. As now this rite proceeds, YOU are the individual focal point of this adventure.

    *   *   *

    You are standing at the center of a vast circular temple, upon a floor of garnet. Completely encompassing the temple is a slowly swirling wall of fiery red light. The ceiling high above you is a billowing vermilion radiance, and represents the veiled portal of Geburah in Yetzirah.

    *   *   *

    As I invoke the Olympic Guardian of the Sphere to open the portal, give your inner affirmation to my words and accept the invocation as your own.

    *   *   *

    O LUMINOUS PHALEGH, SPIRIT OF MARS WHO ART MIGHTY IN THE FIFTH HEAVEN OF YETZIRAH, AND WHO DOST GUARD THE APPROACHES OF THE FIFTH PATH OF THE HOLY TREE OF LIFE: HEAR THE VOICE OF MY POWER AND OPEN UNTO ME THE PORTAL OF THY REALM IN THE DIVINE NAME

ELOHIM GEBOR | SABAO | ISCHYROS
THAT I MAY ASCEND WITHOUT HINDRANCE TO THE HEIGHT OF MA-ON.

*   *   *

The vermilion radiance above you now begins to swirl slowly in a clockwise motion about its center. Gathering momentum, it runs faster and more smoothly, its center opening and lifting away from you so that you are gazing upwards into a receding vortex of vermilion radiance.

*   *   *

And now you are aware of a strong attraction drawing you towards the vortex. You are lifted from the floor of the temple, the attracting force acting more and more strongly. Suddenly, you are drawn completely into the vortex. Immediately it flashes into a new vitality, enwrapping you in a whirling frenzy of vermilion flame, and carrying you swiftly upwards and upwards.

*   *   *

As you continue to ascend, you become aware of the rushing and pulsating sound of the vortex; it is as though the flame itself were uttering the sacred vowel of the Sphere. You catch fragments of other sounds too: sometimes a great shouting mixed with the violent clash of steel striking upon steel; and ever and anon, beaten for marching or as a signal in battle, the deep voice of thunderous drums.

*   *   *

Now the vermilion flame whirling about you seems gradually to decrease in velocity; gradually too you feel the intense speed of your upward movement diminishing. Now you are gliding upwards, in a gently turning vermilion fire which is filled with gradations of scintillant brilliance. More slowly yet you ascend, more slowly swirls the light about you. Now, with a feeling of wondering expectancy, you float in a peaceful region of gleaming vermilion radiance.

*   *   *

In this light and in this vibrant stillness remain without change until I have made the invocation which is to initiate your vision in Ma-on. When the invocation has been made, the light all about you will resolve itself into a scene. Let it unfold and develop in the manner of a waking dream. You may travel therein; or you may remain to witness what befalls. Should you desire greater clarity of vision, make mental utterance of the sacred vowel of the Sphere. Should you be approached by a Being of the Sphere, mentally give it greeting in the divine name of the Sphere; then, if you will, you can accept it as your guide. Seek and explore as you desire, remembering that you have the ability to use astrally all your five senses.

* * *

I will now make the invocation. As I speak the words, give your inner affirmation to them and accept the invocation as your own. Then let the light about you dissolve to reveal the wonders of this astral realm.

* * *

BEHOLD ME, O BRIGHT ONES OF THE FIFTH HEAVEN, YE MINISTERING SPIRITS OF THE FIFTH PATH IN YETZIRAH: FOR I AM THE TRUE CHILD OF MADIM AND WITHIN ME SHINES AND MOVES THE VITAL FLAME OF THE SAME YOUR GOD, THE FLAME-BEARING AND INEXORABLE

ELOHIM GEBOR | **SABAO** | **ISCHYROS**

WHEREFORE, DISSOLVE THE ASTRAL ETHERS OF THIS HEIGHT AND REVEAL TO MY INNER PERCEPTION THE WONDERS OF MA-ON.

* * *

Here the director should allow a space of silence for the development of inward vision by the participants: it will depend upon her feeling as to the progress of the rite, five or ten minutes generally being ample.

* * *

Now your vision fades, giving place at first to a nebulous indistinctness which in turn is transformed once more to vermilion light. Even the ground on which you stand is assimilated into this light, so that again you are floating in a region of peaceful vermilion radiance.

* * *

Remain thus as I now make invocation to access the Briatic level of this Sphere. As I utter the words, give your inner affirmation to them and accept the invocation as your own.

* * *

O GLORIOUS AND MIGHTY

KAMAEL | **DORYXENOS** | **RUTOR**

THOU CELESTIAL INTELLIGENCE WHO DOST RULE IN THE FIFTH MANSION OF BRIAH AND WHO ART PRINCE AND COMMANDER OF THE SPIRITS OF MARS: BEHOLD ME, AND IN THE NAME OF THE SAME YOUR GOD, WHOM I ALSO WORSHIP, EVEN THE FLAME-BEARING AND INEXORABLE

ELOHIM GEBOR | **SABAO** | **ISHCHYROS**

GRANT ME TO ENTER INTO THY REALM AND TO BE ESTABLISHED
IN ZAKOTH.

*   *   *

Now at once, for as far as you can see, the radiance in which you float
is suffused with bright red light, which swirls and sparkles, fluctuating
and diversified all about you. The swirling and fluctuation slowly
diminish; the new and all-pervasive light in which you are floating
becomes steadied to an unvarying radiance of pure and intensely
clear red.

*   *   *

In the profound stillness and peace of this region of red light The
Warrior, the magical image of Geburah, manifests shiningly before
you:
A mighty male figure stands in an iron chariot, in the midst of a dark
and lurid sky of roiling clouds which smolder with inner fire. Each of
the chariot wheels has five spokes, and a long, curved blade projecting from the hub. The rider is clean shaven, and wears a helmet with a
high, flowing horsehair crest and a gleaming breastplate over a
scarlet undertunic. With his left hand he holds, effortlessly, the reins of
the two chestnut roan horses drawing the chariot: of these, the right
hand one is rearing erect in mettlesome impatience, while the other,
with head held low, is moodily pawing at the stormy vapor.

*   *   *

Keeping awareness of the shining form of the Warrior, listen to the
invocation which I shall now make, and accept its words as your
own.

*   *   *

O WARRIOR WHO ABIDEST IN BRIAH, THOU MANTLE OF THE
DIVINE SPIRIT OF GEBURAH, WHO DOST IMPART THE SACRED
ENERGIES OF STRENGTH TO THE LOWER WORLDS: THROUGH
THEE I SEEK PLENITUDE OF BLESSING AND TRUE EXPERIENCE
OF THE MYSTERY OF ZAKOTH. WHEREFORE I SALUTE THEE BY
THE TREMENDOUS MOST EXCELLENT NAME WHICH IS THE
LIGHT OF THY LIFE:
ELOHIM GEBOR | SABAO | ISCHYROS

*   *   *

Now the figure of the Warrior which stands before you is aureoled
with an amber radiance. Rapidly this radiance extends: the figure
glows with it, and bright beams of the same amber light dart piercingly
towards you, becoming continually more brilliant. You are aware of a

swift access of gladness in the influence of the powerful beams. In glorious effulgent waves, more and more of the amber radiance is given forth from the luminous figure. The radiance spreads, then explodes flashingly to fill the whole region. You see nothing in any direction but the amber light itself. You feel transformed, ecstatic, while there reverberates in your ears, clear and ringing, the sacred vowel of the Sphere. In a world of amber radiance you float alone and motionless, exultant and blissful.

*   *   *

For a time the encompassing radiance in which you float is altogether amber: then swirlings of red appear in it. By degrees the red light prevails more and more, until you are floating altogether in a region of luminous red. Now in this red light appear gleams of vermilion. The vermilion light spreads all about you, swirling and flashing, until at last you are floating in a region entirely of vermilion radiance. Suddenly you are floating no longer in a formless world of light. You are standing at the center of a vast circular temple, upon a floor of garnet. Completely encompassing the temple is a slowly swirling wall of fiery red light, and the ceiling high above you is a billowing vermilion radiance.

*   *   *

As I now speak the valediction, give your inner affirmation to my words and accept them as your own.

*   *   *

O GLORIOUS AND MIGHTY
KAMAEL | **DORYXENOS** | **RUTOR**
PRAISE AND HONOR BE UNTO THEE FOR THE SPLENDOR OF THINE OFFICE AND THE MAJESTY OF THY BEING. AND WITH YOU, O MINISTERING SPIRITS OF THE FIFTH PATH IN YETZIRAH, AS LIKEWISE WITH THEE, O LUMINOUS PHALEGH, BE THE BLESSING OF THY GOD AND MINE, EVEN THE FLAME-BEARING AND INEXORABLE
ELOHIM GEBOR | **SABAO** | **ISCHYROS**
AND IN THIS SAME MOST SACRED NAME WHICH IS THE LIGHT OF THY LIFE, I SALUTE THEE, O WARRIOR: WHO ART VEHICLE AND INSTRUMENT OF THE GOOD, THE BEAUTIFUL, AND THE TRUE.

*   *   *

Now the temple in which you are standing fades from your awareness, and you are surrounded by clear yellow light merging into a pale sage green, with swirlings of bright cerise. This too fades, and you become aware once more of yourself, sitting with closed eyes amid your physical surroundings and the other Companions.

*　　　*　　　*

Now open your eyes.

*　　　*　　　*

17. The battery is sounded:　1.
18. At this point, if desired, there may be a discussion, led by the director, of the experience of Ascent and Vision. This is optional; and even when it takes place, individual members may desist from it if they wish to reserve their experiences for further meditation. Following discussion, the battery should again be sounded once.
19. All participants stand, and the director proclaims:
    Companions in Light: in unity this rite began, in unity let us bring it to a close.
20. All link hands and perform one clockwise circumambulation of the place of working. Hands are unlinked.
21. The director now utters the thanksgiving:
    Salutation and thanks be unto thee, O flame-bearing and inexorable
    ELOHIM GEBOR | SABAO | ISCHYROS
    for the virtue and inspiration wherewith thou hast endowed us in this operation of Holy Magick in thy Sphere of Geburah.
    All respond:
    Salutation and thanks.
    The director continues:
    And do thou grant to us, Most Mighty, the continuance of thy regard as now we go forth from this place.
    All respond:
    Thus shall it be.
22. The battery is sounded:　3–5–3.

ASCENT AND VISION IN JUPITER

Temporal Mode:　2
Planetary Time:　Hour of Jupiter
Position of Bomos:　Center of Place of Working
Lights:　1 Blue Light upon the Bomos
Other Requirements:　Chairs for participants, around place of working

(At the opening of the rite all participants stand in a circle around the place of working, in front of their chairs; the director stationed at the East.)

1. The director moves to the West side of the Bomos and faces East. She performs the Rite of Preparation.
2. The battery is sounded: 4.
3. The director makes invocation, as follows:
    O beneficent and most splendid
    ### EL ǀ ZARAIETOS ǀ PANTOKRATOR
    thou dweller in the secret place of Chesed:
    Let shine upon us in this hour the light of thy countenance, and grant us thy blessing and thine aid in this our undertaking. So shall we, ascending in the chariot of our aspiration, penetrate the coruscating gulfs of flame, the living veils of the astral and celestial firmaments of thy Sphere: to achieve true vision in the Yetziratic Heaven of Makon, and to experience thy mystery in the Briatic Sanctuary of Ahabah.
4. The director resumes her place in the circle. The battery is sounded: 1.
5. The director says:
    Companions in Light, let us awaken the vibration of Tzedeq in this place and within ourselves.
6. *If desired, incense is now activated.*
7. All now say:
    Cup that receives and bestows, generous palm
    garnering, scattering,
    Thine are the bountiful rains, thine is the fount
    purpled and perilous:
    Thine is dominion to cast down to the pit,
    thine to give sanctuary—
    Yea, to give liberty!
8. All link hands and vibrate, or chant according to its specified tone, the vowel of the Sphere—
    ♃   (pronounced as German ü)
    Hands are unlinked.
9. Beginning with the director and proceeding clockwise around the circle of participants, each in turn steps forward and, facing the Bomos, performs the Planetary Gesture; then resumes his place in the circle.
10. The last participant having resumed his place, all link hands and circumambulate the place of working four times clockwise;

visualizing as they do so a wall of *blue* light whirling rapidly clockwise about their circle. This done, hands are unlinked and the wall of light is allowed to fade from awareness.

11. The battery is sounded: 1.
12. All now seat themselves, and the director proclaims:
     Let us now seek the deeper mysteries of the Sephirah Chesed, the Fourth Path of the Holy Tree of Life.
13. The battery is sounded: 4.
14. The director utters the following text from the Thirty-two Paths of Wisdom:
     The Fourth Path is the Measuring, Collecting or Receptive Intelligence: so named because it holds within it all the high potencies, and from it issue forth all the successive modalities of spirit in their highest being, each emanated from another through the power of the First Emanation, Kether.
15. The battery is sounded: 1.
16. The Ascent and Vision in Jupiter now proceeds, led by the director who guides the working at a leisurely pace by means of the following text:

     *　　　　　　*　　　　　　*

     Companions in Light, close your eyes and your mind to outer awareness. Breathe evenly and deeply. Let each one of you in this working be aware only of your self, listening to my voice guiding you in your personal experience of Ascent and Vision in this Sphere. As now this rite proceeds, YOU are the individual focal point of this adventure.

     *　　　　　　*　　　　　　*

     You are standing at the center of a vast circular temple, upon a floor of lapis lazuli. Completely encompassing the temple is a slowly swirling wall of white light. The ceiling high above you is a billowing pale royal blue radiance, and represents the veiled portal of Chesed in Yetzirah.

     *　　　　　　*　　　　　　*

     As I invoke the Olympic Guardian of the Sphere to open the portal, give your inner affirmation to my words and accept the invocation as your own.

     *　　　　　　*　　　　　　*

     O LUMINOUS BETHOR, SPIRIT OF JUPITER WHO ART MIGHTY IN THE SIXTH HEAVEN OF YETZIRAH, AND WHO DOST GUARD THE APPROACHES OF THE FOURTH PATH OF THE HOLY TREE OF LIFE: HEAR THE VOICE OF MY POWER AND OPEN UNTO ME THE

PORTAL OF THY REALM IN THE DIVINE NAME
EL | **ZARAIETOS** | **PANTOKRATOR**
THAT I MAY ASCEND WITHOUT HINDRANCE TO THE HEIGHT
OF MAKON.

*   *   *

The pale royal blue radiance above you now begins to swirl slowly in a clockwise motion about its center. Gathering momentum, it runs faster and more smoothly, its center opening and lifting away from you so that you are gazing upwards into a receding vortex of pale royal blue radiance.

*   *   *

And now you are aware of a strong attraction drawing you towards the vortex. You are lifted from the floor of the temple, the attracting force acting more and more strongly. Suddenly, you are drawn completely into the vortex. Immediately it flashes into a new vitality, enwrapping you in a whirling frenzy of pale royal blue flame, and carrying you swiftly upwards and upwards.

*   *   *

As you continue to ascend, you become aware of the rushing and pulsating sound of the vortex; it is as though the flame itself were uttering the sacred vowel of the Sphere. You catch fragments of other sounds too: mighty thunders, pealing and echoing in huge reverberations, and stringed instruments, full-toned and resonant, taking up with their own amplitude the thunder's magnificent music.

*   *   *

Now the pale royal blue flame whirling about you seems gradually to decrease in velocity; gradually too you feel the intense speed of your upward movement diminishing. Now you are gliding upwards, in a gently turning pale royal blue fire which is filled with gradations of scintillant brilliance. More slowly yet you ascend, more slowly swirls the light about you. Now, with a feeling of wondering expectancy, you float in a peaceful region of gleaming pale royal blue radiance.

*   *   *

In this light and in this vibrant stillness remain without change until I have made the invocation which is to initiate your vision in Makon. When the invocation has been made, the light all about you will resolve itself into a scene. Let it unfold and develop in the manner of a waking dream. You may travel therein; or you may remain to witness what befalls. Should you desire greater clarity of vision, make mental utterance of the sacred vowel of the Sphere. Should you be approached by a Being of the Sphere, mentally give it greeting in the divine name of the Sphere; then, if you will, you can accept it as your guide. Seek and explore as you desire, remembering that you have the ability to use astrally all your five senses.

*   *   *

I will now make the invocation. As I speak the words, give your inner affirmation to them and accept the invocation as your own. Then let the light about you dissolve to reveal the wonders of this astral realm.

*   *   *

BEHOLD ME, O BRIGHT ONES OF THE SIXTH HEAVEN, YE MINIS-TERING SPIRITS OF THE FOURTH PATH IN YETZIRAH: FOR I AM THE TRUE CHILD OF TZEDEQ AND WITHIN ME SHINES AND MOVES THE VITAL FLAME OF THE SAME YOUR GOD, THE BENEFICENT AND MOST SPLENDID

EL | ZARAIETOS | PANTOKRATOR

WHEREFORE, DISSOLVE THE ASTRAL ETHERS OF THIS HEIGHT AND REVEAL TO MY INNER PERCEPTION THE WONDERS OF MAKON.

*   *   *

Here the director should allow a space of silence for the development of inward vision by the participants: it will depend upon her feeling as to the progress of the rite, five or ten minutes generally being ample.

*   *   *

Now your vision fades, giving place at first to a nebulous indistinct-ness which in turn is transformed once more to pale royal blue radiance. Even the ground on which you stand is assimilated into this light, so that again you are floating in a region of peaceful pale royal blue radiance.

*   *   *

Remain thus as I now make invocation to access the Briatic level of this Sphere. As I utter the words, give your inner affirmation to them and accept the invocation as your own.

*   *   *

O GLORIOUS AND MIGHTY

TZADQIEL | ORTHOTER | BALEN

THOU CELESTIAL INTELLIGENCE WHO DOST RULE IN THE SIXTH MANSION OF BRIAH AND WHO ART PRINCE AND COM-MANDER OF THE SPIRITS OF JUPITER: BEHOLD ME, AND IN THE

NAME OF THE SAME YOUR GOD, WHOM I ALSO WORSHIP,
EVEN THE BENEFICENT AND MOST SPLENDID
EL | **ZARAIETOS** | **PANTOKRATOR**
GRANT ME TO ENTER INTO THY REALM AND TO BE ESTABLISHED
IN AHABAH.

*　　　　　*　　　　　*

Now at once, for as far as you can see, the radiance in which you float
is suffused with bright spectrum blue light, which swirls and sparkles,
fluctuating and diversified all about you. The swirling and fluctuation
slowly diminish; the new and all-pervasive light in which you are floating becomes steadied to an unvarying radiance of pure and intensely
clear spectrum blue.

*　　　　　*　　　　　*

In the profound stillness and peace of this region of blue light The
Priest King, the magical image of Chesed, manifests shiningly
before you:
A mature male figure, majestic but benign of countenance, is seated
upon a throne of lapis lazuli. This throne, with its dais of four steps, is
securely established in the bright blue firmament. The figure has luxuriant dark hair and beard, his head crowned with a simple gold circlet
which is set with square-cut sapphires. He wears a purple robe,
square-necked and extending to his ankles; this robe has a single
narrow vertical stripe, centrally placed, of electric blue. The sleeves
are full and simple. Upon his feet are sandals. In the right hand of this
figure is a scepter, the head of which is in the shape of an eagle with
outstretched wings. The left hand, raised high and out to the side,
holds a massive goblet. From the four quarters of this goblet there
spring up and over the lip, fountain-wise, streams of clear liquid; these
four streams fall vertically, without touching either the figure or the
throne. Upon the lowest of the four steps of the dais rests a cornucopia,
a Horn of Plenty with ripe and beautiful fruits spilling out from it.

*　　　　　*　　　　　*

Keeping awareness of the shining form of the Priest King, listen to the
invocation which I shall now make, and accept its words as your
own.

*　　　　　*　　　　　*

O PRIEST KING WHO ABIDEST IN BRIAH, THOU MANTLE OF THE
DIVINE SPIRIT OF CHESED, WHO DOST IMPART THE SACRED
ENERGIES OF LOVING KINDNESS TO THE LOWER WORLDS:
THROUGH THEE I SEEK PLENITUDE OF BLESSING AND TRUE

EXPERIENCE OF THE MYSTERY OF AHABAH. WHEREFORE I
SALUTE THEE BY THE TREMENDOUS MOST EXCELLENT NAME
WHICH IS THE LIGHT OF THY LIFE:
EL | ZARAIETOS | PANTOKRATOR

*   *   *

Now the figure of the Priest King which stands before you is aureoled
with a lilac radiance. Rapidly this radiance extends: the figure glows
with it, and bright beams of the same lilac light dart piercingly towards
you, becoming continually more brilliant. You are aware of a swift
access of gladness in the influence of the powerful beams. In glorious
effulgent waves, more and more of the lilac radiance is given forth
from the luminous figure. The radiance spreads, then explodes
flashingly to fill the whole region. You see nothing in any direction but
the lilac light itself. You feel transformed, ecstatic, while there reverberates in your ears, clear and ringing, the sacred vowel of the
Sphere. In a world of lilac radiance you float alone and motionless,
exultant and blissful.

*   *   *

For a time the encompassing radiance in which you float is altogether
lilac: then swirlings of spectrum blue appear in it. By degrees the
spectrum blue light prevails more and more, until you are floating
altogether in a region of luminous spectrum blue. Now in this spectrum blue light appear gleams of pale royal blue. The pale royal blue
light spreads all about you, swirling and flashing, until at last you are
floating in a region entirely of pale royal blue radiance. Suddenly you
are floating no longer in a formless world of light. You are standing at
the center of a vast circular temple, upon a floor of lapis lazuli. Completely encompassing the temple is a slowly swirling wall of white
light, and the ceiling high above you is a billowing pale royal blue
radiance.

*   *   *

As I now speak the valediction, give your inner affirmation to my
words and accept them as your own.

*   *   *

O GLORIOUS AND MIGHTY
TZADQIEL | ORTHOTER | BALEN
PRAISE AND HONOR BE UNTO THEE FOR THE SPLENDOR OF THINE
OFFICE AND THE MAJESTY OF THY BEING. AND WITH YOU, O MINISTER-
ING SPIRITS OF THE FOURTH PATH IN YETZIRAH, AS LIKEWISE WITH
THEE, O LUMINOUS BETHOR, BE THE BLESSING OF THY GOD AND

MINE, EVEN THE BENEFICENT AND MOST SPLENDID
EL | ZARAIETOS | PANTOKRATOR
AND IN THIS SAME MOST SACRED NAME WHICH IS THE LIGHT
OF THY LIFE, I SALUTE THEE, O PRIEST KING: WHO ART VEHICLE
AND INSTRUMENT OF THE GOOD, THE BEAUTIFUL, AND THE
TRUE.

*   *   *

Now the temple in which you are standing fades from your awareness,
and you are surrounded by the bright and changeful blue-green of
abalone shell, merging into luminous and delicate pink. This too fades,
and you become aware once more of yourself, sitting with closed eyes
amid your physical surroundings and the other Companions.

*   *   *

Now open your eyes.

*   *   *

17. The battery is sounded: 1.
18. At this point, if desired, there may be a discussion, led by the
    director, of the experience of Ascent and Vision. This is optional;
    and even when it takes place, individual members may desist
    from it if they wish to reserve their experiences for further
    meditation. Following discussion, the battery should again be
    sounded once.
19. All participants stand, and the director proclaims:
    Companions in Light: in unity this rite began, in unity let us bring
    it to a close.
20. All link hands and perform one clockwise circumambulation of
    the place of working. Hands are unlinked.
21. The director now utters the thanksgiving:
    Salutation and thanks be unto thee, O beneficent and most splendid
    EL | ZARAIETOS | PANTOKRATOR
    for the virtue and inspiration wherewith thou hast endowed us in this
    operation of Holy Magick in thy Sphere of Chesed.
    All respond:
    Salutation and thanks.
    The director continues:
    And do thou grant to us, Most Mighty, the continuance of thy regard
    as now we go forth from this place.
    All respond:
    Thus shall it be.
22. The battery is sounded: 3-5-3.

ASCENT AND VISION IN SATURN

Temporal Mode: 2
Planetary Time: Hour of Saturn
Position of Bomos: Center of Place of Working
Lights: 1 Indigo (or Black) Light upon the Bomos
Other Requirements: Chairs for participants, around place of working

(At the opening of the rite all participants stand in a circle around the place of working, in front of their chairs; the director stationed at the East.)

1.   The director moves to the West side of the Bomos and faces East. She performs the Rite of Preparation.
2.   The battery is sounded: 3.
3.   The director makes invocation, as follows:
      O exalted and vast
         YHVH ELOHIM ∣ **IALDABAOTH** ∣ **AIONOS KYRIOS**
      thou dweller in the secret place of Binah:
      Let shine upon us in this hour the light of thy countenance, and grant us thy blessing and thine aid in this our undertaking. So shall we, ascending in the chariot of our aspiration, penetrate the coruscating gulfs of flame, the living veils of the astral and celestial firmaments of thy Sphere: to achieve true vision in the Yetziratic Heaven of Araboth, and to experience thy mystery in the Briatic Sanctuary of Qadosh Qadoshim.
4.   The director resumes her place in the circle. The battery is sounded: 1.
5.   The director says:
      Companions in Light, let us awaken the vibration of Shabbathai in this place and within ourselves.
6.   *If desired, incense is now activated.*
7.   All now say:
      Thine is the Sign of the End, Being fulfilled
                                 Sum of Existences:
      Thine is the ultimate Door opened on Night's
                                 unuttered mystery:
      Thine, the first hesitant step into the dark
                                 of those but latterly
                   Born to the Labyrinth!
8.   All link hands and vibrate, or chant according to its specified

tone, the vowel of the Sphere—

Ω   (pronounced as "o" in *only*)

Hands are unlinked.

9. Beginning with the director and proceeding clockwise around the circle of participants, each in turn steps forward and, facing the Bomos, performs the Planetary Gesture; then resumes his place in the circle.

10. The last participant having resumed his place, all link hands and circumambulate the place of working three times clockwise; visualizing as they do so, a wall of *indigo* light whirling rapidly clockwise about their circle. This done, hands are unlinked and the wall of light is allowed to fade from awareness.

11. The battery is sounded: 1.

12. All now seat themselves, and the director proclaims:

> Let us now seek the deeper mysteries of the Sephirah Binah, the Third Path of the Holy Tree of Life.

13. The battery is sounded: 3.

14. The director utters the following text from the Thirty-two Paths of Wisdom:

> The Third Path is the Consecrating Intelligence; it is the underlying principle of the Wisdom of the Beginning, which is named the Pattern of Faith and is its root, Affirmation. It is the parent of faith, for from its essential nature faith proceeds.

15. The battery is sounded: 1.

16. The Ascent and Vision in Saturn now proceeds, led by the director who guides the working at a leisurely pace by means of the following text:

*   *   *

> Companions in Light, close your eyes and your mind to outer awareness. Breathe evenly and deeply. Let each one of you in this working be aware only of your self, listening to my voice guiding you in your personal experience of Ascent and Vision in this Sphere. As now this rite proceeds, YOU are the individual focal point of this adventure.

*   *   *

> You are standing at the center of a vast circular temple, upon a floor of black onyx. Completely encompassing the temple is a slowly swirling wall of soft grey light. The ceiling high above you is a billowing soft red-brown radiance, and represents the veiled portal of Binah in Yetzirah.

*   *   *

As I invoke the Olympic Guardian of the Sphere to open the portal, give your inner affirmation to my words and accept the invocation as your own.

*   *   *

O LUMINOUS ARATRON, SPIRIT OF SATURN WHO ART MIGHTY IN THE SEVENTH HEAVEN OF YETZIRAH, AND WHO DOST GUARD THE APPROACHES OF THE THIRD PATH OF THE HOLY TREE OF LIFE: HEAR THE VOICE OF MY POWER AND OPEN UNTO ME THE PORTAL OF THY REALM IN THE DIVINE NAME
YHVH ELOHIM | **IALDABAOTH** | **AIONOS KYRIOS**
THAT I MAY ASCEND WITHOUT HINDRANCE TO THE HEIGHT OF ARABOTH.

*   *   *

The soft red-brown radiance above you now begins to swirl slowly in a clockwise motion about its center. Gathering momentum, it runs faster and more smoothly, its center opening and lifting away from you so that you are gazing upwards into a receding vortex of soft red-brown radiance.

*   *   *

And now you are aware of a strong attraction drawing you towards the vortex. You are lifted from the floor of the temple, the attracting force acting more and more strongly. Suddenly, you are drawn completely into the vortex. Immediately it flashes into a new vitality, enwrapping you a whirling frenzy of soft red-brown flame, and carrying you swiftly upwards and upwards.

*   *   *

As you continue to ascend, you become aware of the rushing and pulsating sound of the vortex; it is as though the flame itself were uttering the sacred vowel of the Sphere. Then across this sound there falls another: a slow succession of deep metallic strokes, strident and ponderous; then complete silence. Gradually you become aware again of the rushing and pulsating articulation of the flame; then again the slow succession of metallic strokes, followed by silence. Gradually once more the rushing pulsation of the vortex establishes itself.

*   *   *

Now the soft red-brown flame whirling about you seems gradually to decrease in velocity; gradually too you feel the intense speed of your upward movement diminishing. Now you are gliding upwards, in a gently turning soft red-brown fire which is filled with gradations of scintillant brilliance. More slowly yet you ascend, more slowly swirls the light about you. Now, with a feeling of wondering expectancy, you float in a peaceful region of gleaming soft red-brown radiance.

*   *   *

In this light and in this vibrant stillness remain without change until I have made the invocation which is to initiate your vision in Araboth. When the invocation has been made, the light all about you will resolve itself into a scene. Let it unfold and develop in the manner of a waking dream. You may travel therein; or you may remain to witness what befalls. Should you desire greater clarity of vision, make mental utterance of the sacred vowel of the Sphere. Should you be approached by a Being of the Sphere, mentally give it greeting in the divine name of the Sphere; then, if you will, you can accept it as your guide. Seek and explore as you desire, remembering that you have the ability to use astrally all your five senses.

*   *   *

I will now make the invocation. As I speak the words, give your inner affirmation to them and accept the invocation as your own. Then let the light about you dissolve to reveal the wonders of this astral realm.

*   *   *

BEHOLD ME, O BRIGHT ONES OF THE SEVENTH HEAVEN, YE MINISTERING SPIRITS OF THE THIRD PATH IN YETZIRAH: FOR I AM THE TRUE CHILD OF SHABBATHAI AND WITHIN ME SHINES AND MOVES THE VITAL FLAME OF THE SAME YOUR GOD, THE EXALTED AND VAST
    YHVH ELOHIM | **IALDABAOTH** | **AIONOS KYRIOS**
WHEREFORE, DISSOLVE THE ASTRAL ETHERS OF THIS HEIGHT AND REVEAL TO MY INNER PERCEPTION THE WONDERS OF ARABOTH.

*   *   *

Here the director should allow a space of silence for the development of inward vision by the participants: it will depend upon her feeling as to the progress of the rite, five or ten minutes generally being ample.

*   *   *

Now your vision fades, giving place at first to a nebulous indistinctness which in turn is transformed once more to soft red-brown light. Even the ground on which you stand is assimilated into this light, so that again you are floating in a region of peaceful soft red-brown radiance.

*   *   *

Remain thus as I now make invocation to access the Briatic level of this Sphere. As I utter the words, give your inner affirmation to them and accept the invocation as your own.

*   *   *

O GLORIOUS AND MIGHTY
TZAPHQIEL | **MENESTHEUS** | **XAIS**
THOU CELESTIAL INTELLIGENCE WHO DOST RULE IN THE SEVENTH MANSION OF BRIAH AND WHO ART PRINCE AND COMMANDER OF THE SPIRITS OF SATURN: BEHOLD ME, AND IN THE NAME OF THE SAME YOUR GOD, WHOM I ALSO WORSHIP, EVEN THE EXALTED AND VAST
YHVH ELOHIM | **IALDABAOTH** | **AIONOS KYRIOS**
GRANT ME TO ENTER INTO THY REALM AND TO BE ESTABLISHED IN QADOSH QADOSHIM.

*   *   *

Now at once, for as far as you can see, the radiance in which you float is suffused with indigo light, which swirls and sparkles, fluctuating and diversified all about you. The swirling and fluctuation slowly diminish; the new and all-pervasive light in which you are floating becomes steadied to an unvarying radiance of pure and intensely clear indigo.

*   *   *

In the profound stillness and peace of this region of indigo light The Ancient, the magical image of Binah, manifests shiningly before you:

An aged male figure with beard and shoulder-length hair of grey is seated on a low outcrop of rock in level, fertile ground. This rock stands between two ancient yew trees, whose dark foliage and pale sinewy branches are densely interwoven so as to form an arch above the seated figure. Beyond this dark arch can be seen a sunlit orchard. The figure wears a draped garment, dusky in color with highlights of gold: this covers the lower part of his body to the ankles and passes over the right shoulder, leaving his arms and part of his chest bare. Upon his brow is a threefold burst of splendor, emitting rays of brilliant light. On the upper part of both arms are heavy barbaric bracelets of gold: his bare feet rest upon the earth. In the palm of his upraised left hand he holds a large faceted diamond, which emits a dazzling radiance: his right arm supports a sheaf of corn.

*   *   *

Keeping awareness of the shining form of the Ancient, listen to the invocation which I shall now make, and accept its words as your own.

*   *   *

O ANCIENT WHO ABIDEST IN BRIAH, THOU MANTLE OF THE DIVINE SPIRIT OF BINAH, WHO DOST IMPART THE SACRED ENERGIES OF UNDERSTANDING TO THE LOWER WORLDS: THROUGH THEE I SEEK PLENITUDE OF BLESSING AND TRUE EXPERIENCE OF THE MYSTERY OF QADOSH QADOSHIM. WHEREFORE I SALUTE THEE BY THE TREMENDOUS MOST EXCELLENT NAME WHICH IS THE LIGHT OF THY LIFE:
YHVH ELOHIM | IALDABAOTH | AIONOS KYRIOS

*   *   *

Now the figure of the Ancient before you is aureoled with a dove grey radiance. Rapidly this radiance extends: the figure glows with it, and bright beams of the same dove grey light dart piercingly towards you, becoming continually more brilliant. You are aware of a swift access of gladness in the influence of the powerful beams. In glorious effulgent waves, more and more of the dove grey radiance is given forth from the luminous figure. The radiance spreads, then explodes flashingly to fill the whole region. You see nothing in any direction but the dove grey light itself. You feel transformed, ecstatic, while there reverberates in your ears, clear and ringing, the sacred vowel of the Sphere. In a world of dove grey radiance you float alone and motionless, exultant and blissful.

*   *   *

For a time the encompassing radiance in which you float is altogether dove grey: then swirlings of indigo appear in it. By degrees the indigo light prevails more and more, until you are floating altogether in a region of luminous indigo. Now in this indigo light appear gleams of soft red-brown. The soft red-brown light spreads all about you, swirling and flashing, until at last you are floating in a region entirely of soft red-brown radiance. Suddenly you are floating no longer in a formless world of light. You are standing at the center of a vast circular temple, upon a floor of black onyx. Completely encompassing the temple is a slowly swirling wall of soft grey light, and the ceiling high above you is a billowing soft red-brown radiance.

*   *   *

As I now speak the valediction, give your inner affirmation to my words and accept them as your own.

*   *   *

O GLORIOUS AND MIGHTY

TZAPHQIEL | MENESTHEUS | XAIS

PRAISE AND HONOR BE UNTO THEE FOR THE SPLENDOR OF THINE OFFICE AND THE MAJESTY OF THY BEING. AND WITH YOU, O MINISTERING SPIRITS OF THE THIRD PATH IN YETZIRAH, AS LIKEWISE WITH THEE, O LUMINOUS ARATRON, BE THE BLESSING OF THY GOD AND MINE, EVEN THE EXALTED AND VAST

YHVH ELOHIM | IALDABAOTH | AIONOS KYRIOS

AND IN THIS SAME MOST SACRED NAME WHICH IS THE LIGHT OF THY LIFE, I SALUTE THEE, O ANCIENT: WHO ART VEHICLE AND INSTRUMENT OF THE GOOD, THE BEAUTIFUL, AND THE TRUE.

*   *   *

Now the temple in which you are standing fades from your awareness, and you are surrounded by a clear grey light glinting with tan and tawny hues. This too fades, and you become aware once more of yourself, sitting with closed eyes amid your physical surroundings and the other Companions.

*   *   *

Now open your eyes.

*   *   *

17. The battery is sounded: 1.
18. At this point, if desired, there may be a discussion, led by the director, of the experience of Ascent and Vision. This is optional; and even when it takes place, individual members may desist from it if they wish to reserve their experiences for further meditation. Following discussion, the battery should again be sounded once.
19. All participants stand, and the director proclaims:
    Companions in Light: in unity this rite began, in unity let us bring it to a close.
20. All link hands and perform one clockwise circumambulation of the place of working. Hands are unlinked.
21. The director now utters the thanksgiving:
    Salutation and thanks be unto thee, O exalted and vast

    ### YHVH ELOHIM | IALDABAOTH | AIONOS KYRIOS

    for the virtue and inspiration wherewith thou hast endowed us in this operation of Holy Magick in thy Sphere of Binah.

    All respond:
    Salutation and thanks.
    The director continues:

And do thou grant to us, Most Mighty, the continuance of thy regard as now we go forth from this place.

All respond:

Thus shall it be.

22. The battery is sounded: 3–5–3.

7 PLANETARY TAROT DIVINATION

Sometimes a question to which an answer is sought through Tarot divination can be seen to lie within the scope and rulership of a particular planet. For example:

> investment, insurance, farming, building, speculation, retirement, divorce, for Saturn;
>
> fatherhood, education, legacies, finance, legal defense, religious matters, civic concerns, for Jupiter;
>
> business relationships, legal action, surgery, phobias, aggression, for Mars;
>
> health generally, loyalties, promotion and matters of reputation, for Sun;
>
> love, luck, romance, marriage, the home, social occasions, the concerns of artists, for Venus;
>
> literary matters, travel, communication, family problems, for Mercury;
>
> dreams, psychism, sex, conception, children, motherhood, the mass media, the self-image, chemical problems, for Moon.

In all such cases the process of divination may be conducted under the positive influence of that planet to enhance the querent's rapport with the true archetypal power thereof and to intensify the focus of the area of concern.

For Tarot readings which are to be made with this intention, the following rites, meant for individual use, provide optimum conditions. Any preferred spread may be employed in Section 16 of these rites; however, the Tree of Life Spread, the Celtic Spread and the Six-pointed Star Spread are particularly recommended.*

---

* Should you wish to look further into the subject of Tarot and its divinatory techniques, see *The Llewellyn Practical Guide to The Magick of the Tarot* (by Dennings and Phillips), where significances of cards, patterns of spreads and methods of interpretation are given; as well as some special types of Tarot Magick.

For each of these rites the operator may, if desired, wear a headband containing a planetary gemstone (as described in Ascent and Vision in the Spheres).

TAROT DIVINATION IN LUNA

Temporal Mode: 1
Planetary Time: Hour of the Moon
Position of Bomos: Center of Place of Working
Lights: Star of Nine Lights
Other Requirements: Tarot Cards, stacked face down upon the Bomos
1. Perform the Rite of Preparation.
2. Standing just West of center, facing East across the Bomos, sound the battery: 3-3-3.
3. Raise both arms in salutation, palms facing forwards, and say:
   I salute thee, O thou Inmost Light of the Foundation.
   Cross arms on breast, right over left and say:
   I acknowledge thy presence within me.
   Now extend your arms downward and slightly forwards, hands horizontal with palms downwards, and say:
   And I call forth thy power from the deeps of my being.
   Maintaining this last position, imagine a continuous spiral of *silver* light ascending from the ground at your feet, whirling clockwise around you and disappearing above your head. Hold this whirling spiral of light in visualization for a few moments, then allow it to fade from your consciousness.
4. Move to the East side of the Bomos and, facing East, trace with your right hand the Presigillum of Luna.
   Now trace, about the Presigillum, the invoking Heptagram of Luna as illustrated. As you trace the Heptagram vibrate the chosen divine name of the Sphere—
   SHADDAI EL CHAI | **IAO** | **AIGLE TRISAGIA**

5. Return to the West side of the Bomos and face East.
6. *If you desire, now activate incense.*
7. Make salutation with your right hand to the East; then circumambulate the Bomos nine times clockwise, concluding West of the Bomos facing East.

8. With your two hands, palms facing forwards, form a triangle to frame the center of your forehead, thumb touching thumb, forefinger touching forefinger. Maintaining this position, incline your head slightly forward towards the Tarot deck. Now visualize a seven-rayed star of brilliant white light upon your forehead, in the triangle framed by your hands. Suddenly fling your hands towards the Tarot deck, slightly separating them, and visualizing the seven-rayed star flying forth to enter into the deck as a burst of light. As you send forth the star vibrate the divine name—
   SHADDAI EL CHAI | IAO | AIGLE TRISAGIA

9. Now take up the Tarot cards and holding them before you at the level of your solar plexus visualize yourself surrounded by an ovoid of *violet* light. In this light, shuffle the cards, reflecting meanwhile upon the matter of your inquiry. When you are ready, allow the violet ovoid to fade from your awareness and place the cards upon the Bomos.

10. Sound the Battery: 1.

11. Now, with your arms at your sides, imagine a continuous spiral of *silver* light ascending from the ground at your feet, whirling clockwise around you and disappearing above your head. As you hold this upward whirling spiral in visualization, vibrate the divine name—
    SHADDAI EL CHAI | IAO | AIGLE TRISAGIA

12. Having completed the vibration of the divine name, allow the whirling spiral to fade from your consciousness.

13. Holding your hands, palms down, above the deck, state aloud the matter of your inquiry, beginning with the words:
    Established upon the first step of the Ziggurat of Light and sustained by the magical forces of Luna, I seek to know . . .

14. Rap nine times upon the deck with the knuckles of your right hand.

15. Cut the deck with your left hand, then re-stack. *But leave the deck uncut if you will.*

16. Now lay out the cards in the chosen spread, and proceed to the interpretation of the Arcana.

17. Having completed the divination, leaving the cards undisturbed sound the battery: 1.

18. Salute the East with your right hand, then proclaim:
    O thou Inmost Light of the Foundation, I thank thee for thine aid whereby I have obtained knowledge and inspiration in this hour. May

the process of this divination strengthen my inner faculties and increase my understanding of thy ways, and may its outcome further the lasting good of my entire being.

19. Sound the battery: 1.
20. Re-stack the Tarot deck.
21. Finally, holding the Tarot deck aloft in both hands, equilibriate the magical current you have imparted to it by uttering the Sacred Vowels of the Cosmic Harmony in the following sequence (which is that of Sun—Jupiter—Mars; Sun—Venus—Mercury; Sun—Saturn—Moon):

> I (pronounced as "ee" in *meet*)
> Υ (as German ü)
> O (as "o" in *hot*)
> I (as "ee" in *meet*)
> H (as "a" in *care*)
> E (as "e" in *set*)
> I (as "ee" in *meet*)
> Ω (as "o" in *only*)
> A (as "a" in *father*)

22. Replace the deck upon the Bomos.
23. Sound the battery: 3-5-3.

TAROT DIVINATION IN MERCURY

Temporal Mode: 1
Planetary Time: Hour of Mercury
Position of Bomos: Center of Place of Working
Lights: Star of Eight Lights
Other Requirements: Tarot Cards, stacked face down upon the Bomos

1. Perform the Rite of Preparation.
2. Standing just West of center, facing East across the Bomos, sound the battery: 2-4-2.
3. Raise both arms in salutation, palms facing forwards, and say:
   I salute thee, O thou Inmost Light of Splendor.
   Cross arms on breast, right over left and say:
   I acknowledge thy presence within me.
   Now extend your arms downward and slightly forwards, hands horizontal with palms downwards, and say:
   And I call forth thy power from the deeps of my being.
   Maintaining this last position, imagine a continuous spiral of

shimmering opalescence ascending from the ground at your feet, whirling clockwise around you and disappearing above your head. Hold this whirling spiral of light in visualization for a few moments, then allow it to fade from your consciousness.

4. Move to the East side of the Bomos and, facing East, trace with your right hand the Presigillum of Mercury.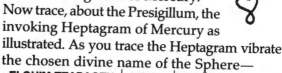

    Now trace, about the Presigillum, the invoking Heptagram of Mercury as illustrated. As you trace the Heptagram vibrate the chosen divine name of the Sphere—

    ELOHIM TZABAOTH | AZOTH | ALETHES LOGOS

5. Return to the West side of the Bomos and face East.

6. *If you desire, now activate incense.*

7. Make salutation with your right hand to the East; then circumambulate the Bomos eight times clockwise, concluding West of the Bomos facing East.

8. With your two hands, palms facing forwards, form a triangle to frame the center of your forehead, thumb touching thumb, forefinger touching forefinger. Maintaining this position, incline your head slightly forward towards the Tarot deck. Now visualize a seven-rayed star of brilliant white light upon your forehead, in the triangle framed by your hands. Suddenly fling your hands towards the Tarot deck, slightly separating them, and visualizing the seven-rayed star flying forth to enter into the deck as a burst of light. As you send forth the star vibrate the divine name—

    ELOHIM TZABAOTH | AZOTH | ALETHES LOGOS

9. Now take up the Tarot cards and holding them before you at the level of your solar plexus visualize yourself surrounded by an ovoid of *orange* light. In this light, shuffle the cards, reflecting meanwhile upon the matter of your inquiry. When you are ready, allow the orange ovoid to fade from your awareness and place the cards upon the Bomos.

10. Sound the Battery: 1.

11. Now, with your arms at your sides, imagine a continuous spiral of *shimmering opalescence* ascending from the ground at your feet, whirling clockwise around you and disappearing above your head. As you hold this upward whirling spiral in visualization, vibrate the divine name—

    ELOHIM TZABAOTH | AZOTH | ALETHES LOGOS

12. Having completed the vibration of the divine name, allow the whirling spiral to fade from your consciousness.

13. Holding your hands, palms down, above the deck, state aloud the matter of your inquiry, beginning with the words:

Established upon the second step of the Ziggurat of Light and sustained by the magical forces of Mercury, I seek to know . . .

14. Rap eight times upon the deck with the knuckles of your right hand.

15. Cut the deck with your left hand, then re-stack. *But leave the deck uncut if you will.*

16. Now lay out the cards in the chosen spread, and proceed to the interpretation of the Arcana.

17. Having completed the divination, leaving the cards undisturbed sound the battery: 1.

18. Salute the East with your right hand, then proclaim:

O thou Inmost Light of Splendor, I thank thee for thine aid whereby I have obtained knowledge and inspiration in this hour. May the process of this divination strengthen my inner faculties and increase my understanding of thy ways, and may its outcome further the lasting good of my entire being.

19. Sound the battery: 1.

20. Re-stack the Tarot deck.

21. Finally, holding the Tarot deck aloft in both hands, equilibriate the magical current you have imparted to it by uttering the Sacred Vowels of the Cosmic Harmony in the following sequence:

I   (pronounced as "ee" in *meet*)
Υ   (as German ü)
O   (as "o" in *hot*)
I   (as "ee" in *meet*)
H   (as "a" in *care*)
E   (as "e" in *set*)
I   (as "ee" in *meet*)
Ω   (as "o" in *only*)
A   (as "a" in *father*)

22. Replace the deck upon the Bomos.

23. Sound the battery: 3-5-3.

TAROT DIVINATION IN VENUS

Temporal Mode: 1
Planetary Time: Hour of Venus

Position of Bomos: Center of Place of Working
Lights: Star of Seven Lights
Other Requirements: Tarot Cards, stacked face down upon the Bomos

1. Perform the Rite of Preparation.
2. Standing just West of center, facing East across the Bomos, sound the battery: 3-1-3.
3. Raise both arms in salutation, palms facing forwards, and say:
   I salute thee, O thou Inmost Light of Victory.
   Cross arms on breast, right over left and say:
   I acknowledge thy presence within me.
   Now extend your arms downward and slightly forwards, hands horizontal with palms downwards, and say:
   And I call forth thy power from the deeps of my being.
   Maintaining this last position, imagine a continuous spiral of *saffron* light ascending from the ground at your feet, whirling clockwise around you and disappearing above your head. Hold this whirling spiral of light in visualization for a few moments, then allow it to fade from your consciousness.
4. Move to the East side of the Bomos and, facing East, trace with your right hand the Presigillum of Venus.

   Now trace, about the Presigillum, the invoking Heptagram of Venus as illustrated. As you trace the Heptagram vibrate the chosen divine name of the Sphere—
   YHVH TZABAOTH | ALBAPHALANA | CHARIS
5. Return to the West side of the Bomos and face East.
6. *If you desire, now activate incense.*
7. Make salutation with your right hand to the East; then circumambulate the Bomos seven times clockwise, concluding West of the Bomos facing East.
8. With your two hands, palms facing forwards, form a triangle to frame the center of your forehead, thumb touching thumb, forefinger touching forefinger. Maintaining this position, incline your head slightly forward towards the Tarot deck. Now visualize a seven-rayed star of brilliant white light upon your forehead, in the triangle framed by your hands. Suddenly fling your hands towards the Tarot deck, slightly separating them, and visualizing the seven-rayed star flying forth to enter into the deck as a burst of light. As you send forth the star vibrate the divine name—

YHVH TZABAOTH | ALBAPHALANA | CHARIS

9. Now take up the Tarot cards and holding them before you at the level of your solar plexus visualize yourself surrounded by an ovoid of *green* light. In this light, shuffle the cards, reflecting meanwhile upon the matter of your inquiry. When you are ready, allow the green ovoid to fade from your awareness and place the cards upon the Bomos.

10. Sound the Battery: 1.

11. Now, with your arms at your sides, imagine a continuous spiral of *saffron* light ascending from the ground at your feet, whirling clockwise around you and disappearing above your head. As you hold this upward whirling spiral in visualization, vibrate the divine name—

YHVH TZABAOTH | ALBAPHALANA | CHARIS

12. Having completed the vibration of the divine name, allow the whirling spiral to fade from your consciousness.

13. Holding your hands, palms down, above the deck, state aloud the matter of your inquiry, beginning with the words:
    Established upon the third step of the Ziggurat of Light and sustained by the magical forces of Venus, I seek to know . . .

14. Rap seven times upon the deck with the knuckles of your right hand.

15. Cut the deck with your left hand, then re-stack. *But leave the deck uncut if you will.*

16. Now lay out the cards in the chosen spread, and proceed to the interpretation of the Arcana.

17. Having completed the divination, leaving the cards undisturbed sound the battery: 1.

18. Salute the East with your right hand, then proclaim:
    O thou Inmost Light of Victory, I thank thee for thine aid whereby I have obtained knowledge and inspiration in this hour. May the process of this divination strengthen my inner faculties and increase my understanding of thy ways, and may its outcome further the lasting good of my entire being.

19. Sound the battery: 1.

20. Re-stack the Tarot deck.

21. Finally, holding the Tarot deck aloft in both hands, equilibrate the magical current you have imparted to it by uttering the Sacred Vowels of the Cosmic Harmony in the following sequence:

    I   (pronounced as "ee" in *meet*)

Υ   (as German ü)
O   (as "o" in *hot*)
I   (as "ee" in *meet*)
H   (as "a" in *care*)
E   (as "e" in *set*)
I   (as "ee" in *meet*)
Ω   (as "o" in *only*)
A   (as "a" in *father*)

22. Replace the deck upon the Bomos.
23. Sound the battery: 3-5-3.

TAROT DIVINATION IN SOL

Temporal Mode: 1
Planetary Time: Hour of the Sun
Position of Bomos: Center of Place of Working
Lights: Star of Six Lights
Other Requirements: Tarot Cards, stacked face down upon the Bomos

1. Perform the Rite of Preparation.
2. Standing just West of center, facing East across the Bomos, sound the battery: 3-3.
3. Raise both arms in salutation, palms facing forwards, and say:
   I salute thee, O thou Inmost Light of Beauty.

   Cross arms on breast, right over left and say:
   I acknowledge thy presence within me.

   Now extend your arms downward and slightly forwards, hands horizontal with palms downwards, and say:
   And I call forth thy power from the deeps of my being.

   Maintaining this last position, imagine a continuous spiral of *gold* light ascending from the ground at your feet, whirling clockwise around you and disappearing above your head. Hold this whirling spiral of light in visualization for a few moments, then allow it to fade from your consciousness.

4. Move to the East side of the Bomos and, facing East, trace with your right hand the Presigillum of Sol.
   Now trace, about the Presigillum, the invoking Heptagram of Sol as illustrated. As you trace the Heptagram vibrate the chosen divine name of the Sphere—

YHVH ELOAH V'DAATH │ ONOPHIS │ THEIOS NOUS

5. Return to the West side of the Bomos and face East.
6. *If you desire, now activate incense.*
7. Make salutation with your right hand to the East; then circum-ambulate the Bomos six times clockwise, concluding West of the Bomos facing East.
8. With your two hands, palms facing forwards, form a triangle to frame the center of your forehead, thumb touching thumb, forefinger touching forefinger. Maintaining this position, incline your head slightly forward towards the Tarot deck. Now visual-ize a seven-rayed star of brilliant white light upon your forehead, in the triangle framed by your hands. Suddenly fling your hands towards the Tarot deck, slightly separating them, and visualizing the seven-rayed star flying forth to enter into the deck as a burst of light. As you send forth the star vibrate the divine name—
   YHVH ELOAH V'DAATH │ ONOPHIS │ THEIOS NOUS
9. Now take up the Tarot cards and holding them before you at the level of your solar plexus visualize yourself surrounded by an ovoid of *yellow* light. In this light, shuffle the cards, reflecting meanwhile upon the matter of your inquiry. When you are ready, allow the yellow ovoid to fade from your awareness and place the cards upon the Bomos.
10. Sound the battery: 1.
11. Now, with your arms at your sides, imagine a continuous spiral of *gold* light ascending from the ground at your feet, whirling clockwise around you and disappearing above your head. As you hold this upward whirling spiral in visualization, vibrate the divine name—
    YHVH ELOAH V'DAATH │ ONOPHIS │ THEIOS NOUS
12. Having completed the vibration of the divine name, allow the whirling spiral to fade from your consciousness.
13. Holding your hands, palms down, above the deck, state aloud the matter of your inquiry, beginning with the words:
    Established upon the fourth step of the Ziggurat of Light and sustained by the magical forces of Sol, I seek to know . . .
14. Rap six times upon the deck with the knuckles of your right hand.
15. Cut the deck with your left hand, then re-stack. *But leave the deck uncut if you will.*
16. Now lay out the cards in the chosen spread, and proceed to the

interpretation of the Arcana.

17. Having completed the divination, leaving the cards undisturbed sound the battery: 1.

18. Salute the East with your right hand, then proclaim:

O thou Inmost Light of Beauty, I thank thee for thine aid whereby I have obtained knowledge and inspiration in this hour. May the process of this divination strengthen my inner faculties and increase my understanding of thy ways, and may its outcome further the lasting good of my entire being.

19. Sound the battery: 1.

20. Re-stack the Tarot deck.

21. Finally, holding the Tarot deck aloft in both hands, equilibriate the magical current you have imparted to it by uttering the Sacred Vowels of the Cosmic Harmony in the following sequence:

    I   (pronounced as "ee" in *meet*)
    ϓ   (as German ü)
    O   (as "o" in *hot*)
    I   (as "ee" in *meet*)
    H   (as "a" in *care*)
    E   (as "e" in *set*)
    I   (as "ee" in *meet*)
    Ω   (as "o" in *only*)
    A   (as "a" in *father*)

22. Replace the deck upon the Bomos.

23. Sound the battery: 3-5-3.

TAROT DIVINATION IN MARS

Temporal Mode: 1
Planetary Time: Hour of Mars
Position of Bomos: Center of Place of Working
Lights: Star of Five Lights
Other Requirements: Tarot Cards, stacked face down upon the Bomos

1. Perform the Rite of Preparation.

2. Standing just West of center, facing East across the Bomos, sound the battery: 2-1-2.

3. Raise both arms in salutation, palms facing forwards, and say:

I salute thee, O thou Inmost Light of Strength.

Cross arms on breast, right over left and say:

I acknowledge thy presence within me.

Now extend your arms downward and slightly forwards, hands horizontal with palms downwards, and say:

And I call forth thy power from the deeps of my being.

Maintaining this last position, imagine a continuous spiral of *fiery red* light ascending from the ground at your feet, whirling clockwise around you and disappearing above your head. Hold this whirling spiral of light in visualization for a few moments, then allow it to fade from your consciousness.

4. Move to the East side of the Bomos and, facing East, trace with your right hand the Presigillum of Mars.

   Now trace, about the Presigillum, the invoking Heptagram of Mars as illustrated. As you trace the Heptagram vibrate the chosen divine name of the Sphere—

   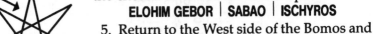
   ELOHIM GEBOR | **SABAO** | **ISCHYROS**

5. Return to the West side of the Bomos and face East.

6. *If you desire, now activate incense.*

7. Make salutation with your right hand to the East; then circumambulate the Bomos five times clockwise, concluding West of the Bomos facing East.

8. With your two hands, palms facing forwards, form a triangle to frame the center of your forehead, thumb touching thumb, forefinger touching forefinger. Maintaining this position, incline your head slightly forward towards the Tarot deck. Now visualize a seven-rayed star of brilliant white light upon your forehead, in the triangle framed by your hands. Suddenly fling your hands towards the Tarot deck, slightly separating them, and visualizing the seven-rayed star flying forth to enter into the deck as a burst of light. As you send forth the star vibrate the divine name—

   ELOHIM GEBOR | **SABAO** | **ISCHYROS**

9. Now take up the Tarot cards and holding them before you at the level of your solar plexus visualize yourself surrounded by an ovoid of *red* light. In this light, shuffle the cards, reflecting meanwhile upon the matter of your inquiry. When you are ready, allow the red ovoid to fade from your awareness and place the cards upon the Bomos.

10. Sound the battery: 1.

11. Now, with your arms at your sides, imagine a continuous spiral of *fiery red* light ascending from the ground at your feet, whirling clockwise around you and disappearing above your head. As you hold this upward whirling spiral in visualization, vibrate the divine name—

ELOHIM GEBOR | SABAO | ISCHYROS

12. Having completed the vibration of the divine name, allow the whirling spiral to fade from your consciousness.

13. Holding your hands, palms down, above the deck, state aloud the matter of your inquiry, beginning with the words:

Established upon the fifth step of the Ziggurat of Light and sustained by the magical forces of Mars, I seek to know . . .

14. Rap five times upon the deck with the knuckles of your right hand.

15. Cut the deck with your left hand, then re-stack. *But leave the deck uncut if you will.*

16. Now lay out the cards in the chosen spread, and proceed to the interpretation of the Arcana.

17. Having completed the divination, leaving the cards undisturbed sound the battery: 1.

18. Salute the East with your right hand, then proclaim:

O thou Inmost Light of Strength, I thank thee for thine aid whereby I have obtained knowledge and inspiration in this hour. May the process of this divination strengthen my inner faculties and increase my understanding of thy ways, and may its outcome further the lasting good of my entire being.

19. Sound the battery: 1.

20. Re-stack the Tarot deck.

21. Finally, holding the Tarot deck aloft in both hands, equilibriate the magical current you have imparted to it by uttering the Sacred Vowels of the Cosmic Harmony in the following sequence:

I	(pronounced as "ee" in *meet*)
Υ	(as German ü)
O	(as "o" in *hot*)
I	(as "ee" in *meet*)
H	(as "a" in *care*)
E	(as "e" in *set*)
I	(as "ee" in *meet*)
Ω	(as "o" in *only*)
A	(as "a" in *father*)

22. Replace the deck upon the Bomos.
23. Sound the battery: 3-5-3.

TAROT DIVINATION IN JUPITER

Temporal Mode: 1
Planetary Time: Hour of Jupiter
Position of Bomos: Center of Place of Working
Lights: Star of Four Lights
Other Requirements: Tarot Cards, stacked face down upon the Bomos

1. Perform the Rite of Preparation.
2. Standing just West of center, facing East across the Bomos, sound the battery: 2-2.
3. Raise both arms in salutation, palms facing forwards, and say:
   I salute thee, O thou Inmost Light of Majesty.
   Cross arms on breast, right over left and say:
   I acknowledge thy presence within me.
   Now extend your arms downward and slightly forwards, hands horizontal with palms downwards, and say:
   And I call forth thy power from the deeps of my being.
   Maintaining this last position, imagine a continuous spiral of *white* light ascending from the ground at your feet, whirling clockwise around you and disappearing above your head. Hold this whirling spiral of light in visualization for a few moments, then allow it to fade from your consciousness.
4. Move to the East side of the Bomos and, facing East, trace with your right hand the Presigillum of Jupiter.
   Now trace, about the Presigillum, the invoking Heptagram of Jupiter as illustrated. As you trace the Heptagram vibrate the chosen divine name of the Sphere—

   EL ⏐ ZARAIETOS ⏐ PANTOKRATOR

5. Return to the West side of the Bomos and face East.
6. *If you desire, now activate incense.*
7. Make salutation with your right hand to the East; then circumambulate the Bomos four times clockwise, concluding West of the Bomos facing East.
8. With your two hands, palms facing forwards, form a triangle to frame the center

of your forehead, thumb touching thumb, forefinger touching forefinger. Maintaining this position, incline your head slightly forward towards the Tarot deck. Now visualize a seven-rayed star of brilliant white light upon your forehead, in the triangle framed by your hands. Suddenly fling your hands towards the Tarot deck, slightly separating them, and visualizing the seven-rayed star flying forth to enter into the deck as a burst of light. As you send forth the star vibrate the divine name—

EL | ZARAIETOS | PANTOKRATOR

9. Now take up the Tarot cards and holding them before you at the level of your solar plexus visualize yourself surrounded by an ovoid of *blue* light. In this light, shuffle the cards, reflecting meanwhile upon the matter of your inquiry. When you are ready, allow the blue ovoid to fade from your awareness and place the cards upon the Bomos.

10. Sound the battery: 1.

11. Now, with your arms at your sides, imagine a continuous spiral of *white* light ascending from the ground at your feet, whirling clockwise around you and disappearing above your head. As you hold this upward whirling spiral in visualization, vibrate the divine name—

EL | ZARAIETOS | PANTOKRATOR

12. Having completed the vibration of the divine name, allow the whirling spiral to fade from your consciousness.

13. Holding your hands, palms down, above the deck, state aloud the matter of your inquiry, beginning with the words:
    Established upon the sixth step of the Ziggurat of Light and sustained by the magical forces of Jupiter, I seek to know . . .

14. Rap four times upon the deck with the knuckles of your right hand.

15. Cut the deck with your left hand, then re-stack. *But leave the deck uncut if you will.*

16. Now lay out the cards in the chosen spread, and proceed to the interpretation of the Arcana.

17. Having completed the divination, leaving the cards undisturbed sound the battery: 1.

18. Salute the East with your right hand, then proclaim:
    O thou Inmost Light of Majesty, I thank thee for thine aid whereby I have obtained knowledge and inspiration in this hour. May the process of this divination strengthen my inner faculties and increase my

　　　understanding of thy ways, and may its outcome further the lasting
　　　good of my entire being.
19. Sound the battery:　1.
20. Re-stack the Tarot deck.
21. Finally, holding the Tarot deck aloft in both hands, equilibrate
　　　the magical current you have imparted to it by uttering the Sacred
　　　Vowels of the Cosmic Harmony in the following sequence:

　　　　　　　　I　(pronounced as "ee" in *meet*)
　　　　　　　　Υ　(as German ü)
　　　　　　　　O　(as "o" in *hot*)
　　　　　　　　I　(as "ee" in *meet*)
　　　　　　　　H　(as "a" in *care*)
　　　　　　　　E　(as "e" in *set*)
　　　　　　　　I　(as "ee" in *meet*)
　　　　　　　　Ω　(as "o" in *only*)
　　　　　　　　A　(as "a" in *father*)

22. Replace the deck upon the Bomos.
23. Sound the battery:　3-5-3.

TAROT DIVINATION IN SATURN

Temporal Mode: 1
Planetary Time: Hour of Saturn
Position of Bomos: Center of Place of Working
Lights: Star of Three Lights
Other Requirements: Tarot Cards, stacked face down upon the Bomos
　1. Perform the Rite of Preparation.
　2. Standing just West of center, facing East across the Bomos, sound
　　　the battery: 3.
　3. Raise both arms in salutation, palms facing forwards, and say:
　　　　I salute thee, O thou Inmost Light of Understanding.
　　　Cross arms on breast, right over left and say:
　　　　I acknowledge thy presence within me.
　　　Now extend your arms downward and slightly forwards, hands
　　　horizontal with palms downwards, and say:
　　　　And I call forth thy power from the deeps of my being.
　　　Maintaining this last position, imagine a continuous spiral of *grey*
　　　light ascending from the ground at your feet, whirling clockwise
　　　around you and disappearing above your head. Hold this whirl-
　　　ing spiral of light in visualization for a few moments, then allow it

to fade from your consciousness.

4. Move to the East side of the Bomos and, facing East, trace with your right hand the Presigillum of Saturn.

Now trace, about the Presigillum, the invoking Heptagram of Saturn as illustrated. As you trace the Heptagram vibrate the chosen divine name of the Sphere—

YHVH ELOHIM ∣ **IALDABAOTH** ∣ **AIONOS KYRIOS**

5. Return to the West side of the Bomos and face East.

6. *If you desire, now activate incense.*

7. Make salutation with your right hand to the East; then circumambulate the Bomos three times clockwise, concluding West of the Bomos facing East.

8. With your two hands, palms facing forwards, form a triangle to frame the center of your forehead, thumb touching thumb, forefinger touching forefinger. Maintaining this position, incline your head slightly forward towards the Tarot deck. Now visualize a seven-rayed star of brilliant white light upon your forehead, in the triangle framed by your hands. Suddenly fling your hands towards the Tarot deck, slightly separating them, and visualizing the seven-rayed star flying forth to enter into the deck as a burst of light. As you send forth the star vibrate the divine name—

YHVH ELOHIM ∣ **IALDABAOTH** ∣ **AIONOS KYRIOS**

9. Now take up the Tarot cards and holding them before you at the level of your solar plexus visualize yourself surrounded by an ovoid of *indigo* light. In this light, shuffle the cards, reflecting meanwhile upon the matter of your inquiry. When you are ready, allow the indigo ovoid to fade from your awareness and place the cards upon the Bomos.

10. Sound the battery: 1.

11. Now, with your arms at your sides, imagine a continuous spiral of *grey* light ascending from the ground at your feet, whirling clockwise around you and disappearing above your head. As you hold this upward whirling spiral in visualization, vibrate the divine name—

YHVH ELOHIM ∣ **IALDABAOTH** ∣ **AIONOS KYRIOS**

12. Having completed the vibration of the divine name, allow the whirling spiral to fade from your consciousness.

13. Holding your hands, palms down, above the deck, state aloud the matter of your inquiry, beginning with the words:

    Established upon the seventh step of the Ziggurat of Light and sustained by the magical forces of Saturn, I seek to know . . .

14. Rap three times upon the deck with the knuckles of your right hand.

15. Cut the deck with your left hand, then re-stack. *But leave the deck uncut if you will.*

16. Now lay out the cards in the chosen spread, and proceed to the interpretation of the Arcana.

17. Having completed the divination, leaving the cards undisturbed sound the battery: 1.

18. Salute the East with your right hand, then proclaim:

    O thou Inmost Light of Understanding, I thank thee for thine aid whereby I have obtained knowledge and inspiration in this hour. May the process of this divination strengthen my inner faculties and increase my understanding of thy ways, and may its outcome further the lasting good of my entire being.

19. Sound the battery: 1.

20. Re-stack the Tarot deck.

21. Finally, holding the Tarot deck aloft in both hands, equilibrate the magical current you have imparted to it by uttering the Sacred Vowels of the Cosmic Harmony in the following sequence:

I	(pronounced as "ee" in *meet*)
Υ	(as German ü)
O	(as "o" in *hot*)
I	(as "ee" in *meet*)
H	(as "a" in *care*)
E	(as "e" in *set*)
I	(as "ee" in *meet*)
Ω	(as "o" in *only*)
A	(as "a" in *father*)

22. Replace the deck upon the Bomos.

23. Sound the battery: 3-5-3.

8

SEVENFOLD RITE OF THE HEART'S DESIRE

This ritual combines several magical methods which, singly or together, are potently effective and which for this reason have been handed down from a considerable antiquity.

As a main category, this is a work of *Talismanic Magick:* it involves the creation of a magical object charged with mighty power and intended to be worn or carried until a particular goal is attained. Besides this, the ritual incorporates the use of *Creative Visualization,* in itself an awesomely powerful key to the fulfillment of one's will. And, too, it is a work of *Cord Magick,* knot magick, whose paramount effectiveness likewise has made it a treasured art from remote times.

Additionally to these factors, this is a *Planetary Rite,* involving the powers and invoking the divine names of all seven of the traditional planets to bring the formulated desire of the magician down through the Spheres, from first concept to realization in materiality. This treatment of the wish is effective whether the "heart's desire" be a specific article such as a house, or a state of affairs such as good health, an educational project or a vacation. Nor is there a necessity to allocate that which is desired to a ruling planet: since in this one ritual the powers of all are involved.

There are, naturally, certain parameters which should be recognized in this work: the most important of which is that you should only employ this method to obtain that which is truly your heart's desire. It should never be undertaken in a spirit of mere experiment: the danger of a discouraging failure, or of success in winning an objective which is no part of one's true will, are alike to be shunned. Apart from this, in magick as elsewhere it is generally advisable to proceed from smaller matters to greater. Practice in working with the powers—

practice in this ritual specifically as well as in magical operations generally—makes for the aptitude and, indeed, the right, to aspire to the greater rewards. Nevertheless the concentration of potent factors in this ritual gives it a conspicuous ascendancy against seemingly high odds.

Of all the positive requirements for the ritual, the foremost is that before attempting anything you should read carefully through these introductory notes and also through the text of the ritual, so as to take heed of what is needed.

As the *materium* for the ritual a piece of slender cord should be obtained, white in color; it should be of sufficient length to go around the waist after having seven simple knots made in it, and to be tied in place there comfortably and securely. Before the rite this cord is further to be prepared by stitching into it, at equidistant points where the knots are going to be tied, seven narrow bands of sewing thread in the Briatic planetary colors:

> *Saturn*—black
> *Jupiter*—spectrum blue
> *Mars*—spectrum red
> *Sun*—spectrum yellow
> *Venus*—green
> *Mercury*—orange
> *Moon*—violet

The yellow band, therefore, can most conveniently be located at about the center point of the length of cord.

Because, as has been said, this is a rite of all seven planetary powers in one, special conditions apply in regard to the choice of time and appurtenances. The rite is conducted on the day of Saturn, in the hour of Luna: that is in the 7th, 14th or 21st magical hour on a Saturday. The lamp, drapes and vestments are to be white, representing the synthesis in light of the seven colors of the spectrum. If incense is employed, it will be of solar attribution.

SEVENFOLD RITE OF THE HEART'S DESIRE

Temporal Mode: 1
Planetary Time: Day of Saturn, Hour of the Moon
Position of Bomos: Center of Place of Working
Lights: 1 White Light upon the Bomos

Other Requirements: The Cord, Seven Planetary Oils,* and a lighting taper upon the Bomos
1.   Standing at the West side of the Bomos facing East, perform the Rite of Preparation.
2.   Move to the East side of the Bomos and face West.
3.   *If you desire, now activate incense.*

(The Knot of Saturn)

4.   (a)   Sound the Battery: 3.
(b)   Take up the cord, keeping it near the surface of the Bomos, and grasping it with both hands, one at each side of the black band.†
(c)   With closed eyes, in imagination surround yourself with the light of the Sphere of Saturn: a cool luminous indigo, with a sense of powerful creativity brooding within it.
(d)   In this light, visualize that which you desire: whether as a single object, or as the representation of a scene, as suitable. Do not attempt at this stage to give it any "animation"; consider it as "an image" simply, latent in the Saturnian creativity.
(e)   Holding this image in mind, raise the cord and breathe on the black band.
(f)   Open your eyes and tie the first knot, saying:
   I tie, tie the Knot of Power: this is the shape of my heart's desire!
(g)   Place the cord upon the Bomos. Light the taper, and trace therewith the Presigillum of Saturn vertically above the knot, meanwhile vibrating the chosen divine name—

YHVH ELOHIM | IALDABAOTH | AIONOS KYRIOS

(h)   Extinguish and replace the taper. Now lightly anoint the knot with the appropriate oil.

(The Knot of Jupiter)

5.   (a)   Sound the battery: 4.
(b)   Take up the cord, keeping it near the surface of the Bomos, and grasping it with both hands, one at each side of the blue band.
(c)   With closed eyes, in imagination surround yourself with the light of the Sphere of Jupiter: a strong blue radiance, with the expansiveness and warmth of summer skies.
(d)   In this light, imagine the joy which the fulfillment of your

---

* Select one pure oil for each planet (see *Entry 29,* Tables of Correspondences).

† As you stand facing West, the cord should be at your left upon the Bomos. Draw it out as needed in the working, and allow it to coil or loop again at your right.

heart's desire will bring you. Feel this joy, not as something hoped for in the future, but as a present emotion because your heart's desire is realized NOW.

(e)   While dwelling upon this joy, raise the cord and breathe once on the blue band.

(f)   Open your eyes and tie the second knot, saying:
        I tie, tie the Knot of Power: in joy I win my heart's desire!

(g)   Place the cord upon the Bomos. Light the taper, and trace therewith the Presigillum of Jupiter vertically above the knot, meanwhile vibrating the chosen divine name—

EL | ZARAIETOS | PANTOKRATOR

(h)   Extinguish and replace the taper. Now lightly anoint the knot with the appropriate oil.

(The Knot of Mars)

6.   (a)   Sound the battery: 5.

(b)   Take up the cord, keeping it near the surface of the Bomos and grasping it with both hands, one at each side of the red band.

(c)   With closed eyes, in imagination surround yourself with the light of the Sphere of Mars: a hot red light which gives forth to you a tremendous feeling of courage and certainty.

(d)   In this light, be conscious of all the longing and resolve with which you look forward to gaining your heart's desire: all the qualities and causes, indeed, which make it your heart's desire. With courage and certainty, know that your desire will prevail.

(e)   While dwelling upon this certainty, raise the cord and breathe once on the red band.

(f)   Open your eyes and tie the third knot, saying:
        I tie, tie the Knot of Power: by will I win my heart's desire!

(g)   Place the cord upon the Bomos. Light the taper, and trace therewith the Presigillum of Mars vertically above the knot, meanwhile vibrating the chosen divine name—

ELOHIM GEBOR | SABAO | ISCHYROS

(h)   Extinguish and replace the taper. Now lightly anoint the knot with the appropriate oil.

(The knot of Sol)

7.   (a)   Sound the battery: 6.

(b)   Take up the cord, keeping it near the surface of the Bomos, and grasping it with both hands, one at each side of the yellow band.

(c)   With closed eyes, in imagination surround yourself with the light of the Sphere of the Sun: a warm yellow radiance which envelops you in inspiring and life-giving power.

(d)   In this light, visualize again that which you desire: much as you did in the Saturnian light, but this time as a reality with dimension, color, movement.

(e)   While visualizing this vivid reality, raise the cord and breathe once on the yellow band.

(f)   Open your eyes and tie the fourth knot, saying:

I tie, tie the Knot of Power: I shall have in truth my heart's desire!

(g)   Place the cord upon the Bomos. Light the taper, and trace therewith the Presigillum of Sol vertically above the knot, meanwhile vibrating the chosen divine name—

YHVH ELOAH V'DAATH │ ONOPHIS │ THEIOS NOUS

(h)   Extinguish and replace the taper. Now lightly anoint the knot with the appropriate oil.

(The Knot of Venus)

8.   (a)   Sound the battery: 7.

(b)   Take up the cord, keeping it near the surface of the Bomos, and grasping it with both hands, one at each side of the green band.

(c)   With closed eyes, in imagination surround yourself with the light of the Sphere of Venus: a strong green radiance, vibrant with the energies of Nature.

(d)   In this light, review the effects the attainment of your heart's desire will have in your life: the changes it will make, the way you feel, the person you will be.

(e)   While holding these effects in imagination, raise the cord and breathe once on the green band.

(f)   Open your eyes and tie the fifth knot, saying:

I tie, tie the Knot of Power: my life enweaves my heart's desire!

(g)   Place the cord upon the Bomos. Light the taper, and trace therewith the Presigillum of Venus vertically above the knot, meanwhile vibrating the chosen divine name—

YHVH TZABAOTH │ ALBAPHALANA │ CHARIS

(h)   Extinguish and replace the taper. Now lightly anoint the knot with the appropriate oil.

(The Knot of Mercury)

9.   (a)   Sound the battery: 8.

(b)   Take up the cord, keeping it near the surface of the Bomos, and grasping it with both hands, one at each side of the orange band.

(c)   With closed eyes, in imagination surround yourself with the light of the Sphere of Mercury: a cool, bright orange light which seems about to flash into electrical sparklings.

(d)   In this light, imagine yourself and the fulfillment of your wish rushing to meet each other, at an immense speed through Time and Space. Because of what you are doing and willing, the meeting—the fulfillment of your heart's desire—is imminent.

(e)   Filled with the sense of this immediacy, raise the cord and breathe once on the orange band.

(f)   Open your eyes and tie the sixth knot, saying:

I tie, tie the Knot of Power: swiftly comes my heart's desire!

(g)   Place the cord upon the Bomos. Light the taper, and trace therewith the Presigillum of Mercury vertically above the knot, meanwhile vibrating the chosen divine name—

ELOHIM TZABAOTH | AZOTH | ALETHES LOGOS

(h)   Extinguish and replace the taper. Now lightly anoint the knot with the appropriate oil.

(The Knot of Luna)

10.   (a)   Sound the battery: 9.

(b)   Take up the cord, keeping it near the surface of the Bomos, and grasping it with both hands, one at each side of the violet band.

(c)   With closed eyes, in imagination surround yourself with the light of the Sphere of the Moon: an intense violet light which is filled equally with a deep red suggesting earthly emotions and enjoyment, and a strong blue quality suggesting spiritual power.

(d)   In this light feel, rather than perceiving, the fulfillment of your wish as a complete reality. The stress of longing, the exertion of will, are at this point no longer relevant: that which you have desired has come to pass.

(e)   Letting this certainty pervade your entire being, raise the cord and breathe once on the violet band.

(f)   Open your eyes and tie the seventh knot, saying:
I tie, tie the Knot of Power: even now fulfilled is my heart's desire!
(g)   Place the cord upon the Bomos. Light the taper,
and trace therewith the Presigillum of Luna vertically
above the knot, meanwhile vibrating the chosen divine
name—
SHADDAI EL CHAI | IAO | AIGLE TRISAGIA
(h)   Extinguish and replace the taper. Now lightly anoint the
knot with the appropriate oil.
11.   Now light the taper and with it slightly sear the ends of the cord.
Extinguish and replace the taper.
12.   Sound the battery: 3–5–3.

*The cord should be tied around your waist during the first magical
hour on the next morning (Sunday). It should be worn next your skin
night and day until your heart's desire is fulfilled: it can in the meantime
be removed, for example when you shower, but otherewise should be
worn consistently.*

*When your heart's desire has been fulfilled, the cord should be
destroyed. Take it off and cut it in two, through the central Solar knot.
Then you have three options: whatever the day, you can cast the two
halves into a river or the sea in the Hour of Saturn, or burn them in the
Hour of the Sun, or bury them in the Hour of the Moon.*

9 BENEFICENT SENDINGS

These group workings give a method by which a beneficent charge of planetary power can be imparted to a person at a distance. The recipient need not be a member of your group and need not have any occult training or, indeed, any special degree of psychic perception. The consent of the recipient is required (as for any form of action which may impinge, however benignly, upon a person's deeds, emotions or energies); also a time needs to be arranged when, during an hour of the planet of the working, the rite can be performed by the group and the recipient can simultaneously sit quietly in a meditative and receptive frame of mind.

For these rites, a photograph of the recipient should be placed upon the Bomos. This will serve as a focal point and an aid in the necessary visualization; any participating member who does not personally know the recipient should, therefore, make a point of looking at and studying the photograph before the ritual work begins.

The sending itself will be of a simple planetary force: its adaptation to individual circumstances will be made partly by the circumstances themselves but also, more particularly, by the psyche of the recipient. For example: a person facing an important interview may feel the need of a special incisiveness in thought and communication for that occasion. If a charge of the energies of Mercury is sent, the total ambience of those enegies will remain latently present with the recipient until called into activity as required: when the special incisiveness is needed, then the planetary energies will become operative in that form. Or a person suffering from a chronic sense of loneliness might receive a charge of Jupiterian energies. That person's craving for company might initially receive the Jupiterian force in the form of a sure and comforting awareness of the unity of life; but an unsuspected talent for leadership might also be awakened, and the resulting expansion of outlook—also Jupiterian—might cause the recipient to find opportunity to exercise benign authority for the general good, as in a youth club for instance.

For the purpose of these rituals the group should certainly take pains to identify the planetary power most suited to the recipient's needs: the power of Venus for one who requires an ambience of harmony or of artistic feeling (for instance), the power of Mars for one who requires courage, initiative or maybe a palpable shield of protection; but no attempt should be made to particularize the benefit which is to result. Such a particularization cannot effectively be made; and this is fortunate, since if it could, it might fall short of the recipient's true needs and also limit the power made available by the planetary charge. The outcome of this type of working can only be good, but factors not immediately apparent may have their rightful part to play in the matter.

It would be great to send a charge of the power of Saturn to one who was apprehensive of losing his or her job. That is the limit of your intervention; but then, if the circumstances are set for it, you may have the reward of beholding that stabilizing force not only securing the position, but infusing the recipient with the ambition, and the aura of reliability, to go on for promotion!

Feel good about sharing the benefits of Planet Power!

RITE OF SENDING IN LUNA

Temporal Mode: 1
Planetary Time: Hour of the Moon
Position of Bomos: Center of Place of Working
Lights: 1 Violet Light or Star of Nine Lights
Other Requirements: Photograph of Recipient upon the Bomos

(At the opening of the rite all participants stand in a circle around the place of working: the director stationed at the West.)

1. The director advances to the West side of the Bomos and performs the Rite of Preparation.
2. The battery is sounded: 1.

3. The director proclaims:

> Companions in Light, our purpose in this hour is to transmit the magical energies of the Moon to _____, that she/he may be encompassed by the benison of the Foundation.

All respond:

> This is our will!

The director continues:

> Let us therefore prepare for this Sending by awakening the vibration of Levanah in this place and within our selves.

4. The battery is sounded: 9.
5. *If desired, incense is now activated.*

6. The director moves to the East side of the Bomos and faces West across it. With her right hand she traces, above the Bomos, the Presigillum of Luna.

Next she traces, about the Presigillum, the invoking Heptagram of Luna as illustrated, meanwhile vibrating the appropriate divine name of the Sphere of operation—

SHADDAI EL CHAI | IAO | AIGLE TRISAGIA

7. The director resumes her place in the West of the circle.
8. The battery is sounded: 1.
9. All now say:

> Great is he and mighty in the infinite heavens,
> Manifest in Light is he, in Light covered wholly.
> His Geburah, his Gedulah, strength his and greatness:
> Might is his, and his dominion, All-Potent, Living!

Therefore most exalted he, whose kingdom over all things is extended.

10. All link hands and vibrate once the appropriate divine name of the sphere—

SHADDAI EL CHAI | IAO | AIGLE TRISAGIA

11. Hands remaining linked, all make nine complete clockwise circumambulations of the place of working; visualizing as they do so, a wall of *violet* light whirling rapidly clockwise about their circle. This done, hands are unlinked and the wall of light is allowed to fade from awareness.
12. The battery is sounded: 9.
13. The director proclaims:

> Companions, upon our bomos rests the likeness of _____, as

witness of her/his participation in this rite. Let us now employ this likeness to establish a magical link between _____ and our selves in the Sphere of the Moon.

14. Beginning with the director and proceeding clockwise around the circle of participants, each in turn advances to the West side of the Bomos and takes up the photograph, holding it before him at heart level. The participant gazes upon the photograph for a few moments, then closes his eyes and surrounds himself with an aura of *lavender* light. In this light he visualizes the photograph, saying:

Unto _____ shall there be blessing upon the first step of the Ziggurat of Light.

The aura of lavender light is allowed to fade from awareness, the photograph is replaced upon the Bomos, and the participant returns to his place in the circle.

15. All link hands and make one complete clockwise circumambulation of the place of working. Hands are unlinked.

16. The battery is sounded: 1.

17. The director says:

Let us now formulate the Astral Plasma that will be the medium for the transmisison of the magical energies of the Moon to _____.

18. All close their eyes and visualize _____ *standing* at the center of the place of working,* within an auric membrane† of pallid white light.

19. When the director judges the formulation to be established, she utters the sacred vowel of the Sphere:

A   (pronounced as "a" in *father*)

As she utters the vowel, all visualize the auric membrane becoming suffused with *violet* light; so that they see it as an ovoid of violet light, within which, and bathed in its radiance, is the image of _____.

20. When the director is ready, she proclaims:

Let there be unto _____ the fullness of the benison of the Foundation.

Immediately following the director's proclamation, all raise their hands, palms towards the ovoid, and vibrate the appropriate

---

* As the focal point of the rite, _____ is at this stage symbolically identified with the Bomos, and is accordingly visualized in the station thereof. Each participant may, as preferred, visualize _____ in profile, half-turned or full face.

† This is the matrix of the Astral Plasma: it is specifically a "membrane" of light, its interior not being as yet suffused with light.

divine name—
SHADDAI EL CHAI | IAO | AIGLE TRISAGIA
As the name is vibrated, all visualize the violet ovoid becoming intensely brilliant, so that the image of _____ can no longer be perceived therein, and flashing with highlights of yellow and red-purple.

Arms are lowered when the vibration of the name has been accomplished.

21. When the director is ready, she proclaims:

     Unto _____ be the fullness of the benison of the Foundation now!

     Immediately, all visualize the scintillant violet light of the ovoid contracting rapidly and disappearing into its own center, leaving the original auric membrane empty. The auric membrane is then allowed to fade from awareness.

22. The director announces:

     It is accomplished in power and truth!

     All respond:

     It is accomplished.

23. All open their eyes, clap their hands once, cross their arms left over right upon their breast, then lower arms to sides.

24. The battery is sounded: 1.

25. The director says:

     In the benison of the Foundation, and in the promise of this hour, be there unto _____ the attainment of the True Will.

     All respond:

     Be it so in power and truth!

26. All link hands and vibrate once the chosen divine name of the Sphere—
SHADDAI EL CHAI | IAO | AIGLE TRISAGIA
     Hands are unlinked.

27. The battery is sounded: 3–5–3.

RITE OF SENDING IN MERCURY

Temporal Mode: 1
Planetary Time: Hour of Mercury
Position of Bomos: Center of Place of Working
Lights: 1 Orange Light or Star of Eight Lights
Other Requirements: Photograph of Recipient upon the Bomos

(At the opening of the rite all participants stand in a circle around the place of working: the director stationed at the West.)

1. The director advances to the West side of the Bomos and performs the Rite of Preparation.
2. The battery is sounded: 1.
3. The director proclaims:

    Companions in Light, our purpose in this hour is to transmit the magical energies of the Mercury to _____, that she/he may be encompassed by the benison of the Splendor.

    All respond:

    This is our will!

    The director continues:

    Let us therefore prepare for this Sending by awakening the vibration of Kokab in this place and within our selves.

4. The battery is sounded: 8.
5. *If desired, incense is now activated.*

6. The director moves to the East side of the Bomos and faces West across it. With her right hand she traces, above the Bomos, the Presigillum of Mercury.

    Next she traces, about the Presigillum, the invoking Heptagram of Mercury as illustrated, meanwhile vibrating the appropriate divine name of the Sphere of operation—

    ELOHIM TZABAOTH | AZOTH | ALETHES LOGOS

7. The director resumes her place in the West of the circle.
8. The battery is sounded: 1.
9. All now say:

    Builded in the heavens are his high habitations,
    Steeps of splendor whence he sendeth rain on the mountains!
    Even they within the deeps, the Fallen, he knoweth:
    Knower of all deeds is he and Lord of the Record.

    Therefore most exalted he, who foundeth in the deeps his habitations.

10. All link hands and vibrate once the appropriate divine name of the sphere—

    ELOHIM TZABAOTH | AZOTH | ALETHES LOGOS

11. Hands remaining linked, all make eight complete clockwise circumambulations of the place of working; visualizing as they do

so, a wall of *orange* light whirling rapidly clockwise about their circle. This done, hands are unlinked and the wall of light is allowed to fade from awareness.

12. The battery is sounded: 8.
13. The director proclaims:

Companions, upon our bomos rests the likeness of _____, as witness of her/his participation in this rite. Let us now employ this likeness to establish a magical link between _____ and our selves in the Sphere of the Mercury.

14. Beginning with the director and proceeding clockwise around the circle of participants, each in turn advances to the West side of the Bomos and takes up the photograph, holding it before him at heart level. The participant gazes upon the photograph for a few moments, then closes his eyes and surrounds himself with an aura of *pale tawny* light. In this light he visualizes the photograph, saying:

Unto _____ shall there be blessing upon the second step of the Ziggurat of Light.

The aura of pale tawny light is allowed to fade from awareness, the photograph is replaced upon the Bomos, and the participant returns to his place in the circle.

15. All link hands and make one complete clockwise circumambulation of the place of working. Hands are unlinked.
16. The battery is sounded: 1.
17. The director says:

Let us now formulate the Astral Plasma that will be the medium for the transmisison of the magical energies of Mercury to _____.

18. All close their eyes and visualize _____ *standing* at the center of the place of working, within an auric membrane of pallid white light.
19. When the director judges the formulation to be established, she utters the sacred vowel of the Sphere:

E   (pronounced as "e" in *set*)

As she utters the vowel, all visualize the auric membrane becoming suffused with *orange* light; so that they see it as an ovoid of orange light, within which, and bathed in its radiance, is the image of _____.

20. When the director is ready, she proclaims:

Let there be unto _____ the fullness of the benison of Splendor.

Immediately following the director's proclamation, all raise their hands, palms towards the ovoid, and vibrate the appropriate divine name—

ELOHIM TZABAOTH ∣ AZOTH ∣ ALETHES LOGOS

As the name is vibrated, all visualize the orange ovoid becoming intensely brilliant, so that the image of _____ can no longer be perceived therein, and flashing with highlights of blue and ochre-yellow.

Arms are lowered when the vibration of the name has been accomplished.

21. When the director is ready, she proclaims:

    Unto _____ be the fullness of the benison of Splendor now!

    Immediately, all visualize the scintillant orange light of the ovoid contracting rapidly and disappearing into its own center, leaving the original auric membrane empty. The auric membrane is then allowed to fade from awareness.

22. The director announces:

    It is accomplished in power and truth!

    All respond:

    It is accomplished.

23. All open their eyes, clap their hands once, cross their arms left over right upon their breast, then lower arms to sides.

24. The battery is sounded: 1.

25. The director says:

    In the benison of Splendor, and in the promise of this hour, be there unto _____ the attainment of the True Will.

    All respond:

    Be it so in power and truth!

26. All link hands and vibrate once the chosen divine name of the Sphere—

    ELOHIM TZABAOTH ∣ AZOTH ∣ ALETHES LOGOS

    Hands are unlinked.

27. The battery is sounded: 3–5–3.

RITE OF SENDING IN VENUS

Temporal Mode: 1
Planetary Time: Hour of Venus
Position of Bomos: Center of Place of Working

Lights: 1 Green Light or Star of Seven Lights
Other Requirements: Photograph of Recipient upon the Bomos

(At the opening of the rite all participants stand in a circle around the place of working: the director stationed at the West.)

1. The director advances to the West side of the Bomos and performs the Rite of Preparation.
2. The battery is sounded: 1.
3. The director proclaims:
    > Companions in Light, our purpose in this hour is to transmit the magical energies of Venus to _____, that she/he may be encompassed by the benison of Victory.

    All respond:
    > This is our will!

    The director continues:
    > Let us therefore prepare for this Sending by awakening the vibration of Nogah in this place and within our selves.
4. The battery is sounded: 7.
5. *If desired, incense is now activated.*

6. The director moves to the East side of the Bomos and faces West across it. With her right hand she traces, above the Bomos, the Presigillum of Venus.

    Next she traces, about the Presigillum, the invoking Heptagram of Venus as illustrated, meanwhile vibrating the appropriate divine name of the Sphere of operation—
    YHVH TZABAOTH | ALBAPHALANA | CHARIS
7. The director resumes her place in the West of the circle.
8. The battery is sounded: 1.
9. All now say:
    > Designate is she the chief of multitudes holy,
    > Glorious before them all, and all-overcoming;
    > Hers the portal of the shrine, within which her path lies,
    > She acclaimed of holiness the Triumph, the Beauty!

    Therefore most exalted she, whose pathway lies within the shrine supernal!
10. All link hands and vibrate once the appropriate divine name of the sphere—
    YHVH TZABAOTH | ALBAPHALANA | CHARIS

11. Hands remaining linked, all make seven complete clockwise circumambulations of the place of working; visualizing as they do so, a wall of *green* light whirling rapidly clockwise about their circle. This done, hands are unlinked and the wall of light is allowed to fade from awareness.
12. The battery is sounded: 7.
13. The director proclaims:

    Companions, upon our bomos rests the likeness of _____, as witness of her/his participation in this rite. Let us now employ this likeness to establish a magical link between _____ and our selves in the Sphere of the Venus.

14. Beginning with the director and proceeding clockwise around the circle of participants, each in turn advances to the West side of the Bomos and takes up the photograph, holding it before him at heart level. The participant gazes upon the photograph for a few moments, then closes his eyes and surrounds himself with an aura of *pale turquoise* light. In this light he visualizes the photograph, saying:

    Unto _____ shall there be blessing upon the third step of the Ziggurat of Light.

    The aura of pale turquoise light is allowed to fade from awareness, the photograph is replaced upon the Bomos, and the participant returns to his place in the circle.

15. All link hands and make one complete clockwise circumambulation of the place of working. Hands are unlinked.
16. The battery is sounded: 1.
17. The director says:

    Let us now formulate the Astral Plasma that will be the medium for the transmisison of the magical energies of Venus to _____.

18. All close their eyes and visualize _____ *standing* at the center of the place of working, within an auric membrane of pallid white light.
19. When the director judges the formulation to be established, she utters the sacred vowel of the Sphere:

    H   (pronounced as "a" in *care*)

    As she utters the vowel, all visualize the auric membrane becoming suffused with *green* light; so that they see it as an ovoid of green light, within which, and bathed in its radiance, is the image of _____.

20. When the director is ready, she proclaims:

Let there be unto _____ the fullness of the benison of Victory.
Immediately following the director's proclamation, all raise their hands, palms towards the ovoid, and vibrate the appropriate divine name—

YHVH TZABAOTH | ALBAPHALANA | CHARIS

As the name is vibrated, all visualize the green ovoid becoming intensely brilliant, so that the image of _____ can no longer be perceived therein, and flashing with highlights of red and greenish-blue.

Arms are lowered when the vibration of the name has been accomplished.

21. When the director is ready, she proclaims:

     Unto _____ be the fullness of the benison of Victory now!

     Immediately, all visualize the scintillant green light of the ovoid contracting rapidly and disappearing into its own center, leaving the original auric membrane empty. The auric membrane is then allowed to fade from awareness.

22. The director announces:

     It is accomplished in power and truth!

     All respond:

     It is accomplished.

23. All open their eyes, clap their hands once, cross their arms left over right upon their breast, then lower arms to sides.

24. The battery is sounded: 1.

25. The director says:

     In the benison of Victory, and in the promise of this hour, be there unto _____ the attainment of the True Will.

     All respond:

     Be it so in power and truth!

26. All link hands and vibrate once the chosen divine name of the Sphere—

     YHVH TZABAOTH | ALBAPHALANA | CHARIS

     Hands are unlinked.

27. The battery is sounded: 3–5–3.

RITE OF SENDING IN SOL

Temporal Mode: 1

Planetary Time: Hour of the Sun
Position of Bomos: Center of Place of Working
Lights: 1 Yellow Light or Star of Six Lights
Other Requirements: Photograph of Recipient upon the Bomos

(At the opening of the rite all participants stand in a circle around the place of working: the director stationed at the West.)

1. The director advances to the West side of the Bomos and performs the Rite of Preparation.
2. The battery is sounded: 1.
3. The director proclaims:
     Companions in Light, our purpose in this hour is to transmit the magical energies of the Sun to _____, that she/he may be encompassed by the benison of Beauty.

   All respond:
     This is our will!

   The director continues:
     Let us therefore prepare for this Sending by awakening the vibration of Shemesh in this place and within our selves.
4. The battery is sounded: 6.
5. *If desired, incense is now activated.*

6. The director moves to the East side of the Bomos and faces West across it. With her right hand she traces, above the Bomos, the Presigillum of Sol.

   Next she traces, about the Presigillum, the invoking Heptagram of the Sun as illustrated, meanwhile vibrating the appropriate divine name of the Sphere of operation—
     YHVH ELOAH V'DAATH | **ONOPHIS** | **THEIOS NOUS**

7. The director resumes her place in the West of the circle.
8. The battery is sounded: 1.
9. All now say:
     Reckoning of days and years unceasing he maketh;
     He to all existence giveth times, giveth seasons,
     Sending glory forth amid the High Lords assembled,
     Giving mind of knowledge clear to hearts that love wisdom.
   Therefore most exalted he, beneath whose burning gaze the rocks are
                                                                parted.

10. All link hands and vibrate once the appropriate divine name of the Sphere—
    YHVH ELOAH V'DAATH | ONOPHIS | THEIOS NOUS
11. Hands remaining linked, all make six complete clockwise circumambulations of the place of working; visualizing as they do so, a wall of *yellow* light whirling rapidly clockwise about their circle. This done, hands are unlinked and the wall of light is allowed to fade from awareness.
12. The battery is sounded: 6
13. The director proclaims:
    Companions, upon our bomos rests the likeness of _____, as witness of her/his participation in this rite. Let us now employ this likeness to establish a magical link between _____ and our selves in the Sphere of Sol.
14. Beginning with the director and proceeding clockwise around the circle of participants, each in turn advances to the West side of the Bomos and takes up the photograph, holding it before him at heart level. The participant gazes upon the photograph for a few moments, then closes his eyes and surrounds himself with an aura of *pale golden yellow* light. In this light he visualizes the photograph, saying:
    Unto _____ shall there be blessing upon the fourth step of the Ziggurat of Light.
    The aura of pale golden yellow light is allowed to fade from awareness, the photograph is replaced upon the Bomos, and the participant returns to his place in the circle.
15. All link hands and make one complete clockwise circumambulation of the place of working. Hands are unlinked.
16. The battery is sounded: 1.
17. The director says:
    Let us now formulate the Astral Plasma that will be the medium for the transmisison of the magical energies of the Sun to _____.
18. All close their eyes and visualize _____ *standing* at the center of the place of working, within an auric membrane of pallid white light.
19. When the director judges the formulation to be established, she utters the sacred vowel of the Sphere:
    I (pronounced as "ee" in *meet*)
    As she utters the vowel, all visualize the auric membrane becoming suffused with *yellow* light; so that they see it as an ovoid of yellow

light, within which, and bathed in its radiance, is the image of
_____.

20. When the director is ready, she proclaims:

Let there be unto _____ the fullness of the benison of Beauty.

Immediately following the director's proclamation, all raise their hands, palms towards the ovoid, and vibrate the appropriate divine name—

YHVH ELOAH V'DAATH | ONOPHIS | THEIOS NOUS

As the name is vibrated, all visualize the yellow ovoid becoming intensely brilliant, so that the image of _____ can no longer be perceived therein, and flashing with highlights of violet and primrose.

Arms are lowered when the vibration of the name has been accomplished.

21. When the director is ready, she proclaims:

Unto _____ be the fullness of the benison of Beauty now!

Immediately, all visualize the scintillant yellow light of the ovoid contracting rapidly and disappearing into its own center, leaving the original auric membrane empty. The auric membrane is then allowed to fade from awareness.

22. The director announces:

It is accomplished in power and truth!

All respond:

It is accomplished.

23. All open their eyes, clap their hands once, cross their arms left over right upon their breast, then lower arms to sides.

24. The battery is sounded: 1.

25. The director says:

In the benison of Beauty, and in the promise of this hour, be there unto _____ the attainment of the True Will.

All respond:

Be it so in power and truth!

26. All link hands and vibrate once the chosen divine name of the Sphere—

YHVH ELOAH V'DAATH | ONOPHIS | THEIOS NOUS

Hands are unlinked.

27. The battery is sounded: 3–5–3.

*   *   *

N.B. It may be decided, in an urgent case of physical sickness whose nature is not yet known, to send a "first aid" charge of beneficent energy. This rite of the Sun can always be so used.

RITE OF SENDING IN MARS

Temporal Mode: 1
Planetary Time: Hour of Mars
Position of Bomos: Center of Place of Working
Lights: 1 Red Light or Star of Five Lights
Other Requirements: Photograph of Recipient upon the Bomos

(At the opening of the rite all participants stand in a circle around the place of working: the director stationed at the West.)

1. The director advances to the West side of the Bomos and performs the Rite of Preparation.
2. The battery is sounded: 1.
3. The director proclaims:

> Companions in Light, our purpose in this hour is to transmit the magical energies of the Mars to _____, that she/he may be encompassed by the benison of Strength.

All respond:

> This is our will!

The director continues:

> Let us therefore prepare for this Sending by awakening the vibration of Madim in this place and within our selves.

4. The battery is sounded: 5.
5. *If desired, incense is now activated.*

6. The director moves to the East side of the Bomos and faces West across it. With her right hand she traces, above the Bomos, the Presigillum of Mars.

Next she traces, about the Presigillum, the invoking Heptagram of Mars as illustrated, meanwhile vibrating the appropriate divine name of the Sphere of operation—

ELOHIM GEBOR ‖ SABAO ‖ ISCHYROS

7. The director resumes her place in the West of the circle.
8. The battery is sounded: 1.
9. All now say:

> Powerfully doth he forge and fashion all beings;
> His the strength that makes them strong; his might magnifies them.
> Great and terrible is he, and true in each scruple:

> To and fro beneath the sun like sparks run his Watchers.
> Might is his, and his dominion, All-Potent, Living!
> Therefore most exalted he austere, who forms and governs every creature.

10. All link hands and vibrate once the appropriate divine name of the sphere—

> **ELOHIM GEBOR** | **SABAO** | **ISCHYROS**

11. Hands remaining linked, all make five complete clockwise circumambulations of the place of working; visualizing as they do so, a wall of *red* light whirling rapidly clockwise about their circle. This done, hands are unlinked and the wall of light is allowed to fade from awareness.

12. The battery is sounded: 5.

13. The director proclaims:

> Companions, upon our bomos rests the likeness of _____, as witness of her/his participation in this rite. Let us now employ this likeness to establish a magical link between _____ and our selves in the Sphere of the Mars.

14. Beginning with the director and proceeding clockwise around the circle of participants, each in turn advances to the West side of the Bomos and takes up the photograph, holding it before him at heart level. The participant gazes upon the photograph for a few moments, then closes his eyes and surrounds himself with an aura of *fiery red* light. In this light he visualizes the photograph, saying:

> Unto _____ shall there be blessing upon the fifth step of the Ziggurat of Light.

The aura of fiery red light is allowed to fade from awareness, the photograph is replaced upon the Bomos, and the participant returns to his place in the circle.

15. All link hands and make one complete clockwise circumambulation of the place of working. Hands are unlinked.

16. The battery is sounded: 1.

17. The director says:

> Let us now formulate the Astral Plasma that will be the medium for the transmission of the magical energies of Mars to _____.

18. All close their eyes and visualize _____ *standing* at the center of the place of working, within an auric membrane of pallid white light.

19. When the director judges the formulation to be established, she utters the sacred vowel of the Sphere:

O (pronounced as "o" in *hot*)

As she utters the vowel, all visualize the auric membrane becoming suffused with *red* light; so that they see it as an ovoid of red light, within which, and bathed in its radiance, is the image of _____.

20. When the director is ready, she proclaims:

Let there be unto _____ the fullness of the benison of Strength.

Immediately following the director's proclamation, all raise their hands, palms towards the ovoid, and vibrate the appropriate divine name—

ELOHIM GEBOR | SABAO | ISCHYROS

As the name is vibrated, all visualize the red ovoid becoming intensely brilliant, so that the image of _____ can no longer be perceived therein, and flashing with highlights of green and amber.

Arms are lowered when the vibration of the name has been accomplished.

21. When the director is ready, she proclaims:

Unto _____ be the fullness of the benison of Strength now!

Immediately, all visualize the scintillant red light of the ovoid contracting rapidly and disappearing into its own center, leaving the original auric membrane empty. The auric membrane is then allowed to fade from awareness.

22. The director announces:

It is accomplished in power and truth!

All respond:

It is accomplished.

23. All open their eyes, clap their hands once, cross their arms left over right upon their breast, then lower arms to sides.

24. The battery is sounded: 1.

25. The director says:

In the benison of Strength, and in the promise of this hour, be there unto _____ the attainment of the True Will.

All respond:

Be it so in power and truth!

26. All link hands and vibrate once the chosen divine name of the Sphere—

ELOHIM GEBOR | SABAO | ISCHYROS

Hands are unlinked.

27. The battery is sounded: 3–5–3.

*　　　　*　　　　*

RITE OF SENDING IN JUPITER

Temporal Mode: 1
Planetary Time: Hour of Jupiter
Position of Bomos: Center of Place of Working
Lights: 1 Blue Light or Star of Four Lights
Other Requirements: Photograph of Recipient upon the Bomos

(At the opening of the rite all participants stand in a circle around the place of working: the director stationed at the West.)

1. The director advances to the West side of the Bomos and performs the Rite of Preparation.
2. The battery is sounded: 1.
3. The director proclaims:

   Companions in Light, our purpose in this hour is to transmit the magical energies of Jupiter to _____, that she/he may be encompassed by the benison of Loving-kindness.

   All respond:

   This is our will!

   The director continues:

   Let us therefore prepare for this Sending by awakening the vibration of Tzedeq in this place and within our selves.

4. The battery is sounded: 4.
5. *If desired, incense is now activated.*

6. The director moves to the East side of the Bomos and faces West across it. With her right hand she traces, above the Bomos, the Presigillum of Jupiter.

   Next she traces, about the Presigillum, the invoking Heptagram of Jupiter as illustrated, meanwhile vibrating the appropriate divine name of the Sphere of operation—

   EL | ZARAIETOS | PANTOKRATOR

7. The director resumes her place in the West of the circle.
8. The battery is sounded: 1.
9. All now say:

   Kingly is his throne established, founded in justice,
   Righteousness, magnificence, and wisdom of judgment.
   Earth and sea are in his hand, the world and the heavens;

All he doth sustain, and all in equity ruleth.

Therefore most exalted he, who nurtureth the souls that long for justice.

10. All link hands and vibrate once the appropriate divine name of the sphere—

EL | **ZARAIETOS** | **PANTOKRATOR**

11. Hands remaining linked, all make four complete clockwise circumambulations of the place of working; visualizing as they do so, a wall of *blue* light whirling rapidly clockwise about their circle. This done, hands are unlinked and the wall of light is allowed to fade from awareness.

12. The battery is sounded: 4

13. The director proclaims:

Companions, upon our bomos rests the likeness of _____, as witness of her/his participation in this rite. Let us now employ this likeness to establish a magical link between _____ and our selves in the Sphere of the Jupiter.

14. Beginning with the director and proceeding clockwise around the circle of participants, each in turn advances to the West side of the Bomos and takes up the photograph, holding it before him at heart level. The participant gazes upon the photograph for a few moments, then closes his eyes and surrounds himself with an aura of *pale royal blue* light. In this light he visualizes the photograph, saying:

Unto _____ shall there be blessing upon the sixth step of the Ziggurat of Light.

The aura of pale royal blue light is allowed to fade from awareness, the photograph is replaced upon the Bomos, and the participant returns to his place in the circle.

15. All link hands and make one complete clockwise circumambulation of the place of working. Hands are unlinked.

16. The battery is sounded: 1.

17. The director says:

Let us now formulate the Astral Plasma that will be the medium for the transmission of the magical energies of Jupiter to _____.

18. All close their eyes and visualize _____ *standing* at the center of the place of working, within an auric membrane of pallid white light.

19. When the director judges the formulation to be established, she utters the sacred vowel of the Sphere:

ϓ (pronounced as German ü)

As she utters the vowel, all visualize the auric membrane becoming suffused with *blue* light; so that they see it as an ovoid of blue light, within which, and bathed in its radiance, is the image of _____.

20. When the director is ready, she proclaims:

    Let there be unto _____ the fullness of the benison of Loving-kindness.

    Immediately following the director's proclamation, all raise their hands, palms towards the ovoid, and vibrate the appropriate divine name—

    EL | ZARAIETOS | PANTOKRATOR

    As the name is vibrated, all visualize the blue ovoid becoming intensely brilliant, so that the image of _____ can no longer be perceived therein, and flashing with highlights of orange and lilac.

    Arms are lowered when the vibration of the name has been accomplished.

21. When the director is ready, she proclaims:

    Unto _____ be the fullness of the benison of Loving-kindness now!

    Immediately, all visualize the scintillant blue light of the ovoid contracting rapidly and disappearing into its own center, leaving the original auric membrane empty. The auric membrane is then allowed to fade from awareness.

22. The director announces:

    It is accomplished in power and truth!

    All respond:

    It is accomplished.

23. All open their eyes, clap their hands once, cross their arms left over right upon their breast, then lower arms to sides.

24. The battery is sounded: 1.

25. The director says:

    In the benison of Loving-kindness, and in the promise of this hour, be there unto _____ the attainment of the True Will.

    All respond:

    Be it so in power and truth!

26. All link hands and vibrate once the chosen divine name of the Sphere—

    EL | ZARAIETOS | PANTOKRATOR

    Hands are unlinked.

27. The battery is sounded: 3–5–3.

RITE OF SENDING IN SATURN

Temporal Mode: 1
Planetary Time: Hour of Saturn
Position of Bomos: Center of Place of Working
Lights: 1 Indigo (or Black) Light or Star of Three Lights
Other Requirements: Photograph of Recipient upon the Bomos

(At the opening of the rite all participants stand in a circle around the place of working: the director stationed at the West.)

1. The director advances to the West side of the Bomos and performs the Rite of Preparation.
2. The battery is sounded: 1.
3. The director proclaims:

    Companions in Light, our purpose in this hour is to transmit the magical energies of Saturn to _____, that she/he may be encompassed by the benison of Understanding.

    All respond:

    This is our will!

    The director continues:

    Let us therefore prepare for this Sending by awakening the vibration of Shabbathai in this place and within our selves.

4. The battery is sounded: 3.
5. *If desired, incense is now activated.*

6. The director moves to the East side of the Bomos and faces West across it. With her right hand she traces, above the Bomos, the Presigillum of Saturn.

    Next she traces, about the Presigillum, the invoking Heptagram of Saturn as illustrated, meanwhile vibrating the appropriate divine name of the Sphere of operation—

    YHVH ELOHIM | **IALDABAOTH** | **AIONOS KYRIOS**

7. The director resumes her place in the West of the circle.
8. The battery is sounded: 1.
9. All now say:

    Therefore through the worlds is he acclaimed: he is mighty!
    Therefore is he praised, who has the patience of ages;
    Anger passes, times go by, his truth is unchanging:

Those who come in trust to him, to new life he bringeth.
Therefore most exalted he, and through the worlds of Life his name is
glorious!

10. All link hands and vibrate once the appropriate divine name of
the sphere—
YHVH ELOHIM | IALDABAOTH | AIONOS KYRIOS

11. Hands remaining linked, all make three complete clockwise circumambulations of the place of working; visualizing as they do
so, a wall of *indigo* light whirling rapidly clockwise about their
circle. This done, hands are unlinked and the wall of light is
allowed to fade from awareness.

12. The battery is sounded: 3.

13. The director proclaims:

Companions, upon our bomos rests the likeness of _____, as
witness of her/his participation in this rite. Let us now employ this likeness to establish a magical link between _____ and our selves in
the Sphere of the Saturn.

14. Beginning with the director and proceeding clockwise around
the circle of participants, each in turn advances to the West side
of the Bomos and takes up the photograph, holding it before him
at heart level. The participant gazes upon the photograph for a
few moments, then closes his eyes and surrounds himself with
an aura of *soft red-brown* light. In this light he visualizes the
photograph, saying:

Unto _____ shall there be blessing upon the seventh step of the
Ziggurat of Light.

The aura of soft red-brown light is allowed to fade from awareness, the photograph is replaced upon the Bomos, and the participant returns to his place in the circle.

15. All link hands and make one complete clockwise circumambulation of the place of working. Hands are unlinked.

16. The battery is sounded: 1.

17. The director says:

Let us now formulate the Astral Plasma that will be the medium for the
transmisison of the magical energies of Saturn to _____.

18. All close their eyes and visualize _____ *standing* at the center of the place of working, within an auric membrane of pallid
white light.

19. When the director judges the formulation to be established, she
utters the sacred vowel of the Sphere:

Ω   (pronounced as "o" in *only*)

As she utters the vowel, all visualize the auric membrane becoming suffused with *indigo* light; so that they see it as an ovoid of indigo light, within which, and bathed in its radiance, is the image of _____.

20. When the director is ready, she proclaims:

Let there be unto _____ the fullness of the benison of Understanding.

Immediately following the director's proclamation, all raise their hands, palms towards the ovoid, and vibrate the appropriate divine name—

YHVH ELOHIM | IALDABAOTH | AIONOS KYRIOS

As the name is vibrated, all visualize the indigo ovoid becoming intensely brilliant, so that the image of _____ can no longer be perceived therein, and flashing with highlights of white and dove-grey.

Arms are lowered when the vibration of the name has been accomplished.

21. When the director is ready, she proclaims:

Unto _____ be the fullness of the benison of Understanding now!

Immediately, all visualize the scintillant indigo light of the ovoid contracting rapidly and disappearing into its own center, leaving the original auric membrane empty. The auric membrane is then allowed to fade from awareness.

22. The director announces:

It is accomplished in power and truth!

All respond:

It is accomplished.

23. All open their eyes, clap their hands once, cross their arms left over right upon their breast, then lower arms to sides.

24. The battery is sounded: 1.

25. The director says:

In the benison of Understanding, and in the promise of this hour, be there unto _____ the attainment of the True Will.

All respond:

Be it so in power and truth!

26. All link hands and vibrate once the chosen divine name of the Sphere—

YHVH ELOHIM | IALDABAOTH | AIONOS KYRIOS

Hands are unlinked.

27. The battery is sounded: 3–5–3.

10 OLYMPIC EVOCATION OF DREAMS

These rituals, examples of one form of traditional mirror magick, are by their nature necessarily designed for individual working. Here the magician conditions the astral substance of the mirror so that the glass becomes a suitable medium for the evocation of the Olympic Planetary Spirit of the Sphere of the working. The charge then laid upon the Spirit affords the magician opportunity to explore the sphere while in the dream state that night, and to obtain personal answers to specific questions on matters governed by the Sphere. These rites also present a means of better acquaintance with the noble and very powerful Olympic Planetary Spirits themselves.

A noteworthy feature of the rites is the need for employing a "cheval mirror," that is a long mirror which, having its own support, can stand in the mid area of a room independently of any wall. These rites require the Bomos to be placed just East of center in the place of working, and the magician by simply turning about must have both Bomos and mirror within reach. The cheval mirror is therefore essential.

A mirror utilized ritually in this way ought to be reserved for magical purposes thereafter, even if it was not so reserved previously. It should when not in use be kept carefully covered, preferably with black fabric; as a piece of magical equipment it can be valuable on varied occasions.

Apart from the mirror, the material requirements for these rituals are simple. So are the non-material requirements. The magician should have studied the form of each of the Olympic Planetary Spirits (*Entry 48*, Tables of Correspondences); but, as indicated in the text of these rituals, an inner awareness of the presence of the invoked Spirit may be preferred to a deliberate visualization of these forms. Again: the

347

magician is required to perform Section 24 of the rite with closed eyes; but while the text may, certainly, be memorized for this purpose, the true need is that the essential points of the text should be grasped so as to be covered in the uttering, no matter what the exact words employed.

For each of these rites the operator may, if desired, wear a headband containing a planetary gemstone (as described in Ascent and Vision in the Spheres).

The rites of this series represent a form of Art Magick which must be *living* if it is to be anything. The action and experience are all: but, with sincere working, the action and experience comprise their own high rewards.

EVOCATION OF DREAMS IN LUNA

Temporal Mode: 2
Planetary Time: Day and Hour of the Moon
Position of Bomos: Just East of Center
Lights: Star of Nine Lights, plus 1 White Light upon the Bomos
Other Requirements: The Mirror, West of Center with its reflecting surface facing East. Anointing Oil for Luna, and a lighting taper, upon the Bomos.

1. Standing at West side of Bomos facing East, perform the Rite of Preparation.
2. Sound the battery: 5–3–1.
3. Visualize yourself encompassed by an ovoid of *violet* light and maintaining this in awareness proclaim:
   O divine and fruitful
   ### SHADDAI EL CHAI | IAO | AIGLE TRISAGIA
   encompass me with the wings of thy protection and fill my soul with thy light, that I may securely and powerfully invoke thy luminous Spirit Phul: to the end that she shall guide me this night in dream for the increase of my true knowledge of the wonders and beauties of the First Heaven.
4. Allow the violet ovoid to fade from your awareness.
5. Sound the battery: 1
6. Visualize yourself encompassed by an ovoid of *red-purple* light and maintaining this in awareness proclaim:

O Phul, sustaining and faithful Spirit! By the power of my desire to advance in Art Magick, bring me to the dream-veiled towers of Kasap and open to me this night the treasury of the sphere of Luna in Yetzirah.

Thine it is O Phul to watch over those who go by land, by air or water. Thou canst empower those who travel in the Astral Light: to the mage who invokes thee in such quests thou showest marvels.

Thou seest secret things, and dost help in recovering that which was stolen: thou hidest not truth from the magician, and dost reveal reality in dreams. Repute is thy domain, and thou art potent to move the voice of the people.

O thou rider upon the Winged Bull of Air, thou of the crescent blade, Phul the resplendent!—upon thee in the mighty name

SHADDAI EL CHAI | IAO | AIGLE TRISAGIA

do I call, that thy will and thy power help bring to full accomplishment this my present working of Art Magick.

7. Allow the red-purple ovoid to fade from your awareness.
8. Sound the battery: 1. *If you desire, now activate incense.*
9. Move to the East, and facing East salute with the right hand; then circumambulate the place of working nine times clockwise, within the Star of Lights and encompassing the Bomos and the Mirror. Conclude the circumambulations in the East, salute, and return to West side of Bomos facing East.
10. Imagine a continuous spiral of *silver* light ascending from the ground at your feet, whirling clockwise around you and disappearing above your head. As you hold this upward whirling spiral in visualization, vibrate the chosen divine name of the Sphere—

SHADDAI EL CHAI | IAO | AIGLE TRISAGIA

11. Having completed the vibration of the divine name, allow the whirling spiral to fade from your consciousness.
12. Turn to face West and, touching the surface of the Mirror with the fingers of your right hand, say:

    Awaken, O Mirror, to the power of Levanah!

    Still touching the Mirror, now utter the sacred vowel of the Sphere:

    A (pronounced as "a" in *father*)
13. Turn to face East, and light the taper.
14. Face West, and proclaim:

    Be attentive, O Mirror to the vibrations which I awaken. Be receptive to them, even as it is thy nature to receive the imprint of form and color.

So receive as thine the sacred characters and the name of power, that thy substance may be harmonious to the astral energies of Levanah and that thou mayest be established in truth upon the first step of the Ziggurat of Light.

With the lighted taper, describe a clockwise circle to encompass the mirror in vertical plane, commencing at the top of the Mirror and returning to the same point. Next, just above the surface of the Mirror, trace with the taper the Presigillum of Luna.

Then, with the taper, trace about the Presigillum the invoking Heptagram of Luna, meanwhile vibrating the chosen divine name of the Sphere—

SHADDAI EL CHAI | IAO | AIGLE TRISAGIA

15. Turn to face East. Extinguish and replace the taper and take up the anointing oil.

16. Turn to face West. With the anointing oil, trace the Sigil of Phul upon the surface of the Mirror, then proclaim:
    Bear this mighty Sigil, O Mirror, and know thyself to be the destined vehicle for the presence of Phul, luminous Spirit of the Moon!

17. Face East and replace the anointing oil.

18. Sound the battery: 1.

19. Face West. With the fingers of both hands, touch the surface of the Mirror and proclaim:
    I touch thee, O Mirror, now token and representative of the Astral Light of Luna, in affirmation of the magical link which exists between that Light and myself.

20. Facing East, sound the battery: 5–3–1.

21. Salute the East with your right hand, then visualize yourself encompassed by an ovoid of *red-purple* light. In this light, vibrate the divine name—
    SHADDAI EL CHAI | IAO | AIGLE TRISAGIA

22. Allow the red-purple ovoid to fade from your awarenes, then turn to face West.
    Take care not to touch the surface of the Mirror until after Section 25 of this rite has been completed.

23. Raise your right hand, palm towards the Mirror, and make invocation as follows:

Come into this Mirror, O luminous Phul, Spirit of the Moon!—for its vibration is in harmony with thine own, and it welcomes thee!

Come, O thou rider upon the Winged Bull of Air, thou of the crescent blade, Phul the resplendent!

Come into this Mirror, O sustaining and faithful Spirit: and in the most sacred name

SHADDAI EL CHAI | **IAO** | **AIGLE TRISAGIA**

be astrally present to my inner perception.

24. (a) Standing with arms at sides *and eyes closed,* visualize before you a portal of soft blue-grey luminescence, co-extensive with the dimensions of the Mirror.

(b) In that luminescence, visualize Phul manifesting before you; or, if you have a spontaneous intimation of the presence of Phul, then without visualization allow this presence to imprint itself upon your awareness.

(c) When you are strongly aware of the manifestation, declare the Charge to the Spirit, as follows:

Thou are welcome, O Phul, illustrious Spirit of the Moon! I give thee salutation in the most sacred name

SHADDAI EL CHAI | **IAO** | **AIGLE TRISAGIA**

that name whereby increase of blessing is extended to thee and to me; and I charge thee in that same most sacred name that thou come to me this night as I sleep and lead me forth, guiding me safely and securely to experience the wonders and beauties of the First Heaven of Yetzirah wherein thou art mighty.

If you seek any special knowledge or experience relevant to the Sphere, conclude the above Charge by stating it, beginning:

And do thou thus reveal unto me . . .

(d) With awareness of the presence of the Spirit, reflect for a few moments upon the potential of the forthcoming dream voyage; then make the following declaration:

I give thee the most sacred name

SHADDAI EL CHAI | **IAO** | **AIGLE TRISAGIA**

as bond and token between us, O Phul! And in that same most sacred name I give thee thanks, and bid thee withdraw in peace from manifestation until we meet again this night for the furtherance of the Great Work.

(e) Now visualize the mirror-portal blazing with a violet radiance, wherein the form of Phul can no longer be seen. Then open your eyes.

25. Now deactivate the mirror-portal by the following procedure: With your right hand, trace just above the surface of the Mirror the Presigillum of Luna.

Then, with your right hand, trace about the Presigillum the banishing Heptagram of Luna, meanwhile vibrating the chosen divine name of the Sphere—

SHADDAI EL CHAI ǀ **IAO** ǀ **AIGLE TRISAGIA**

26. Turn to face East, and sound the battery: 1.

27. Salute the East with your right hand, then proclaim:

O divine and fruitful

SHADDAI EL CHAI ǀ **IAO** ǀ **AIGLE TRISAGIA**

salutation and thanks unto thee for the power with which thou hast endowed me to accomplish this work of Holy Magick. May thy blessing remain with me, O Most Mighty, that on this night, through the guidance of thy Spirit Phul, I shall attain true knowledge of the wonders and beauties of the First Heaven.

28. Sound the battery: 3–5–3.

When you have performed this ritual, one further thing remains to be done. At night when going to bed, anoint your forehead with the oil which you used in the working. Then say:

In dream this night, with the aid of Phul, I will accomplish what today through Art I began; and when I wake I will truly remember this night's showings. So shall it be, in the most sacred name—

SHADDAI EL CHAI ǀ **IAO** ǀ **AIGLE TRISAGIA**

EVOCATION OF DREAMS IN MERCURY

Temporal Mode: 2
Planetary Time: Day and Hour of Mercury
Position of Bomos: Just East of Center
Lights: Star of Eight Lights, plus 1 White Light upon the Bomos
Other Requirements: The Mirror, West of Center with its reflecting surface facing East. Anointing Oil for Mercury, and a lighting taper, upon the Bomos.

1. Standing at West side of Bomos facing East, perform the Rite of Preparation.
2. Sound the battery: 2–2–3–1.
3. Visualize yourself encompassed by an ovoid of *orange* light and

Maintaining this in awareness proclaim:

O divine and fruitful

ELOHIM TZABAOTH | **AZOTH** | **ALETHES LOGOS**

encompass me with the wings of thy protection and fill my soul with thy light, that I may securely and powerfully invoke thy luminous Spirit Ophiel: to the end that he shall guide me this night in dream for the increase of my true knowledge of the wonders and beauties of the Second Heaven.

4. Allow the orange ovoid to fade from your awareness.
5. Sound the battery: 1
6. Visualize yourself encompassed by an ovoid of *yellow ochre* light and maintaining this in awareness proclaim:

O Ophiel, scintillant Spirit! By reason of the magical faculties of my soul, bring me to the lustrous river of Utharud and open to me this night the powers of the Sphere of Mercury in Yetzirah.

Powers of eloquence and of rapid thought are thine to grant, with the arts of persuasion and of the written word. Thine too it is to bring to mind right speech and action, when one amid strange chances looks to thy guidance.

To the magician thou bringest the good and swift conclusion of matters lengthy or intricate; thou bringest the means to win obscure knowledge, thou givest the power to walk invisible, and to pass through doors sealed or forbidden.

O thou Spirit of the shining rod, Ophiel of the wings of music—upon thee in the mighty name

ELOHIM TZABAOTH | **AZOTH** | **ALETHES LOGOS**

do I call, that thy will and thy power help bring to full accomplishment this my present working of Art Magick.

7. Allow the yellow ochre ovoid to fade from your awareness.
8. Sound the battery: 1. *If you desire, now activate incense.*
9. Move to the East, and facing East salute with the right hand; then circumambulate the place of working eight times clockwise, within the Star of Lights and encompassing the Bomos and the Mirror. Conclude the circumambulations in the East, salute, and return to West side of Bomos facing East.
10. Imagine a continuous spiral of *shimmering opalescence* light ascending from the ground at your feet, whirling clockwise around you and disappearing above your head. As you hold this upward whirling spiral in visualization, vibrate the chosen divine name of the Sphere—

ELOHIM TZABAOTH | **AZOTH** | **ALETHES LOGOS**

11. Having completed the vibration of the divine name, allow the whirling spiral to fade from your consciousness.
12. Turn to face West and, touching the surface of the Mirror with the fingers of your right hand, say:

    Awaken, O Mirror, to the power of Kokab!

    Still touching the Mirror, now utter the sacred vowel of the Sphere:

    E   (pronounced as "e" in *set*)
13. Turn to face East, and light the taper.
14. Face West, and proclaim:

    Be attentive, O Mirror to the vibrations which I awaken. Be receptive to them, even as it is thy nature to receive the imprint of form and color. So receive as thine the sacred characters and the name of power, that thy substance may be harmonious to the astral energies of Kokab and that thou mayest be established in truth upon the second step of the Ziggurat of Light.

    With the lighted taper, describe a clockwise circle to encompass the mirror in vertical plane, commencing at the top of the Mirror and returning to the same point. Next, just above the surface of the Mirror, trace with the taper the Presigillum of Mercury.

    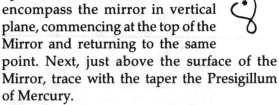

    Then, with the taper, trace about the Presigillum the invoking Heptagram of Mercury, meanwhile vibrating the chosen divine name of the Sphere—

    ELOHIM TZABAOTH | **AZOTH** | **ALETHES LOGOS**
15. Turn to face East. Extinguish and replace the taper and take up the anointing oil.
16. Turn to face West. With the anointing oil, trace the Sigil of Ophiel upon the surface of the Mirror, then proclaim:

    Bear this mighty Sigil, O Mirror, and know thyself to be the destined vehicle for the presence of Ophiel, luminous Spirit of Mercury!
17. Face East and replace the anointing oil.
18. Sound the battery: 1.
19. Face West. With the fingers of both hands, touch the surface of

the Mirror and proclaim:

> I touch thee, O Mirror, now token and representative of the Astral Light of Mercury, in affirmation of the magical link which exists between that Light and myself.

20. Facing East, sound the battery: 2–2–3–1.

21. Salute the East with your right hand, then visualize yourself encompassed by an ovoid of *yellow ochre* light. In this light, vibrate the divine name—

ELOHIM TZABAOTH | AZOTH | ALETHES LOGOS

22. Allow the yellow ochre ovoid to fade from your awareness, then turn to face West.

Take care not to touch the surface of the Mirror until after Section 25 of this rite has been completed.

23. Raise your right hand, palm towards the Mirror, and make invocation as follows:

> Come into this Mirror, O luminous Ophiel, Spirit of Mercury!—for its vibration is in harmony with thine own, and it welcomes thee!
>
> Come, O thou Spirit of the shining rod, Ophiel of the wings of music!
>
> Come into this Mirror, O scintillant Spirit: and in the most sacred name
>
> **ELOHIM TZABAOTH | AZOTH | ALETHES LOGOS**
>
> be astrally present to my inner perception.

24. (a) Standing with arms at sides *and eyes closed,* visualize before you a portal of soft blue-grey luminescence, co-extensive with the dimensions of the Mirror.

(b) In that luminescence, visualize Ophiel manifesting before you; or, if you have a spontaneous intimation of the presence of Ophiel, then without visualization allow this presence to imprint itself upon your awareness.

(c) When you are strongly aware of the manifestation, declare the Charge to the Spirit, as follows:

> Thou are welcome, O Ophiel, illustrious Spirit of Mercury! I give thee salutation in the most sacred name
>
> **ELOHIM TZABAOTH | AZOTH | ALETHES LOGOS**
>
> that name whereby increase of blessing is extended to thee and to me; and I charge thee in that same most sacred name that thou come to me this night as I sleep and lead me forth, guiding me safely and securely to experience the wonders and beauties of the Second Heaven of Yetzirah wherein thou art mighty.

If you seek any special knowledge or experience relevant to the Sphere,
conclude the above Charge by stating it, beginning:

And do thou thus reveal unto me ...

(d)   With awareness of the presence of the Spirit, reflect for a few moments upon the potential of the forthcoming dream voyage; then make the following declaration:

I give thee the most sacred name

ELOHIM TZABAOTH | AZOTH | ALETHES LOGOS

as bond and token between us, O Ophiel! And in that same most sacred name I give thee thanks, and bid thee withdraw in peace from manifestation until we meet again this night for the furtherance of the Great Work.

(e)   Now visualize the mirror-portal blazing with an *orange* radiance, wherein the form of Ophiel can no longer be seen. Then open your eyes.

25.   Now deactivate the mirror-portal by the following procedure:

With your right hand, trace just above the surface of the Mirror the Presigillum of Mercury.

Then, with your right hand, trace about the Presigillum the banishing Heptagram of Mercury, meanwhile vibrating the chosen divine name of the Sphere—

ELOHIM TZABAOTH | AZOTH | ALETHES LOGOS

26.   Turn to face East, and sound the battery: 1.

27.   Salute the East with your right hand, then proclaim:

O divine and fruitful

ELOHIM TZABAOTH | AZOTH | ALETHES LOGOS

salutation and thanks unto thee for the power with which thou hast endowed me to accomplish this work of Holy Magick. May thy blessing remain with me, O Most Mighty, that on this night, through the guidance of thy Spirit Ophiel, I shall attain true knowledge of the wonders and beauties of the Second Heaven.

28.   Sound the battery: 3–5–3.

When you have performed this ritual, one further thing remains to be done. At night when going to bed, anoint your forehead with the oil which you used in the working. Then say:

In dream this night, with the aid of Ophiel, I will accomplish what today through Art I began; and when I wake I will truly remember this night's showings. So shall it be, in the most sacred name—

ELOHIM TZABAOTH | AZOTH | ALETHES LOGOS

EVOCATION OF DREAMS IN VENUS

Temporal Mode: 2
Planetary Time: Day and Hour of Venus
Position of Bomos: Just East of Center
Lights: Star of Seven Lights, plus 1 White Light upon the Bomos
Other Requirements: The Mirror, West of Center with its reflecting surface facing East. Anointing Oil for Venus, and a lighting taper, upon the Bomos.

1. Standing at West side of Bomos facing East, perform the Rite of Preparation.
2. Sound the battery: 2–2–2–1.
3. Visualize yourself encompassed by an ovoid of *green* light and maintaining this in awareness proclaim:

    O divine and fruitful

    YHVH TZABAOTH ｜ **ALBAPHALANA** ｜ **CHARIS**

    encompass me with the wings of thy protection and fill my soul with thy light, that I may securely and powerfully invoke thy luminous Spirit Hagith: to the end that she shall guide me this night in dream for the increase of my true knowledge of the wonders and beauties of the Third Heaven.

4. Allow the green ovoid to fade from your awareness.
5. Sound the battery: 1
6. Visualize yourself encompassed by an ovoid of *greenish blue* light and maintaining this in awareness proclaim:

    O Hagith, wonderful Spirit! For love of the limitless beauty of Art Magick, bring me to the roseate grotto of Nechsheth and open to me this night the potencies of the sphere of Venus in Yetzirah.

    Thine it is to accord joyous gifts of love and friendship, thine to grace the lives of those who seek thee with wonder, gladness and festal laughter.

    Thine it is, O Hagith, to bring favor where skill alone could not promise success: in the fall of dice, in the sweepstakes of advancement, in the unexpected glance of an eye. Those who invoke thee in the workings of Art Magick thou dost endow with the grace and power of the sacred dance, with the art to unite purpose to flowing gesture and captivating chant.

    O thou Spirit of life-renewing loveliness, Hagith moving in radiance!— upon thee in the mighty name

    YHVH TZABAOTH ｜ **ALBAPHALANA** ｜ **CHARIS**

> do I call, that thy will and thy power help bring to full accomplishment this my present working of Art Magick.

7. Allow the greenish blue ovoid to fade from your awareness.
8. Sound the battery: 1. *If you desire, now activate incense.*
9. Move to the East, and facing East salute with the right hand; then circumambulate the place of working seven times clockwise, within the Star of Lights and encompassing the Bomos and the Mirror. Conclude the circumambulations in the East, salute, and return to West side of Bomos facing East.
10. Imagine a continuous spiral of *saffron* light ascending from the ground at your feet, whirling clockwise around you and disappearing above your head. As you hold this upward whirling spiral in visualization, vibrate the chosen divine name of the Sphere—

    YHVH TZABAOTH | ALBAPHALANA | CHARIS

11. Having completed the vibration of the divine name, allow the whirling spiral to fade from your consciousness.
12. Turn to face West and, touching the surface of the Mirror with the fingers of your right hand, say:

    Awaken, O Mirror, to the power of Nogah!

    Still touching the Mirror, now utter the sacred vowel of the Sphere:

    H   (pronounced as "a" in *care*)

13. Turn to face East, and light the taper.
14. Face West, and proclaim:

    Be attentive, O Mirror to the vibrations which I awaken. Be receptive to them, even as it is thy nature to receive the imprint of form and color. So receive as thine the sacred characters and the name of power, that thy substance may be harmonious to the astral energies of Nogah and that thou mayest be established in truth upon the third step of the Ziggurat of Light.

    With the lighted taper, describe a clockwise circle to encompass

the mirror in vertical plane, commencing at the top of the Mirror and returning to the same point. Next, just above the surface of the Mirror, trace with the taper the Presigillum of Venus. Then, with the taper, trace about the Presigillum the invoking Heptagram of Venus, meanwhile vibrating the chosen divine name of the Sphere—

YHVH TZABAOTH | ALBAPHALANA | CHARIS

15. Turn to face East. Extinguish and replace the taper and take up the anointing oil.

16. Turn to face West. With the anointing oil, trace the Sigil of Hagith upon the surface of the Mirror, then proclaim:

> Bear this mighty Sigil, O Mirror, and know thyself to be the destined vehicle for the presence of Hagith, luminous Spirit of Venus!

17. Face East and replace the anointing oil.

18. Sound the battery: 1.

19. Face West. With the fingers of both hands, touch the surface of the Mirror and proclaim:

> I touch thee, O Mirror, now token and representative of the Astral Light of Venus, in affirmation of the magical link which exists between that Light and myself.

20. Facing East, sound the battery: 2–2–2–1.

21. Salute the East with your right hand, then visualize yourself encompassed by an ovoid of *greenish blue* light. In this light, vibrate the divine name—

YHVH TZABAOTH | ALBAPHALANA | CHARIS

22. Allow the greenish blue ovoid to fade from your awarenes, then turn to face West.

Take care not to touch the surface of the Mirror until after Section 25 of this rite has been completed.

23. Raise your right hand, palm towards the Mirror, and make invocation as follows:

> Come into this Mirror, O luminous Hagith, Spirit of Venus!—for its vibration is in harmony with thine own, and it welcomes thee!
> Come, O thou Spirit of life-renewing loveliness, Hagith moving in radiance!
> Come into this Mirror, O wonderful Spirit: and in the most sacred name

YHVH TZABAOTH | ALBAPHALANA | CHARIS

> be astrally present to my inner perception.

24. (a) Standing with arms at sides *and eyes closed,* visualize before you a portal of soft blue-grey luminescence, co-extensive with the dimensions of the Mirror.

(b) In that luminescence, visualize Hagith manifesting before you; or, if you have a spontaneous intimation of the presence of Hagith, then without visualization allow this presence to imprint itself upon your awareness.

(c)   When you are strongly aware of the manifestation, declare the Charge to the Spirit, as follows:

Thou are welcome, O Hagith, illustrious Spirit of Venus! I give thee salutation in the most sacred name

YHVH TZABAOTH | ALBAPHALANA | CHARIS

that name whereby increase of blessing is extended to thee and to me; and I charge thee in that same most sacred name that thou come to me this night as I sleep and lead me forth, guiding me safely and securely to experience the wonders and beauties of the Third Heaven of Yetzirah wherein thou art mighty.

If you seek any special knowledge or experience relevant to the Sphere, conclude the above Charge by stating it, beginning:

And do thou thus reveal unto me . . .

(d)   With awareness of the presence of the Spirit, reflect for a few moments upon the potential of the forthcoming dream voyage; then make the following declaration:

I give thee the most sacred name

YHVH TZABAOTH | ALBAPHALANA | CHARIS

as bond and token between us, O Hagith! And in that same most sacred name I give thee thanks, and bid thee withdraw in peace from manifestation until we meet again this night for the furtherance of the Great Work.

(e)   Now visualize the mirror-portal blazing with a *green* radiance, wherein the form of Hagith can no longer be seen. Then open your eyes.

25.   Now deactivate the mirror-portal by the following procedure:

With your right hand, trace just above the surface of the Mirror the Presigillum of Venus.

Then, with your right hand, trace about the Presigillum the banishing Heptagram of Venus, meanwhile vibrating the chosen divine name of the Sphere—

YHVH TZABAOTH | ALBAPHALANA | CHARIS

26. Turn to face East, and sound the battery: 1.

27. Salute the East with your right hand, then proclaim:

O divine and loving

YHVH TZABAOTH | ALBAPHALANA | CHARIS

salutation and thanks unto thee for the power with which thou hast endowed me to accomplish this work of Holy Magick. May thy blessing remain with me, O Most Mighty, that on this night, through the guidance of thy Spirit Hagith, I shall attain true knowledge of the wonders and beauties of the Third Heaven.

28. Sound the battery: 3–5–3.

When you have performed this ritual, one further thing remains to be done. At night when going to bed, anoint your forehead with the oil which you used in the working. Then say:

In dream this night, with the aid of Hagith, I will accomplish what today through Art I began; and when I wake I will truly remember this night's showings. So shall it be, in the most sacred name—
YHVH TZABAOTH | ALBAPHALANA | CHARIS

EVOCATION OF DREAMS IN SOL

Temporal Mode: 2
Planetary Time: Day and Hour of the Sun
Position of Bomos: Just East of Center
Lights: Star of Six Lights, plus 1 White Light upon the Bomos
Other Requirements: The Mirror, West of Center with its reflecting surface facing East. Anointing Oil for Sol, and a lighting taper, upon the Bomos.

1. Standing at West side of Bomos facing East, perform the Rite of Preparation.
2. Sound the battery: 3–2–1.
3. Visualize yourself encompassed by an ovoid of *yellow* light and maintaining this in awareness proclaim:

O divine and jubilant
YHVH ELOAH V'DAATH | ONOPHIS | THEIOS NOUS
encompass me with the wings of thy protection and fill my soul with thy light, that I may securely and powerfully invoke thy luminous Spirit Och: to the end that he shall guide me this night in dream for the increase of my true knowledge of the wonders and beauties of the Fourth Heaven.

4. Allow the yellow ovoid to fade from your awareness.
5. Sound the battery: 1
6. Visualize yourself encompassed by an ovoid of *pale greenish-yellow* light and maintaining this in awareness proclaim:

O Och, triumphant and noble Spirit! By the truth of my heart and the steadfastness of my purpose, bring me to the radiant pavillion of Zahab and open to me this night the glories of the Sphere of Sol in Yetzirah.

Gifts in profusion, O Och, whether earthly or other are thine to confer, and the genial warmth of friendship wherein the talents of humankind flourish and increase. Thou givest the soul's clear vision, and that inner comprehension thereof which is called prophetic. Thou dost inspire and prosper undertakings of discovery and adventure, and the questing mind which would ever illumine what has been dark or unknown: those who hazard new paths, those who love rare knowledge, thou dost bless.

O thou who dost control the red lion of energy most active, incomparable Och!—upon thee now in the mighty name

YHVH ELOAH V'DAATH | ONOPHIS | THEIOS NOUS

do I call, that thy will and thy power help bring to full accomplishment this my present working of Art Magick.

7. Allow the pale greenish-yellow ovoid to fade from your awareness.

8. Sound the battery: 1. *If you desire, now activate incense.*

9. Move to the East, and facing East salute with the right hand; then circumambulate the place of working six times clockwise, within the Star of Lights and encompassing the Bomos and the Mirror. Conclude the circumambulations in the East, salute, and return to West side of Bomos facing East.

10. Imagine a continuous spiral of *gold* light ascending from the ground at your feet, whirling clockwise around you and disappearing above your head. As you hold this upward whirling spiral in visualization, vibrate the chosen divine name of the Sphere—

YHVH ELOAH V'DAATH | ONOPHIS | THEIOS NOUS

11. Having completed the vibration of the divine name, allow the whirling spiral to fade from your consciousness.

12. Turn to face West and, touching the surface of the Mirror with the fingers of your right hand, say:

Awaken, O Mirror, to the power of Shemesh!

Still touching the Mirror, now utter the sacred vowel of the Sphere:

I (pronounced as "ee" in *meet*)

13. Turn to face East, and light the taper.

14. Face West, and proclaim:

Be attentive, O Mirror to the vibrations which I awaken. Be receptive to them, even as it is thy nature to receive the imprint of form and color.

So receive as thine the sacred characters and the name of power, that thy substance may be harmonious to the astral energies of Shemesh and that thou mayest be established in truth upon the fourth step of the Ziggurat of Light.

With the lighted taper, describe a clockwise circle to encompass the mirror in vertical plane, commencing at the top of the Mirror and returning to the same point. Next, just above the surface of the Mirror, trace with the taper the Presigillum of Sol.

Then, with the taper, trace about the Presigillum the invoking Heptagram of Sol, meanwhile vibrating the chosen divine name of the Sphere—

YHVH ELOAH V'DAATH | **ONOPHIS** | **THEIOS NOUS**

15. Turn to face East. Extinguish and replace the taper and take up the anointing oil.

16. Turn to face West. With the anointing oil, trace the Sigil of Och upon the surface of the Mirror, then proclaim:
     Bear this mighty Sigil, O Mirror, and know thyself to be the destined vehicle for the presence of Och, luminous Spirit of the Sun!

17. Face East and replace the anointing oil.

18. Sound the battery: 1.

19. Face West. With the fingers of both hands, touch the surface of the Mirror and proclaim:
     I touch thee, O Mirror, now token and representative of the Astral Light of Sol, in affirmation of the magical link which exists between that Light and myself.

20. Facing East, sound the battery: 3–2–1.

21. Salute the East with your right hand, then visualize yourself encompassed by an ovoid of *pale greenish-yellow* light. In this light, vibrate the divine name—
     YHVH ELOAH V'DAATH | **ONOPHIS** | **THEIOS NOUS**

22. Allow the pale greenish-yellow ovoid to fade from your awareness, then turn to face West.
     Take care not to touch the surface of the Mirror until after Section 25 of this rite has been completed.

23. Raise your right hand, palm towards the Mirror, and make invocation as follows:

> Come into this Mirror, O luminous Och, Spirit of the Sun!—for its vibration is in harmony with thine own, and it welcomes thee!
>
> Come, O thou who dost control the red lion of energy most active, incomparable Och!
>
> Come into this Mirror, O triumphant and noble Spirit: and in the most sacred name
>
> **YHVH ELOAH V'DAATH | ONOPHIS | THEIOS NOUS**
>
> be astrally present to my inner perception.

24. (a) Standing with arms at sides *and eyes closed,* visualize before you a portal of soft blue-grey luminescence, co-extensive with the dimensions of the Mirror.

(b) In that luminescence, visualize Och manifesting before you; or, if you have a spontaneous intimation of the presence of Och, then without visualization allow this presence to imprint itself upon your awareness.

(c) When you are strongly aware of the manifestation, declare the Charge to the Spirit, as follows:

> Thou are welcome, O Och, illustrious Spirit of the Sun! I give thee salutation in the most sacred name
>
> **YHVH ELOAH V'DAATH | ONOPHIS | THEIOS NOUS**
>
> that name whereby increase of blessing is extended to thee and to me; and I charge thee in that same most sacred name that thou come to me this night as I sleep and lead me forth, guiding me safely and securely to experience the wonders and beauties of the Fourth Heaven of Yetzirah wherein thou art mighty.

If you seek any special knowledge or experience relevant to the Sphere, conclude the above Charge by stating it, beginning:

> And do thou thus reveal unto me . . .

(d) With awareness of the presence of the Spirit, reflect for a few moments upon the potential of the forthcoming dream voyage; then make the following declaration:

> I give thee the most sacred name
>
> **YHVH ELOAH V'DAATH | ONOPHIS | THEIOS NOUS**
>
> as bond and token between us, O Och! And in that same most sacred name I give thee thanks, and bid thee withdraw in peace from manifestation until we meet again this night for the furtherance of the Great Work.

(e) Now visualize the mirror-portal blazing with a *yellow* radiance, wherein the form of Och can no longer be seen. Then open your eyes.

25. Now deactivate the mirror-portal by the following procedure:

With your right hand, trace just above the surface of the Mirror the Presigillum of Sol.

Then, with your right hand, trace about the Presigillum the banishing Heptagram of Sol, meanwhile vibrating the chosen divine name of the Sphere—

YHVH ELOAH V'DAATH | ONOPHIS | THEIOS NOUS

26. Turn to face East, and sound the battery: 1.

27. Salute the East with your right hand, then proclaim:

O divine and jubilant

YHVH ELOAH V'DAATH | ONOPHIS | THEIOS NOUS

salutation and thanks unto thee for the power with which thou hast endowed me to accomplish this work of Holy Magick. May thy blessing remain with me, O Most Mighty, that on this night, through the guidance of thy Spirit Och, I shall attain true knowledge of the wonders and beauties of the Fourth Heaven.

28. Sound the battery: 3–5–3.

When you have performed this ritual, one further thing remains to be done. At night when going to bed, anoint your forehead with the oil which you used in the working. Then say:

In dream this night, with the aid of Och, I will accomplish what today through Art I began; and when I wake I will truly remember this night's showings. So shall it be, in the most sacred name—

YHVH ELOAH V'DAATH | ONOPHIS | THEIOS NOUS

EVOCATION OF DREAMS IN MARS

Temporal Mode: 2
Planetary Time: Day and Hour of Mars
Position of Bomos: Just East of Center
Lights: Star of Five Lights, plus 1 White Light upon the Bomos
Other Requirements: The Mirror, West of Center with its reflecting surface facing East. Anointing Oil for Mars, and a lighting taper, upon the Bomos.

1. Standing at West side of Bomos facing East, perform the Rite of Preparation.

2. Sound the battery: 2–2–1.
3. Visualize yourself encompassed by an ovoid of *red* light and maintaining this in awareness proclaim:

> O divine and impelling
> ### ELOHIM GEBOR | SABAO | ISCHYROS
> encompass me with the wings of thy protection and fill my soul with thy light, that I may securely and powerfully invoke thy luminous Spirit Phalegh: to the end that he shall guide me this night in dream for the increase of my true knowledge of the wonders and beauties of the Fifth Heaven.

4. Allow the red ovoid to fade from your awareness.
5. Sound the battery: 1
6. Visualize yourself encompassed by an ovoid of *amber* light and maintaining this in awareness proclaim:

> O Phalegh, mighty Spirit! For the fulfillment of my true will and by the strength of my magical resolve, bring me to the sable fortress of Barzel and open to me this night the energies of the Sphere of Mars in Yetzirah.
>
> Courage and confidence abounding, O Phalegh, thou dost bestow, and thou art the tutelary champion of those that seek justice. For the magician thou findest allies unfaltering and loyal to aid in works which require a dauntless heart; in every craft also thou dost forge a bond of unity between hand and instrument, that the will of the wielder work through them unhindered.
>
> O thou of the all-prevailing sword, thou Spirit of the invincible protecting shield, fiery and vigorous Phalegh!—upon thee in the mighty name
> ### ELOHIM GEBOR | SABAO | ISCHYROS
> do I call, that thy will and thy power help bring to full accomplishment this my present working of Art Magick.

7. Allow the amber ovoid to fade from your awareness.
8. Sound the battery: 1. *If you desire, now activate incense.*
9. Move to the East, and facing East salute with the right hand; then circumambulate the place of working five times clockwise, within the Star of Lights and encompassing the Bomos and the Mirror. Conclude the circumambulations in the East, salute, and return to West side of Bomos facing East.
10. Imagine a continuous spiral of *fiery red* light ascending from the ground at your feet, whirling clockwise around you and disappearing

above your head. As you hold this upward whirling spiral in visualization, vibrate the chosen divine name of the Sphere—
ELOHIM GEBOR | SABAO | ISCHYROS

11. Having completed the vibration of the divine name, allow the whirling spiral to fade from your consciousness.

12. Turn to face West and, touching the surface of the Mirror with the fingers of your right hand, say:

    Awaken, O Mirror, to the power of Madim!

    Still touching the Mirror, now utter the sacred vowel of the Sphere:

    O   (pronounced as "o" in *hot*)

13. Turn to face East, and light the taper.

14. Face West, and proclaim:

    Be attentive, O Mirror to the vibrations which I awaken. Be receptive to them, even as it is thy nature to receive the imprint of form and color. So receive as thine the sacred characters and the name of power, that thy substance may be harmonious to the astral energies of Madim and that thou mayest be established in truth upon the fifth step of the Ziggurat of Light.

    With the lighted taper, describe a clockwise circle to encompass the mirror in vertical plane, commencing at the top of the Mirror and returning to the same point. Next, just above the surface of the Mirror, trace with the taper the Presigillum of Mars.

    Then, with the taper, trace about the Presigillum the invoking Heptagram of Mars, meanwhile vibrating the chosen divine name of the Sphere—
    ELOHIM GEBOR | SABAO | ISCHYROS

15. Turn to face East. Extinguish and replace the taper and take up the anointing oil.

16. Turn to face West. With the anointing oil, trace the Sigil of Phalegh upon the surface of the Mirror, then proclaim:

    Bear this mighty Sigil, O Mirror, and know thyself to be the destined vehicle for the presence of Phalegh, luminous Spirit of Mars!

17. Face East and replace the anointing oil.

18. Sound the battery: 1.

19. Face West. With the fingers of both hands, touch the surface of the Mirror and proclaim:

> I touch thee, O Mirror, now token and representative of the Astral Light of Mars, in affirmation of the magical link which exists between that Light and myself.

20. Facing East, sound the battery: 2–2–1.

21. Salute the East with your right hand, then visualize yourself encompassed by an ovoid of *amber* light. In this light, vibrate the divine name—

> ### ELOHIM GEBOR | SABAO | ISCHYROS

22. Allow the amber ovoid to fade from your awareness, then turn to face West.

Take care not to touch the surface of the Mirror until after Section 25 of this rite has been completed.

23. Raise your right hand, palm towards the Mirror, and make invocation as follows:

> Come into this Mirror, O luminous Phalegh, Spirit of Mars!—for its vibration is in harmony with thine own, and it welcomes thee!
>
> Come, O thou of the all-prevailing sword, thou Spirit of the invincible protecting shield, fiery and vigorous Phalegh!
>
> Come into this Mirror, O mighty Spirit: and in the most sacred name
>
> ### ELOHIM GEBOR | SABAO | ISCHYROS
>
> be astrally present to my inner perception.

24. (a) Standing with arms at sides *and eyes closed,* visualize before you a portal of soft blue-grey luminescence, co-extensive with the dimensions of the Mirror.

(b) In that luminescence, visualize Phalegh manifesting before you; or, if you have a spontaneous intimation of the presence of Phalegh, then without visualization allow this presence to imprint itself upon your awareness.

(c) When you are strongly aware of the manifestation, declare the Charge to the Spirit, as follows:

> Thou are welcome, O Phalegh, illustrious Spirit of Mars! I give thee salutation in the most sacred name
>
> ### ELOHIM GEBOR | SABAO | ISCHYROS
>
> that name whereby increase of blessing is extended to thee and to me; and I charge thee in that same most sacred name that thou come to me this night as I sleep and lead me forth, guiding me safely and securely to experience the wonders and beauties of the Fifth Heaven

of Yetzirah wherein thou art mighty.
If you seek any special knowledge or experience relevant to the Sphere,
conclude the above Charge by stating it, beginning:
And do thou thus reveal unto me . . .
(d)   With awareness of the presence of the Spirit, reflect for a
few moments upon the potential of the forthcoming dream
voyage; then make the following declaration:
I give thee the most sacred name
ELOHIM GEBOR | SABAO | ISCHYROS
as bond and token between us, O Phalegh! And in that same most
sacred name I give thee thanks, and bid thee withdraw in peace from
manifestation until we meet again this night for the furtherance of the
Great Work.
(e)   Now visualize the mirror-portal blazing with a red radiance,
wherein the form of Phalegh can no longer be seen. Then open
your eyes.
25.   Now deactivate the mirror-portal by the following procedure:

With your right hand, trace just
above the surface of the Mirror the
Presigillum of Mars.
Then, with your right hand, trace
about the Presigillum the banishing Heptagram
of Mars, meanwhile vibrating the chosen divine
name of the Sphere—
ELOHIM GEBOR | SABAO | ISCHYROS
26.   Turn to face East, and sound the battery: 1.
27.   Salute the East with your right hand,
then proclaim:
O divine and impelling
ELOHIM GEBOR | SABAO | ISCHYROS
salutation and thanks unto thee for the power with which thou hast
endowed me to accomplish this work of Holy Magick. May thy blessing remain with me, O Most Mighty, that on this night, through the
guidance of thy Spirit Phalegh, I shall attain true knowledge of the
wonders and beauties of the Fifth Heaven.
28.   Sound the battery: 3–5–3.
When you have performed this ritual, one further thing remains to be
done. At night when going to bed, anoint your forehead with the oil which you
used in the working. Then say:
In dream this night, with the aid of Phalegh, I will accomplish what

today through Art I began; and when I wake I will truly remember this night's showings. So shall it be, in the most sacred name—
ELOHIM GEBOR | SABAO | ISCHYROS

EVOCATION OF DREAMS IN JUPITER

Temporal Mode: 2
Planetary Time: Day and Hour of Jupiter
Position of Bomos: Just East of Center
Lights: Star of Four Lights, plus 1 White Light upon the Bomos
Other Requirements: The Mirror, West of Center with its reflecting surface facing East. Anointing Oil for Jupiter, and a lighting taper, upon the Bomos.

1. Standing at West side of Bomos facing East, perform the Rite of Preparation.
2. Sound the battery: 3–1.
3. Visualize yourself encompassed by an ovoid of *blue* light and maintaining this in awareness proclaim:
    O divine and clement
    EL | ZARAIETOS | PANTOKRATOR
    encompass me with the wings of thy protection and fill my soul with thy light, that I may securely and powerfully invoke thy luminous Spirit Bethor: to the end that he shall guide me this night in dream for the increase of my true knowledge of the wonders and beauties of the Sixth Heaven.
4. Allow the blue ovoid to fade from your awareness.
5. Sound the battery: 1
6. Visualize yourself encompassed by an ovoid of *lilac* light and maintaining this in awareness proclaim:
    O Bethor, majestic Spirit! By the greatness of my spiritual heritage and the force of my aspiration, bring me to the shining portals of Bedil and open to me this night the abundance of the sphere of Jupiter in Yetzirah.
    O Bethor, among thy gifts are honor and success, convivial rejoicing and the power of peaceful leadership. Thou dost inspire the mage to frame rites of magical worship, thereby to ascend to greater renown, to increased acuity of mind and greater earthly well-being.
    O thou regal Spirit, thou who bearest the vase of smoking incense, thou who carriest upon thy brow the sapphire of celestial magnificence,

most splendid Bethor!—upon thee in the mighty name
EL | ZARAIETOS | PANTOKRATOR
do I call, that thy will and thy power help bring to full accomplishment this my present working of Art Magick.

7. Allow the lilac ovoid to fade from your awareness.
8. Sound the battery: 1. *If you desire, now activate incense.*
9. Move to the East, and facing East salute with the right hand; then circumambulate the place of working four times clockwise, within the Star of Lights and encompassing the Bomos and the Mirror. Conclude the circumambulations in the East, salute, and return to West side of Bomos facing East.
10. Imagine a continuous spiral of *brilliant white* light ascending from the ground at your feet, whirling clockwise around you and disappearing above your head. As you hold this upward whirling spiral in visualization, vibrate the chosen divine name of the Sphere—
EL | ZARAIETOS | PANTOKRATOR
11. Having completed the vibration of the divine name, allow the whirling spiral to fade from your consciousness.
12. Turn to face West and, touching the surface of the Mirror with the fingers of your right hand, say:

    Awaken, O Mirror, to the power of Tzedeq!

    Still touching the Mirror, now utter the sacred vowel of the Sphere:

    Υ (pronounced as German ü)
13. Turn to face East, and light the taper.
14. Face West, and proclaim:

    Be attentive, O Mirror to the vibrations which I awaken. Be receptive to them, even as it is thy nature to receive the imprint of form and color. So receive as thine the sacred characters and the name of power, that thy substance may be harmonious to the astral energies of Tzedeq and that thou mayest be established in truth upon the sixth step of the Ziggurat of Light.

    With the lighted taper, describe a clockwise circle to encompass the mirror in vertical plane, commencing at the top of the Mirror and returning to the same point. Next, just above the surface of the Mirror, trace with the taper the Presigillum of Jupiter.

    Then, with the taper, trace about the Presigillum the invoking Heptagram of Jupiter, meanwhile vibrating

the chosen divine name of the Sphere—
EL | ZARAIETOS | PANTOKRATOR

15. Turn to face East. Extinguish and replace the taper and take up the anointing oil.
16. Turn to face West. With the anointing oil, trace the Sigil of Bethor upon the surface of the Mirror, then proclaim:

Bear this mighty Sigil, O Mirror, and know thyself to be the destined vehicle for the presence of Bethor, luminous Spirit of Jupiter!

17. Face East and replace the anointing oil.
18. Sound the battery: 1.
19. Face West. With the fingers of both hands, touch the surface of the Mirror and proclaim:

I touch thee, O Mirror, now token and representative of the Astral Light of Jupiter, in affirmation of the magical link which exists between that Light and myself.

20. Facing East, sound the battery: 3–1.
21. Salute the East with your right hand, then visualize yourself encompassed by an ovoid of *lilac* light. In this light, vibrate the divine name—
EL | ZARAIETOS | PANTOKRATOR

22. Allow the lilac ovoid to fade from your awareness, then turn to face West.

Take care not to touch the surface of the Mirror until after Section 25 of this rite has been completed.

23. Raise your right hand, palm towards the Mirror, and make invocation as follows:

Come into this Mirror, O luminous Bethor, Spirit of Jupiter!—for its vibration is in harmony with thine own, and it welcomes thee!

Come, O thou regal Spirit, thou who bearest the vase of smoking incense, thou who carriest upon thy brow the sapphire of celestial magnificence, most splendid Bethor!

Come into this Mirror, O majestic Spirit: and in the most sacred name

EL | ZARAIETOS | PANTOKRATOR

be astrally present to my inner perception.

24. (a) Standing with arms at sides *and eyes closed,* visualize before

you a portal of soft blue-grey luminescence, co-extensive with the dimensions of the Mirror.

(b)   In that luminescence, visualize Bethor manifesting before you; or, if you have a spontaneous intimation of the presence of Bethor, then without visualization allow this presence to imprint itself upon your awareness.

(c)   When you are strongly aware of the manifestation, declare the Charge to the Spirit, as follows:

> Thou are welcome, O Bethor, illustrious Spirit of Jupiter! I give thee salutation in the most sacred name
>
> ### EL | ZARAIETOS | PANTOKRATOR
>
> that name whereby increase of blessing is extended to thee and to me; and I charge thee in that same most sacred name that thou come to me this night as I sleep and lead me forth, guiding me safely and securely to experience the wonders and beauties of the Sixth Heaven of Yetzirah wherein thou art mighty.

If you seek any special knowledge or experience relevant to the Sphere, conclude the above Charge by stating it, beginning:

> And do thou thus reveal unto me . . .

(d)   With awareness of the presence of the Spirit, reflect for a few moments upon the potential of the forthcoming dream voyage; then make the following declaration:

> I give thee the most sacred name
>
> ### EL | ZARAIETOS | PANTOKRATOR
>
> as bond and token between us, O Bethor! And in that same most sacred name I give thee thanks, and bid thee withdraw in peace from manifestation until we meet again this night for the furtherance of the Great Work.

(e)   Now visualize the mirror-portal blazing with a *blue* radiance, wherein the form of Bethor can no longer be seen. Then open your eyes.

25. Now deactivate the mirror-portal by the following procedure:

With your right hand, trace just above the surface of the Mirror the Presigillum of Jupiter.

Then, with your right hand, trace about the Presigillum the banishing Heptagram of Jupiter, meanwhile vibrating the chosen divine   name   of   the   Sphere—

EL | ZARAIETOS | PANTOKRATOR

26. Turn to face East, and sound the battery: 1.
27. Salute the East with your right hand, then proclaim:

O divine and clement

EL | ZARAIETOS | PANTOKRATOR

salutation and thanks unto thee for the power with which thou hast endowed me to accomplish this work of Holy Magick. May thy blessing remain with me, O Most Mighty, that on this night, through the guidance of thy Spirit Bethor, I shall attain true knowledge of the wonders and beauties of the Sixth Heaven.

28. Sound the battery: 3-5-3.

When you have performed this ritual, one further thing remains to be done. At night when going to bed, anoint your forehead with the oil which you used in the working. Then say:

In dream this night, with the aid of Bethor, I will accomplish what today through Art I began; and when I wake I will truly remember this night's showings. So shall it be, in the most sacred name—

EL | ZARAIETOS | PANTOKRATOR

EVOCATION OF DREAMS IN SATURN

Temporal Mode: 2
Planetary Time: Day and Hour of Saturn
Position of Bomos: Just East of Center
Lights: Star of Three Lights, plus 1 White Light upon the Bomos
Other Requirements: The Mirror, West of Center with its reflecting surface facing East. Anointing Oil for Saturn, and a lighting taper, upon the Bomos.

1. Standing at West side of Bomos facing East, perform the Rite of Preparation.
2. Sound the battery: 2-1.
3. Visualize yourself encompassed by an ovoid of *indigo* light and maintaining this in awareness proclaim:

O divine and inscrutable

YHVH ELOHIM | IALDABAOTH | AIONOS KYRIOS

encompass me with the wings of thy protection and fill my soul with thy light, that I may securely and powerfully invoke thy luminous Spirit Aratron: to the end that he shall guide me this night in dream for the increase of my true knowledge of the wonders and beauties of the

Seventh Heaven.
4. Allow the indigo ovoid to fade from your awareness.
5. Sound the battery: 1
6. Visualize yourself encompassed by an ovoid of *dove grey* light and maintaining this in awareness proclaim:

> O Aratron, august and lofty Spirit! By my soul's quest for wisdom and the deep intimations of destiny, bring me to the grey mountains of Abar and open to me this night the grandeur of the Sphere of Saturn in Yetzirah.
>
> Thine to bestow are endurance and sublime perseverance, the clear light of remembered experience, the happiness of stability and of long continuance in serenity. Thou dost enable the mage to seal threefold with adamantine locks that which is to be kept secret, and thou givest the sleep in which works of the Art may be performed or learning and skill gained.
>
> O thou Spirit of most venerable aspect, exalted Aratron!—upon thee in the mighty name
>
> **YHVH ELOHIM | IALDABAOTH | AIONOS KYRIOS**
>
> do I call, that thy will and thy power help bring to full accomplishment this my present working of Art Magick.

7. Allow the dove grey ovoid to fade from your awareness.
8. Sound the battery: 1. *If you desire, now activate incense.*
9. Move to the East, and facing East salute with the right hand; then circumambulate the place of working three times clockwise, within the Star of Lights and encompassing the Bomos and the Mirror. Conclude the circumambulations in the East, salute, and return to West side of Bomos facing East.
10. Imagine a continuous spiral of *grey* light ascending from the ground at your feet, whirling clockwise around you and disappearing above your head. As you hold this upward whirling spiral in visualization, vibrate the chosen divine name of the Sphere—

> **YHVH ELOHIM | IALDABAOTH | AIONOS KYRIOS**

11. Having completed the vibration of the divine name, allow the whirling spiral to fade from your consciousness.
12. Turn to face West and, touching the surface of the Mirror with the fingers of your right hand, say:

> Awaken, O Mirror, to the power of Shabbathai!

Still touching the Mirror, now utter the sacred vowel of the Sphere:

Ω   (pronounced as "o" in *only*)

13. Turn to face East, and light the taper.

14. Face West, and proclaim:

> Be attentive, O Mirror to the vibrations which I awaken. Be receptive to them, even as it is thy nature to receive the imprint of form and color. So receive as thine the sacred characters and the name of power, that thy substance may be harmonious to the astral energies of Shabbathai and that thou mayest be established in truth upon the seventh step of the Ziggurat of Light.

With the lighted taper, describe a clockwise circle to encompass the mirror in vertical plane, commencing at the top of the Mirror and returning to the same point. Next, just above the surface of the Mirror, trace with the taper the Presigillum of Saturn.

Then, with the taper, trace about the Presigillum the invoking Heptagram of Saturn, meanwhile vibrating the chosen divine name of the Sphere—

YHVH ELOHIM | **IALDABAOTH** | **AIONOS KYRIOS**

15. Turn to face East. Extinguish and replace the taper and take up the anointing oil.

16. Turn to face West. With the anointing oil, trace the Sigil of Aratron upon the surface of the Mirror, then proclaim:

> Bear this mighty Sigil, O Mirror, and know thyself to be the destined vehicle for the presence of Aratron, luminous Spirit of Saturn!

17. Face East and replace the anointing oil.

18. Sound the battery: 1.

19. Face West. With the fingers of both hands, touch the surface of the Mirror and proclaim:

> I touch thee, O Mirror, now token and representative of the Astral Light of Saturn, in affirmation of the magical link which exists between that Light and myself.

20. Facing East, sound the battery: 2–1.

21. Salute the East with your right hand, then visualize yourself encompassed by an ovoid of *dove grey* light. In this light, vibrate the divine name—

YHVH ELOHIM | **IALDABAOTH** | **AIONOS KYRIOS**

22. Allow the dove grey ovoid to fade from your awareness, then

turn to face West.

Take care not to touch the surface of the Mirror until after Section 25 of this rite has been completed.

23. Raise your right hand, palm towards the Mirror, and make invocation as follows:

Come into this Mirror, O luminous Aratron, Spirit of Saturn!—for its vibration is in harmony with thine own, and it welcomes thee!

Come, O thou Spirit of most venerable aspect, exalted Aratron!

Come into this Mirror, O august and lofty Spirit: and in the most sacred name

YHVH ELOHIM | IALDABAOTH | AIONOS KYRIOS

be astrally present to my inner perception.

24. (a) Standing with arms at sides *and eyes closed,* visualize before you a portal of soft blue-grey luminescence, co-extensive with the dimensions of the Mirror.

(b) In that luminescence, visualize Aratron manifesting before you; or, if you have a spontaneous intimation of the presence of Aratron, then without visualization allow this presence to imprint itself upon your awareness.

(c) When you are strongly aware of the manifestation, declare the Charge to the Spirit, as follows:

Thou are welcome, O Aratron, illustrious Spirit of Saturn! I give thee salutation in the most sacred name

YHVH ELOHIM | IALDABAOTH | AIONOS KYRIOS

that name whereby increase of blessing is extended to thee and to me; and I charge thee in that same most sacred name that thou come to me this night as I sleep and lead me forth, guiding me safely and securely to experience the wonders and beauties of the Seventh Heaven of Yetzirah wherein thou art mighty.

If you seek any special knowledge or experience relevant to the Sphere, conclude the above Charge by stating it, beginning:

And do thou thus reveal unto me . . .

(d) With awareness of the presence of the Spirit, reflect for a few moments upon the potential of the forthcoming dream voyage; then make the following declaration:

I give thee the most sacred name

YHVH ELOHIM | IALDABAOTH | AIONOS KYRIOS

as bond and token between us, O Aratron! And in that same most sacred name I give thee thanks, and bid thee withdraw in peace from manifestation until we meet again this night for the furtherance of the

Great Work.

(e)   Now visualize the mirror-portal blazing with a *indigo* radiance, wherein the form of Aratron can no longer be seen. Then open your eyes.

25.   Now deactivate the mirror-portal by the following procedure: With your right hand, trace just above the surface of the Mirror the Presigillum of Saturn.

Then, with your right hand, trace about the Presigillum the banishing Heptagram of Saturn, meanwhile vibrating the chosen divine name of the Sphere—

YHVH ELOHIM | IALDABAOTH | AIONOS KYRIOS

26.   Turn to face East, and sound the battery: 1.

27.   Salute the East with your right hand, then proclaim:

O divine and inscrutable

YHVH ELOHIM | IALDABAOTH | AIONOS KYRIOS

salutation and thanks unto thee for the power with which thou hast endowed me to accomplish this work of Holy Magick. May thy blessing remain with me, O Most Mighty, that on this night, through the guidance of thy Spirit Aratron, I shall attain true knowledge of the wonders and beauties of the Seventh Heaven.

28.   Sound the battery: 3–5–3.

When you have performed this ritual, one further thing remains to be done. At night when going to bed, anoint your forehead with the oil which you used in the working. Then say:

In dream this night, with the aid of Aratron, I will accomplish what today through Art I began; and when I wake I will truly remember this night's showings. So shall it be, in the most sacred name—

YHVH ELOHIM | IALDABAOTH | AIONOS KYRIOS

APPENDIX A

THE PLANETARY SEPHIROTH
IN "THE THIRTY-TWO PATHS OF WISDOM"
OF JOANNES STEPHANUS RITTANGELIUS

"The Thirty-two Paths of Wisdom" is a Qabalistic work of considerable interest, whose paragraphs relating to the planetary Sephiroth
are given in translation in Section 9 of our Tables of Correspondence.

Valuable for ritual or meditative use, this work has, nonetheless,
frequently been considered altogether obscure, or even spurious, by
critics who have not possessed the keys to its interpretation. At a cursory
reading, many of its statements seem limited in thought, arbitrary in
judgment; but, as is often the case with Qabalistic literature, the
immediate sense of the words is by no means their entire message or
even, in some instances, their main import.

Gematria, the art of associating or interpreting letters, words or
even whole passages according to their accepted numerical values, is
a feature of considerable antiquity in Hebrew mystical texts. It can be
employed in various ways, some very complex: the simplest is to
"reduce" a number by adding its digits, then to explore the affinities of
the reduced number.

For instance, the number 996 can be reduced, first to 24, then to 6.
Among words or phrases which are considered relevant, a closer
kinship of numeration is generally held to be more notable than a
lesser one. The word BTh (402), "a daughter," might be associated in a

particular context with RTzVN (996) "delight," since both reduce to 6; but BTh would be accorded a closer affinity with DR (204), "a pearl," because the numerical value of the one word mirrors that of the other. However, the single-digit association, although scorned by some authorities, is used by many learned Qabalists; particularly, and of necessity, when words are to be linked to one of the ten Sephiroth. Here Rittangelius is no exception.

Gematria provides only one of the sources of ideas for the present comments: we include references to both Hebrew and general philosophic thinking of medieval and Renaissance times, to show the particular mental and imaginative environment in which "The Thirty-two Paths" is to be understood. These notes do not by any means exhaust the numerical and other associations which can be found, still less the implications which may be meditatively drawn from them; it is sufficient here to show the method and the main lines of Rittangelius' thinking, with regard to the planetary Spheres; to point the way for the student's personal researches on these passages.

The Thirty-two Paths alluded to comprise the ten Sephiroth followed by the Twenty-two Paths properly so called: thus the "First Path" is the first Sephirah, Kether. As we are concerned here only with the seven Planetary Sephiroth we begin with the Third Path which is the Third Sephirah, Binah, and which is also the Sphere of Saturn.

The Third Path is the Consecrating Intelligence: it is the underlying principle of the Wisdom of the Beginning, which is named the Pattern of Faith and is its root, Affirmation (Amen). It is the parent of faith, for from its essential nature faith proceeds.

Thomas Aquinas, who was (besides much else) a pupil of Albertus Magnus, defined *faith* as "the substance of things hoped for." In medieval philosophy "substance" is always that which "underlies" material being: it is the reality in the Causal Worlds which can result in material manifestation. Above, Rittangelius is telling us that faith properly understood is a creative act, bringing the light of divine causality (of Kether and Chokmah) into form by the power of affirmation; he is also saying that this creative affirmation, which in human mind-processes is active in faith, is in essence one with the power of that holy Understanding, the feminine Wisdom, the divine Sophia, through whose agency the lower Spheres have their genesis. (See

Proverbs 8:14, 22-23.) *Amen,* AMN, the word of affirmation, is a title of Kether, the Supreme Source; but its numeration (741) is also linked, by reduction, to the 3rd Sephirah. In planetary terms that Sephirah is the Sphere of Saturn, which planet indicates condensation, crystallization, materialization.

The Fourth Path is the Measuring, Collecting or Receptive Intelligence: so named because it holds within it all the high potencies, and from it issue forth all the successive modalities of spirit in their highest being, each emanated from another through the power of the First Emanation, Kether.

The 4th Sephirah is Chesed, the Sphere of Jupiter: the corresponding letter of the Hebrew alphabet is Kaph, whose two forms represent the cupped (receptive) and the open (giving) palm respectively. This Sphere has a strong association with water, whether contained in a cup, well or sea, or falling, as rain or dew: likewise with such skyey phenomena as thunder and lightning (Zeus, Thor, Jupiter Pluvius etc.).

The Measuring, Collecting or Receptive Intelligence—Some interesting words have numerations which reduce to 13 and thence to 4: MAZNYM (148, taking final M as 40), "a pair of scales"; MDH (49), "measuring"; TzNVR (346), "a water channel"; PK (580), "a flask, container for liquid." Another group has digits adding directly to 4: ShY (310), "tribute"; RB (202), "abundance"; NVLA (121), "it is filled"; and YAR (211) " a flood."

It holds within it all the high potencies—Reference here is to the Sephiroth above Chesed, that is, the three Supernals: KThR, ChKMH and BYNH. Adding their numerations, 620 + 73 + 67, the total is 760 which reduces to 13 and thus to 4, so that they are "held within" the domain of the 4th Sephirah.

And from it issue forth all the successive modalities—Descending through the subsequent Sephiroth, and giving to Malkuth its mystical title of Shar, "the Gate," we have GBVRH, 216; ThPARTh, 1081; NTzCh, 148; HVD, 15; YSVD, 80; ShOR, 570. The total of these is 2110, reducing to 4. Again, all these subsequent Sephiroth are a progressive LYDH (49), "a bringing forth" from the 4th Sephirah. It is said of all the Sephiroth that they are MQBYL V-MThQBL (760), "both active and passive." This is here exemplified by Chesed, which in receiving and giving forth may be said to act as intermediary: HGH (13) "to mediate" in the course of HARH (211) "the Lightning Flash" which is the whole range of the Sephiroth. One sometimes sees a traditional diagram which shows the ten Spheres, in their proper positions united within a zigzag flash of lightning, which in turn is ATzL (121) "emanated from," PH (85) "the mouth," of a venerable figure representing Kether.

In their highest being. That is, in the Atziluthic purity of their YSh (310), their "essential nature."

Through the power of the First Emanation, Kether—This is indicated above in the matter of the Lightning Flash, a symbol closely associated with the skyey forces of Chesed. Titles of Kether which reduce to 13 include OLVYN (166), "Most High," and RVM MOLH, "Inscrutable Height."

The Fifth Path is the Root Intelligence, so named because it is itself the essence equalling the Unity. It is linked with Binah, the Intelligence which emanates from the unfathomed deeps of Wisdom, Chokmah.

The 5th Path or Sephirah is Geburah, signifying "Strength." This title, GBVRH, has the numeration 216; it thus has a great gematric affinity with BRYTh (612) "covenant," and an affinity also with ShBTh (702), "Sabbath."

The 5th Path is the Root Intelligence—ShRSh (800), "root," has the identical numeration of QShTh, "a bow," the meaning of the latter word including the rainbow, the celestial sign of the covenant. (Genesis 9:13-14.)

It is itself the essence equalling the Unity—MZL (77) is "the force of destiny," a mysterious influence from Kether which, by reason of its numeration, can be associated with the 5th Sephirah. Again, AChD (13) is "Unity," a title of Kether, while MDYM (94, taking each M as 40) is "Madim," the Hebrew name of Mars the planet of Geburah. *The 5th Path is the Root Intelligence . . . because . . . equalling the Unity* can also be interpreted by the affinity between the numeration of ShRSh (800), "root," and that of KThR (620), "Kether."

It is linked with Binah—Apart from the position of Geburah below Binah on the column of Severity, there are some noteworthy gematric links between these two Sephiroth. BYNH (67), "Binah," reduces to 13 as does MDYM (94), but this is not the most significant affinity. The relationship of the "root" i.e., Geburah, with "Covenant" and "Sabbath" is indicated above; now the direct relationship of each of these concepts with Binah is to be shown.

From the Zohar, I,71b: "And the rainbow is therefore called 'covenant' because they [rainbow and covenant] embrace one another. Like the firmament it is a supernal resplendent glory, a sight of all sights, resembling the hidden one (the Shekinah), containing colors undisclosed and impossible to reveal. Hence it is not permitted to gaze at the rainbow . . ."

The title *shekinah* refers to the outward manifestation of the invisible glory of the Divine Presence. Sometimes it refers to the Tenth Sephirah, Malkuth; but most often, as in this passage, it refers to a manifestation which is itself supernal; that is, of the formative and coalescing power of Binah.

Somewhat less abstrusely Geburah, in being linked with the Sabbath, is again linked with Binah. The Hebrew name of the planet Saturn, whose Sphere is the 3rd Sephirah, is Shabbathai, attesting to the close association of Binah with the Sabbath. Again, however, we look to the Zohar for a mystical and poetic expression of their relationship:

Zohar I, 48a: "But on the Sabbath a tabernacle of peace is spread over the world . . ." And (48b): "This tabernacle of peace is the Matron [i.e., the supernal Mother] of the World, and the souls which are the celestial lamp abide in her . . ."

Of words which relate the sephirothic number of Geburah, 5, to Binah, some are particularly notable: AChLB (41), "fecundity"; AM (41), "mother"; while MShKN (410, taking N as 50) is "tabernacle," recalling the passage just quoted from the Zohar wherein the tabernacle of peace "is" the Mother. 86, a number of a different group which reduces through 14 to 5, is the numeration of KVM. This word means "cup," but in particular the Cup in the sense of the supreme female symbol, the Grail of Binah which is often seen as contrasted to the Spear of Chokmah. ChYM, "life," mirrors it with the numeration 68 if—as Qabalistic numerations often require—the final M is given the value 40.

From the unfathomed deeps of Wisdom, Chokmah—ChKM, "to be wise," has also the numeration 68. ThHMVh (851) is "the deeps"; the singular form of the word, ThVM, is both by meaning and by numeration a unique attribution of the 3rd Sephirah. But Chokmah, ChKMH (73) both suggests the 10th Sephirah and resolves back numerically to the Unity of Kether, and therefore is indeed *unfathomable*.

The Sixth Path is the Intelligence of the Mediatory Influence: it is so named because therein is gathered the influx from all the Emanations, so

that it in turn causes the mediatory influence to flow into the founts of each of the benign Powers, with which they are linked.

On a simple reading, this paragraph might seem a summary interpretation of the position of the 6th Sephirah upon the Tree of Life. Gematria however shows there is more cause than might appear for the choice of imagery. The principal title of the 6th Sephirah, Tiphareth, ThPARTh (1081), "Beauty," reduces numerically to 10; the numbers 6 and 10 thus give us keys to the main underlying ideas of the text. In this instance the celestial body associated with the Sphere does not give us an additional key number, for it is the Sun, whose Hebrew name is ShMSh (640), the numeration of this reducing to 10 also.

The Mediatory Influence—Reducing to 6 are: RBK (222), taking K as 20), "to be mingled"; YShR (510), "just measure"; MAZNYM (708), "scales for measuring." Reducing to 10: DYN (64), "justice"; ChLP (838), "to renew or change"; and, very notably, MChY TBAL (100), "Mitigation of one by the other."

Therein is gathered the influx—Reducing to 6 are: GBA (6), "to collect"; or ASP (861), "collected"; QBL (132) "to receive" (whence *Qabalah*); ChYBTh (420), "a receptacle for new wine"; LG (33), "a basin." Reducing to 10, BVR (208) is "a cistern." Since this influx is gathered into the sphere of the sun, it may be termed MY ZHB (64), "Golden Water."

From all the emanations—This totality might be deduced in principle, since the title of Tiphareth reduces to 10 which is the total number of the Sephiroth. Proceeding according to our plan, however, we have, reducing to 6: ShBYLYN (402, taking N as 50), "paths"; OVLM (141, with M as 40), "world, universe"; ATzYLVTh (537), literally meaning "nobility," the name of the highest spiritual World which comprises the ten Sephiroth in their full divine perfection. Reducing to 10 are OTz-H-ChYM (1603), "Tree of Life": ThM (1000), "whole, perfect"; while 1495 is the sum of the numerations of all 22 letters of the Hebrew alphabet and hence, by ascription of the letters, the Paths encompassing every part of the Tree of Life.

Causes . . . to flow into the founts—Reducing to 6 are: GL (33), "a spring, fountain"; ChDSh (312), "to renew"; KBR (222), "to increase"; ZVB (15) "copious, plentiful." Reducing to 10 is KP (820), "palm of the hand," whose two functions of receiving and giving have been noted above in connection with the 4th Path; there is also ZKVTh (433), "a due portion."

Each of the benign Powers—ChH ChSYDH (100), "A benign, just, holy, living force." This phrase has the same numeration as MChY TBAL, "Mitigation of one by the other"; and so has KP, "palm of the hand" if P is taken as 80. The ideas of balance, of giving and receiving, of compensation, are thus carried throughout this paragraph.

The Seventh Path is the concealed Intelligence, so named because it is the dazzling resplendence of all the qualities of Mind, which are discerned by intellectual vision and by the gaze of faith.

The 7th Sephirah is the Sphere of Venus and of the forces of Nature. The familiar image of the Goddess with her mirror calls to mind how the mystics have unanimously attested the vivid reflection in the lower Worlds of the powers and wonders of the higher. A supplementary interpretation of the present text is provided by current research which is discovering, in the human psyche as in the natural world at large, numberless examples of the subtle directive power of Mind in the organization of the subrational.

This Sephirah is titled Netzach, NTzCh (148), "Victory": the numeration reducing through 13 to 4. The planet Venus is associated with the 4th letter, Daleth: this strengthens the importance of the 4. The planet's Hebrew name is Nogah, NVGH (64), the numeration reducing to 10, again significantly.

The concealed Intelligence—Of words whose numeration reduces to 13, ChMQ (148), "to retire, retreat" is remarkable here because it has exactly the same numeration as NTzCh. The word ChN, "love, graciousness, grace" (pre-eminent Venusian qualities) is composed of the initials of the words ChKMH NSThRH, "Secret Wisdom"; this use of initial letters, *Notariqon*, being another important Qabalistic device, the sense of the longer phrase being carried by the shorter one. DBVB (76) is "a hiding place; while AVR MVPLA (364), "Concealed Light," is a title of Kether.

It is the dazzling resplendence—YHY AVR (232), "Let there be light," and ADR," resplendent," both relate by numeration to the 7th Sephirah. BVTzYNA DQRDYNVThA (934), "a most brilliant shining," reduces to 7 through 16 which is 4 × 4. GBVH (16), ZQP (907), and MRVM (286, with each M as 40), all meaning "exalted, raised up," reduce similarly. So does MNRH (295), "a candlestick"; the original *Menorah* had seven branches. The numeration 10 gives us NH (55), which is both "splendor" and "eminence." The numeration 211, which links with NTzCh by reducing simply to 4, is shared by two interesting words: HARH, "a flash" as of lightning, and YRA, which signifies that "wonder or awe" towards Deity which we are told is the beginning of wisdom.

Of all the qualities of Mind—Relating to the sephirothic 7, NR (250) means both "a lamp" and "instruction." RVCh (214) signifies "air," "the breath of life," or "Mind" itself: that part of the psyche whose high destiny it is to receive intuitions from the Supernals, thereby (as well as by its own reason) to govern the emotional and physical levels of the person.

Intellectual vision and the gaze of faith—OYN (130, with N as 50), "an eye" is the literal and the pictographic significance of the letter Ayin: and since that letter has the numerical value of 70, the 7 is represented here as well as the 4 to which 130 reduces. The 16 is represented here too, because Ayin is the sixteenth letter. Since RVCh, "mind," also reduces to 7, this Eye sees with intellectual vision. Reducing to 10, AVR PNYMY (397), "Inward Light, Illumination," is a title of Kether; so likewise is AMN (91), "Amen"; and this word, as has been indicated earlier, has a special significance of "affirmation, faith."

The Eighth Path is called the Absolute or Perfect Intelligence, because it is the Instrument of the Primordial, which has no root by which it can hold fast or abide save in the hidden regions of Gedulah, Magnificence, which emanate from its own nature.

The Absolute or Perfect Intelligence—The 8th Path is the Sephirah Hod, HVD, this title having the numeration 15, reducing to 6. The planet Mercury, the luminary of the Sphere, has the Hebrew name Kokab, KVKB; the numeration of this name is 48, which is 6 × 8. The importance here of the numbers 6 and 8 is emphasized. This path HVD is called *perfect* because by ancient tradition 6 is a "perfect number"; the term *absolute* relates to the 8. This Path is called *absolute*, of supreme and universal authority, because ThVRH (611), "Law," is thus absolute. According to tradition, the entire text of the Torah (i.e., the Pentateuch) is composed of the letters of the supreme Divine Name.

It is the instrument of the Primordial—KLY (60) is "instrument." OYLAH, "Primordial," a title of Kether, has the numeration 116 which mirrors the 611 of ThVRH and, of course, reduces to 8.

Which has no root by which it can hold fast or abide—ShRSh (800) is "root"; MKVN, which like OYLAH has the numeration 116, means "emplacement" or "prepared resting place."

Save in the hidden regions of Gedulah, Magnificence—MKVN, "prepared resting place," is the title of the "Heaven" or *hidden region* of Chesed (Gedulah). It is in Makun the Heaven of Chesed, that the 8th Path finds its "Root."

Which emanates from its own nature—That is, from the nature of the 8th Path. Chesed is in the text given its alternative title of *Gedulah* because the numeration of that title, GDVLH (48) is identical with that of KVKB, the planet Mercury, and is made up of 6 × 8. The affinity of the 8th Path with MKVN is said to *emanate from* its nature, because 8 is the number to which, as we have seen, OYLAH (116) "the Primordial," also reduces; and this is a title of Kether the source of all emanation.

A futher point relevant to 6 × 8 is that, as indicated by their positions on the Tree, the 6th Sephirah is the necessary intermediary between the 8th Sephirah and its "Root."

The Ninth Path is called the Pure Intelligence, because it purifies the manifestations of the Sephiroth: it proves and governs the formation of their similitude, and disposes in exact measure the unity which is intrinsic to them, not lessened nor divided.

The Ninth Path is the Sephirah Yesod, Sphere of the Moon, ruler of the World of Yetzirah, the Astral Light.

The number 9, from ancient times pre-eminently associated with the number of lunar months of human gestation, is thereby linked also with the idea of the soul's descent into earthly manifestation: whence the same number comes to represent also the descent through the Worlds of the creative sephirothic impulses, to find astral manifestation in Yetzirah and in many cases also a further concretion of that manifestation in Assiah.

Besides these associations, the ideas of justice, purification and renewal are conveyed by the Moon's own psychic and physical associations, notably by the cyclic progress of the phases. The Hebrew numerations reflect all these factors: to cite many would be a digression but, as examples, ShPTYM (999) is the Hebrew title of the Book of Judges, while the text of the "Ten Commandments" gives a numerical value of 16011.

LBNH (87), the Hebrew name of the Moon, reduces to 6 and thus looks to the 6th Sephirah, the Sun Sphere, which has its numerical connotations of times and chronicles, glory, abjection and exaltation.

The Pure Intelligence—ZK (27 when K is reckoned as 20) is "pure, innocent."

It purifies the manifestations of the Sephiroth—BRK (702) is "tried, refined"; while PZ (87), "pure gold," has the identical numeration of LBNH, "the Moon." SPYRVTh (756) is here translated "the manifestations of the Sephiroth" because this word can equally be rendered (besides "Spheres") as "Numerations" or "Emanations," and in the present context evidently signifies the varied manifestations of the Sephiroth in the lower Worlds, not the pure perfection of their essential natures in Atziluth.

It proves and governs the formation of their similitudes—DN (54, with N as 50) is both "prove" and "govern," while BChN (60), similarly, is "tried by fire" and, reducing to 6, carries on the idea of PZ (87), "pure gold." YTzYRH (315), "Formation," is the Hebrew name of the Astral World, amid whose shifting illusions the archetypal images can become distorted and corrupt; its numeration is identical with that of OMRH, the true name of Gomorrah. 45, the "mystic number" of Yesod, mirrors the 54 of DN; 45 is also the numeration of MH, the syllable which not only asks "How?" "What?" "Why?" but is also the Secret Name of the World of Yetzirah. DMVTh (450) is "similitude."

Disposes in exact measure—YShR (510) is "just measure"; MAZNYM (708) is "scales"; MN (90, with N as 50) is "a portion."

The Unity which is intrinsic to them, neither lessened nor divided—Philosophically, the Unity in which the manifestations participate when restored to their pure sephirothic nature can by no means be lessened or divided; for it is the divine and primal unity of Kether, NQDH PShVTh (945), "The Small Point," which subsists whole and entire in each of its emanations. [2 = 2 × 1, 3 = 3 × 1, etc.]

AChD, "unity," can normally have the numeration 13; but in the *Sepher Sephiroth* a numeration for AChD is given as 963, this being achieved by spelling out the names of each of the three letters, thus: ALP = 111, ChYTh = 418, DLTh = 434; 111 + 418 + 434 = 963 if the P in ALP is taken as 80. If final P is used, the total is 1683; this or 963 alike reduces to 18, and thence to 9.

However, upon this theme the numeration of the title of the 9th Sephirah, YSVD (80), "Yesod, the Foundation" comes into its own. VOR (80) is "unity" in the sense of "union, unitedness"; ThM (440) is "wholeness, completeness, perfection"; TzMTzM (260) is "to gather together"; and MLA (71) is "plenitude."

APPENDIX B

ADDITIONAL NOTES ON THE PLANETARY GESTURES

Significances of the Seven

The seven Gestures given in the Tables of Correspondences (*Entry 36*) are named for the Mithraic degrees of initiation. Each of these Gestures is in its own right a mode of evocation of the planetary power to which it is harmonious, and directly involves the body, the emotional-instinctual nature, the rational mind and the will in the dramatic action.

KORAX, the Gesture of Luna

The curve of the arms and hands when they are raised above the head, then lowered and raised again, is indicative of the waxing and waning of the Moon. These movements therefore need unhurried, steady and even timing.

KRYPHIOS, The Gesture of Mercury

The "Priest of Babylon" is visibly a *Yin-Yang* sign; as such, indicating the union of opposites, it is particularly significant in this Mercurial evocation. The use of the hood represents (1) the concealment of the Mithraic Kryphios, (2) the "helmet of invisibility" of myth, and (3) the astronomical phases of invisibility of the planet Mercury.

MILES, the Gesture of Venus

This Gesture is associated with Netzach-Victory, and also with the relationship of the Morning Star to the Sun. The initial actions of the two arms mime Mithraic ritual: the right arm sweeps aside a sword upon which a crown is offered, the left arm indicates the higher glory which is preferred: "I aspire to the light of a spiritual crown," or "Crown not the herald of day, for behold, the glorious Sun is rising!" The signing of the Tau on the brow also follows the significance of the Mithraic rite. The gesture Psi accompanied by the stamping foot indicates the Victory over the lower nature.

LEO, the Gesture of Sol

The spiritual action represented is as follows. The Cup Formulation indicates the operator as initially receptive. The Fire Triangle overhead denotes the divine Fire; the passive backwards movement indicates the reception thereof. The Divine Fire is thereafter indicated as having been received in the heart of the operator, whose next act is to transmit this spiritual force, by touch, to the earth; thus becoming a participant in the Solar Work.

PERSIS, the Gesture of Mars

The total action of this evocation formulates the Mars, Persis or Anhur gesture, representing the poising of a spear for throwing. The force of Mars is here directed to the eradication of adverse influences, from a stance of positive dynamism.

HELIODROMOS, the Gesture of Jupiter

The Mithraic degree associated with Jupiter sees the cosmic Jupiterian powers as related to those of the Sun. "TheThunderer" formulates the violent aspect of the Skyfather. "Chesed" betokens the correspondence of Jupiter to the left shoulder and acknowledges the beneficent aspect of the Skyfather. "Kaph" formulates the "generous palm garnering, scattering" and proclaims the normal form of the letter (the cupped hand) and the final form of the letter (the open hand).

PATER, the Gesture of Saturn

Despite the Mithraic title, the divine force signified is not limited as to sex. The Sephirah in question is both the Sphere of Saturn and that of the Supernal Mother. In Qabalistic psychology the corresponding function, the Neshamah, in some contexts is "triune," carrying the powers of all three Supernals. After "Orante," the operative sign here is triune: a traditional Attis gesture indicating the glory and ecstasy of Power Divine, a traditional Cybele gesture of blessing, and the Uplifting of the World—or of the Universe—in offering to its Original Source which is also its supreme destiny. Cybele, the Great Mother, is a deity typical of this Sphere, and her son Attis was always regarded as the manifestation of her power; their mysteries were harmonious to those of Mithras and existed in alliance therewith in Rome.

Further Applications in the Planetary Rites

These Planetary Gestures are employed in Section 9 of the Rites of Ascent and Vision; but they may be incorporated into other of the rites, as follows:

In each of the Rites of Contact, the appropriate Planetary Gesture may be performed following Section 7 and preceding Section 8.

In each of the Rites of Attunement, the appropriate Planetary Gesture may be performed following Section 3 and preceding Section 4.

In each of the Rites of Tarot Divination, the appropriate Planetary Gesture may be performed following Section 12 and preceding Section 13.

In each of the Rites of Evocation of Dreams, the appropriate Planetary Gesture may be incorporated into Section 9, adapting the text thus:

9.   Move to the East, and facing East salute with the right hand. Perform the Planetary Gesture; then circumambulate the place of working *(planetary number of)* times clockwise, within the Star of Lights and encompassing the Bomos and the Mirror. Conclude the circumambulations in the East, salute, and return to West side of Bomos facing East.

GLOSSARY

(Words which have their own entry in this Glossary are indicated by italics when they occur in the text of another entry.)

ABAR   Hebrew name of lead (ABR), alchemical metal of Saturn.

AEGIS   In general, a piece of armor made according to ancient custom of hardened goatskin. Term used for the shield of Zeus, but most often for the breastplate of Athene. The Gorgon head thereon (represented also on the robes of priestesses) is meant as a caution to the overbold.

ANCILLARY   Noun or adjective, used of a person or thing which gives assistance as a subordinate factor.

ARCHETYPAL IMAGE   The form in which an *archetype* is clothed by a particular culture, mythology, religion or individual.

ARCHETYPE   A universal and, in itself, imageless concept. In the philosophies of Philo of Alexandria and Augustine of Hippo, the archetypes are discerned as subsisting within the Divine Mind; in the psychology of C.G. Jung they are discerned as within the Collective *Unconscious* of humanity. These insights do not exclude each other, and can be taken as mutually complementary.

ASTRAL   Relating or belonging to the level of being which is "beyond" and causal to the material world but is denser than the mental level. The "Astral Plane" is equivalent to the *Qabalistic* World of *Yetzirah*.

ASTRAL PLASMA,   *see* **PLASMA.**

ASTRO-PHYSICAL   Relating to, or affecting, existence at both *astral* and material levels, particularly in the experience of a human being.

393

ATZILUTH   The highest of the Four Worlds of *Qabalah*, the World of Spirit, of the divine Mind wherein the pure *Archetypes* subsist.

BARZEL   Hebrew name of iron (BRZL), alchemical metal of Mars.

BEDIL   Hebrew name of tin (BDYL), alchemical metal of Jupiter; probably connected with the word "bdellium" which has been applied to various crystalline substances.

BENISON   A beneficent conveying of divine influence, either as a "blessing" bestowed by a person or as a spontaneous action of divine force for which a suitable channel has been opened.

BRIAH   The second of the Four Worlds of *Qabalah*, the World of Mind which is next below *Atziluth*.

CADUCEUS   The staff of Hermes. In early times wreathed with ribbons as a herald's wand of office, the Caduceus became stylized with crowning wings and entwining serpents as the unique insignia of the Divine Messenger.

CHARITES   The Graces, attendants of Aphrodite. The three are Aglaia ("Brightness"), Euphrosyne ("Joy") and Thalia ("Blossom"). Since Charis—grace or charm—is a title of Aphrodite herself, the Charites can be considered as minor manifestations of the Goddess of Love and Beauty.

COLLECTIVE UNCONSCIOUS, *see* **UNCONSCIOUS**

COUNTERPART   In general, the counterpart is the *astral* component or reflection of any object or entity which exists, has existed or will exist. In *Planetary Magick* it is the potent reflection in the *Deep Mind* of any one of the planetary *archetypes*.

CRUCIBLE   A laboratory pot of iron, clay etc., to contain material for treatment by dry heat. Probably so named for the cross-shaped support within the pot, to keep the contents (if necessary) from touching the sides. In medieval alchemy the crucible is important symbolically as well as for practical work: the vessel represents the outer nature of the alchemist, and the contents the inner nature standing upon the cross of the Four Elements.

DARK NIGHT OF THE SOUL   Term now familiar in Western mystical psychology: 16th-century Spanish Carmelite St. John of the Cross (whose writings reveal much *Qabalistic* understanding) used it to describe the intense desolation which characterizes the eighth of his ten stages of spiritual ascent, corresponding to the experience of Binah, the Third *Sephirah*.

DEEP MIND   The *Unconscious* area of emotional and instinctual nature in the *psyche* of each individual. It is the source of all *psychic* powers, the full extent of which is as yet unmeasured and perhaps immeasurable. It comprises also for each person the *counterparts* of the planetary *archetypes*.

DEOSIL In a sunwise and clockwise direction. (Celtic word: rhymes with "facial.")

DIVINATION Any method of bringing conditions in the *Astral Light* into manifestation in the material world, so as to trace past, future or terrestrially distant happenings, or the emotional trend of persons, etc. The *Deep Mind* of the operator registers these astral conditions and transmits some part of their significance, through material symbols (as in Tarot, Geomancy, etc.), or conveys it directly to the conscious personality (as in Psychometry, Scrying, etc.).

EGREGORE An energized *astral* form produced consciously or unconsciously by human agency. In particular, (a) a strongly characterized form, usually an *archetypal image*, produced by the imaginative and emotional energies of a religious or magical group collectively, or (b) an astral shape of any kind, deliberately formulated by a magician to carry a specific force.

EIDOLON An image, whether existing in the material world or formulated in the *astral*, designed to represent the character of a deity or other spiritual being. An eidolon is a representation simply, and should not be confused with an *egregore.*

ENGRAM An effect in the *Deep Mind*, caused by an exceptional stimulus producing an indelible recollection.

EVOKE To call forth [a force or influence] from within the *psyche*. Compare with **INVOKE**, which means "to call [the power or presence of, for instance, a deity] in from outside the psyche."

EVOLUTION A progressive development; an improvement is implied in the word. One's "spiritual evolution" is one's progress on the Way of Return, after the initial "involution" of the spiritual self into earthly life.

INHIBIT To forbid or prevent by a *psychic* process. Inhibition may be unconscious, or a person may cultivate an inhibition by self-training against undesired actions, thoughts, etc.

INVOKE *see* **EVOKE.**

KASEP Hebrew name of silver (KSP), alchemical metal of the Moon.

KATHARSIS Purification, cleansing. The word is most often associated with an "emptying" of the emotional nature by experience of an overwhelming emotion. This association comes from Aristotle's description of the effect of tragic drama, "a katharsis of pity and terror."

NACREOUS   Iridescent, like mother-of-pearl. The term is used not simply to indicate a lustrous quality in the many-colored surface, but pre-eminently to denote the living, vibrant, changeful play of hues therein.

NECHSHETH   Hebrew name of copper (NChShTh), alchemical metal of Venus. (Compare the Arabic word "Nuhas," copper).

NEOPLATONIST   Of or relating to one of the philosophies developed from Platonism, which in turn like much other Greek philosophy, adapted certain Oriental material to Western modes of thinking. Neoplatonism, being "emanationist" in its theories (as against "creationist"), became strongly integrated with the growing *Qabalistic* structures.

PLANETARY MAGICK   The art of *invoking* and *evoking*, directing and experiencing, the forces related to the luminaries of our Solar System: a magical art developed though more than two millennia.

PLASMA   In the physical sciences, a primal fluidic substance. An **ASTRAL PLASMA** is a simple uncharacterized astral substance, formed into a "shell" for reception of a force which is to be directed into it.

PSYCHE   The non-material part of a psycho-physical being. The psyche includes rational and non-rational, conscious and *unconscious* functions. The *Deep Mind* is comprised within the individual psyche; the Collective *Unconscious*, as its name implies, lies beyond the bounds of individuality.

PSYCHIC   (Adjective.) This word has two meanings, and must be interpreted according to context. It signifies: (1) relating to the psyche, as when we say "The cause of a malady may be physical or psychic"; or (2) relating to a special use of the faculties of the psyche, as in "a psychic communication," "a psychic healer."

PSYCHOSOMATIC   Adjective describing a bodily disorder which is caused or intensified by a disorder (conscious or not) within the *psyche*. Frequently such a bodily disorder will in turn intensify the condition in the psyche. Treatment is necessarily addressed to the whole person: hence "psychosomatic treatment."

PSYCHOPOMPOS   "Guide of Souls." Greek title given to several deities—but particularly to Hermes—to signify the function of leading the souls of the departed to their appointed place.

QABALAH, QABALISTIC   The adjective "qabalistic," often used with various spellings by non-occult writers to mean simply "mystical" or "mysterious," properly relates to the Qabalah, a specific and venerable Wisdom Tradition formulated chiefly in Mediterranean regions. Hebrew and Greek are its principal languages: one of its primal tenets is the descent of Divine power (as knowable to us) in ten successive emanations—the Sephiroth—which exist in all four Worlds or levels of being, but in their primal perfection in *Atziluth.*

SEPHIRAH (plural, **SEPHIROTH**)   The ten Sephiroth are modalities of being, as experienced by the human investigator of states of consciousness. The Sephiroth are diagrammatically represented as ten spheres or circles upon the *Qabalistic* "Tree of Life": and of the ten, seven relate to the traditional Seven Planets.

SISTRUM   An instrument used in sacred rites and dances, usually in honor of a Goddess (Isis, Hathor, Ishtar, Cybele), but also of Dionysos. It consists of a frame or loop of rigid metal which runs through perforated metal rods or disks. The whole is fitted with a handle, so the rods or disks can rattle sharply together when the sistrum is shaken.

STERNUM   The breastbone, the flat blade of bone and cartilage which extends from below the collarbone vertically to the pit of the stomach, where it ends in a narrow rounded tip. The upper seven pairs of ribs are attached along its course. Occultly, the sternum bridges the area between Heart Chakra and Throat Chakra.

SUBLIMINAL   "Below the threshold"—a psychological term used of material which is in, or which enters, the *psyche* without the conscious mind being aware of it; as examples, an impression unconsciously retained from infancy, or an image flashed upon a screen which a person is watching, but lasting for too brief an interval for the conscious mind to grasp it. The impressions from both examples can however influence feeling and action through their presence in the *unconscious.*

SUPERNAL   "Of the higher regions"; in particular in *Qabalistic* language, pertaining to any one of the three highest *Sephiroth*: Kether, Chokmah and Binah. The two first-mentioned, and Binah apart from its planetary (Saturnian) aspect, are accessible only to mystical experience beyond the range of ordinary earthly life. Nevertheless their powers and influences flow through all levels of being.

SYNTHESIS   A combining of previously existing phenomena or concepts to produce a phenomenon or concept with a new identity, which may have characteristics differing from those of the phenomena or concepts which produced it.

TEMPORAL MODE   The classification as to lunar phases and Seasonal Tides, which identifies the requirements for performing specific magical rites. Three Temporal Modes cover the requirements for all rituals given in this book.

UNCONSCIOUS   Those great areas of the *psyche* which are not within the knowledge, and so not within the direct control, of the conscious and rational mind. This term is used to comprise: (a) the Higher Unconscious, Higher Self or "Supermind"; (b) the Lower Unconscious, the *Deep Mind,* the unconscious region of the emotional and instinctual nature; (c) the Personal Unconscious, an individual's personal deposit of forgotten and, often, repressed material, therefore to that extent an abnormal development in the psyche; (d) the Collective Unconscious, the repository of the totality of all human experience, beyond the domain of the individual psyche; and, beyond the Collective Unconscious of humanity, the Collective Unconscious of all life. Any part of these depths may in certain circumstances become accessible to the individual psyche.

URAEUS (Plural, **URAEI**)   The sacred cobra of Ancient Egypt, emblem of divine energy and royal authority.

UTHARUD   Hebrew name of quicksilver (VThRVD), alchemical metal of Mercury. (Compare the angelic name "Uthrodiel," and one of the Arabic alchemical names for quicksilver, "Utarit.")

YETZIRAH   The third of the Four Worlds of the *Qabalah:* the *Astral* World, less dense than the material World but less subtle and elevated than *Briah,* the World of Mind.

ZAHAB   Hebrew name of gold (ZHB), alchemical metal of the Sun.

ZIGGURAT OF LIGHT   An occult term which incorporates the imagery of the Mesopotamian Tower-temple, the Ziggurat, to represent the ascending order, Moon through Saturn, of the seven planetary Spheres.

SELECT BIBLIOGRAPHY

Aurum Solis: *Rite of Integration* (Second Hall Initiation) (Unpublished.)
Budge, E.A. Wallis: *The Gods of the Egyptians* (Dover, 1969).
Cumont, Franz: *The Mysteries of Mithra,* (Dover, 1966).
Cunningham, Scott: *Encyclopedia of Magical Herbs,* (Llewellyn, 1985).
Denning & Phillips: *The Magical Philosophy (5 vols). (Llewellyn, 1974-1981).*
          Practical Guide to Magick of the Tarot (Llewellyn, 1983).
Dodds, E.R.: *The Greeks and the Irrational,* (Beacon Press, Boston, 1957).
d'Olivet, Abbé: *Thoughts of Cicero:* transl. from the French, with Latin text. (Glasgow, MDCCLIV).
Ficino, Marsilio: *Liber de Vita, The Book of Life:* transl. by Charles Boer (Spring, Texas, 1980).
George, Llewellyn: *The Planetary Hour Book,* Llewellyn, revised 1975).
Godwin, David: *Godwin's Cabalistic Encyclopedia,* (Llewellyn, 1989).
Graves, Robert: *The Greek Myths* (2 vols.), (Penguin, revised 1957).
Hall, Manly P.: *Astrological Keywords,* (Peter Owen, London, 1959).
Holy Scriptures (The), according to the Masoretic Text (2 vols.), (Jewish Publication Society of America, Philadelphia, 1955).
James, E.O.: *Myth and Ritual in the Ancient Near East,* (Thames & Hudson, 1958).
Jung, C.G.: *Structure & Dynamics of the Psyche,* (Princeton University Press, 1968).
          Psychology and Alchemy, (Princeton University Press, 1968).
Larousse Encyclopedia of Mythology, (Prometheus, New York, 1959).

Leyden Papyrus (The), an Egyptian Magical Book: ed. F.L1., Griffith & Herbert Thompson, (Dover, 1974).

Meunier, Mario: *Hymnes philosophiques: Aristote, Cléanthe, Proclus.* French transl. & notes. (L'Artisan du Livre, Paris MCMXXXV).

Moore, Thomas: *The Planets Within,* (Assoc. University Presses, London & Toronto, 1982).

Murray, Alexander S.: *Manual of Mythology,* (Tudor, New York, 1935).

Pallotino, M.: *The Etruscans,* (Penguin, 1955).

Pinches, Theophilus G., LL.D.: *Religion of Babylonia and Assyria,* (Constable, London 1906).

Pindar: *The Odes,* (Penguin, 1969).

Reuchlin, Johann: *La Kabbale (De Arte Cabalistica),* French transl. Francois Secret (Aubier-Montaigne, Paris, 1973).

Rougier, Louis: *La Religion astrale des Pythagoriciens,* (Presses universitaires, Paris, 1959).

Scott, Walter: *Hermetica, Vol. I: Introduction,* Greek & Latin texts and transl., (Shambhala, Boston, 1985).

Spence, Lewis, F.R.A.I.: *Myths & Legends of Babylonia & Assyria,* (Gale, Detroit, 1975).

"Sources orientales" Various Authors: *Le Monde du Sorcier* (Egypte, Babylone, Hittites, Israël, Islam, Asie centrale, Inde, Nepal, Cambodge, Vietnam, Japon). (Edns. du Seuil, Paris, 1966).

Tyl, Noel: *Astrology 1—2—3,* (Llewellyn, 1984).

Zohar (The) Transl. Harry Sperling & Maurice Simon (5 vols.) (Soncino Press, London, 1933).

STAY IN TOUCH

On the following pages you will find listed, with their current prices, some of the books now available on related subjects. Your book dealer stocks most of these and will stock new titles in the Llewellyn series as they become available. We urge your patronage.

To obtain our full catalog, to keep informed about new titles as they are released and to benefit from informative articles and helpful news, you are invited to write for our bimonthly news magazine/catalog, *Llewellyn's New Worlds of Mind and Spirit*. A sample copy is free, and it will continue coming to you at no cost as long as you are an active mail customer. Or you may subscribe for just $7.00 in the U.S.A. and Canada ($20.00 overseas, first class mail). Many bookstores also have *New Worlds* available to their customers. Ask for it.

Stay in touch! In *New Worlds'* pages you will find news and features about new books, tapes and services, announcements of meetings and seminars, articles helpful to our readers, news of authors, products and services, special money-making opportunities, and much more.

Llewellyn's New Worlds of Mind and Spirit
P.O. Box 64383-193, St. Paul, MN 55164-0383, U.S.A.
* * *

TO ORDER BOOKS AND TAPES

If your book dealer does not have the books described on the following pages readily available, you may order them directly from the publisher by sending full price in U.S. funds, plus $3.00 for postage and handling for orders *under* $10.00; $4.00 for orders *over* $10.00. There are no postage and handling charges for orders over $50.00. Postage and handling rates are subject to change. UPS Delivery: We ship UPS whenever possible. Delivery guaranteed. Provide your street address as UPS does not deliver to P.O. Boxes. UPS to Canada requires a $50.00 minimum order. Allow 4-6 weeks for delivery. Orders outside the U.S.A. and Canada: Airmail—add retail price of book; add $5.00 for each non-book item (tapes, etc.); add $1.00 per item for surface mail.

FOR GROUP STUDY AND PURCHASE

Because there is a great deal of interest in group discussion and study of the subject matter of this book, we feel that we should encourage the adoption and use of this particular book by such groups by offering a special quantity price to group leaders or agents.

Our Special Quantity Price for a minimum order of five copies of *Planetary Magick* is $45.00 cash-with-order. This price includes postage and handling within the United States. Minnesota residents must add 6.5% sales tax. For additional quantities, please order in multiples of five. For Canadian and foreign orders, add postage and handling charges as above. Credit card (VISA, MasterCard, American Express) orders are accepted. Charge card orders only ($15.00 minimum order) may be phoned in free within the U.S.A. or Canada by dialing 1-800-THE-MOON. For customer service, call 1-612-291-1970. Mail orders to:

LLEWELLYN PUBLICATIONS
P.O. Box 64383-193, St. Paul, MN 55164-0383, U.S.A.

THE MAGICAL PHILOSOPHY, VOLUME 1
The Foundations of High Magick
by Denning & Phillips
The long-awaited re-publication of *The Magical Philosophy Series* is now complete—this time improved and revised with additional material. *The Foundations of High Magick* is a structured and progressive curriculum of Qabalistic and Ogdoadic Magick based upon the wide practical experience and extensive researches of the Order Aurum Solis. The *Foundations of High Magick* contains the revised Book I, "Robe and Ring," which explores the philosophy of the magical art and the ethics of Western Occultism. It also contains Book II, "The Apparel of High Magick," which discusses the symbolism and introduces the concept of "the correspondences." It makes a preliminary study of some of the objective materials of the magical art, both on the physical and other levels, and introduces some of the laws which link those levels.

The Aurum Solis was founded in 1897 as a practical school of ceremonial magick. Its philosophy is rooted deeply in the Western esoteric tradition. Founded on the Ogdoadic Tradition rather than on the Rosicrucian mold, the Aurum Solis is distinctive and unique, yet remains harmonious with the work of other Qabalistic orders.
0-87542-174-1, 408 pgs., 6 x 9, illus., softcover   **$15.00**

THE MAGICAL PHILOSOPHY, VOLUME 2
The Sword and the Serpent
by Denning & Phillips
This is the comprehensive guide to the Magical Qabalah, with extensive correspondences as well as the techniques for activating the centers, use of images and the psychology of attainment.

In this volume, histories from contemporary life, together with references to the works of mystics, poets, artists, philosophers and authorities in psychology are cited to illustrate the action and interaction of the functions of the psyche as identified in Qabalistic teaching.

The real meaning of adepthood is clearly set forth: in relation to this, frequent enigmas of occult literature such as the Abyss, the Knowledge and Conversation of the Holy Guardian Angel, and the supernal attainments are presented in their true meaning and significance. The natural dignity and potential of life in this world is your birthright. In this volume, its splendor and power are manifested.
0-87542-197-0, 540 pgs., 6 x 9, illus., softcover   **$15.00**

THE MAGICAL PHILOSOPHY, VOLUME 3
Mysteria Magica
by Denning & Phillips

For years, Denning and Phillips headed the international occult Order Aurum Solis. In this book, they present the magickal system of the order so that you can use it. Here you will find rituals for banishing and invoking plus instructions for proper posture and breathing. You will learn astral projection, rising on the planes, and the magickal works that should be undertaken through astral projection. You will learn the basic principle of ceremonies and how to make sigils and talismans. You will learn practical Enochian magick plus how to create, consecrate and use your magickal tools such as the magickal sword, wand and cup. You will also learn the advanced arts of sphere-working and evocation to visible appearance.

Filled with illustrations, this book is an expanded version of the previous edition. It is now complete in itself and can be the basis of an entire magickal system. You can use the information alone or as the source book for a group. If you want to learn how to do real magick, this is the place you should start.

0-87542-196-2, 480 pgs., 6 x 9, illus., softcover **$15.00**

THE LLEWELLYN PRACTICAL GUIDE TO ASTRAL PROJECTION
The Out-of-Body Experience
by Denning & Phillips

Yes, your consciousness can be sent forth, out of the body, with full awareness and return with full memory. You can travel through time and space, converse with nonphysical entities, obtain knowledge by nonmaterial means, and experience higher dimensions.

Is there life after death? Are we forever shackled by time and space? The ability to go forth by means of the Astral Body, or Body of Light, gives the personal assurance of consciousness (and life) beyond the limitations of the physical body. No other answer to these ageless questions is as meaningful as experienced reality.

The reader is led through the essential stages for the inner growth and development that will culminate in fully conscious projection and return. Not only are the requisite practices set forth in step-by-step procedures, augmented with photographs and visualization aids, but the vital reasons for undertaking them are clearly explained. Beyond this, the great benefits from the various practices themselves are demonstrated in renewed physical and emotional health, mental discipline, spiritual attainment, and the development of extra faculties.

Guidance is also given to the Astral World itself: what to expect, what can be done—including the ecstatic experience of Astral Sex between two people who project together into this higher world where true union is consummated free of the barriers of physical bodies.

0-87542-181-4, 266 pgs., 5 1/4 x 8, illus., softcover **$8.95**

THE LLEWELLYN PRACTICAL GUIDE TO CREATIVE MONEYMAKING
Become a Money Magnet
by Denning & Phillips
The world is full of people who "wish" they had more money. This book is for those who really *want* to have more money. It shows you how to direct your natural powers in such a way that you *will* make money.

This is a creative program of money making, saving and investment—with no encounter, unless one chooses, with the bulls and bears of the financial arena. Equally, readers who are business people, but who suspect there is a "psychic edge" to be gained, will find that edge here. There are no tedious preliminary exercises or specialized metaphysical or occult vocabulary to wade through. Instead, you will receive simple instructions on: how to use vision and imagination to will money to you, the practical and psychic value of regular saving, how to make a "Talisman of Increase," why you should never borrow or lend, how to form a partnership with your powerful Deep Mind, how to use your dreams to attract money, how to increase your psychic powers, how to invest creatively and much, much more.
0-87542-173-3, 208 pgs., 5 1/4 x 8, illus., softcover **$8.95**

THE LLEWELLYN PRACTICAL GUIDE TO THE MAGICK OF THE TAROT
by Denning & Phillips
"To gain understanding, and control, of your life"—can anything be more important? To gain insight into the circumstances of your life—the inner causes, the karmic needs, the hidden factors at work—and then to have the power to change your life in order to fulfill your real desires and true will: that's what the techniques taught in this book can do.

Discover the shadows cast ahead by coming events. Yes, this is possible, because it is your DEEP MIND—that part of your psyche, normally beyond your conscious awareness, which is in touch with the world soul and with your own higher (and divine) self—that perceives the astral shadows of coming events and can communicate them to you through the symbols and images of the ancient and mysterious Tarot cards.

Your Deep Mind has the power to shape those astral shadows—images that are causal to material events—when you learn to communicate your own desires and goals using the Tarot.
0-87542-198-9, 252 pgs., 5-1/4 x 8, illus., softcover **$8.95**

THE LLEWELLYN PRACTICAL GUIDE TO THE DEVELOPMENT OF PSYCHIC POWERS
by Denning & Phillips

You may not realize it, but you already have the ability to use ESP, astral vision and clairvoyance, divination, dowsing,prophecy, and communication with spirits.

Written by two of the most knowledgeable experts in the world of psychic development, this book is a complete course—teaching you, step-by-step, how to develop these powers that actually have been yours since birth. Using the techniques, you will soon be able to move objects at a distance, see into the future, know the thoughts and feelings of another person, find lost objects and locate water using your no-longer latent talents.

Psychic powers are as much a natural ability as any other talent. You'll learn to play with these new skills, working with groups of friends to accomplish things you never would have believed possible before reading this book. The text shows you how to make the equipment you can use, the exercises you can do—many of them at any time, anywhere—and how to use your abilities to change your life and the lives of those close to you. Many of the exercises are presented in forms that can be adapted as games for pleasure and fun, as well as development.

0-87542-191-1, 272 pgs., 5 1/4 x 8, illus., softcover **$8.95**

THE LLEWELLYN PRACTICAL GUIDE TO PSYCHIC SELF-DEFENSE AND WELL-BEING
by Denning & Phillips

Psychic well-being and psychic self-defense are two sides of the same coin, just as are physical health and resistance to disease. Each person (and every living thing) is surrounded by an electromagnetic force field, or AURA, that can provide the means to psychic self-defense and to dynamic well-being. This book explores the world of very real "psychic warfare" of which we are all victims.

Every person in our modern world is subjected to psychic stress and psychological bombardment: advertising promotions that play upon primitive emotions, political and religious appeals that work on feelings of insecurity and guilt, noise, threats of violence and war, news of crime and disaster, etc.

This book shows the nature of genuine psychic attacks—ranging from actual acts of black magic to bitter jealousy and hate—and the reality of psychic stress, the structure of the psyche and its interrelationship with the physical body. It shows how each person must develop his weakened aura into a powerful defense-shield, thereby gaining both physical protection and energetic well-being that can extend to protection from physical violence, accidents ... even ill health.

0-87542-190-3, 306 pgs., 5 1/4 x 8, illus., softcover **$8.95**

THE LLEWELLYN PRACTICAL GUIDE TO CREATIVE VISUALIZATION
For the Fulfillment of Your Desires
by Denning & Phillips

All things you will ever want must have their start in your mind. The average person uses very little of the full creative power that is his, potentially. It's like the power locked in the atom—it's all there, but you have to learn to release it and apply it constructively.

IF YOU CAN SEE IT ... in your Mind's Eye ... you will have it! It's true: you can have whatever you want, but there are "laws" to mental creation that must be followed. The power of the mind is not limited to, nor limited by, the material world. *Creative Visualization* enables Man to reach beyond, into the invisible world of Astral and Spiritual Forces.

Some people apply this innate power without actually knowing what they are doing, and achieve great success and happiness; most people, however, use this same power, again unknowingly, incorrectly, and experience bad luck, failure, or at best an unfulfilled life.

This book changes that. Through an easy series of step-by-step, progressive exercises, your mind is applied to bring desire into realization! Wealth, power, success, happiness even psychic powers ... even what we call magickal power and spiritual attainment ... all can be yours. You can easily develop this completely natural power, and correctly apply it, for your immediate and practical benefit. Illustrated with unique, "puts-you-into-the-picture" visualization aids.
0-87542-183-0, 294 pgs., 5 1/4 x 8, illus., softcover **$8.95**

THE INNER WORLD OF FITNESS
Psychic Strength and Inner Health
by Melita Denning

Because the artificialities and the daily hassles of routine living tend to turn our attention from the real values, *The Inner World of Fitness* leads us back by means of those natural factors in life which remain to us: air, water, sunlight, the food we eat, the world of nature, meditations, sexual love and the power of our wishes—so that through these things we can re-link ourselves in awareness to the great nonmaterial forces of life and of being which underlie them.

The unity and interaction of inner and outer, keeping body and psyche open to the great currents of life and of the natural forces, is seen as the essential secret of "youthfulness" and hence of radiant fitness. Regardless of our physical age, so long as we are within the flow of these great currents, we have the vital quality of youthfulness; but if we begin to close off or turn away from those contacts, in the same measure we begin to lose youthfulness.

This book will help you to experience the total energy of abundant health. Also included is a metaphysical examination of AIDS.
0-87542-165-2, 224 pgs., 5 1/4 x 8, illus., softcover **$7.95**

THE MAGICAL DIARY
A Personal Ritual Journal
by Donald Michael Kraig

Virtually every teacher of magic, whether it is a book or an individual, will advise you to keep a record of your magical rituals. Unfortunately, most people keep these records in a collection of different sized and different looking books, frequently forgetting to include important data. *The Magical Diary* changes this forever. In this book are pages waiting to be filled in. Each page has headings for all of the important information including date, day, time, astrological information, planetary hour, name of rituals performed, results, comments, and much more. Use some of them or use them all. This book was specially designed to be perfect for all magicians no matter what tradition you are involved in. Everybody who does magic needs *The Magical Diary*.

0-87542-322-1, 240 pgs., 7 x 8 1/2, otabound $9.95

MAGIC AND THE WESTERN MIND
Ancient Knowledge and the Transformation of Consciousness
by Gareth Knight

Magic and the Western Mind explains why intelligent and responsible people are turning to magic and the occult as a radical and important way to find meaning in modern life, as well as a means of survival for themselves and the planet.

First published in 1978 as *A History of White Magic*, this book illustrates, in a wide historical survey, how the higher imagination has been used to aid the evolution of consciousness—from the ancient mystery religions, through alchemy, Renaissance magic, the Rosicrucian Manifestoes, Freemasonry, 19th-century magic fraternities, up to psychoanalysis and the current occult revival. Plus it offers some surprising insights into the little-known interests of famous people.The Western mind developed magic originally as one of the noblest of arts and sciences. Now, with the help of this book, anyone can defend a belief in magic in convincing terms.

0-87542-374-4, 336 pgs., 6 x 9, illus., softcover $12.95

MODERN MAGICK
Eleven Lessons in the High Magickal Arts
by Donald Michael Kraig

Modern Magick is the most comprehensive step-by-step introduction to the art of ceremonial magic ever offered. The eleven lessons in this book will guide you from the easiest of rituals and the construction of your magickal tools through the highest forms of magick: designing your own rituals and doing pathworking. Along the way you will learn the secrets of the Kabbalah in a clear and easy-to-understand manner. You will discover the true secrets of invocation (channeling) and evocation, and the missing information that will finally make the ancient grimoires, such as the "Keys of Solomon," not only comprehensible, but usable. This book also contains one of the most in-depth chapters on sex magick ever written. *Modern Magick* is designed so anyone can use it, and it is the perfect guidebook for students and classes. It will also help to round out the knowledge of long-time practitioners of the magickal arts.

0-87542-324-8, 592 pgs., 6 x 9, illus., index, softcover $14.95

THE GOLDEN DAWN
The Original Account of the Teachings, Rites & Ceremonies
of the Hermetic Order
As revealed by Israel Regardie
Complete in one volume with further revision, expansion, and additional notes by Regardie, Cris Monnastre, and others. Expanded with an index of more than 100 pages!

Originally published in four bulky volumes of some 1,200 pages, this 6th Revised and Enlarged Edition has been entirely reset in modern, less space-consuming type, in half the pages (while retaining the original pagination in marginal notation for reference) for greater ease and use.

Corrections of typographical errors perpetuated in the original and subsequent editions have been made, with further revision and additional text and notes by noted scholars and by actual practitioners of the Golden Dawn system of Magick, with an Introduction by the only student ever accepted for personal training by Regardie.

Also included are Initiation Ceremonies, important rituals for consecration and invocation, methods of meditation and magical working based on the Enochian Tablets, studies in the Tarot, and the system of Qabalistic Correspondences that unite the World's religions and magical traditions into a comprehensive and practical whole.

This volume is designed as a study and practice curriculum suited to both group and private practice. Meditation upon, and following with the Active Imagination, the Initiation Ceremonies are fully experiential without need of participation in group or lodge. A very complete reference encyclopedia of Western Magick.
0-87542-663-8, 840 pgs., 6 x 9, illus., softcover $19.95

A GARDEN OF POMEGRANATES
by Israel Regardie
What is the Tree of Life? It's the ground plan of the Qabalistic system—a set of symbols used since ancient times to study the Universe. The Tree of Life is a geometrical arrangement of ten sephiroth, or spheres, each of which is associated with a different archetypal idea, and 22 paths which connect the spheres.This system of primal correspondences has been found the most efficient plan ever devised to classify and organize the characteristics of the self. Israel Regardie has written one of the best and most lucid introductions to the Qabalah. *A Garden of Pomegranates* combines Regardie's own studies with his notes on the works of Aleister Crowley, A. E. Waite, Eliphas Levi and D. H. Lawrence. No longer is the wisdom of the Qabalah to be held secret! The needs of today place the burden of growth upon each and every person . . . each has to undertake the Path as his or her own responsibility, but every help is given in the most ancient and yet most modern teaching here known to humankind.
0-87542-690-5, 160 pgs., 5 1/4 x 8, softcover $8.95

THE MIDDLE PILLAR
by Israel Regardie

Between the two outer pillars of the Qabalistic Tree of Life, the extremes of Mercy and Severity, stands the Middle Pillar, signifying one who has achieved equilibrium in his or her own self.

Integration of the human personality is vital to the continuance of creative life. Without it, man lives as an outsider to his own true self. By combining Magic and Psychology in the Middle Pillar Ritual/Exercise (a magical meditation technique), we bring into balance the opposing elements of the psyche while yet holding within their essence and allowing full expression of man's entire being.

In this book, and with this practice, you will learn to: understand the psyche through its correspondences of the Tree of Life; expand self-awareness, thereby intensifying the inner growth process; activate creative and intuitive potentials; understand the individual thought patterns which control every facet of personal behavior; and regain the sense of balance and peace of mind—the equilibrium that everyone needs for phsyical and psychic health.

0-87542-658-1, 176 pgs., 5-1/4x8, softcover $8.95

THE NEW MAGUS
The Modern Magician's Practical Guide
by Donald Tyson

The New Magus is a practical framework on which a student can base his or her personal system of magic.

This book is filled with practical, usable magical techniques and rituals which anyone from any magical tradition can use. It includes instructions on how to design and perform rituals, create and use sigils, do invocations and evocations, do spiritual healings, learn rune magic, use god-forms, create telesmatic images, discover your personal guardian, create and use magical tools and much more. You will learn how YOU can be a New Magus!

The New Age is based on ancient concepts that have been put into terms, or metaphors, that are appropriate to life in our world today. That makes *The New Magus* the book on magic for today. If you have found that magic seems illogical, overcomplicated and not appropriate to your lifestyle, *The New Magus* is the book for you. It will change your ideas of magic forever!

0-87542-825-8, 368 pgs., 6 x 9, illus., softcover $12.95

THE LLEWELLYN ANNUALS

Llewellyn's MOON SIGN BOOK: Approximately 400 pages of valuable information on gardening, fishing, weather, stock market forecasts, personal horoscopes, good planting dates, and general instructions for finding the best date to do just about anything! Articles by prominent forecasters and writers in the fields of gardening, astrology, politics, economics and cycles. This special almanac, different from any other, has been published annually since 1906. It's fun, informative and has been a great help to millions in their daily planning. **State year $4.95**

Llewellyn's SUN SIGN BOOK: Your personal horoscope for the entire year! All 12 signs are included in one handy book. Also included are forecasts, special feature articles, and an action guide for each sign. Monthly horoscopes are written by Gloria Star, author of *Optimum Child*, for your personal Sun Sign and there are articles on a variety of subjects written by well-known astrologers from around the country. Much more than just a horoscope guide! Entertaining and fun the year around. **State year $4.95**

Llewellyn's DAILY PLANETARY GUIDE: Includes all of the major daily aspects plus their exact times in Eastern and Pacific time zones, lunar phases, signs and voids plus their times, planetary motion, a monthly ephemeris, sunrise and sunset tables, special articles on the planets, signs, aspects, a business guide, planetary hours, rulerships, and much more. Large 5-1/4 x 8 format for more writing space, spiral bound to lay flat, address and phone listings, time-zone conversion chart and blank horoscope chart. **State year $6.95**

Llewellyn's ASTROLOGICAL CALENDAR: Large wall calendar of 48 pages. Beautiful full-color cover and full-color paintings inside. Includes special feature articles by famous astrologers, and complete introductory information on astrology. It also contains a Lunar Gardening Guide, celestial phenomena, a blank horoscope chart, and monthly date pages which include aspects, Moon phases, signs and voids, planetary motion, an ephemeris, personal forecasts, lucky dates, planting and fishing dates, and more. 10 x 13 size. Set in Central time, with fold-down conversion table for other time zones worldwide. **State year $9.95**

Llewellyn's MAGICAL ALMANAC: This beautifully illustrated almanac explores traditional earth religions and folklore while focusing on magical myths. Each month is summarized in a two-page format with information that includes the phases of the moon, festivals and rites for the month, as well as detailed magical advice. This is an indispensable guide is for anyone who is interested in planning rituals, spells and other magical advice. It features writing by some of the most prominent authors in the field. **State year $7.95**

ARCHETYPES OF THE ZODIAC
by Kathleen Burt
The horoscope is probably the most unique tool for personal growth you can ever have. This book is intended to help you understand how the energies within your horoscope manifest. Once you are aware of how your chart operates on an instinctual level, you can then work consciously with it to remove any obstacles to your growth.

The technique offered in this book is based upon the incorporation of the esoteric rulers of the signs and the integration of their polar opposites. This technique has been very successful in helping the client or reader modify existing negative energies in a horoscope so as to improve the quality of his or her life and the understanding of his or her psyche.

There is special focus in this huge comprehensive volume on the myths for each sign. Some signs may have as many as four different myths coming from all parts of the world. All are discussed by the author. There is also emphasis on the Jungian Archetypes involved with each sign.

This book has a depth often surprising to the readers of popular astrology books. It has a clarity of expression seldom found in books of the esoteric tradition. It is very easy to understand, even if you know nothing of Jungian philosophy or of mythology. It is intriguing, exciting and very helpful for all levels of astrologers.
0-87542-088-5, 576 pgs., 6 x 9, illus., softcover **$14.95**

WICCA
A Guide for the Solitary Practitioner
by Scott Cunningham
Wicca is a book of life, and how to live magically, spiritually, and wholly attuned with Nature. It is a book of sense and common sense, not only about Magick, but about religion and one of the most critical issues of today: how to achieve the much needed and wholesome relationship with out Earth. Cunningham presents Wicca as it is today: a gentle, Earth-oriented religion dedicated to the Goddess and God. This book fulfills a need for a practical guide to solitary Wicca—a need which no previous book has fulfilled.

Here is a positive, practical introduction to the religion of Wicca, designed so that any interested person can learn to practice the religion alone, anywhere in the world. It presents Wicca honestly and clearly, without the pseudo-history that permeates other books. It shows that Wicca is a vital, satisfying part of twentieth century life.

This book presents the theory and practice of Wicca from an individual's perspective. The section on the Standing Stones Book of Shadows contains solitary rituals for the Esbats and Sabbats. This book, based on the author's nearly two decades of Wiccan practice, presents an eclectic picture of various aspects of this religion. Exercises designed to develop magical proficiency, a self-dedication ritual, herb, crystal and rune magic, recipes for Sabbat feasts, are included in this excellent book.
0-87542-118-0, 240 pgs., 6 x 9, illus., softcover **$9.95**

TEMPLE MAGIC
Building the Personal Temple: Gateway to Inner Worlds
by William Gray

This important book on occultism deals specifically with problems and details you are likely to encounter in temple practice. Learn how a temple should look, how a temple should function, what a ceremonialist should wear, what physical postures best promote the ideal spiritual-mental attitude, and how magic is worked in a temple.

Temple Magic has been written specifically for the instruction and guidance of esoteric ceremonialists by someone who spent a lifetime in spiritual service to his natural Inner Way. There are few comparable works in existence, and this book in particular deals with up-to-date techniques of constructing and using a workable temple dedicated to the furtherance of the Western Inner Tradition. In simple yet adequate language, it helps any individual understand and promote the spiritual structure of our esoteric inheritance. It is a book by a specialist for those who are intending to be specialists.

0-87542-274-8, 288 pgs,, 5 1/4 x 8, illus., softcover   **$7.95**

YOUR PLANETARY PERSONALITY
Everything You Need to Make Sense of Your Horoscope
by Dennis Oakland

This book deepens the study of astrological interpretation for professional and beginning astrologers alike. Dennis Oakland's interpretations of the planets in the houses and signs are the result of years of study of psychology, sciences, symbolism, Eastern philosophy plus the study of birth charts from a psychotherapy group. Unlike the interpretations in other books, these emphasize the life processes involved and facilitate a greater understanding of the chart. Includes 100-year ephemeris.

Even if you now know *nothing* about astrology, Dennis Oakland's clear instructions will teach you how to construct a complete and accurate birth chart for anyone born between 1900 to 1999. After you have built your chart, he will lead you through the steps of reading it, giving you indepth interpretations of each of your planets. When done, you will have the satisfaction that comes from increased self-awareness *and* from being your *own* astrologer!

This book is also an excellent exploration for psychologists and psychiatrists who use astrology in their practices.

0-87542-594-1, 580 pgs., 7 x 10, softcover   **$19.95**

HOW TO PERSONALIZE THE OUTER PLANETS
The Astrology of Uranus, Neptune & Pluto
Edited by Noel Tyl

Since their discoveries, the three outer planets have been symbols of the modern era. Representing great social change on a global scale, they also take us as individuals to higher levels of consciousness and new possibilities of experience. Explored individually, each outer planet offers tremendous promise for growth. But when taken as a group, as they are in *How to Personalize the Outer Planets*, the potential exists to recognize *accelerated* development.

As never done before, the seven prominent astrologers in *How to Personalize the Outer Planets* bring these revolutionary forces down to earth in practical ways.

* Jeff Jawer: Learn how the discoveries of the outer planets rocked the world
* Noel Tyl: Project into the future with outer planet Solar Arcs
* Jeff Green: See how the outer planets are tied to personal trauma
* Jeff Jawer: Give perspective to your inner spirit through outer planet symbolisms
* Jayj Jacobs: Explore interpersonal relationships and sex through the outer planets
* Mary E. Shea: Make the right choices using outer planet transits
* Joanne Wickenburg: Realize your unconscious drives and urges through the outer planets
* Capel N. McCutcheon: Personalize the incredible archetypal significance of outer planet aspects

0-87542-389-2, 288 pgs., 6 x 9, illus., softcover **$12.00**

ATTAINMENT THROUGH MAGIC
by William G. Gray

In this newly titled re-release of the classic *A Self Made by Magic*, the author presents a "Self-Seeking System" of powerful magical practice designed to help seekers become better and more fulfilled souls. The source material is taken from standard procedures familiar to most students of the Western Inner Tradition, procedures that encourage the best of our potential while diminishing or eliminating our worst characteristics. To that end, Gray deals extensively with the dangers and detriments of maleficent or "black" magic.

The lessons follow the pattern of the Life-Tree, and guide the student through the four elements and their connection of Truth, the Ten Principles of "Spheres" of the Life-Tree, and the associations which bind these together. Gray includes an in-depth study of the Archangelic concepts with exercises to "make the Archangels come true" for us through the systematic use of appropriate words of power.

0-87542-298-5, 308 pgs., 5 1/4 x 8, illus., softcover **$9.95**

ANCIENT MAGICKS FOR A NEW AGE
Rituals from the Merlin Temple, the Magick of the Dragon Kings
by Alan Richardson and Geoff Hughes
With two sets of personal magickal diaries, this book details the work of magicians from two different eras. In it, you can learn what a particular magician is experiencing in this day and age, how to follow a similar path of your own, and discover correlations to the workings of traditional adepti from almost half a century ago.

The first set of diaries are from Christine Hartley and show the magick performed within the Merlin Temple of the Stella Matutina, an offshoot of the Hermetic Order of the Golden Dawn, in the years 1940-42. The second set are from Geoff Hughes and detail his magickal work during 1984-86. Although he was not at that time a member of any formal group, the magick he practiced was under the same aegis as Hartley's. The third section of this book, written by Hughes, shows how you can become your own Priest or Priestess and make contact with Merlin.

The magick of Christine Hartley and Geoff Hughes are like the poles of some hidden battery that lies beneath the Earth and beneath the years. There is a current flowing between them, and the energy is there for you to tap.
0-87542-671-9, 320 pgs., 6 x 9, illus., softcover $12.95

SECRETS OF A GOLDEN DAWN TEMPLE
The Alchemy and Crafting of Magickal Implements
by Chic Cicero and Sandra Tabatha Cicero
Foreword by Chris Monnastre
Afterword by Donald Michael Kraig

A Must-Have for Every Student of the Western Magickal Tradition! From its inception 100 years ago, the Hermetic Order of the Golden Dawn continues to be *the* authority on high magick. Yet the books written on the Golden Dawn system have fallen far short in explaining how to construct the tools and implements necessary for ritual. Until now.

Secrets of a Golden Dawn Temple picks up where all the other books leave off. This is the first book to describe *all* Golden Dawn implements and tools in complete detail. Here is a unique compilation of the various tools used, all described in full: wands, ritual clothing, elemental tools, Enochian tablets, altars, temple furniture, banners, lamens, admission badges and much more. This book provides complete step-by-step instructions for the construction of nearly 80 different implements, all displayed in photographs or drawings, along with the exact symbolism behind each and every item. Plus, it gives a ritual or meditation for every magickal instrument presented. It truly is an indispensable guide for any student of Western Magickal Tradition.
0-87542-150-4, 592 pgs., 6 x 9, 16 color plates, softcover $19.95

ARCHETYPES ON THE TREE OF LIFE
The Tarot as Pathwork
by Madonna Compton

The "Tree" is the Kabbalistic Tree of Life, the ageless mystical map to the secrets of the Universe. By working with its 10 circular paths and 22 linear ones, you can find answers to life's most profound questions. By mapping archetypes on the Tree, you can trace mythological and religious themes as well as those symbols that stir the psyche on deep inner levels. It can help you bring out your latent powers and develop your full potential.

Archetypes on the Tree of Life symbolically examines the meanings and uses of the 22 paths based upon their correspondences with the Tarot trumps and Hebrew letters. The first half of the book is a scholarly approach to deciphering the archetypal symbols behind the etiology of the Hebrew letters, names and numbers. The second half is designed to enhance creativity and intuition through meditations and exercises that bring the material alive in the reader's subconscious.

Along the way, you will investigate the mystical and allegorical interpretations of the Old and New Testaments and compare these and other mythologies worldwide to the Tarot archetypes.

0-87542-104-0, 336 pgs., 6 x 9, illus., softcover $12.95

THE BOOK OF GODDESSES & HEROINES
by Patricia Monaghan

The Book of Goddesses & Heroines is a historical landmark, a must for everyone interested in Goddesses and Goddess worship. It is not an effort to trivialize the beliefs of matriarchal cultures. It is not a collection of Goddess descriptions penned by biased male historians throughout the ages. It is the complete, non-biased account of Goddesses of every cultural and geographic area, including African, Egyptian, Japanese, Korean, Persian, Australian, Pacific, Latin American, British, Irish, Scottish, Welsh, Chinese, Greek, Icelandic, Italian, Finnish, German, Scandinavian, Indian, Tibetan, Mesopotamian, North American, Semitic and Slavic Goddesses!

Unlike some of the male historians before her, Patricia Monaghan eliminates as much bias as possible from her Goddess stories. Envisioning herself as a woman who might have revered each of these Goddesses, she has done away with language that referred to the deities in relation to their male counterparts, as well as with culturally relative terms such as "married" or "fertility cult." The beliefs of the cultures and the attributes of the Goddesses have been left intact.

Plus, this book has a new, complete index. If you are more concerned about finding a Goddess of war than you are a Goddess of a given country, this index will lead you to the right page. This is especially useful for anyone seeking to do Goddess rituals. Your work will be twice as efficient and effective with this detailed and easy-to-use book.

0-87542-573-9, 456 pgs., 6 x 9, photos, softcover $17.95

CUNNINGHAM'S ENCYCLOPEDIA OF CRYSTAL, GEM & METAL MAGIC
by Scott Cunningham
Here you will find the most complete information anywhere on the magical qualities of more than 100 crystals and gemstones as well as several metals. The information for each crystal, gem or metal includes: its related energy, planetary rulership, magical element, deities, Tarot card, and the magical powers that each is believed to possess. Also included is a complete description of their uses for magical purposes. The classic on the subject.
0-87542-126-1, 240 pgs., 6 x 9, illus., color plates, softcover $12.95

SACRED SOUNDS
Transformation through Music & Word
by Ted Andrews
Sound has always been considered a direct link between humanity and the divine. The ancient mystery schools all taught their students the use of sound as a creative and healing force that bridged the different worlds of life and consciousness.

Now, *Sacred Sounds* reveals to today's seekers how to tap into the magical and healing aspects of voice, resonance and music. On a physical level, these techniques have been used to alleviate aches and pains, lower blood pressure and balance hyperactivity in children. On a metaphysical level, they have been used to induce altered states of consciousness, open new levels of awareness, stimulate intuition and increase creativity.

In this book, Ted Andrews reveals the tones and instruments that affect the chakras, the use of kinesiology and "muscle testing" in relation to sound responses, the healing aspects of vocal tones, the uses of mystical words of power, the art of magical storytelling, how to write magical sonnets, how to form healing groups and utilize group toning for healing and enlightenment, and much, much more.
0-87542-018-4, 240 pgs., 5 1/4 x 8, illus., softcover $7.95